THE
WINDSOR
PLOT

Novels by Pauline Glen Winslow

GALLOWS CHILD
DEATH OF AN ANGEL
THE BRANDENBERG HOTEL
THE WITCH HILL MURDER
COPPERGOLD
THE COUNSELLOR HEART
THE ROCKEFELLER GIFT
THE WINDSOR PLOT
I, MARTHA ADAMS

THE
WINDSOR
PLOT

Pauline Glen Winslow

St. Martin's Press
New York

THE WINDSOR PLOT

Mass market edition/May 1986

ISBN: 0-312-90389-8
Can. ISBN: 0-312-90390-1

"I see no reason why this war should go on."
Adolf Hitler, speech to the Reichstag, July 1940

"England for the good of the world must remain unchanged in its present form.

Consequently, after final victory, we must effect a reconciliation.

Only the King must go—in his place the Duke of Windsor. With him we will make a permanent treaty of friendship instead of a peace treaty."
Adolf Hitler, handwritten note. From the Müllern Schönhausen Collection

CAST OF CHARACTERS

THE DUKE OF WINDSOR Former King Edward VIII (David)

THE DUCHESS OF WINDSOR Née Bessiewallis Warfield; formerly Mrs Winfield Spencer, Mrs Ernest Simpson (Wallis)

KING GEORGE VI Formerly Duke of York (Bertie)

QUEEN ELIZABETH Formerly Duchess of York (Betty)

WINSTON SPENCER CHURCHILL Prime Minister of England and Minister of Defence

ADOLF HITLER, THE FÜHRER Dictator of Germany

GENERALISSIMO FRANCISCO FRANCO Dictator of Spain

ADMIRAL CANARIS Chief of Germany's senior espionage agency, the Abwehr

JOACHIM VON RIBBENTROP German Foreign Minister

SIR WALFORD SELBY British Ambassador to Portugal

BARON OSWALD VON HOYNINGHEN-HUENE German Minister to Portugal

RICARDO ESPERITO SANTO E SILVA Portuguese banker, host to Duke and Duchess

WALTER MONCKTON British Under-Secretary of State for Foreign Affairs, lawyer, friend of the Duke

MIGUEL PRIMO DE RIVERA Leader of Madrid's Fascist party

EBERHARD VON STORER German Ambassador to Spain

SIR SAMUEL HOARE British Ambassador to Spain

MARTIN BORMANN Hitler's Secretary

REINHARD HEYDRICH Head of Gestapo, SD and Criminal Police, Deputy Reich Protector

HERMANN GÖRING Head of the Luftwaffe

MAJOR ERWIN VON LAHOUSEN Chief of Sabotage Division, Abwehr

COLONEL HANS OSTER Chief Assistant to Admiral Canaris, leader of anti-Hitler plot

HANS VON DOHNANYI Abwehr lawyer, part of anti-Hitler plot

DAVID LLOYD GEORGE British statesman, former Prime Minister

MR NEVILLE CHAMBERLAIN Lord President of the Council

MR CLEMENT R. ATTLEE Lord Privy Seal

LORD HALIFAX Secretary of State for Foreign Affairs

MR ARTHUR GREENWOOD Minister Without Portfolio

MR A. V. ALEXANDER First Lord of the Admiralty

MR ANTHONY EDEN Secretary of State for War

LORD BEAVERBROOK Minister of Aircraft Production

MR L. S. AMERY Secretary of State for India and Burma

SIR HASTINGS LIONEL ISMAY Lieutenant-General, Chief of Staff to Minister of Defence, Deputy Secretary to War Cabinet

SIR ARCHIBALD WAVELL General, Commander of Middle East Command

SIR JOHN G. DILL Chief of Imperial General Staff (CIGS)

MR HUGH DOWDING Chief of Fighter Command

EVA BRAUN Hitler's mistress

DETECTIVE-INSPECTOR THOMPSON Churchill's bodyguard

FRAULEIN BUMKE German agent in Great Britain

Fictional Characters

SERGEANT REX BARNEY Holder of Victoria Cross, highest award for bravery in the British Army

DETECTIVE-INSPECTOR ALFRED BARNEY Formerly Churchill's bodyguard, retired from Special Branch

HORST HOLSTEIN Also known as Henry Holbrook and Peter Hainault. Untersturmführer, SS and Abwehr agent

OBERFÜHRER SCHREIG Holstein's Commanding Officer

JOHANN METZ (deceased) Abwehr agent and scout who recruited Holstein

JEAN SINCLAIR Maid in small Royal house at Deeside

THE GRAF FRIEDRICH VON AUERBACH German diplomat, connection of British Royal Family

DETECTIVE-INSPECTOR HILLIARD One of Churchill's bodyguards, Special Branch

MAJOR LEITER Abwehr bureaucrat

ECKHARDT Radio operator, Major Leiter's assistant in London

IDA London barmaid, Rex Barney's mistress

GEORGE GUMM } Members Local Defence Volunteers
HENRY BODGER }   (Home Guard)

JACK KEMP Civilian

LARRY GREEN (deceased) Friend of Rex Barney

NEVILLE JARNDYCE British Abwehr agent

MARIAN JARNDYCE His daughter

DAI LEWIS Welsh Nationalist, Chief of Operation Whale

EVANS Dai Lewis' son-in-law, member Operation Whale

MALONEY Chief assassin, Operation Whale, IRA soldier

MACLEISH Scottish Nationalist, member Operation Whale

SEAN O'CONNOR Member Operation Whale, IRA soldier

MICHAEL O'CONNOR Sean's brother, IRA soldier, working for Major Leiter in London

FRANK PURCELL IRA saboteur trained by Major Lahousen at Quenzee, Bavaria

CAPTAIN STANGEL

DIETZ

KLEIST

BRUNER

BECKER   Paratroops *(Fallschirmjäger)*

MULLER

SCHMIDT

SCHURMER

MEISTER German pilot

GILES CARRUTHERS King George's equerry

PARSONS King George's chauffeur

BURNS King George's valet

DONALDSON Queen Elizabeth's maid

MRS GORDON Housekeeper at Scottish Royal house

ARTHUR BROWN Outdoor man

SIR EWEN MACBRIDE Scottish landowner

MRS RAE Cottage landlady

MARIA Housemaid in Cascais

JORGE Maria's son

MANUEL Butler in Cascais, Maria's lover

FERDI Houseboy in Cascais

GIBBONS British spy in Lisbon

RODRIGUES Chauffeur in Lisbon

Contents

AUTHOR'S NOTE

This work is, obviously, fiction. The events described in it never took place. The story of the actual attempt by Adolf Hitler to use the Duke of Windsor for his own purposes is too well known to need recounting here. It has been remarked, however, by at least one historian of the period that Hitler's emissary, Walter Schellenberg of the SS, was half-hearted in his efforts, which were clumsy and betrayed his ignorance of the British in general and the Duke in particular. This leads to the question: What if the emissary had been eager, deft and knowledgeable?

The Windsor Plot is one attempt to answer that question.

PROLOGUE
The Mouth Of Hell

The lighthouse at the Cape of Roca stands at the western-most tip of Europe. A strong salt wind blows in off the sea, spinning the sand like a veil across the sky, withering all green things along its path. On the beach at Guincho the strong pull of the tides throws up a wall of water, but a little further south the sea itself is sucked down between the rocks to a whirling foam-ridden vortex at the place called the Boca Do Inferno, the Mouth of Hell.

Close by the chasm, on a high point overlooking the coast road, is a house of the same name. There, in the summer of 1940, lived Edward Albert Christian George Andrew Patrick David, the man who, by the Grace of God, of Great Britain, Ireland and the British Dominions Beyond the Seas, had been King, Defender of the Faith, Emperor of India.

Great Britain was at war. The former King, now the Duke of Windsor, had been ordered home. But at the Mouth of Hell, in the company of his wife, he remained.

Through the long, warm summer days, two British flying boats sat in Lisbon harbour, waiting to take him home. The powerful four-engined craft, conspicuously glittering, sat helpless under the surveillance of German U-boats. The fishermen, who sat and mended their nets along the shore, gossiped about this strange Englishman.

The Germans were triumphant everywhere; Great Britain was fighting for her life, but these valuable planes were held at the pleasure of the Duke.

In Lisbon itself, the speculation was even greater—from the dinner tables of the rich and great, to the little café on the Rua Gambetta where spies of all nations congregated. The knowledgeable were aware that the Germans, through 'non-belligerent' emissaries, had approached the Duke, suggesting that he return to Spain for the duration of the war. Over the wine, the talk was blunt. Would the Duke and Duchess ever return to England, under the present rule? The Duke himself could not have answered them.

He and his wife were waiting. They waited in the summer house they had borrowed from the banker, Ricardo Esperito Santo e Silva. It was a charming house, but they had little interest in its charms. The Duke sent his telegrams to London and waited for the replies that would spell out his destiny. The wait seemed most unreasonably long.

After a late Portuguese luncheon, he and the Duchess sat and sipped their coffee on the balcony that overlooked a garden, the Lisbon road, and the sea. The Duke gazed at the road. Unsheltered from the sun, it blazed a long, dusty trail over the village and on from there to Lisbon. Not an attractive sight, yet it was an irresistible magnet to the Duke's somewhat crooked eyes.

"I was sure we'd get word today," he said.

In spite of the awning that shaded the balcony and the breeze coming up from the sea, he looked hot, vexed and restless. He wore a loose shirt, Bermuda shorts and espadrilles. From a distance he still looked boyish, but a close observer would see the fine lines like a net of age settling over the youthful features.

The luncheon sat heavily inside him. He preferred not to eat luncheon at all. A good English breakfast was enough to sustain him until dinner, but he could not get

2

a decent English breakfast here. He disliked Lisbon and would be glad to leave. The resentment he felt at being trapped, added to his other resentments, made a dull persistent ache in his belly.

"I was very strong this time in my cable to Winston. No point in him sending Selby to dither again."

Sir Walford Selby, the British Ambassador, had the task of passing on the Prime Minister's replies. It had become as difficult for him as it was painful for the Duke. The Duke's demands were two-fold. He must be given a job in accordance with his position as he saw it, and his wife *must* be acknowledged as a Royal Highness. The present King, the fount of all honours, had not granted the title. And the Government had its own view of the position of a king who had abdicated.

"If we go back," the Duke went on, "you will have your proper standing as my wife. As my wife," he repeated, enjoying the sound.

The Duchess lay back in her chair, cool in deep blue linen and pearl earrings, perfectly groomed, her eyes closed, her face impassive.

"I was strong," he said again, "But my demands are perfectly just. I felt I could get away with that."

"You thought that before," the Duchess murmured, using a minimum of energy. "And how wrong you were."

The Duke winced. It was something he could not bear to think about, or talk about, and yet, in spite of all their agreements not to do so, they went back to it, again and again. For the hated subject was—and would be—the basis of his life, their lives always.

He had been so happy, carefree, confident when, at his beloved home of Fort Belvedere, he had told this woman that he must marry her. In the place he had made a retreat, where the stuffiness of the Court had never been allowed to penetrate, surrounded only by his close friends, his plan had seemed perfectly feasible. For once his wife-to-be, who knew so little of English ways, had been more prescient than the King.

"They'll never let us do it," she had said.

She had not needed to explain who 'they' were. The King had always seen himself, though he was now approaching fifty, as the leading representative of all that was modern and young, the very spirit of a new age. As had many others seen the charming young Prince of Wales —the 'Golden Prince'. He became used to the adulation and was contemptuous of the nay-sayers, the old Palace Household of his father's day, the leaders in government and the armed forces who did not understand the modern world. The people, especially the young, were with him. He had done what he pleased, and, in his own mind, he had 'got away with it'.

But in this matter so important to him, to his surprise and ultimate consternation, he had not. He had under-estimated his opposition, all the old 'revereds' he had despised. And he had over-estimated his friends—never separating the friends of the King from the friends of the man. With the fatal documents signed, he was to learn his lesson quickly. In the leisure that was so suddenly his, with all the time for contemplation, his first proud sense of sacrifice had turned to bitterness. The unyielding strength of those who continued to oppose him caused the Duke to suspect a plot against him—cunning, widespread, with deep implications.

The sound of a door, opening or closing, inside the house brought him back to the present. He gazed at his wife, hoping she was not angry. But she looked merely withdrawn, which hurt more. His resentment burst out into words.

"Yes, but then I didn't know about the Windsor Plot."

She glanced at him but did not speak. The idea of this plot had become an obsession. But it was hardly a useful obsession. It was not going to remove them from the

4

tedium of Lisbon back to place and position with all of London Society fawning on her once again.

David looked a mess, she thought. She had not realised, until he had been separated from his valet, how helpless he was. The man who once had swept her across Europe like an empress, with a magnificent yacht for her pleasure and luxury trains held to suit her convenience, cheered by the people and courted by foreign governments and royalty, now kept his room in a shambles and could not find a pair of matching socks.

The Duke was brooding bitterly. The Windsor Plot. It all seemed so clear now. Of course, they had wanted him to go. It was not only the matter of his marriage—far from it. They did not like his new ideas, his plan of an active reign where the monarch was not wasted entirely on the tedium of ceremonial. They were jealous of his statesmanship: he, the friend of Germany, influential with Hitler, would never have allowed the country to drift into this insane war that would ultimately only mean a victory for communism.

And how artfully it had been done! They had trapped him into inquiring about a morganatic marriage—itself an insult, where Wallis would be his wife but not his Queen. Then he had been told, very calmly, that there was no such thing in English law. A man's wife must take her husband's rank and title. And the Dominions wouldn't hear of it. He must give up Mrs Simpson, or abdicate. How he had been outmanoeuvred! For they had known he would never give her up. Abdication—yes, he had been prepared at the last to give up the Crown. But he had not realised that what was intended was his extinction.

In his deep concern not to threaten the monarchy itself, he had played right into their hands. When he wanted to broadcast to the nation, to explain to his people, everyone had been surprisingly agreeable: he could certainly broadcast—after the Instrument of Abdication was signed.

5

Now he stared out over the dusty road, hearing, seeing nothing, his fingers tapping restlessly on the balustrade. Of course, he had agreed. Then, with elaborate casualness, some underling from the BBC raised a question of protocol. How should he be introduced to the nation? He was no longer King Edward. Other voices took up the cry. Walter Monckton for one, the lawyer who had also been a friend. The matter of his new title would have to be settled immediately, for though he was no longer King, he could not be Mr Windsor. After all, he had been born Prince Edward.

Up until then he had thought little about it. Apart from being King, he had possessed the Duchy of Cornwall since his father's accession to the throne. Wallis, in her charming naîveté, had suggested he retain the title of His Royal Highness the Duke of Cornwall, with Wallis as Her Royal Highness the Duchess.

But it had been put to him that if his sister-in-law had a son—hardly likely at that point in time!—her son would be entitled to the Duchy. His brother Bertie, now King George, had suggested a new dukedom using the Anglicised family name of Windsor. He had never liked the name but he had agreed—anything to get away quickly, to join Wallis when he could. Even then he had not realised the extent of the machinations against him. It would take time to issue Letters Patent. Thus he was introduced to the listeners as His Royal Highness, Prince Edward.

On the week of his wedding, Letters Patent had been issued. King George had been pleased to 'declare that the Duke of Windsor . . . be entitled to hold and enjoy *for himself only,* the title, style or attribute of Royal Highness, so however that his wife and descendants, if any shall *not . . .*'

His marriage had been made morganatic. His wife was not recognised as royal. In these days, he thought, when any Jew with money could be made a lord, his wife was merely a titled commoner. He had given up the throne

6

for—nothing at all. The trap was sprung. The Windsor Plot was complete.

And his wife, who now looked so remote, how did she feel, with all the bright promise left behind them? He could not bear to think any more.

"I wish we'd stayed in Spain," he said bitterly. "At least we were properly served there. Primo de Rivera was very charming. And he really pressed us to stay. Perhaps we should have gone to see that Caliph's palace the Generalissimo wanted to give us—at Rondo, was it?"

He remembered very clearly that there had also been mention of fifty million Swiss francs for its upkeep. It was certainly tempting. All his adult life, as Prince and King, he had been a very rich man. One of his great pleasures was to shower Wallis with jewels and watch the matching sparkle in her eyes. At the time of the Abdication he had made an agreement with his brother about a financial settlement. Or he thought he had. But there had been months of haggling, months when he, who had never had to think of money at all, had not known if he would be able to pay his bills. It had been settled at last, but part of the money came as a yearly payment. Who could know if, at some future time, it might not be stopped?

"I enjoyed Madrid," the Duchess said, absently.

Certainly, she thought, it was more agreeable being flattered by Spaniards than insulted by the English. Of course it was more pleasant in Spain. But the Duke had been frightened. He had not minded the attentions of the leader of Madrid's Fascist party, Miguel Primo de Rivera, but he had been warned that de Rivera's offers originated with the Germans. The very last thing the Duke wanted was to be branded a traitor to his country.

"I tried to call Bertie this morning," the Duke said suddenly. The new King had been the greatest hero-worshipper of his eldest brother. "Even when I said it was urgent and important, he wouldn't take the call. And

7

Winston expects us to rush back when he whistles—and in those boats!"

His wife shuddered. She was afraid of flying and didn't care for the idea of the flying boats for many reasons.

"I tell you, Dolly," he used the name as a diminutive of darling, "if the Spanish invite us there again, I think we will go." He spoke with a new energy. "Take the plunge. And let people say what they like."

The Duchess did not believe him. What people would say was that he was a royal Quisling, eager to see Great Britain crushed under the Nazi jackboot. Why should he care? After all the humiliations that had been heaped upon them. But care he did. He would never do it. Or so she thought. She did not trouble to reply.

But upstairs a maid, who had been an inordinate time in closing the shades of a bedroom window, had listened with far more interest. The German agent who had transmitted the Führer's offer through de Rivera in Spain, had followed the Windsors to Lisbon. Among other arrangements, he had made sure of informants at the Boca Do Inferno. The maid Maria was one who received a small, but useful, regular payment.

Before the day was over, von Ribbentrop in Berlin was listening with satisfaction to the talk of the disaffected Duke. It had been a lovely day after all, he thought, sunny but not too warm. The Foreign Minister, in his official residence, once the palace of the Reich President, felt himself to be a happy man, now he had this news. Churchill could brag all he wished of the loyalty of the British people to himself, and of their desire to fight this war to a finish. He, von Ribbentrop, had lived there long enough to know the truth and he had so advised the Führer. Certainly he had always said that the former King would remain their friend, an important friend. And now this friend was ready to take the final step. Von Ribbentrop went to the telephone at once. He must inform the Führer that his plot was racing to its climax. The ex-King would be theirs.

ONE

Move By A Master

The sun was shining, the air was crisp and clean at Ober-salzberg, but Admiral Canaris, head of the mighty Abwehr, the secret intelligence service of the High Command, was not enjoying his visit to the Berghof. Not at all. The Führer had left him to cool his heels in an ante-room for the last four hours.

Canaris was stiff and tired; tired from his journey, tired from his intensive preparations for *Barbarossa*—the projected invasion of Germany's ally, Russia. Tired because he was fifty-three years-old and felt much older. Tired because he feared and loathed the man who had summoned him to his presence. He could only fret and wonder—what now?

When at last he was shown into the room with the great window overlooking the mountains, he saw Hitler seated between Eva Braun and Martin Bormann. Bormann, that palace lackey, was only to be expected, but the presence of Eva Braun was not a good sign. True, she was only displayed to the Führer's intimates, yet her being there was a hint that the Admiral was not considered a person of high importance. Appearances did not need to be kept up before him.

Hitler sent Bormann off on some business before he greeted Canaris. Then, rather grudgingly, he asked him to

9

be seated, but continued to talk to Eva Braun. She looked fresh and healthy from the mountain air, tidily dressed in a woollen jumper, a tweed skirt and low-heeled shoes—a typical housewife of the lower middle-class, the Admiral thought. But the Führer was unusually tender towards her, patting her arm. "My *Tschapperl*," he said, smiling.

His 'little thing' looked pleased enough with the condescending intimacy, but the Admiral did not care for that smile. It soon vanished and she was dismissed, her task accomplished.

Immediately the Führer jumped to his feet. His face was dark and a line of sweat sprang to his forehead as he faced the Admiral, who rose in turn. What in God's name . . . His thoughts rushed through his mind, behind the pale, impassive face. Oster . . . Oster must have been betrayed. Canaris' chief assistant, Colonel Hans Oster, had been working with the Zossen conspirators in their hopeless attempt at a *putsch*. He had gone so far as to approach the British and warn them of the coming invasion of the Lowlands. Not that they had paid attention. They had been busy with their Cabinet crisis.

But if Oster had been betrayed, he, Canaris, would not be here now. The Gestapo would have come for both of them in Berlin. Gradually, the Admiral's heart stopped racing and his breathing went back to normal. This temper must be one of Hitler's ploys. There was something disagreeable to be done, no doubt. The Führer was following his usual pattern. Terrify a man with unknown dangers, and he will be relieved to agree to some lesser abomination than his own fears. Some development of 'Felix' perhaps, the pet plan of the Führer's to take Gibralter—with Franco's agreement, if possible. The Führer knew of his liking for Spain, his good relationship with the Generalissimo. Perhaps Hitler knew also of his secret dream of retiring in that warm and friendly land. Was he planning treachery there? But behind this dismaying thought the darker one persisted. *Could* the Führer suspect Oster?

Suddenly, Hitler was shouting. "The Duke is still in Lisbon!"

For a moment the Admiral was bewildered. The Duke? Then he understood. The Abwehr was not in charge of the attempted seduction of the Duke of Windsor. That job had been given to Heydrich's SD, the Security Service of the SS, always growing in power and importance. Canaris had slipped a few of his own men into SD headquarters, and had read the cables from Lisbon. They were claiming success. So why was he here being castigated? Quietly he pointed out the facts which the Führer must already have known.

"And why should you have been given this job?" came the reply.

He was lashing himself into a fury, real or feigned. Beyond the window the sweep of mountains piercing the sky looked less noble than menacing. The Admiral was shivering. Here, no matter the temperature, he never felt warm. Here he was completely at this man's mercy.

"You failed with Churchill in '39."

His voice was high-pitched, almost screaming now.

Outwardly the Admiral looked calm. But with the Führer bringing up the Churchill affair, certainly there was trouble. The Führer had an obsession about Winston Churchill. Even when the man had been out of office, out of power, something of a joke in his own country, the Führer's obsession had grown. Just before the war Churchill, at the invitation of the French Government, had gone to inspect a section of the Maginot Line. And German agents had learned that he intended to visit the Duke of Windsor, then in the South of France. The Führer had ordered his assassination—cunningly contrived so as not to cause anti-German feeling in Great Britain.

At that time it had seemed a particularly senseless murder. But there was nothing to be done, except to follow orders. The Abwehr had arranged that the actual killing be done by a group of criminals from Marseilles.

11

But the plot, after all, had come to nothing. After lunching with General Georges in Paris, Churchill had suddenly changed his plans and flown directly to London.

"We were betrayed!"

The Admiral himself had wondered about the French *Action Service*. Churchill was known to be a friend of France.

"He might merely have changed his mind," the Admiral said quietly. "The Duke was being difficult—it is his way."

Hitler stared. His eyes, normally dull as currents in that pasty face, were brilliant and dangerous.

"Changed his mind—and sent a message to England recalling his old bodyguard. Warned. *Warned!* And future attempts frustrated."

The Admiral sighed. That bodyguard business had meant nothing. Churchill was used to having some doddering old Special Branch man about him. The man had been retired years before from Scotland Yard, and was in fact, a grocer. Hardly someone to daunt the Abwehr! But it was no use talking now.

Besides, events, as they so often did, had proved the Führer right. No other man could have turned his complacent country into a bulwark of defiance against Germany. At this very moment, the Admiral knew, there were members of Churchill's own Cabinet hankering to make a peace, but they would not dare to raise their voices in public against the Prime Minister. Privately they would call him a fire-eater, a warmonger, totally unrealistic—but it would all come to nothing. They could not oppose him now any more than the High Command dare oppose Hitler, for all their plots and plans.

The Führer's gaze, once more opaque, was still upon him. The Admiral wondered if he saw a trace of mockery in the stern lines of his face. The Führer talked and talked and finally talked himself into a lighter mood. Abruptly, he changed the subject. Or so it seemed.

"We are going ahead with Operation Green," he said.

The Admiral thought he knew the man before him, with his quick changes of humour, his plans and alternate plans. But operation Green? He remembered the projected scheme quite well, but it had never been seriously considered. An invasion of Great Britain through Ireland and Wales, using the German supporters in those countries, including the IRA and certain Welsh Nationalists. How could this possibly be done in connection with *Barbarossa*? The British Home Army was small and almost without weapons, but they would be fighting on their own soil . . .

"There will be differences," the Führer said, smiling now. Suddenly relaxed and happy, he summoned a servant. Today he would not join the household at the teahouse; he ordered tea for himself and the Admiral. Tea at the Berghof meant a lot of sweet things. The Führer asked for cream cakes, which he insisted the Admiral eat. The Admiral—something of a gourmet—detested such stuff but forced himself to eat it.

Some of the cream clung to Hitler's moustache and gave him a clownish look, but he was not a clown. His new plan took the Admiral's breath away. There was to be no invasion. His supporters in Great Britain were to be used in quite another way. Operation Green was to be joined with the Windsor Plot. What the Führer proposed was, simply, a coup d'état in Great Britain. And Admiral Canaris was to arrange it.

Having been led all round the cart, Canaris now got a good view of the horse. As the Führer explained his ideas, already worked out in some detail, the Abwehr head realised what had happened. Hitler had always thought of the former King of England as his friend—with reason. And he had always thought of him as important, perhaps more important than he really was. Certainly at the time of Germany's invasion of the Rhineland, Edward's friendly attitude had encouraged the Führer to assume that England would not march against him. And the Führer believed it was because of Edward that England, and therefore France, had been so accommodating.

With Edward as King, the Führer had always said, there would be friendship between England and Germany. His dismay at the Abdication had been profound. But he had received the Duke and Duchess graciously when they had toured Germany in 1937 and remarked that the Duchess would have made a good Queen. The Duke had continued to say publicly that war between Great Britain and Germany would be a great mistake—and when war was actually begun he deplored it. Always lurking in Hitler's mind was the idea of using the Duke to embarrass the British Government. The Duke's careless words, spoken in his house in Lisbon and reported back to Hitler, had apparently elated him and this plan exploded in his imagination.

The Admiral was horrified. But perhaps the Führer was not serious.

"We can't wipe out the entire Royal Family!" he protested.

"Why not?" Hitler sounded quite calm and reasonable. "The Russians wiped out theirs. One good clean wipe at Ekaterinberg." He chuckled. "And who cared? The Empress' cousin, this man's father? When a plan was made to send a destroyer to get the Romanovs away, it was George V himself who forbade it. The English Royal Family must not get involved!"

The Admiral, surprised at this incursion into history, reflected that no-one was ever sure what the Führer, ill-educated as he was, actually knew. He himself had heard this story—almost certainly untrue. That devious mind . . . The thought made his nerves quiver again. How much did the Führer suspect of the Zossen conspiracy? How many senior OKW officers were involved? It might just suit him to play like a cat among the mice, while they served him.

14

"It might not be necessary to kill them all," Hitler said, casually. "Just the King would probably do. With him dead, and Churchill . . ." he spat the name out ". . . it will be easy enough to get Edward back on the throne. Repeal that Abdication Act. Ribbentrop tells me he is sure Lloyd George would be ready enough to accept my peace offer."

Canaris' face, already furrowed, puckered further in perplexity.

"But how can you be sure it would be Lloyd George called upon to form a government?"

Hitler shrugged.

"It's a coalition government. They must find someone they can agree on. The Conservatives will never take someone from the Labour Party. It could be Halifax—he would do just as well. But those men of Labour probably would reject him. So who is left? The great old man of the Liberals. Their Hindenberg, Lloyd George."

He smiled. He looked as though he could have said more. Canaris knew that the Führer had kept in touch with the old Welsh wizard, whose admiration for him had been almost embarrassing in its openness. Canaris, himself, had an agent, the redoubtable Fraulein Bumke, in touch with the former Prime Minister.

Canaris tried another move.

"As you say, *mein Führer*," he replied with deep respect. "But in such a case, do we need to kill the King?"

Hitler scowled.

"Edward is our friend. Our goal is to smash Communist Russia and we need England to be neutral. He will help us. King George could be a rallying point for our enemies."

"Yet the British Constitution would prevent the Crown reverting to an abdicated king," Canaris argued, without much hope, and waited for another tongue-lashing.

15

It did not come. The Führer sounded sweetly reasonable.

"Constitution! Did Churchill think of the British Constitution when he, one man, offered to join France and Great Britain into one nation? Without a word to the Cabinet, the Parliament, the Law Lords or one cat and dog in the Empire? Admiral, Constitutions are what rulers decide they should be. Besides," he took another cream cake and bit into it happily, "I have consulted experts in this matter."

The Admiral wondered who his experts were. The Duke of Coburg, perhaps.

"There is great legal confusion as to the next heir to the British throne, with there being no male heir and *two* daughters. Nothing in British law gives the eldest daughter the sole right to the kingdom. I have confidence in you to make the most of all this, little *Kieker,*" he said, with a sudden switch from the orator to a giggling intimate.

Canaris flinched. The nickname from his childhood, 'the Peeper', still haunted him.

"You *can* do it," the Führer went on. He gazed at the Admiral intently. "You are the one person who has the brains and the knowledge. I rely on you."

Behind the warm smile, the beaming brown eyes, the Admiral saw the menace, as cold as the mountain peaks surrounding the eyrie. Yes, the Führer relied on him. He needed him—now. But if the Admiral should refuse this bloodthirsty business, or should he fail . . . He shivered again. Someone had walked over his grave.

"But it must be soon. Very soon." The Führer's gaze went to his calendar. "By the first week in August. Say—August 3. Otherwise, we prepare *Adlerangriff!*"

Adlerangriff. The attack of Göring's 'eagles' to weaken Great Britain for invasion. An invasion that Canaris had hoped against hope would never be attempted. Already the Luftwaffe was raiding the coast shipping and the ports.

16

"One way or another, we must have settled peace with Great Britain before next spring. The German army will be marching—*Aufbau Ost!* It must not be caught in the Russian winter. So—get to work at once."

The Admiral was dismissed.

Canaris left the Berghof, for once without a feeling of disdain for Hitler's transformation of what had been a pleasant mountain-top retreat into an ugly complex surrounded by barbed wire fences. He was in no condition to think of aesthetics. On the way back to Berlin his 'plane was buffeted by high winds unusual for the time of year, but he hardly noticed the turbulence. His car was waiting for him at the Templehof airfield and he was driven through the dark streets of Berlin, shaken in mind and body. He went straight to the Abwehr building on the Tirpitz Ufer, the quay along the Landwehrkanal. It was no use going home to try to sleep that night.

The corporal who admitted him thought that 'Der Alte' looked ill. It was a pity he didn't wear his naval uniform and make a smarter appearance. His civilian clothes hung limply on his body and his prematurely white hair stuck up in wisps under his shabby felt hat as if he'd seen a ghost.

In his office on the top floor, his orderly tried to take his coat but Canaris waved him away. Despite the heat of Berlin, he was still shivering. These days it seemed he could never get warm. He had not dined, yet he felt no hunger. Telling the orderly to bring him coffee, he settled himself at his desk, his accustomed work place in the small, familiar room. The room seemed bleak to anyone but the Admiral; to him it brought ease.

As he sipped his coffee, his body recovered from the buffeting in the 'plane, and the turbulence in his mind also subsided. When he had left the Berghof, he had thought the Führer mad. The Admiral had thought so before and still believed that, sometimes, he was. Yet there was no question that, on occasion, the man was inspired.

There were few decorations in the office. But on the wall, next to the signed portrait of Generalissimo Francisco Franco, there hung a Japanese painting vividly depicting the devil. It seemed to stare down at him. The Admiral smiled grimly. Inspired by something. For the idea that at first had seemed so outrageous had begun to show certain logical features, then to seem reasonable, until at last, as he stirred the cream into a third cup of coffee, desirable. So much so that Canaris wondered tiredly why the Führer could not have just explained it like an ordinary human being, instead of turning on all his *sturm* and *drang*. But then, of course, he wasn't an ordinary human being. He was more like Genghis Khan. With as little regard for human life. Images of Poland rose up before the Admiral's mental gaze, and he rubbed his forehead as if to push them away.

He had long been reluctant to serve Hitler. Yet if he resigned he knew that Heydrich would take his place—Heydrich, the Gestapo head, whom he sometimes feared even more than Hitler himself. It would be the end of Oster, Dohnanyi. But it was Poland that had broken his spirit. He had seen the devastation of Warsaw; he had learned of the mass executions. Rushing to the Führer who was in his special train, at least the Admiral had the comfort of knowing that in this, certainly, the SS was exceeding its authority. Hitler would stop this abomination.

There, at a railway siding in Ilnau, he had learned the truth. This was the basis for the Thousand Year Reich. Afterwards he told his friends bleakly, "We have seen these events; at some future time the world will hold us responsible for them."

Germany was at war. The generals of the OKW could not bring themselves to move against the Führer. They talked, but would not act. Oster had failed.

Now, in one thing at least, Canaris agreed with Hitler. There should be no more war against England. He had been opposed to it from the beginning. Although he had outwitted Churchill in the race for Norway, Canaris never confused a battle with the war. If this war continued, the United States would surely come in on England's side. Germany would be crushed—and probably all the good before the bad. If there could be peace with England, the war against Russia could be won. Then the High Command, victorious, would have the courage to move against Hitler. Or so he hoped.

He poured the last of the coffee and watched the black liquid swirling in his cup. A dark business. Inciting to treason. The murder of a Prime Minister. The murder of a king. King George, a family man, struggling with infirmities to do a duty that should not have been his. He was to be put down like an unwanted animal.

But the Admiral was not a sentimental man. Two deaths would be a small price to pay compared with the evils of an invasion of England, its occupation and all that would follow. Two deaths against, very likely, millions. And the end of Europe, of the world as he had known it.

If it could be done. But could it be done?

He sat, thinking, deep into the night. A summer rain blew down on the Tirpitz Ufer, but he was not aware of it. This was not a matter of a kidnap and two assassinations. This was a matter of diplomacy as well as an act of war. The Führer had been insistent—and he was right— this coup must be disguised. It must be carried out in such a way that the British public would not suspect that Germany was involved. The deaths of Churchill and King George must seem either natural or accidental. The Duke must be persuaded to return to England of his own free will. And all this in scarcely a month.

As he sat puzzling over his problem alone, in his usual fashion, he realised with a certain detachment that he was almost enjoying it. Although his business was morally repugnant, the difficulties intrigued his mind. Secrecy, subtlety, timing. The three separate actions must move forward to synchronise perfectly at their climax—to the mover it was like a game of three-dimensional chess.

The part that would be simplest was the one that would seem to the world at large the most difficult: the murder of the most important man in England. Churchill was sanguine, headstrong, contemptuous of advice and caution. He was a good shot, walked about armed and was convinced he could protect himself, declaring that he needed a bodyguard only when he was asleep. And he had the odd English trait—Canaris could only think of it now as odd—of feeling safe in his own country, no matter how much he might know and talk of the possibilities of enemy agents and imminent peril.

The protection given him by Special Branch of Scotland Yard could never guard against a really determined assassin. He could have been killed at almost any time since he took office. The IRA had bragged of this and even offered to do the job. The only problem *there* was discretion. Those wild men were good for acts of open sabotage —they were doing excellent work in Birmingham and London in armaments factories—but in this case the death must look accidental. A downed 'plane perhaps, a car crash, even falling down the stairs of his own house in the dark . . .

Then there was King George. King George had never been strong. He suffered badly from delicate nerves; in his youth he was tormented by duodenal ulcers, and he was plagued by a stammer. His youngest brother had died of epilepsy . . . The public could be made to believe that he died of natural causes—even his own family, if it were done skilfully. Failing health culminating in a heart attack, perhaps. There were ways to make a sudden death appear like heart attack; actually indeed to cause a heart attack. The Abwehr had done it before.

But the King would be more difficult than the Prime Minister. The Royal Family were equally foolhardy as regards their personal safety, but on the other hand, by the very nature of their position, they were always surrounded by people. And people that they knew. Family, friends, the Palace Household, officials of all sorts. True, he had managed to slip an agent over in the entourage of Queen Wilhelmina, but the agent had not been housed in the palace and had been sent to a country house where he was of little use to anyone. For the moment, the Admiral could not think how that part of the problem could be handled, and he put it aside.

Dawn approached, grey at first as the stone of the Abwehr building itself, then the sun rose to sparkle on the quay; but the light was still on in the Admiral's office as he turned his mind to the matter of the Duke. When Hitler had first proposed the change in the English Royal Family it had seemed to Canaris unnecessary for the plan, once Churchill was gone. And yet, now, he had to admit the Führer was right again. Certainly Edward would be a rallying point for all those who wanted to make peace with Germany, from the poor who had believed he was their champion, to the aristocracy who in their hearts feared what he feared, that the war would mean at last a victory for Communism.

Edward, as King, had been a magnetic man. Foolish and ineffectual as he was now, the resumption of majesty would restore him to greatness. As he had learned, he was a man fitted for one thing only, but given a second chance he would do it well. He was willing, eager, to be given this chance. But would he have the stomach to take the throne and supplant his younger brother? The Duke's angry words, spoken privately in his house near Lisbon and reported back to the Führer, had inflamed that ready imagination. But they did not impress the Admiral. As head of a great spy system, he knew how agents puffed reports to make them seem important. The Duke was no Tudor monarch, able to face the prospect of his family's blood on his hands.

Canaris knew the man Heydrich had been sent to arrange the Duke's seduction. He was his most brilliant spy, but in this case he would fail. The Duke would talk and talk, but he would obey orders at the last. Of course, Canaris realised, Hitler himself, in his own strange way, was aware of this. That was why he had been sent for. The Duke *could* be persuaded—but directly, by someone who understood him. Someone who could gloss over unpleasantness and make the action appear to be the Duke's patriotic duty. A man of his own class, someone from the old German aristocracy, a connection perhaps of the English Royal House. The Nazi Duke of Coburg. Or, better still—an image came to Canaris' mind—the young Graf von Auerbach. A subtle schemer. And attractive to women—that would help with the all-important Duchess.

Suddenly, the Admiral was very tired. He shuffled over to the old iron bedstead he kept in the office, unlaced his boots, took off his outer garments and huddled under two blankets. For four hours he slept, until the noise of the daytime staff at their work finally jarred him awake. Instantly he was aware it was July 4.

He sat up, blinking, somewhat refreshed but his problem had not, as it so often did, resolved itself. The threads still ran through his mind as they had before he slept. The Duke possibly, if all else went well. Churchill—that could be done, with care. But King George . . .

After washing and dressing, he had breakfast at his desk and asked his orderly to send down for Colonel Piekenbrock. Although the Führer wanted this matter to be known to as few people as possible, certainly Canaris felt he could use Piekenbrock's help. 'Pieki', second only to Canaris himself in the Abwehr, a brilliant, worldly, vastly capable man, chief of espionage as well as administration, would certainly have something useful to suggest. And in this, the Admiral would not dare use Oster, the firebrand. He had tried to warn the British once . . . But the orderly returned with disappointing news. The day before Colonel Piekenbrock had been dispatched to Norway on special orders of the Führer.

Canaris sighed in vexation. There was nothing to be done; this was the Führer's habit. It pleased him to ignore his official representatives abroad and send someone else, whoever struck his fancy at the moment. Göring, Martin Bormann, even himself, regardless of the effect this had on his messenger's regular duties. Now there was no-one who could take 'Pieki's' place.

Canaris looked at his incoming correspondence with disfavour. It would have to wait. Who, under Piekenbrock, was in charge of espionage in Great Britain? Of course, it was the man he had brought in from Hamburg, Major Leiter.

The Admiral sighed. Leiter was a good man in his way. He had risen to the rank of Major, but he had never seen action in his Army service. For all that he had the stiff bearing of the strutting Army officers of the Kaiser's time. A big, burly body with a head that did not seem to belong to it, small, with a mouse face, and a large moustache to give it importance. He had been a useful man in Hamburg, well respected for his ability to turn enemy agents into good workers for the Abwehr. And he did it without torture, which he considered only worthy of Hitler's riff-raff, the *Lumpengesindel,* and said so.

Doubtless, that had inspired 'Pieki' with confidence. Like all of the Abwehr, he was wary of Himmler's spies. He had brought Leiter to the Tirpitz Ufer as the chief coordinator of all British operations, and there Leiter had really found his niche. He was the perfect bureaucrat, bringing in order where 'Pieki' himself, impatient of detail, had failed to do so. Yes, a good man on a team. But not a man to spark off a new idea . . .

He sent for him, and asked for all the files of agents still operating in the British Isles. 'Pieki' could have sorted through them and saved him much work, but he could not tell Leiter to do it. He didn't know what he was looking for himself.

This unexpected request sent Major Leiter into a flutter. He wished the Colonel had been there to explain, or someone from Sophien Terrace in Hamburg that had the actual running of the agents. The long row of filing cabinets for 'Golf Course'—England—looked impressive, but so many of the files were marked 'inactive' now. Since war had been declared, Scotland Yard's Special Branch and MI5, British Counter-Intelligence, had been busy. Armed with special powers, they had arrested all enemy aliens, then many friendly aliens, as well as all persons they had found suspicious, even those of British nationality—a grand sweep. Yet to take a small group of files in to 'Der Alte' as covering the whole of Great Britain would make it appear that the department had been lax. Appearances meant a great deal to the Major.

His staff brought out the main files, each one of a *Haupt-V-Mann*. He sent them scurrying back. Not only the Chief Agents—all of them, he insisted. It was fortunate that for a long time the Abwehr had made a policy of working with British nationals—not only professional agents but Fascist sympathisers, IRA, Welsh Nationalists. The Scottish Nationalists had been disappointing—in fact the Scottish section was deplorably thin. To make it look more substantial, Leiter himself went to the cabinet and took out the remaining Scottish files. These were contacts of small importance, casual informers.

"Junk," one secretary muttered to his fellow worker as the stiff-backed Major left the room. The other man spat into his handkerchief. "Brass hat!"

When the Major entered the office, the heart of what the staff called the *Fuchsbau*—the fox's lair—the Admiral was bending over a map of the British Isles. It was a huge, detailed map which would have distressed the British Admiralty very much if they had seen it. Prepared by Colonel Ulrich Liss of *Fremde Heere West*, it showed on the two

24

thousand miles of British coast, every bay, inlet and estuary marked with all its fortifications or lack of them, certainly equal to any charts in Great Britain. But the Admiral was looking inland, his pencil point tapping at Windsor, and he had a discouraged air.

He glanced up at the Major: tall, stout, his face freshly shaven, his grey hair neatly brushed, his uniform fit for the parade ground. With a shrug of his shoulders that was hardly perceptible, he told the Major to leave the files and sent him back to his administrative tasks.

All that day, and the next night, Canaris spent going through the files. When he tired he took a short nap on the bed and then rose, drank coffee and went back to work. By dawn the next day he had come to the smallest pile, the Scottish section. His eyes were red and burning. The first file he saw was the one that Leiter had added last and placed on top of the heap.

By its code it was obviously of the least importance, one of a group of informants, some of them unpaid and unwitting, correspondents from all over Great Britain whose chatty letters to friends and relatives in Germany, put together, had provided useful knowledge to the Abwehr. The Admiral gave it an irritated glance—so like Leiter to waste his time. It was coded, facetiously no doubt, 'Röslein'. A monstrously large file, stuffed with letters—it looked like hundreds of them. One more cook or housemaid sending information home—troop movements and anti-aircraft posts mixed up with legs of lamb and fur coats bought in the sales. Then he noticed a cross-index number.

He was a meticulous man and for all his weariness looked up the reference. It was to one of Lahousen's men, in Abwehr II. When he got the man's file, the Admiral looked at it with some perplexity. This was the 'Black Knight', one of the Abwehr's most skilled assassins.

Canaris took up the correspondence from the 'Röslein' file and began at the beginning. The first letter was

25

dated 1936. Reading through, at first, was not as time-consuming as it might have been. Someone had carefully marked out the passages of interest—someone with a brain. Canaris seemed to remember the handwriting of the notations. It was that of a successful *Förscher,* a scout for spies . . . Yes, the Admiral recalled—Johann Metz, of Munich. Where was he now?

Metz had circled the name of the house on top of 'Röslein's' writing paper. It meant nothing to the Admiral, but as he read on, the red-circled passages suddenly struck him with their meaning. He looked at the name of the house again, and the address—a simple address, a name, a county, a country. After August of 1939, the careful, intelligent marking ceased. Some Abwehr clerk had checked for the obvious data for a time, but 'Röslein' was a poor observer, and came up with nothing of value to him. Very soon her letters had merely been numbered and thrown in the file. Except for the cross-reference number on the original file cover, there was nothing obvious to connect her with anything of importance, or 'Black Knight'.

Whatever had happened to Metz, whose game apparently this had been? Suddenly, the Admiral remembered. Of course. A chill touched him. No-one would ever know. Metz, like so many others, had disappeared without trace.

But the chill was forgotten in his rising excitement. The two most recent letters, dated in June, he read three times. The last words he read in a blur. *"And if only I could be sure you were getting my letters, my darling, I wouldn't even mind so much that you can't write to me . . ."*

He got up and stood once more over his map, peering, marking. Although he had not slept properly for forty-eight hours, suddenly his mind was sharp and clear. He sent for Leiter.

"Signal Sophien Terrace. I want every detail that can be scraped up on Röslein and Black Knight. Anyone who

26

was there in '36 is to be questioned. And they'll need to contact the SS—if there are any problems there, refer them to me at once. Report back to me here as soon as you have the information."

The next day he knew as much as anyone alive about Jean Sinclair, code-named Röslein, and Horst Holstein, the Black Knight.

* * *

For Horst Holstein, the SS had been a dream come true. How he had longed to be one of that noble band! He had been afraid he could never qualify, with his mother an Englishwoman. But Reichsführer Himmler, in his wisdom, had ordered that some foreign blood, provided it was suitably Nordic, was not a bar for the SS.

And his happiness had been complete when he had been made an officer. He had been invited to the Schloss Wewelsburg, had participated in the ceremonies of the Teutonic Knights, even the secret chapter, and had been seated in his own armchair, with the silver plate. His name had been engraved there. That had been as precious to him as receiving his sword with the two lightning flashes on the scabbard.

How proud he had been—he, the son of a caretaker, there with the lawyers and the socialities. He wished his father had been alive to see it. His mother, after all, had been only lukewarm in her appreciation. Governess. Englishwoman. Annoying him all through his childhood to pronounce his English *properly*. "Make the 'R' with your tongue and your palate, not in the back of your throat." She had had to go to a camp, eventually, for re-education. It had taken two years. But for him there had been all the bright lights of Munich.

The summer of '36 had been warm with marching, parades and music everywhere. It was far too exciting for the very young tourist, Jean Sinclair. In the evening, there were the beerhalls and cafés, and more music and the handsome young men. Never had she known anything like that. Particularly the SS, in their smart uniforms, the shining boots, their black cars with the red leather seats . . .

The Highlands where she had grown up had been all too thin of young men. Some said it was the last war that had killed off so many Highlanders who should have fathered families, others complained that all the men had to go off to find work, for crofting was almost finished now. No small croft could keep a family alive these days. Donald Sinclair, Jean's father, was fortunate: he had always worked as a ghillie on the Balmoral estate.

Jean, a child born late to middle-aged parents, had been a spoiled one, people said. And when she had wanted to go into Aberdeen to be a nurse, her parents had agreed. But Aberdeen was not the paradise of boys, dancing and the cinema that she had hoped it would be. The hours at the hospital were long, the work hard. All she did was scrub the ward floors, only to have the matron tell her to 'Scrub that floor again, Sinclair. There's dirt yet in the corners.'

The young men of Aberdeen had little interest in the probationer nurses who slept like captives in the grim old hospital. She had been glad enough to give up and go home. Her mother soon found her a place as under-house-maid in one of the great houses nearby. Jean found the work light after the hospital; she was naturally neat-fingered and won approbation. Her parents were relieved that she had settled to something and also, perhaps, for they were feeling their years, relieved that the high-spirited girl was no longer under their roof.

This did not last long, as Jean's employers, in a burst of economy, gave up their Highland house. They were not the only ones to economise: the new King, who had little interest in Balmoral, cut down relentlessly on the staff, and Donald Sinclair was one of those who lost his position. The King's economies, though reasonable from his point of view, were not received well in the area where so much poverty existed, and it was rumoured that the King was spending hundreds of thousands of pounds on jewels for an American woman who, it was said, had two husbands already.

His brother, the Duke of York, a very different kind of man, was extremely perturbed about these economies. He had not been consulted and could only remain silent, but he was concerned for the old family servants. When Jean Sinclair was recommended for a vacant position in the Ducal house at Deeside, Birkhall, the Duchess was happy to offer it to her. As Birkhall House was used mostly for the shooting season, only a skeleton staff was kept, augmented when the family arrived. The work was no hardship, but it was a somewhat lonely life for a young girl.

However, Jean settled in. The hospital had been a lesson. She liked a place where she had her rest, the food was good and the cook never minded if she sat down at any hour of the day to have a cup of tea and a piece of cake or shortbread. And the two of them listened to the wireless when there wasn't too much crackling from the atmospherics. Her wages were not large, but her parents felt there was honour in her position, for when the Duchess came up for a few days, Jean soon became quite a favourite.

So it was that when Jean, rather daringly, asked permission to take her summer holiday with some young people who were going on a hiking tour of Germany, her parents agreed. A good girl should have a treat. And she was to have rather more of a treat than they intended.

Several of the girls of the hiking party, entranced by the glamorous SS, managed to pick them up in the cafés. The young officers were quite willing. Hitler had been concerned that marriage was not producing enough pure Nordic babies for the Reich. The SS were encouraged to spread the seed without benefit of clergy, and if they amused themselves with a few pretty foreigners, their seniors looked upon them with benevolence. After all, did not the Führer himself have a young English lady friend?

From admiring all, Jean quickly fell in love with one —the fair, blue-eyed, most handsome Horst Holstein, Untersturmführer. His perfect English—better than hers, Jean said, laughing—helped the romance along. He, in turn, was attracted to the Scots girl with her freckles, her tiny nose and the wild rose flush on her cheeks. She would have been extremely pretty, except that her mouth was too often parted, giving her the look of a trustful puppy. When it was time for the group to move on, Jean, the former nurse, faked a sprained ankle very credibly, and the hiking party, hoping to do a little mountain climbing, went on without her, promising to meet her on the way back.

Young Jean had been so long in an almost completely female society that she was very ready for love. After a long, happy day when she had been driven through the streets of Munich in the SS car, with the siren screaming and all traffic giving way before them, she had been duly seduced on its red leather cushions. So enthusiastic was she that Holstein had been moved to vainglory.

It was a cheerful custom among his band of brother officers, as they gathered in their favourite café of an evening, to chalk up, on a convenient board, their 'score' from the previous night. A weekly tally was kept and the winner was the recipient of free drinks. Holstein was so often a winner that his claims had been questioned, but those who knew him best spoke up in his defence. He was indeed a priapic young man, even considering his youth, and women were drawn to his angelic countenance. And no sentiment ever hindered him in his conquests. One night, quite soon after the beginning of this affair, he marched into the café and quietly chalked up the figure nine. His admirers broke into a round of applause.

Holstein, plied with drinks, described his amorous *Mädchen* in detail, even to the light dusting of freckles

30

covering her small, but high and firm breasts and her lively haunches. The intriguing freckles lingered in the minds of the young men, as well as the Scots girl's erotic energy. The matter was widely discussed and came to the ears of Holstein's Commanding Officer, Oberführer Schreig. To the dismay of Untersturmführer Holstein, he was summoned to answer certain questions. But it was not the Oberführer who wished to question him. He was most lenient with his men and had brought about Holstein's trouble by bragging about his prowess at a dinner the night before.

The man in civilian clothes who questioned him was an Abwehr agent. He asked a good many questions about the Scots girl. Holstein could not know it, but at that time the agent's action was mere routine. His interest in the girl was very slight.

Admiral Canaris and the Abwehr were in annoying difficulties regarding Great Britain. The Führer wanted peace with that nation and refused to allow any spy system to operate there. Admiral Canaris himself wanted peace with Great Britain, but did not believe that ignorance of what was happening was the best way to get it. Also he knew that should the Führer ever change his mind, he would want an apparatus ready to work for him. But such an apparatus was not built in a day, or even a year. A first-rate network was a slow growth.

But a network could not be built without money, and in the circumstances there could be no appropriation. Canaris had had to bleed what he could from other budgets, but in the mid-thirties none of them was ample. And so he had instructed his people to gather a network as cheaply as possible. Apart from the important professionals who had to be reasonably well paid, there was an assortment of petty peeping Toms, stringers, sleepers, cutouts and go-betweens, some willing partners, some dopes or dupes.

Scotland was remarkably thin of informants. The Abwehr agent was only interested because Jean Sinclair came, he thought, from Aberdeen. All that he wanted was a correspondence to be established with the girl on her return. The letters would be dictated by an agent to elicit cautiously what she observed as to fortifications on the port and along the river, troop movements and other such useful bits of information that could be checked against others.

Holstein answered the questions put to him with great frankness. It was explained to him that he was to become a correspondent.

"You will write to the girl through a London address," he was informed. "Promise her marriage to keep her interested. But persuade her to keep her mouth shut."

The Untersturmführer had been aghast. He did not want to promise Jean marriage—he had ambitions which rose higher than marrying a servant girl. And though he was sure she would write, he could hardly imagine that silly girl keeping quiet about anything. She talked constantly; even, in a rather irritating way, in his own most breathless moments. And giggled.

He protested. As an SS officer he had acquired a good opinion of himself and his own importance. The Abwehr agent, Johann Metz, a professional, had taken a dislike to this Holstein. Perhaps because of his foul tongue—Metz had three daughters himself. This young man with his bright hair, his light blue eyes, his fresh and ingenuous look . . . Grimly, Metz wondered what this Jean Sinclair would have thought could she have heard her angel describing every part of her body to his companions, among their roars of laughter, and declaring that she butted him with her haunches like a bitch in heat.

It would be good to turn the tables on him, to let him have some of the treatment he was so fond of giving. After a word, the Oberführer left the office. Two Gestapo men were sent for and ordered to persuade the young Holstein, without in any way marring that golden beauty. They had little trouble.

He was taken to the nearest camp, just a short way out of the town, where 'undesirables' and uncooperative citizens were being held. Some had been there for several months, awaiting final disposition of their cases, and their general looks did not cheer Holstein, in whom the only strong emotion was one of self-preservation. He was left to cool his heels for an hour or two in a hut that served as a cell and was foul from its last occupant. The hut was one of a number round what was known as the exercise yard, and into this yard a prisoner was brought for punishment.

Nothing was said to Holstein, but he could see what happened through an open hatch. The Gestapo men took up their positions, about ten yards apart, in a wide circle. Each was armed with a truncheon. A man, thin, naked, was pushed through a wooden gate, and it was only after a few moments of confused recollection that Holstein could place his still familiar look.

The man had once been an SS officer, living in Munich, but he had disappeared. There had been whispers that he had proved 'unreliable'. Holstein, if he had thought about it at all, had assumed he was dismissed, and had left the area in shame.

The ex-officer was beaten on the rump and forced to run the circle. As he came to one of the armed men he was beaten until he fell, and after he fell he was beaten again and driven on. It took four hours, but he died at last. Holstein had seen many such deaths, but of *Untermenschen*, Communists, Social Democrats. For the first time it was borne in on him that no-one was sacrosanct. *No-one*. Not even Horst Holstein. When he was driven back to Munich he was very ready to do what he was told. Somehow.

For underneath his attempt at coolness, he was close to panic. In spite of his willingness, he simply did not see how he could do what was wanted. His Commanding Officer, the Oberführer, was sorry for this young man whom he had found valuable, and reflected that women had been the ruin of too many good young men. Heydrich himself had been cashiered from the Navy because of some trouble with a girl.

He sent for Holstein, gave him a drink and some fatherly advice. Of course, the order must be obeyed. But there was nothing in it to his detriment, quite the reverse. If he managed well, there would be promotion. Holstein pointed out that there was no way he could manage well. He couldn't keep Jean quiet. Already she had taken a hundred photographs, cut off a bit of his hair to put in a locket, and showed every sign of making a public scandal of herself.

The Oberführer entered into the spirit of the thing. He would handle the girl, he promised. Holstein should go and make his proposal, and then bring her to him for his permission. After all, there was Holstein's *Sippenbuch* to be considered. The girl had to be given a certificate under the racial laws, and the result entered in his Clan Book.

Holstein, though he didn't like taking orders from a civilian, was very willing to obey his Oberführer. Armed with a bouquet of red roses, provided by his obliging senior, he went and made his proposal. Jean had been in ecstasy. She had longed, hoped . . . but she had not dared to believe . . .

Then the Oberführer, very grim, had refused permission. Jean had returned to her lodging in tears. The next day Holstein took her back, and the girl pleaded with this terrifying officer. Gradually, he allowed himself to be worn down. He had a long interview with her, alone. Jean, flushed with worry and agitation, her hazel eyes shining with tears, was most attractive. The Oberführer was tempted to ask a few favours on his own account. He believed in the circumstances they might have been forthcoming, but he restrained himself.

He told Jean that though it was utterly forbidden, he would allow the engagement but it must remain secret. Holstein would be in the greatest danger if there was the

34

slightest hint. Even back in Scotland she must tell no-one. The SS had many enemies, and should they learn that this fine young SS officer had disobeyed the laws of the élite band, they would be happy to make sure he was ruined and disgraced. It was easy for Jean to be convinced of this, for already her room had been rifled, her photographs and mementos of her beloved stolen, even to the film in her camera.

She explained anxiously all this to the Commanding Officer. Gravely, he assured her that all would be well, as long as she kept silent. He would track down and deal with the perpetrators of the robbery. It certainly was an easy task, he reflected, since he had arranged it himself. Once Holstein achieved the rank of Sturmbannführer, he went on, his position would be different. Then he could apply openly for permission to marry a foreigner and he, as his Oberführer, would recommend it. Then Frau Holstein could come and live in Munich.

At those magic words 'Frau Holstein', Jean's eyes had shone with love and hope. Also, the very young girl was intrigued and thrilled. The Oberführer, grown benign, drove her round Munich and pointed out a house that might be her own. It was only occupied at the moment by a family of Jews. He took her inside and had the mistress of the house show her round. Jean's eyes were wide at the luxury of it all—the carpets, the curtains, the fine furniture, the crystal chandelier in the drawing-room, four bedrooms and a bathroom, and all for her and Horst. Then he took the lovers to a café and regaled them with sweet Rhine wine. The two had ended the evening content enough, back on the red leather seats.

Six months to a year was all that the Abwehr had hoped for from Jean Sinclair. Eventually she would talk to her parents and the correspondence would be stopped. Or she would find another lover, and simply forget. But if Holstein forgot her from the day she left, she cherished him to her heart. Every day of separation, back in the quiet of Deeside, made him more a combination of Siegfried, Young Lochinvar and Bonnie Prince Charlie. And she wrote. And wrote.

The agent, Metz, grew irritated by the file. It was not worth the trouble of so much paper work. The girl rarely went into Aberdeen and though she lived in a house close to the Dee, she didn't know a fortification if she saw one. He decided to close the file, and glanced through the correspondence to see if there was anything worth saving when he burnt the rest. Two letters had just come in and he scanned them quickly, but they were like the rest. The girl was entirely taken up with her own thoughts and dreams, observed nothing and said little except to pour out a love that apparently thrived on absence.

But as he put the last letter down, something stuck in his mind and he took it up again and glanced at it, frowning. Not guns, ships or aeroplanes but: "*Everything here is exactly the same as it always is. Of course, the family haven't been up, with all the fuss. It's strange to think that when I next see my lady she'll be 'Her Majesty'. And she from Glamis Castle. Mrs Donald is in the most terrible fidget, but I can only think of you, my darling, and how long it will be before your promotion . . .*"

He realised for the first time just who this girl's employers were. Of course, six months ago when the file was opened it would not have seemed such a great matter—but the six months had brought great change. Even then, it had been worth more trouble than he had taken.

He went into a burst of activity. At that time, the Abwehr was by far the most powerful of the secret services, and he had no trouble in transferring Holstein into its service, and putting him through training as an agent. Holstein was furious, but there was nothing he could do. He had forgotten 'Röslein'—apart from his routine duty of copying the letters that Metz sent him. But though he missed his old companions, he had found himself well suited to certain aspects of his new work.

He had distinguished himself in training with Lahousen's saboteurs, but reached his pinnacle as an assassin. His superiors found him useful in that he combined great physical skills with an emotional state not often found in adults: the sufferings of others had no meaning to him at all, except as they affected his personal convenience. He was an infant with the intelligence and body of a man. His code name was 'Black Knight' and Lahousen used him often, many times with a degree of repugnance.

Now that 'Röslein' had grown in importance, money was spent. When she had holidays, her lover was sent to meet her at a safe house in London. This kept her happy and interested and enabled the Abwehr to establish Holstein's new identity. He had been given a new cover story which he fed to Jean, between the sheets. Now he knew he could trust her fidelity, she could know the truth. He was a British Secret Service agent, and had been when they met. Although his father, who had died long ago, had been German, he had been brought up to be entirely British. Because of his birth and his perfect command of both languages, he had been asked early to work with the British Secret Service, to infiltrate the SS. His real name, he told her, was Henry, and his mother had changed the German Holstein to Holbrook.

Jean, intrigued before, was now lifted to seventh heaven. The charms of the SS were all forgotten. It was far better, after all, that Horst—Henry—was an Englishman. Though not as good as if he had been a Scot, she said, giggling. Of course, their engagement still had to remain secret, until his work was done. Now she realised that his very life depended on her discretion, she became quite solemn.

She begged him not to go back to Germany, but he pointed out that a man must do his work. Had she not been very scornful of the former King who had given up his work for the woman he loved? Indeed she had. For that Mrs Simpson!

37

The correspondence continued through the address, though Jean didn't realise it, of the Hungarian Embassy. Their marriage was often talked of, always postponed. Just before the invasion of Poland, Johann Metz of Hamburg fell from grace and disappeared. The Black Knight grew in prestige, but his records were kept with those of Lahousen's sabouteurs. His part in the Röslein matter was forgotten. His letters to her stopped, but hers continued, assuring him she knew it was the war that prevented his correspondence. She would wait for him for ever.

She might have done so. Metz had been a close-mouthed agent, and Röslein's importance could have been completely forgotten. It was not until Leiter brought in the dusty file to Admiral Canaris as make-weight that the game, begun by Metz in '36, at last came to its climax.

The Admiral looked again at Röslein's last two letters. All his puzzling and confusion were gone. The solution to his problem lay before him, as though his chess game were already played and he was familiar with every move. By July 7, the file of the silly little Röslein beside him, the head of the Abwehr knew, with a sense almost of awe, that he held the fate of Great Britain in his hands.

TWO

Fred Karno's War [i]

In London, July 7 was a day of occasional sunshine and sudden showers. From Horse Guards Parade, the rain pattered against the windows of the book-lined room at 10 Downing Street where Winston Spencer Churchill presided over a meeting of the War Cabinet Defence Committee. He sat halfway down the table behind the fortification he had built up of pens, pencils, blotters, a paper punch, tags, a bottle of glue and a pile of red labels that read: ACTION THIS DAY. The labels were ready for his orders that would govern the day-to-day living of about a quarter of the population of the world. Pink-faced, round-shouldered, the Prime Minister looked smaller and more delicate than he did in his photographs. His brow was dark. He felt unaccountably depressed.

To anyone else his depression would have seemed accountable enough. The subject of the meeting was the imminent invasion of England. While the British Expeditionary Force had been in France the Chief of Staff had made the position clear:

"Should the Germans succeed in establishing a force with its vehicles in this country, our Army forces have not got the offensive power to drive it out."

Well, then it had been expected that they would only save twenty or thirty thousand men from the Belgian coast. Instead they had three hundred thousand! But it was a broken army, with all its equipment lost. And now Italy was in the war, and Wavell facing superior numbers on five fronts, calling for men and equipment. From Gibralter, Malta, Hong Kong, Singapore, India, Burma and West Africa, as well as all the small outposts, requests were coming in for reinforcements and supplies. Supplies —for the moment the Prime Minister pushed that thought aside.

The First Lord of the Admiralty finished making his report. The Navy, at least, would be able to do its job, despite heavy losses to the U-boats, and all that had been lost at Narvik. Narvik—he hated to think of that. But this was not like '14–'18, when the Navy could be relied on for the defence of the country. Air power, also, was essential now.

He glanced up at Dowding, his Air Chief Marshal. 'Stuffy' Dowding had protested for years that Fighter Command was starved of men, money and machines. Well, since he had taken over as Prime Minister he'd done his best to get things moving. 'Get cracking', as the young men of the RAF would say. Yet the men he had to deal with would agree about the emergency and then go off to the country from Friday—or even Thursday—to Monday, where they did no work at all.

He thought of his own weekends of constant work. One of his Private Secretaries had burst in upon him in the bath that morning—two fully equipped Canadian Divisions were on their way to Iceland. Iceland! The Secretary, a rather prudish young man, had taken down an urgent note while carefully keeping his gaze somewhat above the Ministerial person. Even when the Prime Minister splashed his elegant trousers . . .

Well, he'd put Beaverbrook in charge of aircraft production, and that had trodden on a lot of toes. But even Beaverbrook could not provide the 'planes to make the difference now. Dowding's voice was unemotional as he

40

gave the figures, but the lines on his face from nose to mouth were deep and dragged downwards. At least, the Prime Minister thought ruefully, Dowding's protests had saved him from sending the last of the air reserves to France, to fight a battle already lost.

It had been a nasty business with the dog, this morning, he thought. That was enough to sour his mood. With so many despatches, they'd been late getting off from Chequers, and his chauffeur had been driving at a smart pace to get him to the meeting. There had been no policeman that day to clear the traffic before them, but his chauffeur needed only to press a pedal to ring the large railway bell that Churchill himself had had installed to warn anything that could hear on the country lanes. He had seen the cheerful little fox terrier breaking through the hedgerow before the chauffeur.

"Sound the bell! Sound the bell!" he had shouted, but the mechanism had stuck and although the chauffeur tried to swerve they had bumped over the poor beast, leaving the Prime Minister with a sense of melancholy. But that was not the only thing depressing his spirits.

General Ismay, having given the figures of the Home Army, got onto the wretched state of available weapons. Most of the figures Churchill knew already. There had not been one real armoured division in the whole of the British Expeditionary Force. Chamberlain, when he was still Prime Minister, had pointed that out. He had never believed that Great Britain could fight Germany. No-one had wanted rearmament, he'd said. And now we were in no position to take on Hitler's conquering army.

Chamberlain sat in his place silently. His juniors had always referred to him as 'the Boiling Fowl'. Now he looked old and ill—too far gone for the pot. Churchill would have pitied his former rival, but he could not forgive him. Hardly a month ago he had supported Halifax, when he had suggested the benefits of making peace with Hitler before France fell.

41

"We will not get such good terms three months from now," he had said.

Peacemonger!

Ismay was still reciting his tale of doom.

"I must remind you, gentlemen, that this is all the equipment in our possession, not stored reserves. Two-pounder anti-tank guns: fifty-four; Bren guns: 2300, but as you know, they proved almost useless in France."

Not surprising, Churchill thought, as many of them had been taken from museums. He had given the order himself. Better than nothing, he had thought.

"Two- and three-inch mortars, very few, and little ammunition reserve . . ."

The Prime Minister growled quietly, bit down on his cigar and stopped listening. That infamous Chamberlain-Halifax proposal. Italy would stay neutral and Mussolini would get good peace terms for Great Britain from Hitler, guaranteeing her independence. *Great Britain*'s independence! And Mussolini didn't want much. Only Malta, Cyprus, a share in Gibralter, Egypt, Syria, Iraq and the Sudan. And from France: Nice, Savoy, Corsica and Tunis. A modest proposal.

"Armoured cars: thirty-seven in England, fifteen in Ireland . . ." Ismay was chanting and so the list went on.

The Prime Minister, forced to hear again the figures that made the peace proposal seem reasonable, glared at Chamberlain. He himself had appointed him President of the Council. Politics—it had been essential. His own position had been so precarious. And still was.

The King hadn't wanted to summon Winston Churchill, he was certain of that. The King much preferred Halifax. So did the Conservative Party. Only the fact that the new Government had to be a Coalition, that Labour would not stomach Halifax, had given Winston Churchill his chance at last. Sometimes he had to think—what a chance!

He knew that Chamberlain, his former chief, still

hankered after a negotiated peace. It was Attlee and Greenwood, Labour men both, who had joined Churchill in squashing Hitler's peace proposal. Two very strange bedfellows for him but they had served.

There had been rumours of peace talks, and a split in the Government. Chamberlain had had to take to the wireless to deny that peace negotiations had ever been considered. His voice, widely broadcast, had sounded entirely sincere. The wireless had its uses. Churchill wondered if 'the Boiling Fowl' still wanted to be Prime Minister.

Well, best to put a good face on it. There was trouble enough without disunion at home. The great mass of the public seemed loyal. The most prominent Nazis had been jailed. All aliens were registered and some would be interned. He would put spirit into the nation! And yet . . .

The door opened—a telegram for him. It must be marked 'Most Urgent' to interrupt the meeting. He looked with foreboding. It came from the Duke of Windsor. He scowled and groaned. The other men at the table looked up, startled. They didn't know if he had received more bad news, of which there was always plenty, or if he were groaning at the undeniable facts Ismay was giving them: simply, there were not enough weapons of any kind for the men already in the Army, small as it was, before any more were called up.

Churchill regarded the paper in his hand with exasperation and weariness. These messages had been coming to him almost daily since he had taken this high office, as indeed they had before. The Lowlands had fallen, the King of the Belgians had made a treacherous peace, the BEF fought their way to the beach at Dunkirk to avoid extinction, but still these messages showered upon him like rice on a bride and groom.

While he was worrying whether von Runstedt would pounce on the poor remains of the once proud British force—and why he hadn't the Prime Minister would never fathom—during all his own strenuous efforts to save France, still the messages came. Five flights Churchill had made to France. He had even proposed to unite France with Great Britain—but the French had refused even that. So like them: better be raped by the Germans than embraced by the British. He remembered the words of Reynaud, repeated over and over, dogged with defeat:

"We have been defeated. We are beaten. We have lost the battle."

Now the Prime Minister was left with nothing but de Gaulle and his Cross of Lorraine—the heaviest cross he had to bear. Except for the Duke. The Duke, it seemed, wanted a post with more prestige. He would not come home unless his wife would be acknowledged as a Royal Highness. And the Duchess wanted her maid, left behind somewhere in France.

He closed his mind, as well as his ears, to General Ismay's voice. No use dwelling on the grim probability of defeat. Sometimes, in facing facts, one had to follow Lord Nelson and raise the telescope to one's blind eye! He would make his own facts. He barked out a few suggestions, closed his ears again and huddled into his seat.

He had had one pleasant message that morning. Thompson, his bodyguard, had told him that today Sergeant Barney would be receiving his Victoria Cross from the King. The Prime Minister wished he had the time to attend the ceremony. He relaxed slightly as, smiling, he thought of that rascally young man, whom he'd known as a lively, red-headed boy.

From the beginning he'd been sure there was good in him, and so it had proved. He had known Rex Barney nearly all his life, the son of Detective-Sergeant Alfred Barney, now retired with a wound, who had once been his own bodyguard. Young Rex, after a few wild years—and what young man worth his salt was never wild?—had joined the army in '38, and his conduct with the BEF in the retreat and on the beach had justified all the Prime Minister's expectations.

He had read the despatches, and had actually spoken to a frightened young private who had served with him. Barney had stayed on the beach until the last, after Lord Gort himself had gone. He had stuck with his gun, driving off the low-flying Stukas, and almost got left behind.

But it was his action on the retreat that had won him the VC. Barney's company had been in the rearguard. Under orders, they had fallen further and further back, their officers killed, the men mowed down, until there had been a mere handful of men left, about twenty-four led by Barney himself. There was no food, but he had foraged and found a pig. The men had butchered it, and cooked it on a carefully concealed fire. After eating, they'd found shelter in the ruins of some outbuildings near a burned-out farmhouse. While they slept, young Barney had stayed on guard. As the twilight deepened, Barney, always keen-eyed, spotted dark shapes, spaced at regular intervals, moving towards them. He'd caught his breath—there were at least two hundred and fifty men. Quietly, he roused his small squad. They had nothing heavier than their Bren gun. They had a few rifles, little ammunition and no hope of reinforcements.

"Right!" Barney had yelled. "Let's get a bit closer, chums."

He leapt forward, his whistle shrilling, as though for all the world he was playing some football game, moving in to tackle. His squad followed him, howling. Startled, the Germans had fallen back. Scrambling to the roof of a barn, Barney had picked off nineteen Germans—then, seizing the Bren gun from a fallen man, he pelted forward again. One lance-corporal had reported that "when we ran out of ammo we kicked, choked and bit 'em. That German infantry had never seen nothing like it. Fair flummoxed they was and fell back—if you can call it falling back. Running from the devil, they was."

The Prime Minister thought dourly that that was one of the few victories in England's most terrible defeat since —his mind shied away from the thought of Hastings. Not exactly the methods of a Guards' officer perhaps, but . . . this war was not going to be won by gentlemen. He knew that. He wondered how long it would take for others to realise it.

"Rifles . . ." Ismay was still reciting.

Churchill's mind slid back to his Boer War days. Some of these Boer farmers had learned to fight—fight the British Army—with almost no weapons. A few rifles. They attack by night in small parties, catching odd pockets of troops unawares. He decided that he would form some small, élite units to work the same way. With fit, strong young men of high courage, like Rex Barney, he thought.

With a sigh, he put that happy thought away, and read the telegram. Most of it was as usual, except that a new demand had been added. The Duke insisted that his valet be released from the armed forces and sent to him in Lisbon. He simply could not manage without him. Churchill frowned. The man who sent this message had been his Prince and his King and had received his complete loyalty.

On the day of Abdication, Churchill, with tears in his eyes, had quoted:

"He nothing common did or mean, Upon that memorable scene." But now, the man who had left his job and did nothing but fuss about his domestic problems seemed, if not common or mean, something perilously close to it. The Prime Minister would have liked to order that these messages no longer be brought to him, but his old allegiance lived on in present courtesy and he couldn't say the words.

His eyes looked with suspicion on another urgent summons that came in, but it was for the First Lord of the Admiralty. Churchill saw his face turn pale. He asked to see it and Alexander passed him the message. A convoy had been attacked, a destroyer and a tanker torpedoed and sunk, blazing. All hands had been lost, burned in the blazing oil.

The two men glanced at each other and looked away. The Prime Minister felt tears pricking the back of his eyes. He gulped and collected himself.

"Don't give it to the newspapers," he said gruffly. "The British public have had enough bad news lately without this."

And in giving orders he forgot the Duke for that day.

It was four am before the Prime Minister got to bed. He could manage with little sleep for he had always been a good sleeper. But that morning sleep would not come. No arrangement of pillows would suit him; a brandy did not induce the needed rest. The depression of the morning was back on him, a dreary agitation. It was not the real problems of the war . . . he was a warrior and despite his swiftly passing sentiment, he enjoyed the battle. No, it was something else.

But what? Things were better than last month and far better than they had been in May. Even the King, who had been so stiff in his manner, was said to be coming round. The public was not blaming him for Norway; Chamberlain had got the blame for that, though the former First Lord knew his own responsibility. The German spy-master, Canaris, had beaten him there. He thought of him with grim respect. Another former naval person. No— that was the luck of war. He thrashed round in his bed. It was those damned telegrams. That was it. He sat up and lit a cigar in disgust.

There had been stories when the Duke was in Spain, sent on to him from the Secret Service—or what was left of it after the fiasco in Holland—that the Germans were sniffing round him. Hardly surprising! But the Duke had left to go to Lisbon as ordered, and the Prime Minister had not been seriously concerned. He had sent the flying boats and orders that the Duke should come home. Something could be arranged about the Duchess that would keep him happy.

But every day the Duke failed to leave. And those telegrams, more and more absurd, the man who sent them seeming not to realise the country was at war. Why the devil *didn't* he come home? That was the nagging question keeping the Prime Minister awake.

From the remnants of the Secret Service he got no information that was of any use. Embassy chatter. The gossip of the gun clubs of Europe. For a moment he thought of Admiral Canaris again, and envied Hitler his luck there. Something would have to be done about the Secret Service. Now they had a new Chief perhaps they could get organised . . . as long as Menzies didn't stick to hiring only ex-army officers and realised this war was not a game between well-bred opponents. It was going to be a dirty business before it was done.

What *was* the Duke up to? He took a last, non-refreshing pull at his cigar and put it down beside him. He would think of something less disturbing. His idea that he'd had that morning and not thought of since—his Storm Troops, or Leopards, he would call them. Or Commandos, as they had been called in South Africa. Fine young men like Rex Barney.

Rex Barney. He wished he had someone like Barney to send to Lisbon. He'd soon find out what was going on. No respecter of persons. Why, young Barney had once told him—and he was Chancellor of the Exchequer then, he remembered—that his face was like a blister with wrinkles. And when he had reproached the lad for whistling, for that was the one thing that set his nerves on edge, the impudent rascal had stared right in his face and told him, "Then shut your ears!"

He chuckled into his pillow. "Shut your ears!" He *would* send Barney himself. He would get him seconded to his personal staff. Sergeant Rex Barney, on the Prime

48

Minister's service. He felt better. And he went to sleep.

His valet, who had been watching and waiting outside for that moment, came in. He quietly removed the still smouldering cigar, and left, closing the door without a sound. He would have to take in breakfast at eight o'clock. Well, he thought to himself, can't let the old man burn himself to death. King and country need him.

THREE

Fred Karno's War [ii]

Rex Barney had spent the night more pleasantly than the Prime Minister. He was in the upstairs bedroom of the Fox and Hounds, a room properly belonging to the owner of the pub, on his excellent mattress, by the side of the publican's wife. The two were woken early, after a night of strenuous love-making, by shouting and martial noises from the pub yard below.

Rex was out of his bed and at the window in one bound. His eyes took in the scene before his companion had sleepily opened her eyes.

"Oh, for Crissake!" he said, somewhere between amusement and disgust.

Half a dozen elderly men, in civilian dress, were engaged in what they apparently hoped was military exercise. Although the sun was shining, there was mud in the yard from the previous day's showers and already the men were splashed up to their knees. The man barking the orders was old George Gumm, a pompous ass if ever there was one, who had risen to the rank of Captain in 1918.

Rex watched sardonically as they shouldered broomsticks; he grinned as Henry Bodger, the shoe-mender, whose hands seemed to be afflicted with palsy that morning, stuck his broomstick handle into Gumm's eye on attempting an about turn.

"Don't worry, darling," he said to the sleepy Ida. "It's the LDV. Getting ready to save you from Jerry, that's all."

"Home Guard, they call them now," she said. Yawning, she stretched her pink, sturdy arms above her head.

She looked towards the window, watching the sun shine on Rex's rumpled brown hair, turning it to a coppery mop over his face, which was still tanned from Dunkirk. His nose, which had been broken once in a street fight and once in the ring, was peeling, but that battered feature made him no less attractive in her eyes. He was naked and the sight of his strong, athletic body added to her sense of pleasure in the remembrance of the night, but it was when he looked at her and grinned that her heart turned over.

"I'll get us a cup of tea," she said hastily, and jumped up.

Their affair was one of long standing. Ida, older than Rex and settled in her marriage, was a sensible woman and would not let her love become cloying—or demanding. She shuffled off in her slippers to get the tea—the girl usually brought it up, but with Rex there she had to head her off, though God knows, she thought, the little bitch probably knew everything. With Sid in the Army, she hadn't been as careful as she used to be. Getting Rex back after Dunkirk—well!

Rex, smoking his first cigarette of the day, was not feeling his usual content. He watched his father propelling his wheelchair through the yard gate. Come to give his advice, no doubt. His cronies were glad to see him, and forgot their drill to shake his hand.

"Good old Alf," floated up to the window.

George Gumm now was strictly an also ran. Alf Barney had come prepared to lecture on the use of the pistol. None of them had a pistol, but his father had brought some charts and notes that he'd got somehow

51

from the police college. His old mates would still do him a turn like that.

They liked him. Old Barney was someone they could go to and have a pint and a jaw—always at home and knew what they were talking about. That lot could only talk to each other. And it cheered him up. Well, his father ought to get something. All those years of service. Crippled in the line of duty—Irish sods. And if it wasn't for him, Rex, the old chap wouldn't have enough nicker from his pension to keep his little house and have a woman come in to look after him.

What a mug a man had to be to join the police! Spend his life protecting a lot of nobs—and for what? He expressed his feelings forcibly to Ida when she returned with two steaming cups of tea.

"Your mum was glad when he got the job," she pointed out. "Steady wages, that's what a woman looked for then. Poor woman," she added as Mrs Barney had died when Rex was fourteen. Perhaps that's what made him turn out a bit wild like, she thought. Nothing like his mum or dad. Though sometimes she thought it was just his nature.

"Anyway," she added. "You *didn't* join the p'lice, whatever your dad wanted. Tell the truth," she said dispassionately, "don't suppose they'd have wanted you. Not the sort to knuckle under."

She'd heard a few words over the years from old Special Branch men down in the Public Bar, when Alf had gone off to the Gents.

"Born for trouble, that boy. Poor old Alf," had been their judgement.

"Don't know how you've managed in the Army, that's a fact," she added.

She looked at the arrogant line of his head and neck over his powerful shoulders, and meant what she said. Rex had never knuckled under to anything. From the day he'd left school he'd been in one scrape after another. Alf declared he didn't know where he'd got him from. Lucky for Rex, he was a local favourite through playing in the football team—Bellingdon Orient had been champions in those years—and boxing in the club. Got in real trouble mixing it up with the Blackshirts in the East End—but that had only been to help his friend, poor old Larry.

After his dad's getting shot he had decided to make money. Got a stall in the market, and he'd done well. Grab the women and chat them up, he would, and they'd buy anything from him. Soon he'd had four stalls and two shops. Made a mint—even if some people did talk about where the stuff came from. He was a good boy. Looked after his father.

He'd been enjoying himself, with his motor bikes and then racing cars—she'd been terrified he'd kill himself, mad young devil. But he'd chucked it up to join the Army with Larry. Now Larry was dead. She wondered how he was going to stick the Army without him.

"Got my stripes up three times and lost 'em twice," Rex answered her with a shrug. "But it's got to be done, darling. What can you do? Leave it to the old buggers like them down there? I've seen the Germans," he said grimly.

The room was full of fumed oak furniture that must have cost Ida's old man a packet. Big bedstead, two wardrobes, chest of drawers. But there was no comfortable chair so he went back to lie on the bed, propping himself up on the pillows and the thick bolster. Ida sat beside him and he patted her shoulder comfortingly.

No use frightening the women. But from what he'd seen, England didn't have a chance in hell. People liked to talk about Dunkirk—what did they know? The British Army had been smashed to bits. And the French and the Belgians. The Germans had just tanked all over them. If they'd moved in just a bit faster, there wouldn't have been one British soldier left to take off from Dunkirk. The BEF had no tanks—he'd seen the artillery with plywood jobs, for God's sake. As for the RAF—what was that?

When the King had given him his medal the day before, he'd felt like saying a mouthful. But the King had looked as pale and ill as his own father. Poor sod. He'd got dragged into this because his brother wouldn't do his job. Just as he, Rex Barney, had been dragged in because of Larry.

He felt real pain, an unfamiliar sensation in his blithe existence, when he thought of Larry. Rex had wept when his mother died, that large, friendly, placid woman. But no other woman had caused him grief; his loves had been uncomplicated. He enjoyed and liked women, though he usually felt rather sorry for them, just as he felt sorry for Ida, now. Not much of a life.

But Larry . . . He and Larry had knocked about together as kids and as youngsters. Larry had had brains. It was different, talking to Larry. Never knew what he might come up with. Always full of surprises. He had been —well, now he was dead.

Ida looked at him speculatively.

"Thought you might have wanted to get out, now Larry's gone. There are ways."

The thought of Rex being at home while her husband was gone, perhaps for several years, made Ida's heart beat faster.

"Plenty of money to be made now, and easy," she said, very much in earnest. "The war's only on a year and already people are mad to get hold of stuff. All the women working, a lot of them got more money than they ever saw in their lives, and can't find anything to buy. But there's still stuff around to be bought, if you know where to get hold of it."

Rex closed his eyes. He knew all about it. Though it wasn't easy to get out of the Army with the war on. But there were fortunes going to be made in this war. On leave only a few days, and some of his old grafters had been around, asking him if he was interested in a lorry load or two. NAAFI stuff. He couldn't tell Ida that his

54

first impulse had been to break their necks.

Stupid bastards. Johnny Walsh had laughed at his uniform. Said it would make no difference to him if the Government was German—all governments were swines, he'd said. That was what he thought. But there were swine and swine.

Ida, sensitive to his mood if she could not follow his thought, went on.

"Remember how you and Larry used to argue," she said. "Gawd, I remember you saying that war was only to look after the nobs. That you'd be just like your father, getting yourself shot up so that the big pots could live in comfort and not even remember your name when you weren't no more use to 'em."

So he had. But it was different now. He'd been at war and seen for himself.

It was the way Larry had died that made his anger stay hot. Rex had not spoken to anyone about it. If Larry had just died in the retreat or on the beach from the bombardment with all the others it would have been bad, but bearable. But those treacherous Nazi bastards—

He'd first noticed Larry Green the day he'd started school. Larry had started a few days late because of the Jewish holidays. Five years old, on the floor of the playground with three kids on top, pummelling his head. Jew boy. Rex had been with Larry in a lot of fights in their lives. When Larry had decided to join the army in '38 to be ready in time to have a crack at Hitler, Rex sold his businesses, his cars and even his motor-bike to provide for the old man, kissed his women good-bye and went with him.

And they had been ready when war started. They'd thanked God for that, when they saw what happened to the untrained troops who got caught up in the fighting. One rifle to a hundred men, and if they had the ammo they didn't know how to use it. Larry had fought with the best. Their whole unit had fought their arses off. But it was no

55

use. And then the retreat, fighting all the way. At last, they'd been ordered to leave everything, move light and get to the beach. The orders came, he'd heard, from Winnie himself. He'd saved the British Army; he knew how it was done. Not like those chairwarmers at Whitehall.

Rex's lot had got to the beach on the 29th May, a bloody beautiful day, marvellous for a holiday, marvellous for the Luftwaffe. They'd known where the Luftwaffe was all right. They'd come in flying low and mowed down the mob on the beach until there was more blood and ripped carcasses than ever there was at Smithfield Market. He'd brought one of the bastards down for sure and he'd thought he'd got another.

Some of the men not yet in line for the boats had set up scraggy little camps in the dunes—dune dwellers, the officers called them. Everyone scrounging for food—he saw twelve men eat from a tin of bully beef that was soaked through with diesel oil, carving it up with a bayonet.

On the 30th it had been another lovely day for the Germans, but some RAF had turned up and they'd been able to get some men into the boats alive. He could have got a boat himself that day but Larry hadn't got there yet. Larry hadn't done too well on the last leg of the retreat. He'd been wounded in one arm—not too badly, but something was wrong. He'd looked almost yellow. It had been hot and their canteens were empty. Larry wanted water badly. Then the Stukas had come and the group was scattered when they ran for cover. Someone had told him that Larry and Corporal Cade had gone for water and would catch up. He should have gone after him then, Rex thought bitterly. But he'd been busy with his gun—the Messerschmitt 109's had been coming after them as if the Luftwaffe had an endless supply. So he had waited for Larry on the beach.

He'd got his men off, but he couldn't go and maybe leave Larry to be taken prisoner. They all knew what would happen to the Jews. Somebody thought he might be with the men waiting on the Eastern Hole. Ten thousand men there, packed in, waiting for the big ships. But Rex had seen too many men turned away from the embarkation points if they weren't on the manifest of a unit. He had to be sure.

The beachmaster, anxious to get the stragglers in line, let Rex take a lorry and go back into the town. All day he went back and forth, picking up groups of wounded, tired and hopeless men, but Larry was never among them. The town was an unbelievable sight—what was left of it. Men who'd given up on getting back, drunk in the streets on looted wine and spirits, men lining up at the doors of basement brothels in burned-out buildings.

On the 1st of June three destroyers went down and a lot of good men with them, and most of the small boats. After that the bombing was so bad, men could be taken off only at night. Still Larry didn't turn up. On the 4th, Rex was told it was his last chance. The Germans were pressing in too close, the evacuation was to be ended. But by that time he'd found Corporal Cade, riding into Dunkirk in a stolen French van, just in time for the last embarkation. And he had learned what had happened to Larry.

Corporal Cade and Larry had tried to get water at a farmhouse a few hundred yards off the road where he had lost them. Most of the Belgian women, angry that the armies were leaving, or perhaps just afraid, kept their doors locked while they peered out of the windows. The rest of the unit had given up trying, but Cade and Larry persisted. They didn't know it then, but the Germans were right behind them.

The old man in the farmhouse had taken them in and given them water. He had not seemed too unfriendly until Larry, sweating heavily, had loosed his collar. Round his neck was his gold chain and the Star of David. The old man had looked hard. Then the knock came at the door —German soldiers. Cade and Larry had made a run for it, each taking a different path to the road. As Cade reached the shelter of a clump of trees, he heard the old man shout and looked back. He was pointing out to the Germans the path Larry had taken.

For a while Cade had stood motionless. There were six Germans, all armed and carrying a light machine gun. The Germans dragged Larry from a little copse. They'd killed him, but not before they'd had a little sport with their bayonets.

Cade had escaped, but got a bullet in his leg on the way to the coast. If he hadn't have grabbed the van, he'd have been a prisoner for sure. He tried to comfort Rex. It was bad, but better than if Larry had been taken prisoner. They'd made a mistake, trusting the Belgian. Too many Nazis everywhere. The Sarge must remember what it had been like in France. You couldn't be sure of anyone.

Sergeant Barney remembered. If German tanks started rolling down Bellingdon Road, he wondered who would turn out to be Jerry's friends right here. There'd been plenty of British Fascists parading about right up until the war started, and there were those who didn't wear the uniform who might still turn out worse.

No, in spite of what he'd said himself before the war, he knew now that it wasn't being fought just for the big pots. Besides, though he'd never trusted the nobs, old Winnie was in now. Winnie—he was different.

At breakfast in Ida's parlour, he said as much to her. Ida gave her deep, pleasant laugh.

"Oh, you say that because he got round you. Same as he did your father. Your mother used to complain that your father, and all the others—Thompson, Hilliard and the rest—they would kill themselves for him. Above and beyond the call of duty, she always said."

Rex considered as he ate, unknowingly, Ida's week's ration of bacon. True in a way, old Winnie was a slave driver all right. But he was decent to his people. His father had been guarding someone else when he'd caught it, but the old man had sent inquiries, money, and had gone to see him in hospital. And remembered him still at Christmas, every year.

Chancellor of the Exchequer the old man had been then. Special Branch thought the Micks were after him, and his father had had one hell of a job. Worked all the hours God sent, so that his mother used to send him, Rex —a young lad in those days—round to 11 Downing Street to try to get a word to Detective-Sergeant Barney.

Sometimes the staff would take a message, sometimes they wouldn't. Supercilious bastards. And one day he'd really wanted his father. His mother had come down with the 'flu, all chills and fever, but she wouldn't have the doctor. They'd given him the quick heave-ho at No. 11— his father wasn't there and he should run along. Well, he'd never run along for them or anyone else. A window was open and when no-one was looking he'd hopped in.

They'd told the truth—his father wasn't there. He found out later that he'd been sent on an errand. The Chancellor used his staff as he saw fit. But he bumped into Churchill himself in the library. Churchill had not been surprised at the irruption of a boy into his sanctum. A family man, he took children calmly. He counselled waiting for the absent Detective-Sergeant Barney and commended him for spirit and enterprise.

Then, thinking that the child might be nervous in his august presence, he considered what he could do to amuse him. He decided to do what had pleased his own children the most. Dropping to his knees on the carpet, he waved his hands about menacingly and made roaring noises. These noises were supposed to represent the sounds of a gorilla—frightening, but not unpleasantly so.

Rex at ten years-old was a tall child, advanced for his age, already with a certain skill in barter among his fellows. Seeing the great man on his knees, pawing and roaring, made him want to laugh. But he was a polite guest and, not wanting to hurt the feelings of his host, he dropped down on his own knees and pawed and roared in return. He laughed, the Chancellor laughed, and they alternately laughed and roared at each other. So the Chancellor's Private Secretary had found them, and they were still roaring away when Detective-Sergeant Barney returned.

It was that afternoon, rather than the boxes of iron soldiers and the books on military history that Churchill was to send Rex later, that had won the old man his allegiance. Yes, Rex thought now, after a breakfast cigarette, Winnie was all right. But you couldn't explain it to a woman.

"Time I opened up," Ida said regretfully. "It's eleven, and the Guard'll be wanting to wet their whistles. We're getting low on beer," she added, sighing. "Breweries don't deliver. It's only the tied houses getting their supplies regular and I don't know how long that'll be. But Sid wants to keep a free house. I'll hang on as long as I can."

Rex said nothing but his discomfort returned. It wasn't pleasant to be reminded that old Sid was in the Army. He'd never liked him much—Sid had thrown Master Rex Barney out of the Fox years before, when he'd tried to go in with his mates before he was eighteen. And the old so-and-so had tried to show him up with a lot of rudery. It had been a lark to carry on an affair with his wife right under his nose and his handlebar moustache. But now—it had bothered Rex the night before. Sleeping in a man's bed while he was in a tent somewhere on the south coast, waiting for Jerry. Rex stayed for Ida's sake more than his own. All excited, she was. The medal. The hero of Dunkirk—a lot of bollocks, but women liked to think that way.

He grinned at her—fond of old Ida he was. He liked the look of her big fair body, her bleached blonde curls, the look of that fine pair she had as she leaned over the table, same as she leaned over the bar. A cheerful, smiling woman. His father, who had been faithful to one woman all his life, could say she was a tart, but Rex didn't think so. When she'd come to work at the Fox times were bad, and she'd been lucky to get the job. Sid was old enough to be her father, but when he'd taken a fancy to her and offered marriage, she'd been sensible to have him. But they'd had no children, and it was only natural after a few years she would look round a bit. She kept the bar and cooked his meals—not a bad wife, as wives go.

Rex had a pint of ale in the Public with his father and the Guard, and a few others who had drifted in. Old Gumm was arguing as usual with Jack Kemp—thirty years-old, still in civvies with his red tie and not even in the Guard. There was talk that when his age group was called he was going to file as a Conchie.

"We all have to pull our weight," Gumm was saying.

"Pull our weight in what?" Kemp replied. "We went in to save Poland for the Poles. But it was lost. You don't really think we're going to invade the Continent and give it back to them, do you?"

Old Gumm always lost the arguments but there wasn't a man in the bar who wouldn't have liked to take a smack at Jack Kemp.

Gumm snorted. "Not after your bloody Russia marched in and grabbed what she could. But we will at the finish, don't you worry."

"The Soviets had to defend their borders," Kemp said, as cool as if he were addressing a meeting, and Gumm chewed on his moustache.

Ida, with the ease of long practice, distracted them.

"The sign's been painted out on the Bellingdon Odeon. What d'you think of that?"

"Quite right," Gumm said instantly. "No use giving the enemy information."

"Well, if they come by parachute I don't suppose they'll be wanting to go to the pictures," Henry Bodger said, puzzled.

"They've changed the signs of the High Street and up

the avenue," Ida told them, "and the lorry that was coming up from Charrington's was half over to Brixton before he knew he'd gone wrong."

"You'd think the driver would know his way," Gumm expostulated. "Been coming here Gawd knows how long . . ."

"All the regular drivers have been called up," Ida said, "the ones that didn't go with the Territorials last summer. They had to send some old codger they'd scraped up, a Scotch fellow, used to work on the Clyde. And the police held him up at the station when he went in to ask directions 'cause he'd lost his identity card."

While the men were arguing whether British subjects should or should not have to carry identity cards—"There goes your bloody freedom," Jack Kemp said, "See what it's worth as soon as trouble starts. Now you can understand Russia. She's been threatened for over twenty years—" Alf Barney spoke to his son in an undertone.

"Thought I might find you 'ere," he said gruffly.

He didn't approve of Rex's 'carrying on'. On the other hand, Rex wasn't a married man, and it was shocking the way the women ran after him. He couldn't help seeing the way that silly little Molly Price, who should have been sleeping after doing the night shift, was ogling him from the window seat. What a sight she was for a pretty young woman, her hair half tied up with a scarf, and the front all puffed out and fastened with enough hair clips to make a battleship. Not that Rex was taking any notice, any more than he took notice of Jack Kemp.

It was the same as in the last war. It was never the men back from the front who wanted to punch up the Conchies. Alf couldn't help feeling swollen with pride as he looked at his son in his battle dress. When he'd gone to see him get the VC at the hands of the King, Alf had been proud enough to burst. He only wished his wife had been alive to see it. Margaret had always said he worried for nothing: Rex was a good lad. Hard to think he was twenty-seven now.

"These came just before I left."

'These' were two War Office telegrams. Leave cancelled, Rex thought. He found he was not sorry. He was too impatient these days to potter round the house at 19 Bellingdon Grove with his father. The talk in the bar no longer interested him—the blind leading the blind. And he couldn't really enjoy himself now on old Sid's fumed oak bedstead, and Ida couldn't get away. He took a pull on his ale and opened the envelope.

He read it, put his tankard down and read it again. His father, always anxious, wondered what it could be. The message was simple enough. Sergeant Rex Barney was to report to 10 Downing Street at 9:30 am the next morning. It had come from the Prime Minister himself. Rex opened the second one impatiently. It was from his Commanding Officer. His leave from the regiment was extended while he was on special duty. The special duty was not named.

What could the Prime Minister want with him? Rex thought about it, but came up with no answer. Obviously, by the look on his father's face, he'd had nothing to do with it. Rex didn't know if this was supposed to be confidential, so he merely said he had to go and report the next morning, and joined in the discussion on the chances of what was left of Bellingdon Orient.

He had a quiet dinner with his father, refraining from comment during the six o'clock news when the treacle-voiced announcer seemed to be talking about a war quite different from the one he'd been in. After his father had gone to bed, he returned to the fumed oak bedroom after all. Ida's china blue eyes, her pink round breasts and plump thighs were more alluring now he knew his leave was ended and there was something unknown on the way.

In the morning he left early. With no car and no bike, he had to make the slow crawl to the other side of the river by bus. The bus was full, but as he was in uniform the conductor let him stand on the outside. The passengers were mostly women workers, getting off at factories and offices along the way, and the bus was frequently delayed by other buses stopping in front of them to disgorge loads of their own.

About half of the women were middle-aged house-wives, the rest young girls with their faces bright with make-up, giggling and chattering like London sparrows, all with an eye for the big soldier. Outside Wormwood Scrubbs prison, another mob of girls was scrambling to the pavement, giggling just as loudly, but their voices, to Rex, sounded 'lah-di-dah'.

The very jovial conductor of their bus was shouting, "All off for MI5" and the girls exploded into even louder shrieks, before disappearing into the old grey building. Rex's eyes met those of another soldier, their expressions identical. What a Fred Karno act that lot was, Rex thought in disgust. Special Branch was the police arm of MI5. His father could get twenty years if he talked about their HQ but here they were, screaming their presence to all the odds and sods in earshot.

The other soldier was looking after the shriekers with great puzzlement, but Rex knew all about them. His father rarely complained, even to him, but his fury at what was going on made him unable to contain himself. The Major-General who ran the Security Service was one of his pet dislikes, but when the Major-General announced his policy of staffing the offices only with well-bred girls with good legs he became a joke to the police—a grim joke.

The only valuable thing about MI5 was its files. And these files were in the hands of girls who didn't know a filing cabinet from a chest of drawers, who couldn't type and many of whom couldn't even spell. They thought it all great fun, and took shooting sticks and hampers of food to picnic outside the prison on the grass. It was rumoured that they chanted a song of their own composition: *'I'm*

*just a girl from MI5, and heading for a virgin's grive, My
legs it was what got me in—I'm waiting for my bit of sin.'*

For all the delay, he was at 10 Downing Street and
rapping the lion-head knocker on the plain black door, in
good time. Not that it mattered. It was past eleven that
night before he got to see the old man.

The conference was private. Not even a Secretary or
typist was present and old Thompson, still on the job, was
left to wait outside the door. Rex gave him a wink, but
Thompson had kept his perfect on-duty poker face,
though it must have surprised him a bit to see Rex Barney
turn up. Bad penny.

Rex had a pang when he came face to face with the
Prime Minister. He hadn't seen him for ten years, and it
was a shock to see how much older and how worn he
looked, oddly doll-like in his dark romper-suit. But when
he smiled he was the same old Winnie.

The Prime Minister, who had known a brash boy,
now saw a man. Confident in bearing, with a confidence
born of ability, not privilege, and still the uncomfortable
intelligence in the bright brown eyes. Churchill felt a sense
of pride in 'his' boy.

He greeted Barney with affection, and gave him his
instructions briefly—there was a lot more work to be done
that night. Rex was surprised when he heard him out, but
only that he was the one to be sent. It was time someone
had a good dekko at what the Duke and Duchess were up
to in Lisbon. But you'd think they'd come up with someone more likely than a sergeant in the foot-sloggers. What
was the bloody Secret Service for?

But he remembered wryly that his father despised the
Service, MI6 even more than '5'. The old codgers knew
about each other. A lot of thick heads from the Indian
police, his father said. There were whispers that the whole
Continental outfit had been in a big bust-up in Holland.
Jerry copping the lot. And people thought they were protected. It was like the tanks with the plywood bodies in the

65

BEF. Yes, this was a real Fred Karno's war. So much for the glory of the British Empire. He'd go if the old man wanted him to.

But he couldn't see the Duke letting him within a mile of his Royal presence. Sergeant Barney was not impressed by rank. In the field and on the retreat he'd seen officers as brave as Errol Flynn in the pictures; some who'd gone to pieces; some who'd run away. And the same with the men. But when they'd lost their officers, it was the non-coms who'd kept the units together, who'd fought off Jerry, and who'd done as well as any lot of officers, or better. England would be different after this lot, he thought. For better or worse. But while he was taking on the job, he looked at all the trouble he was liable to get into, which he saw as clearly as he saw the man before him.

"He was a Fieldmarshal, guv," he said. "Not likely to chat much with a sergeant."

"I'm sending you out as his chauffeur," the Prime Minister said airily, as if that solved everything. "He's been asking for his man back. We'll infiltrate the position," he said and chuckled. He didn't add that the Duke was notoriously careless for talking before the servants. He usually forgot they were there at all.

"And you'll report directly to me."

He paused. That was a problem. He didn't want Barney going to the Embassy—the Embassy staff chattered like birds, the Duke would know it at once. But, with all the trouble with the Germans in Lisbon, the only official telecommunication now was from the wireless room at the Embassy through their scrambler system. Not that that had proved safe, despite changing the code constantly.

Of course, there was the ultra-secret transmitter used by Military Intelligence. Its location was moved every month. But no-one was allowed to know about that. There was not even a record kept of funds expended. No-one . . . He made up his mind quickly.

"No going through channels."

Rex thought that was a bloody miracle.

The Prime Minister gave him a telephone number.

"I'll make the arrangements. You call this number from anywhere in Lisbon. Don't ask any questions, just give your code name. They'll relay your call to me!" He brooded for a moment. "They have a scrambler, but you'd better be discreet. Use a code name for the Duke. What name shall we use? Peter Pan?" For a moment he looked grim. Then he started to laugh. "No, call him 'Il Duce'. That'll mix up the Germans if they listen in."

Rex nodded.

"What's my code name?"

The Prime Minister's laugh now sounded like a giggle.

"Oh, say, 'Dirty Dog'. Easy for me to remember."

Rex gave him a long look. He was glad the old man was enjoying himself. Rex was very sure he had little idea of what he was asking. Winston Spencer Churchill had never been told by the police to move along because he was in the 'wrong part' of London.

The Prime Minister patted Rex's shoulder and grinned cheerfully when they parted. Rex had grinned back, knowing how his father and the rest felt when they were ready to bust their guts for the old boy. Outside, in the dark and quiet, he thought of what he had taken on. At least he wouldn't have to go through a bunch of striped trousers or brass hats. He would have a straight road to the PM. At that moment his foot hit an obstruction that turned out to be a pillar box. While he swore at the pain of his stubbed toe, he still thought the dodge might work. Anyway, most likely he was a lunatic, but he'd said yes.

At seven o'clock next morning, July 19, he boarded the 'plane from Whitechurch to Lisbon.

FOUR

The Ginger Man [i]

Admiral Canaris had not been laggard. While Rex Barney was getting his move order, and signing a chit for fifty pounds in Portuguese escudos—from the Prime Minister's private funds to save time—the suave young Graf von Auerbach had already arrived in Lisbon after a night flight and had gone straight to the German Minister. This Minister, the Baron Oswald von Hoyninghen-Huene, was no great friend of the Nazis, but he could hardly refuse to cooperate with von Ribbentrop's emissary. Though for the moment von Auerbach hardly needed his help. He had been in touch with a woman related to his own family and the Duke's. The night before, at a Lisbon gathering, she had murmured to the Duke and Duchess that dear Friedrich was arriving and would love to call on them.

   The Minister invited von Auerbach to stay for luncheon, but they agreed it would be more suitable, in the circumstances, if the Graf did not stay at the Legation. It took the rest of the day to get the Graf settled in a suitable hotel, and so, after all, it was Sergeant Barney who saw the Duke first, soon after he arrived in the blazing sun of Lisbon. The heat rose from the tarmac as he jumped down the steps of the 'plane and hit him like a blast. At first he thought he was in the heat from the engine before he realised that ninety degrees was the normal heat of Lisbon.

He sweated under his thick battle dress, and inside the room where Portuguese officials looked over his papers, it was not much cooler. When he was released, the sun outside the building seemed even fiercer.

Carrying his kit made him sweat more. Something had been said about a train to Cascais, but when he saw the line of waiting taxis he hailed the first one and told the driver to make for the Boca Do Inferno. The driver did not speak English. There was some gesticulation back and forth while he tried to find out if this English soldier wanted to visit the chasm of that name along the coast. Rex, patient, reiterated 'Cascais' trying to sketch a house with his hands.

Soon the driver understood. The *soldado* wished to go to the summer house of the Esperito de Santos. The driver was not quite sure where it was—there were few calls for taxis to go there. The people who visited the banker, or the Duke who was now in residence, usually went in their own cars. But he would find it—for a price. He wrote the price on a piece of paper and Rex nodded.

It was not very far to Cascais from the *Aeroporto*. The driver, mindful of the somewhat excessive sum he had asked, made a loop through the town and then went up the coast road, passing the chain of old forts that stood guarding the shore. After war-time England, Portugal had a strangely peaceful appearance to Rex's eyes. The forts looked empty, fishermen were out in their boats, a few children were bathing on the beach.

When the taxi turned off the shore road to the house, the driver missed his way and muttered to himself. At last he found the private roadway and they came to an iron gate. It stood open. Happy at accomplishing his mission and being sure of his fare, the driver bowled along the drive between the flower beds, having made a very bad turn, and nicked his car and the gates of the drive.

The chief manservant of the house, Manuel the butler, happened to be talking to the gardener cum odd-job-man, and saw, to his astonishment and fury, this damage to his absent master's property. He protested in a flood of Portuguese. The driver answered hotly. Rex tried to end it by paying the man off, but although the money soothed, it did not entirely satisfy.

The argument continued and grew raucous. Cries of "*Grande Cabrā*" and "*Filho da Puta*" rang out. Manuel, though the driver couldn't know it, was venting some of his frustration at having to serve his master's guests, whom he disliked. Now a common English soldier had come, and the gates had been trampled. While they argued, Rex walked round the house. He might as well present himself to the Duke now as later.

He had taken the path to the left instead of the one to the right. Before him was a garden and in its centre, set against patterned blue-on-white tile, the water of a swimming pool sparkled invitingly. A small boy was splashing about but jumped out and bolted like a rabbit as footsteps approached. From the house a little man appeared, clad in a cotton dressing-gown which he threw off at once.

The Duke had decided to bathe to cheer himself. His spirits had been low. The night before had begun well with an agreeable dinner in Lisbon. Ena, an attractive woman whom he'd always liked, and a family connection, had been there, and Ena had won the Duchess' regard by her great sympathy for their position. It was always soothing for him to find family connections who gave Wallis her due. After a time some of the appalling chill cast upon them by the English side would seem less deadly.

Then Ena had invited them, quite casually, to come for a holiday on her estate to do some hunting. But her estate was in Granada. The Duke, humiliated, had had to explain that he had surrendered his passport to the British Embassy with a request for Spanish and French visas, but they were clearly unwilling to grant them.

Ena had pooh-pooh'd this nonsense. Certainly the Spanish required no visas, and she could arrange it so that he would have no trouble at all. She suggested to the Duchess that they go, as so many Portuguese did, to a mountain resort just by the border, and she would meet them there. In lowered tones, she had told the Duchess all that the Spanish would be prepared to do to make them comfortable should they decide to stay. El Caudillo had great respect for Royalty—nowhere in the world, Ena insisted, would the Duchess receive more honour than in Spain.

Turning again to the Duke, Ena had mentioned that young Friedrich von Auerbach had arrived in Lisbon and would certainly be calling on them. The Duke had been non-committal. It was true that the von Auerbachs were also distantly related to the Saxe-Coburg-Gothas—though he would have to ask his mother exactly how—but he was certain he remembered that von Auerbach was in the diplomatic corps. He was not sure if he could receive him. It was a difficult decision—like the business of going to Spain. A pleasant visit away from the tensions of Lisbon would be most agreeable but he decided that he would not go. When the Duchess inquired directly, he had had to tell her that. Wallis had been sparkling all evening in the lively party but the sparkle had quickly subsided. She developed a very bad headache and when they got back to the house she went straight to her room. Her maid had reported to him that morning that the headache was still bad.

The water of the pool looked pleasant. He wished Wallis would come and bathe, it would do her good. Nostalgically, he remembered their bathes off the *Nahlin* when he was King. What fun they'd had then! It seemed a long time ago. Suddenly he became aware of someone standing close by watching him.

He glanced up to see a young British sergeant, in battle dress, so-called—the Duke thought it deplorably casual. The sergeant's hair gleamed red under his forage cap, and his big, broken nose gave him an oddly impudent look. The man was staring down at him with a look far from respectful in a pair of too-bright brown eyes.

"What the devil are you doing here?" he snapped.

It wasn't until the Duke spoke that Rex realised who he was. The Duke spoke with authority, and as he looked directly at him his face was familiar, although he looked much older than Rex had expected. He had not realised, from newspaper photographs, that the Duke was of such slight build. Rex was a ribald young man and he could not help being rather amused. The great Royal lady killer.

The Duke had seen that look before. His animosity against this unknown sergeant was absolute, even before the man had been able to utter a single word.

"Sorry, sir," Rex said genially. "Your man out there seems to be busy so I came in. I have my orders here. Sent in place of the man you requested, for chauffeur duty."

The Duke was torn between rages of several different kinds. First, that this sergeant did not address him as 'Your Royal Highness'. Of course, in his military capacity, the Duke having a rank of Major-General, he supposed the fellow had a right to address him as 'sir'. But he had not saluted either.

"*You*—you sent here in place of Fletcher! You're no valet!"

"No, sir. My orders are to act as chauffeur, sir."

"But I don't need a chauffeur." The Duke was exasperated. "I have one already." The Esperito Santos had left him their Bentley and chauffeur, and a skeleton staff of indoor and outdoor servants.

"I need my valet. You're of no use at all." A fellow like that would not be employed in a decent house as boot-boy, he thought angrily.

Rex looked down at him, considering. It's not going well, mate, he told himself. The old man wasn't going to like it.

"Dare say there's a mix-up in the orders, sir. Army muck-up as usual," he smiled engagingly but the Duke was not charmed. He examined the man's orders and saw

72

that they had been issued on a very high level. Churchill's doing, of course. It was just another trick to annoy and torment him. The Windsor Plot, still going on, and Churchill joining it. But he would not get away with this.

"Certainly a mistake has been made," he said coldly.

The man had Army orders to report to him. He could not just dismiss him, much as he wanted to do so. But he would get on to the Ambassador that very afternoon. He was not going to be chauffered by this minion of Churchill's—and certainly he was not going to give up Fletcher. Fletcher was the only man who could turn him out to the Duchess' satisfaction.

"Manuel. Manuel!" he shouted.

The butler glided to his side, his face impassive. The taxi had finally taken itself off.

"Take this man to the servants' quarters. He will remain there until I give fresh instructions."

Manuel led the intruder away. The Duke, with keen dislike, watched the lithe stride, the arrogant line of head and shoulders. In his day he had been considered a friend of the working man. But if he could have put his feelings into words, he might have said he was a friend of the working man—when he knew his place.

Obviously, this young man did not. He had looked upon him as one man to another—and certainly without admiration or even respect. Gloomily, his swim spoiled, the Duke splashed about the pool, and left only when a servant brought him a message that the Duchess, who had refused luncheon, was now taking coffee on the balcony. She had not sent for him, but he had previously asked as he always did, to be told when the Duchess left her room.

It was hot on the balcony. There was no breeze and the birds were silent in the trees. The Duchess was dressed all in white, and was lying back in her chair, her eyes closed, a look of suffering upon her face. The Duke was not usually imaginative, but where his wife was concerned his fancy became charged, and now he thought she looked like a creature ready for the sacrifice. He had not told her all of his humiliations, in which she would have to share, and his heart became more anxious and heavy.

An empty coffee cup was on a table beside her, and a brandy bottle, unopened. Contrary to his habit, the Duke poured himself a glass, and found the courage to meet his wife's dark gaze as she opened her eyes.

"Any news?" she asked, with an inflexion that suggested little hope.

"Not from Selby. I telephoned earlier but they *said* he wasn't in the office. Perhaps he's taken to the siesta habit. And the telegrams sitting there waiting."

The Duchess did not reply.

"I can't understand why Bertie hasn't answered any of my messages. Neither the personal ones nor those about the peace." He repeated what he had said already, perhaps a hundred times. "He must want peace. He knows as well as I do that this war is insane. We've discussed it many times. It'll ruin us all. He knows how many monarchies were left after the last war. This is the last chance: the last time in history that a king will be able to act."

His expression, which his wife did not see, was passionate and sincere.

"We're at the crossroads," he said heavily, "the crossroads."

"Your brother the King hasn't troubled to write since the Abdication, has he? At least Winston answers, even if his answers are always the wrong ones."

The Duke had been leaning over the balcony in his accustomed attitude, staring down the Lisbon road. Now his eyes narrowed and he leaned forward.

"Is that someone coming? You have such sharp eyes, Dolly."

The Duchess sighed slightly. In a quick, sinuous movement she rose and stepped to the balcony rail.

"Again?" she protested. "I feel like Bluebeard's wife. Sister Anne, Sister Anne, is Winston approaching at the head of the cavalry—or should it be the Marines?"

She laughed, without turning. Her laughter hung in the warm air, a sound with some real amusement, but it was a private joke that surrounded her more closely than her fine French scent.

The Duke, sensitive, felt his exclusion. The net of lines on his face dug in deeper as if someone had pulled the drawstring.

"I hope I don't seem like Bluebeard to you already, my dear. I know this place is rather dull . . ."

The Duchess laughed again.

"I'm the Bluebeard, remember? It was my husbands, not your ladies, that aroused the wrath of Jehovah and all his bishops. Did Jehovah have bishops? Anyway, you would certainly have thought, from the papers, that I had Win and Ernest hanging in a closet by their hair. And we could hardly have stayed on the Riviera. It would have been no fun there with everyone run off. Can you imagine Willie Maugham in that Polish coal boat? I hope he found some husky seaman for consolation. I wonder what he thought the Germans would do to him? I am so tired of escaping. I don't *want* to be rescued. Look at what happened last time. I ran away from perfectly amiable Germans to be insulted by the implacable English."

The Duke's face darkened as he thought of their return to England the year before. A muscle in his jaw twitched. Still his eyes scanned the road. "That's why I've been determined—"

The Duchess, now that she had started, went on without heed.

"The English!" She twisted her wedding ring. "All those women who ran after me when they thought I was your mistress, so anxious to cut me as soon as I was your wife. The Wedding of the Year . . . with all the guests detained by the Ancient Mariner. And some of those women I had thought were my friends before you and I had even met."

75

The light, artificial tone was replaced by the harshness of real feeling. For a second or two, the smooth mask of her face shattered, showing for an instant a woman curiously younger, alive with hurt. Her husband, gazing down the coast road, did not see the change. Attuned as he was to his wife's hopes and wishes, he would not have recognised this other woman, a girl, soft and vulnerable.

He had never known Bessiewallis Warfield, of Baltimore. Nor could he have loved her. The man who longed to be ruled in love could only desire a woman well versed in the art of subjection. He had met Mrs Ernest Simpson, a soignée, poised creature, with the worldliness of Washington, Peking, London, a woman already making her own way with quiet determination into Society. Bessiewallis, she devoutly hoped, was laid to rest. Only in dreams, sometimes, did she return.

In the city of Baltimore, Bessiewallis had been born of good family, but very poor. Her parents made a love match; her father had died in the year of her birth. She and her mother had lived on the charity of a rich uncle, a charity that seemed to them capricious. Surrounded by the well-born and rich, Bessiewallis, receiving her fears from her mother, felt as though her life was a long walk upon a tightrope. She and her mother struggled and contrived, but to keep up with other girls of her class seemed more than they could possibly achieve.

Bessiewallis was terrified of falling into the pit of the 'other people', the common folk, the girls who were not invited to the Cotillion Balls, who could not marry well, who were really not much better than the Negroes huddled together in the shanty-like slums of the town. But she had her loyalty—she was invited to go and live with her uncle and could have been safe forever, yet she chose to stay with her mother.

Her uncle sent her to a 'good' school. Bessiewallis tried. She was brighter, livelier, made more jokes, was more friendly than any other girl. She even joined in the sports, which she hated, and one of the happiest moments of her life was when she was chosen to play on the baseball team. Sometimes she thought it *was* the happiest moment. Very early she learned she was unusually attractive to boys, more than her plump, pleasant looks with her loose brown hair seemed to justify. She already knew this was a two-edged sword.

Her mother had such sexual charm, and it did not help their condition. A widow, especially a poor widow, should not be fascinating. Bessiewallis had seen the eyes of Uncle Sol linger on her mother; she had felt the weight of the disapproval of the town when that unfortunate lady took a lover. Even the fact that the lover married her at last did not wipe out the blot. Bessiewallis' name, put down on invitation lists by old school friends, was firmly scratched off by the mamas, and Bessiewallis stayed at home and cried. In private. She didn't let her mother see her tears.

She tried harder to be pleasing—too hard. Men responded too well, and the word went out that Bessiewallis Warfield was fast. Her invitations from the best families dropped to none. She was going to be an outsider after all.

Desperate, her mother went to the Warfields, to Uncle Sol. Family pressure was exerted. When the time came for the Cotillion Ball, Bessiewallis was invited after all. She glittered with happiness, was a belle at the ball, and went home tired but joyous, believing her troubles were over. Accepted at last, she was one of the group. A girl whom not only the men in good society would chase, but also the women. The women, most powerful, with their nods and smiles so carefully bestowed, so easily withdrawn. Now it would be her turn to smile, or not smile, on other debutantes.

But just as it seemed that the shining doors had opened with a flourish, slowly, subtly she learned that after all they had not. Only some women accepted her. People still whispered. She was her mother's daughter, and there were houses to which she was never invited. Despite her popularity, the right kind of proposal, from the right kind of man, never came.

It was then she began to dream the dream that was to haunt her all her life, with only a brief respite. In her happiest times, in Washington when she was in love, in Peking where she found herself again a belle, after sparkling days, she would sink into sleep and find herself gripped by terror.

First it was dark. Her heart pounding, her feet trying desperately to find a hold, she was balancing above a deep pit, walking across a high wire. Then the lights came, brighter and brighter, but they brought no lessening of the terror, it intensified and her body shook from both the fear and the fear of fear. She was dressed only in gauze and a few spangles, a bright tent was round her, below was the pit, lions and tigers, elephants with their piercing shrieks, and a crowd pointing, cheering.

She was afraid to move, unable to stay still. The sweat poured from her, and her feet became slithery in her thin slippers. Somehow she inched across the wire, her calf muscles knotting with spasms of cramp, her toes almost breaking with the pain of panic. Across her face her smile was fixed in determination, desperation.

The cheers grew louder and louder. She could not hold on, waves of dread were drowning her, she shrieked madly for someone to hold, to grasp, to clutch, but the noise only came up in one greater wave that flung her from the wire; the candy-striped walls tilted crazily and she was hurled down, down into the pit.

Suddenly the dream changed. The terror was almost gone. Her fall was over. Miraculously, she was unharmed. But now everything was topsy-turvy. The crowd was all above her. Much closer now, they were pointing, jeering, laughing. Closer and closer they came; she could see the individual faces as they grinned and snickered. Her flimsy costume had ripped off as she fell; she was naked, but the soft pit where she had fallen was full of mud, straw and ordure which clung to her, smearing her body, sinking into her hair and mouth, while the jeering faces and the pointing fingers came close enough to touch—

At that moment she always woke. With a slight shiver, even now, the Duchess, perhaps the most elegant woman in the world, touched her pearly skin, her silk and linen, her sleek and shining hair. No-one was more meticulous in her grooming than the Duchess, it was said. Even in France, no-one was more demanding of a maid, a *lingère,* a coiffeur.

Now her eyes took in the figure of the Duke, who smelled of brandy. Her first husband had been a weakling. Attracted by her strength, he soon crumbled under it and took to drink. A stupid marriage, it had been merely a bolt from the troubles of home. Once she had loved, but it had been Baltimore all over again. She could be the man's mistress, never his wife. Felipe. Then with Ernest Simpson she had found quiet and peace, the strains of her girlhood almost forgotten. With the attentions of the Prince, her life had become glamorous; when he became King and offered marriage she was incandescent with glory. Bessiewallis Warfield, who would have gone on her knees to be invited to the Cotillion Ball in Baltimore, was to be Queen of England, Empress of India, to reign over a fourth of the globe.

She had begun to do so. When she entered a room, the women of the cream of Society would come to her and greet her with a respectful kiss. She would stand there, gracious, receiving but never returning the embrace. The jewels which the King had given her, and which she proudly wore, gave her the illusion that the Crown jewels would be hers to command. And then . . .

The Abdication itself need not have been a tragedy. In their discussions beforehand, the King had made it clear that in the event of his stepping down, his position, as he saw it, would officially be one of a Royal younger

brother. But because of Bertie's great dependence upon
him, he would still be King in all but name. Certainly he
would keep Fort Belvedere. It might be preferable to
reigning formally, he had said, to be the acknowledged
Royal leaders of Society, with someone else to do the dull,
humdrum business of protocol and ceremony.

How wrong he was. And how much worse it had been
for her. She could have borne the people—the common
people—seeing fit to throw stones at her windows. But her
friends—friends! With a stroke of the King's pen on the
Instrument of Abdication, while the ink was still wet, she
had lost every English friend and many others besides. She
became—no-one. Sometimes she felt if she looked in the
engagement books of these old friends she would find
every trace of herself erased.

Her letters were not answered. Her telephone calls
were not returned. The eyes of many women who knew
her well slid away when they met. But unlike the Duke,
she did not complain. She hid her wounds. Long ago she
had learned her lesson, taking it in with her mother's milk.
One did not whine. Whining made one tiresome, more
than ever an outsider to be left among outsiders. In a way
it was worse than the dream. Instead of being reviled she
was non-existent. The Royal Family had said so, and so
it was.

She began to dream the dream again. Her time was
spent in bathing, having her hair washed and arranged,
buying clothes and more clothes, sleek, elegant, fashion-
able, decking herself with her glittering gems. This
caused another scandal. A Government official was dispatched from England. It was claimed that a set of emeralds the former King had given her was part of the
dowry Queen Alexandra had brought from Denmark—
Crown property that must be returned. The Duke was
still in Austria while she waited for her divorce. When
he heard of this he was so angry that he ordered an emerald and diamond brooch from a famous jeweller for

which he paid twenty thousand pounds—long before his financial affairs were settled—and he was afraid to pay wages and household bills.

When he came to her at last, and she saw him for the first time since the Abdication, he seemed shrunken and aged. The day was warm, he was sweating with haste and emotion, and in the bright sun of Tours he looked curiously tarnished and slightly soiled. He fell into her arms, saying grimly:

"The drawbridges are up. I have taken you into a void."

And he had. Every honour that had been showered upon her was taken away—and all for such a strange reason: because the King had proposed marriage. Because he had thought her too fine to be merely a mistress. Once again her sexual power had brought her to disaster, in a new way, in the topsy-turvy English world.

With the discipline of long practice, she pulled herself together. The crack into the distant past was sealed, her face smoothed out into its accustomed brittle calm. She shrugged, resumed her usual manner and went on before her husband had taken his mournful glance from the road.

"In America it would be *quite* the other way round. Nasty old vulgar America respects a man's wife more than his mistress."

The Duke swatted angrily at an intrusive fly, that was intrigued by his almost naked body in the wet swimming trunks.

"It didn't mean that, you know it didn't. It's not that they don't like and respect you. It's the Court. They owe their respect and duty to the present Court and they'll take their guidance from the Palace. That's why I've been so insistent in my cables to Winston and Bertie. Equal treatment as man and wife. And they'll have to agree." He gave a short laugh. "Maybe the Germans' buzzings will give them a jolt. I'm certain we're spied on wherever we go— by both sides. It's worse here than in Spain."

He thought with resentment of the impudent sergeant.

"Hullo, what's that?"

A large black car rolled with stately haste along the Lisbon road.

"Not Sir Walford," the Duchess said, settling into her chair with an attitude proclaiming that boredom was her daily lot and accepted gracefully. "It's a Mercedes."

"Oh. You don't suppose it's Hoyninghen-Huene calling? That would send all the chickens scurrying. But he wouldn't do that. The man's a gentleman. Not like some of those fellows we met in Germany. I haven't forgotten Ley. Hitler is one thing and Göring and Hess are all right, but I draw the line at Ley. Drunken sot. Shall I let the Germans make you a Queen, Dolly?"

The Duke spoke idly, with a little wry smile for his joke, still searching the Lisbon road for the expected English envoy.

"Queen of what? The Channel Islands? I can just see me, Queen of Jersey and Guernsey . . . No, it's no use, it sounds like a prize cow." The Duchess ran a hand lightly over her slim flanks.

"Anyway, it won't be Hoyninghen-Huene. Haven't you heard? Now, if you listened to hairdressers, instead of ministers, you would know what was happening, and you wouldn't have to wait for me to tell you."

"Tell me what?" The Duke's pale blue eyes blinked in puzzlement.

The Duchess smiled to herself, willing to let his enlightenment wait.

"If I'd listened to my hairdresser in London, instead of your so-called advisers, you'd still be on the throne. He told me over and over, 'Modom, you have to understand the English'." She managed a good imitation of a Cockney voice larded over with an attempt at gentility.

"He said they would stand anything, as long as it didn't move and looked as if it had always been there.

82

They don't care what it is, as long as they're used to it. Think of pork pies." She laughed. " 'Take my word, Modom, you don't do nothing, nothing at all, just go on like nothing's happening. And one day you'll wake up and you'll be Queen and no-one will've noticed anything'." She laughed again, her private, excluding laugh.

The Duke huddled into his chair, his shoulders slumped, and then rushed over to the brandy. He poured himself a large double and drank deeply. The Duchess observed him silently for a moment.

"The gossip is that Hoyninghen-Huene is being recalled," she told him at last. "Perhaps this is the new man. No, it could hardly be so soon. It must be that relation of yours that Ena was talking about."

"Recalled? Huene recalled?" The Duke put his glass down. "But why? Everyone says he is a fixture here. Loves the place."

"Berlin didn't love him when one of their wizards broke the Portuguese code. They found that Salazar is bargaining with the British about the Azores. Hoyninghen-Huene is going to be spanked. I bet they want someone more energetic anyway—the type who'd ginger you up a bit, among other things."

The black car turned in at the gate.

"I wonder if this is a ginger type," the Duke looked down with a displeased frown. "It would be grossly impudent, coming here. I won't receive whoever it is—unless it's von Auerbach."

"If it is, he hasn't wasted much time," the Duchess observed. "Why is it that the enemy is so much more prompt than our British friends?"

"German efficiency," the Duke said. "Great workers. I remember years ago when I used to be sent to my Aunt Augusta, the Grand Duchess, at Neu Strelitz, how that Court worked at being dull! I would run off to Berlin for a little fun, and how hard the Berliners worked at that! I would go home from my 'rest' exhausted . . . Now all

Europe's crumbled about them. It's not surprising. And in England, even now, war or no war, Friday to Monday is sacred."

He sighed. "Do you suppose that's why von Auerbach came to Lisbon, to ginger? I *think* I recognise him. He hasn't changed much. Perhaps I should refuse to see him. One has to keep these fellows in their place."

"As we are kept in ours," the Duchess retorted.

The Duke's face darkened. He remembered one suggestion that had come from London. A governorship in an obscure outpost. An insult to himself and his wife. He had not even mentioned it to Wallis, and he would not now. London had not taken it seriously, it seemed, the continued presence of the flying boats was proof of that.

"Well, it's a pity if we're losing Hoyninghen-Huene. I suppose some of the delicate propositions we've received come from him, but they were nicely done. Remind me of all the years when I was pursued—with much delicacy— by so many charming ladies." He smiled in reminiscence. "That was before I found you to pursue, my dear."

"I think that was the entire secret of my charm," the Duchess said, as though the thought gave her no special pleasure. "The not-pursuing. Though every little girl in Baltimore knows enough for that."

Sounds came from below of the door being opened, and voices, indistinct.

"Well, the new stage of the courtship is on," the Duke said, resignedly.

"Perhaps," the Duchess looked up, brightening a little, "perhaps this time it will be rape?"

FIVE

The Ginger Man [ii]

Manuel, left with Sergeant Barney, had given him into the charge of a harassed youth. This youth, whose name Rex was to learn was Ferdi, had been doing most of the work of the underservants who normally served the family. The rest were at their master's house in Lisbon. The Ducal visit had been expected to last only two days, and the small staff remaining had to struggle as best they could. Even the chef was gone, and all the cooking for upstairs was being done by the Italian pastry chef. The demanding Duke and Duchess did not make all this easier.

The trained eye of Manuel immediately saw what the Duke in his anger had guessed: this soldier had never seen domestic service of any kind. He would be of no help, but merely more work.

The telephone rang; the Duke was shouting from the pool, but despite these noisy demands on his attention, Manuel drew himself up to his full dignity, which always cowed the other servants, and told the sergeant that under no circumstances was he allowed above stairs except when the Duke and Duchess should ring for him, and that he must not chatter to the staff during their working hours. He then gave him a piercing look to see if these warnings had sunk in.

Rex saw a stiff old codger who was trying to seem

85

impressive while his head turned to the various noises, like a tall rabbit not knowing which way to jump. The startled Manuel recognised the gleam of amusement in the soldier's eyes, and his stomach burned. Although there were several rooms available, he told Ferdi to take him to one of the smallest and most cramped. Then he could show the soldier the kitchen, but afterwards—he swelled with authority—Ferdi must return to his work. At once!

Following the youth, Rex offered him an English cigarette, which he liked, and together they had a comfortable smoke. Ferdi sat on the bed in Rex's cubby-hole, and tried to make himself understood. Rex listened, after making sure that the room was clean and the linen, though old and thin, was spotless. He'd be glad of his bed that night, he'd been up before dawn and the 'plane journey had been long.

Ferdi's English was poor but Rex understood his dissatisfaction with Manuel, the Duke, and his life in general. He would leave now, he said gloomily, but it was hard for him to get work—he had once had a little trouble. The damned *policia*. When they got a down on you—perhaps the *soldado* understood. He did.

With a more jaunty air, Ferdi pointed out the kitchen, a large basement room where the servants sat when they were not working. Rex was heartened as he saw him go, the free-talking Ferdi might be a useful ally. When he entered the basement room, staring about in the dim light, it seemed empty. Then he saw the small boy who had been in the pool, playing now with a little grey cat on a large basket chair. The cat looked bored and ready to jump off, and as the boy moved forward with his hands full of the struggling ball of fur he saw the soldier and looked up. He had large dark eyes and a wary expression, but the hands that held the cat were gentle. She flicked her tail and he let her go. Rex smiled down at him and the boy smiled back.

There was a bar of chocolate in his battle dress pocket, a little the worse for the Lisbon heat, but good

English chocolate. The boy, speechless, approved, and his face and hands were soon smeared and his eyes were shining. He pointed to Rex's uniform, his forefinger jabbing into his chest.

"Militar?" He pointed to himself. *"Soldado!"*

Picking up a loaf of bread, he brandished it at Rex. Rex obligingly took a banana and they duelled briskly, with Rex on his knees and the boy standing on the chair. The boy, after a sturdy jab to the armpit, jumped down and kicked all the wooden chairs into a barricade, hurling apples across it. His piercing shriek accompanied each of his 'grenades', and then triumphantly, he shouted 'Boom' as one apple struck Rex in the shoulder. Rex howled and staggered about convincingly, and the boy shrieked in delight.

The noise caught the ear of his mother. Maria, the only female servant left in the house, was kept busy by the Duchess. The Duchess had demanded aspirin, and Maria had had to come to the larder to get the special bottled water that the Duchess liked to drink. She was in a hurry to get back, as she must make the Duchess' bed. Besides, while she was in the bedroom she could hear the talk on the balcony—she might learn something interesting. Maria had not yet heard of the new addition to the household. Wondering what could be happening to Jorge, she rushed into the kitchen.

Relieved, she saw he was shrieking merely from laughter. He was astride the back of a soldier, whooping and calling. She gestured at once for quiet—if the Duchess should hear! A ray of sunlight came through the window just above the level of the ground and shone red on the soldier's hair. How kind, her first thought was, for no-one in the house ever played with Jorge. Ferdi was not the age to play with children, and Manuel quite plainly thought her son a nuisance and told her pointedly that when the master returned she would have to send him to her sister in the old quarter of the Alfama.

Rex looked up, saw her in the doorway and smiled.

Maria gazed at the stranger. Her errand for the Duchess, even Jorge were forgotten. Oddly, for the first time since she had been in service here, the kitchen seemed a pleasant place. It would be good to stay a few moments, to talk . . . She patted her hair and smiled like a shy young girl.

Obviously, this was the child's mother, Rex thought. She was an attractive woman. Dark-haired, well-curved, with the same liquid brown eyes as the boy. Rex saw the invitation in her glance and was cheered with the thought that this job was not going to be all problems.

"Hello," he said agreeably and was pleased, though not surprised, when she answered him in English.

"Hello, Senhor."

But Manuel was calling; the Duchess was impatient. Maria got the water, and also quickly poured a glass of wine from a bottle that Manuel had left for himself and placed it in front of the exciting stranger. Then she gave him a sidelong look and walked away slowly, her full hips swaying.

Rex smiled. He settled down in the comfortable chair —Manuel's, although he didn't know it—lit a second cigarette and sipped the wine. He would have preferred a glass of beer but the girl's intentions had been sound. If he couldn't drive the Duke, he thought composedly, well, there were going to be other ways to get information. More than one way to skin a cat. The cat, forgotten by little Jorge who was playing with a handful of English pennies, gave a petulant cry. Rex stroked it absent-mindedly and it sprung up on his knee, arched its back and purred in satisfaction. Sergeant Barney had arrived.

Manuel, who had been extremely rushed, was annoyed at Maria's slowness. The telephone was ringing again and he was the only one who answered it. The Duchess was ringing the bell from the balcony and there was a caller at the front door. He answered the telephone, opened the door, then took the water from Maria, put it on a salver, and made his dignified way upstairs. The

Duke was roaring with laughter at the Duchess' sally, his face for a moment regaining its youth, and he slapped his naked thigh. Manuel stared at him in surprise that was quickly masked by his habitual grave courtesy. Dressed in his dark clothes, neatly groomed, he looked adult next to the boyish, rumpled figure.

"Your Grace, Your Royal Highness—"

"You will address the Duchess as 'Your Royal Highness,' " the Duke interrupted coldly. He muttered an aside to his wife. "We're not in England now."

"Yes, Your Royal Highness. His Excellency the Graf von Auerbach is below. He sends his compliments and asks if Her Royal Highness will receive him."

The Duke was vexed, Manuel saw, by his blunder.

"Present my compliments to the Graf, and inform him that we do not receive members of the German Legation."

The stiffness of the speech came oddly from his undignified person.

"Yes, Your Royal Highness. So the Graf was informed. But he says he is not with the Legation, he is here privately, with a most urgent message, and begs that you will receive him as a family connection. And, sir, the British Ambassador is on the telephone."

"On the telephone!" The three words were an explosion. "Now, what's this? Too much trouble for him to come out, d'you think, Wallis?"

The servant looked uncomfortable.

"Sir Walford said it was important that he speak to you, and that he has been tied up with business because of some possible changes in the German Legation. He wishes to explain it all to you. Perhaps my English . . ." His English was faultless.

"Too busy because of the German changeover. But you notice there's a German here, waiting to pay his respects. It's typical, Wallis, typical."

"Why don't you find out what it is? Perhaps it's the

news you've been waiting for." His wife grinned. "Come home, all is forgiven."

Manuel had tactfully withdrawn. The Duke followed him, grumbling. He must speak to the Ambassador about his man. He was not going to keep that insolent sergeant. One espadrille flopped loosely as he walked. The fly, following the tempting exposed skin, buzzed after him.

The Duchess relaxed, her hands hanging limply over the side of her chair. Her eyes were closed, and she showed no sign of curiosity, or even interest, at the events taking place inside the house. Manuel, removing the coffee cups, was seized by the uncomfortable sensation of a memory disturbed, yet not quite brought to consciousness.

What was it? he wondered, as he walked with professional quiet down the long tiled corridors. The Duke's voice was coming loudly and angrily from the north sitting-room that he used as an office, and the servant tried to shut the sounds away while he traced his recollection.

"I won't do it," the Duke was shouting. "I won't go!"

And then the memory came. It was years ago, when Manuel had been working as a daily servant, a combination valet and butler, to a rich but unpleasant South American who was living in Estoril. One morning, after kissing his wife good-bye he had started out for work, not briskly as usual, but slowly, brooding over his resentment against his ill-tempered master. Deeply abstracted, he had stumbled into a tree that grew along the path, though he had seen it there every day for years. Now he stared at it, as though seeing it for the first time. The muddy grey bark on the gnarled branches looked tired and old. His resentment turned to depression. The tree reminded him of old age, coming as surely as next winter, reminding him that life was short and slipping away fast.

'I won't do it any more,' he had thought. 'I won't go. There are other men and other jobs. I don't have to be a servant.'

And he had turned round and gone home. Even at

that age, he had walked softly. His wife had not heard him return. He found her sitting in her usual chair, with the small embroidered cushion, just as when he left. Her eyes were closed. But she had a look about her that he had never seen, of complete, perfect relaxation. Immediately, with a pain that went deep, he understood. She was relieved, relieved he had gone for the day, relieved to be rid of his company. He was young and in love. Somehow he could not break the peace that rejoiced in his absence. He left as quietly as he had come and was only ten minutes late for the bad-tempered South American. It was after that he had suspected his wife and the new torero who had come down for the season from Madrid.

Long ago, and now it all seemed nonsense. His five children were growing up and his wife was fat and wheezed when she walked. He had Maria . . . there was always a Maria. Young and docile. And the South American had not been so bad, apart from his temper. He had died ten years later and left some fine gifts and a respectable sum for his manservant.

Why should the Duchess have reminded him of that morning, he mused. The mind is a strange and silly thing. What did his wife, a former servant girl, have in common with a lady that was almost a Queen? The memory left a bad taste on his tongue. Those years of jealousy were sour. He would have a glass of his master's best wine, he decided. His master's, not the Duke's, for his master, though absent, was still the host and made all provision. These Royals made no contribution to the household. In the eyes of the staff, their master was the superior man.

Neither did their master shout childishly, thought the servant as he approached the north sitting-room. The Duke was roaring:

"And you can tell Winston I won't budge! Orders or no orders, I won't be threatened!"

He banged the receiver down hard enough to break the instrument. The servant felt offended. *Imprudente,* he thought, and had to jump back three feet in an instant as the Duke charged out of the room and almost impaled himself on the tray. The cups hardly rattled, the man noticed with professional pleasure at his own skill, while the Duke's eyes boggled at him.

"Bring something cool to the balcony," he ordered, and loped off towards his Duchess.

"Yes, Your Royal Highness," the man murmured to the air. What kind of drink? he wondered. Lemonade, or something stronger? He shrugged. For such a temper, something stronger. And he longed for the orderly life of his master, and he wished these visitors, who had been invited for a night or two, would leave. After three days, fish and guests both stink. Yes, like Mr Churchill, he wished they would go. Crossly, he wondered what had happened to Ferdi who should have taken the order down to the kitchen.

The Duke slammed onto the balcony.

"I won't do it. We won't go home like this. The boats can stay there forever. We'll go only when this matter is settled. Not before. And I don't go anywhere without Fletcher."

The Duchess wasn't paying attention to his words. The first thing she noticed was that the fly, that noxious impudent fly, had followed the Duke back. She wondered what attracted the fly so much. Some creatures were hard to shake off.

Manuel appeared with glasses, ice and a tall jug of something that looked delicious with sprigs of mint floating by the frosty rim.

"The Graf von Auerbach is still waiting, Your Royal Highness," he said.

"I can't see him," the Duke answered, irritably.

"Oh, I don't know," the Duchess murmured. "We've no engagements until nine o'clock. Perhaps he'll be amusing. We could use a little fun, after one more snub from the British."

Manuel's temper restorer had some effect on the Duke. Besides, the Duchess' word was law.

"Well, if you think so, my dear. Let's get it over. Show the Graf up," he ordered.

The breeze had failed, and the sun shone brassily on the awning. Even on the balcony the air seemed used and tired as lethargy followed anger, and the banished couple sank back gloomily in their chairs. The fly settled close to the jug, droning monotonously.

The sharp ring of heels along the terrace was startling. The double doors were flung open, and the servant announced, "His Excellency, the Graf von Auerbach." The tall, well-built man bowed deeply to the Duke and Duchess.

Although he wore the usual black coat and striped trousers, his bearing and manner suggested the military rather than the diplomatic man. He looked young, the Duchess thought with favour, in his early thirties perhaps, with a fresh and vigorous look. His clear complexion, bright eyes and his fair hair cut *en brosse,* together with his brisk movements, brought a quickening of life to the somnolent place.

"Your Royal Highness, Your Royal Highness, Friedrich von Auberbach at your service."

The Duchess glowed at being addressed by the contested title. Both she and the Duke beamed on the visitor.

"It would be more correct—" he bowed again, "If I addressed you as 'Your Majesties'."

"Oh, no, no," the Duke responded, smiling but firm. "That is gone forever. There can be only one King of England."

The German inclined his head courteously.

"Quite so. That is one of the important matters I have come to discuss. I did not disturb your Royal Highnesses on some trivial matter."

"Please be seated," the Duchess said.

Her look of boredom had gone and her eyes sparkled.

The servant had already withdrawn and von Auerbach found himself a chair and sat between the Duke and Duchess. His energy vitalised the Duke who sprang to his feet and poured a drink for the visitor.

"You must try this," he said genially. "I don't know what's in it, but it seems a cure for the heat." As he handed him the glass, he looked at his guest ruminatively. "Von Auerbach. We have met before."

"Your Royal Highness is gracious to remember. Very briefly, in Berlin in '32. At my brother Leopold's house."

The Duke smacked his hand on the table. "Leo, of course. He was one of my good friends. You are the younger brother. Army, wasn't it then?"

Von Auerbach looked impressed at the Duke's memory.

"Quite right. My first love. Leopold was the diplomat. But after his accident I was the only son. Our father wished me to follow the family tradition."

The Duke nodded in understanding.

"We don't have our choices. I tell you, I would have preferred to stay in the Navy but . . ."

He turned to the Duchess.

"We must bring you up to date, my dear. Leo was a very old friend of mine and Dickie Mountbatten's, from the days at Aunt Augusta's Court in Strelitz. We had a lot of fun together. A great rider, a keen sportsman. It was a real tragedy when he was killed. An accident on a shoot, up in Scotland, not far from Balmoral. Dreadful loss. Well, von Auerbach, very glad to see you again."

"The pleasure is mine, and particularly as I am bringing you news that must be deeply interesting. I think Leo would have been glad that I have the opportunity."

The Duke looked puzzled but polite. Like the Duchess, he had brightened up, and he refilled his glass and drank with more zest.

"I have just left Hoyninghen-Huene," von Auerbach

continued, "He's on his way to Berlin. An urgent summons."

The Duke frowned.

"A very decent fellow. I hope . . . ?" he suggested delicately.

"No, contrary to rumour . . ." von Auerbach said and smiled with a flash of strong white teeth, "he did not leave under a cloud. Quite frankly, and between ourselves, he is to be replaced eventually—I have it from the Foreign Minister. But not yet. There *was* some talk of my taking the post but . . . in view of the delicacy of the discussions, if I may call them that, with you, Sir, it was felt better that I should be here in a private capacity and not as a Minister of a . . . foreign power."

"There are no discussions," the Duke said, suddenly very cold.

"Naturally not," von Auerbach went on smoothly, "as you have not yet the benefit of my information. And Hoyninghen-Huene, like your host, felt friendship to *all* members of the English Royal House. Just at this time it could be difficult. Incidentally, I know I can trust your discretion, but your host should not know of our talk. He is in some ways a friend of ours, but as you probably know, just a week before your own arrival he entertained your brother, George. He and the Duke of Kent are close friends."

The Duke still looked puzzled. The Duchess was still and quiet but her eyes were sharp with interest.

"I'm afraid I don't see . . ." the Duke said stiffly. "You seem to misunderstand. There are no differences between my family and myself."

For most of his life his brother George had been his closest friend. But the friendship had dwindled after their marriages. It had not been his wish. He turned to his visitor as though he would look down upon him sternly. Unfortunately von Auerbach, even seated, appeared to tower over him. With controlled force, the German leaned

95

forward and directing his remarks to the Duchess as much as the Duke, he spoke slowly and distinctly.

"The news I have come to tell you is something we have suspected but could not be sure of until we had checked, re-checked and collated all our information. Now we are sure. It is my painful duty to point out that there are differences between members of your family, though you have not known of it."

He paused, making sure of the attention of his listeners. The Duchess had moved closer, not bothering to conceal her interest. The Duke gazed at him with an air that was a mixture of curiosity and affront, but he said nothing and waited for von Auerbach to continue.

"Your brother Albert, King George, is very ill. As long as he possibly could, he stayed in London so that he could be seen. But while he was officially resting at Royal Lodge, the Queen took him, unknown not only to the public but also to almost everyone else, to Scotland so that his decline would not be witnessed. Unfortunately, he should not have been moved and his condition quickly worsened. Now it is known to us that his illness is fatal and he will probably not live out this month."

The Duke looked shocked. His brother had never been the strongest of men but this was totally unexpected.

"But what is it?"

Von Auerbach hesitated. "His nerves were always bad, I understand. And you know your brother, Prince John . . ."

The Duke turned white under his tan. This was something about which he had never talked to his wife. John had been epileptic from birth and had had to live a life secluded from his family in a quiet house on the Windsor estate, until his early death.

"But Bertie is not . . ."

"No, but the strain of the throne and the war have brought on nervous seizures of the motor system which have affected his heart. It is believed that he will not survive the summer."

"Good God, how awful!" The Duke looked stunned. "Can you really be sure?"

Von Auerbach coughed.

"Sir, we have had word of this for some time. Actually we have . . . shall I say correspondents? . . . in the area. But we waited for the confirmation."

At the word 'correspondents' the Duke gave him a startled look. For a moment he was an officer hearing about the successful intelligence service of the enemy.

The German continued as though he had noticed nothing.

"As his illness has progressed, the King has become increasingly unhappy about all the problems of the succession. Important questions have been raised on legal matters, but in any event the King does not believe that in the present chaotic state of things his daughter Elizabeth should succeed to the throne under a Regency. The Queen is upset about this and he is being kept up in the Highlands incommunicado."

"Now that could be true, Wallis. You know I've said how strange it is that Bertie won't talk to me on the telephone, and he hasn't answered my letters since—well. And any messages I do get make no sense. That's not like him. By God, it isn't."

The Duke rose and walked about the terrace excitedly. Von Auerbach had caught him on an exposed nerve. From childhood his younger brothers had admired him to the point of hero worship, but Bertie had worshipped him most of all. Even the night before his Abdication, on their last dinner at the Fort, Bertie had been staring at him admiringly. He had been in good form, he remembered rather proudly; he had known he looked his most dazzling as he had dressed for dinner in his white kilt, and he had heard Bertie's whisper to Monckton: "Look at him! Is this the man we are to lose?"

It had been a thunderous blow when he had been told, as far back as his stay at the Schloss Enzesfeld, immediately following the Abdication, that his brother wanted him to cease from telephoning. He could not, even then, believe that this message came from Bertie himself. Now he was beginning to understand. He turned to von Auerbach.

"I am convinced he has never seen my letters, for he certainly would have answered them."

Von Auerbach followed up.

"The Queen is trying desperately to hide his condition. The King wants the succession settled. He had thought of your younger brothers. But in these last weeks, at death's door, he has been troubled in his mind, very troubled. He has asked to see you. This is the best kept secret in Great Britain."

"What?" the Duke said. "*He* wants me to come home?" He looked at the Duchess significantly.

"Of course, there are those in England who know of it," the German said. "Prime Minister Churchill for one. And he knows why."

"Why?" the Duchess chimed in, all eagerness.

"The King has flatly stated that the Abdication was illegal. He knows it was brought about by lies and intimidation. Promises about the future that were never intended to be kept, threats to interfere with Her Royal Highness' divorce—"

"That is certainly true," the Duke interjected.

"And even bodily harm to you, Ma'am."

"I always said it was the Secret Service who threw those stones at my window in Cumberland Terrace," the Duchess said excitedly.

The Duke winced. He remembered that insult and injury to his beloved. A proud man, he had been infuriated that this could have happened to her in his own kingdom. It had been necessary to take her into the protection of Fort Belvedere, which had caused more insult. At this hateful recollection his face was very dark.

"The King has said, over and over again, to his family and to such Cabinet members as he was still allowed to see while he was in London, that the whole thing was a monstrous error and a fraud, and that he was wrong, wicked even, to comply. The Abdication Act must be repealed."

The Duke looked not unbelieving, but puzzled.

"The present Government would never allow the Abdication Act to be repealed and—"

"The present Government is about to fall," von Auerbach said. "It was an unhappy coalition from the beginning, as you can well believe."

"Most coalitions are," the Duke said, nodding.

"You know that Halifax and Chamberlain wanted to accept the Führer's peace offer—they have stated so openly enough. And they have a large majority with them. The King wants Halifax to form a Government. If that is not possible, then it might be Lloyd George. But whichever it is, he believes that repeal would not be difficult. He has said that you must come home and resume your rightful place which never truly passed from you. He feels you are still properly King today. That is why I ventured to address you as Your Majesties, for if you are King, Sir, then obviously your wife is Queen."

There was a long pause. The balcony was very quiet, but it was not the quiet of heat and lethargy. The Duke had been too confused for speech, but the last words lingered in his mind and he responded.

"Yes, that undoubtedly is settled for ever. If I am King, Wallis is certainly Queen. That matter can never be brought up again."

Von Auerbach had been watching him carefully, and decided that his point had been made.

"With your permission, I will now take leave of Your Royal Highnesses. You have much to consider and discuss. But, if you will allow me, I will call again."

And with a bow and a click of his heels, he departed gracefully, leaving the Duke and Duchess to gaze at each other in wild surmise.

"Perhaps," the Duchess said slowly at last, "we should take those flying boats after all."

SIX

The Ginger Man [iii]

Maria, listening from the inside room, was pondering also. Her English was enough to allow her to serve an English lady, but much of what she had heard she had not understood. And of the rest, she was not sure if it meant what it seemed to mean. She gathered up the Duchess' nightgown, the underclothes she had worn the day before, three different sets, and her stockings. All must be washed and, except for the stockings, pressed. The stockings were merely to be touched up, very lightly, with a cool iron. Once she had spoiled a pair and the Duchess was very angry.

What she had heard, although interesting, was probably not useful. The Senhor at the German Legation would not pay for this. The Graf was German, and so certainly the Germans would know of this Royal story.

In the Duke's room, all was confusion. Ferdi had not been there at all. She wondered where he could be. Leaving the unmade bed for the moment, she gathered up soiled clothes that were scattered all over the room and the bathroom. None of the socks seemed to match. When she washed them, she thought, she would also do the things of the English soldier.

Then the idea came. Perhaps the British might be willing to pay her something for what she had heard. She knew that Manuel, although he had not told her, took a little money from both sides. Nothing wrong with that. Their master, after all, had friends among the Germans as well as the British. Naturally, that was the nature of his business. Perhaps it would be hers? A maid's wages were small. She had Jorge to think of. Manuel, her lover, was not the father of Jorge. He had five children of his own, and he didn't care for the boy. Not like the Englishman. Who was he? she wondered. He had liked her little Jorge, she could see that. Such a man, young, strong. With a look in his eyes . . .

Perhaps, she considered, as she made her way down the stairs, if she could get him in a little private talk away from Manuel she might discover whether the British would want to know about this business. Was it worth anything? *If* she could get away from Manuel. Even in her own room, she thought crossly now, she had no privacy. Manuel looked upon it as he did his own. It struck her that Manuel thought too much was his own. She *would* manage to talk alone to this young Senhor with the reddish hair. There was, after all, she remembered brightening, his room. She wondered which one it was.

When she got to the kitchen, she found it in chaos. The chef was shouting, Manuel was growling, Jorge was crying and the cat was squealing—the chef was treading on its tail; the gardener, who should not have been there at that hour, was shouting also.

She was soon enlightened. Ferdi had gone. Manuel had gone to Ferdi's room and found all his things were missing. Manuel's first thought had been merely to thank heaven that the Duke and Duchess were dining out—by tomorrow he would arrange something. But when he had gone to check the time on his watch—his gold watch, a gift from the South American, which he always left on his bedside table—that, too, was gone. Also a silver cigarcase, slightly dented, passed on to him by his master. And all the escudos he had stuffed away under his mattress.

101

The other servants had similar tales, from the chef's gold cuff-links to the very valuable holy medal belonging to the gardener. Maria exclaimed, rushed to her room and examined everything so quickly that her room soon looked as bad as the Duke's. Yes, the gold cross and chain, which she wore only on feast days—vanished!

Rex missed most of the excitement as he had left the house and gone down to Cascais. He had been looking around, chatted with those people who knew a few words of English, and arranged to hire a motor-bike. The young fellow who owned it looked rather down and out and was happy to make the deal. Rex checked over the old but still serviceable BSA. It wasn't like riding his Harley-Davidson but it had been reasonably well cared for, and it would take him where he wanted to go. He might not have the use of the car, but he wasn't going to be tied by the leg.

There was a lot of clucking over the servants' dinner about the absconding Ferdi, but Rex's attention was directed balefully at the food. Manuel cooked the food for the kitchen: a Portuguese version of paella with the fish of the region. The Cockney Rex termed it to himself as 'diabolical'. He was horrified when Maria and Manuel poured olive oil all over it. *Some* foreign food was all right, in his opinion, but this was going too far.

Maria, between her moments of anguish about her gold cross and chain, had been casting many languorous looks in Rex's direction—Manuel had seen them too and didn't like it. So Rex was not surprised that night to hear the rustle of Maria's dress at his door. Foreigners might not be able to cook, but he was to have no complaints about their ways of making love. Maria, used to coping with the demands of the ageing and tired Manuel, was full of pleasant tricks. She herself was agreeably surprised.

Unfortunately for her plan, she found it much easier to make love than to talk. Rex did think of his business —he had heard a little in Cascais, but no more than he had gathered already. He had not missed the pennant on von

Auerbach's Mercedes as it stood in the drive of the Boca Do Inferno. So while he complimented Maria on her charms and erotic talents, he tried to get her to talk about the Duchess—but met with little success.

Maria understood his compliments and giggled. She ran her hands down Rex's back as the muscles rippled and sighed in pleasure. For once she would not change places with Her Royal Highness.

The next day there was no chance for private talk. The servants had not gone to the police about Ferdi but Manuel had mentioned the thefts when he told the Duchess of Ferdi's departure. The Duchess, predictably, had become excited and made an inventory of her jewels. The Duchess had a great many jewels. But, eagle-eyed, she soon noticed the absence of one piece that she had worn recently and not locked up—a brooch of diamonds and emeralds in the shape of a snake.

Almost instantly it seemed the house was crawling with police—about half a dozen different kinds of police. There were policemen from Cascais, the Guarda Nacional Republicana, their faces rather worried under their peaked caps; the Seguranca Publica from Lisbon, smart in light grey and efficient looking; some men in plain clothes with a fish-eyed stare like the CID, only shabbier. A few of the road police came in for good measure, and there were others, unidentified, except that their presence made the servants nervous.

Although they had been robbed themselves, the servants were all searched, bullied and their rooms turned over. The police looked at Rex as though they'd like to bully him too, but he was a foreigner and had to be treated with more consideration. Also he was the personal servant of the Duke.

There was another fuss when a call came from Lisbon that the master required the services of his chauffeur for a few days. The chef, much distressed by the questioning of the *policia*, told the others he believed this was a gesture by his master to show that he was angry at this harassment of his staff. The Duchess had shopping to do in the town and Sergeant Barney had to be called after all to drive the Ducal pair.

The Duke, except to give instructions, ignored his new chauffeur completely, but Rex's first meeting with the Duchess was a strange one. As she left the house, beautifully turned out in cream-coloured linen and a tiny straw hat, she had shot him a look of intense interest that he was accustomed to receiving from women, but in this case the look was not followed by warmth and invitation, but instead a swift hostility behind the mask of calm. He had only held open the door of the car, but it was as if he had attempted rape.

At the start of the journey, the Duke and Duchess were quiet, his alien presence inhibiting. But the car was equipped with speaking tube and glass panel which gave them confidence, and as the day advanced and he drove them from place to place, following the Duke's impatient and often erroneous direction, they began to chatter normally—rather excitedly, Rex thought. The panel, as it happened, was not soundproof, and he could hear some of their talk.

The Duke referred again and again to 'the Ginger Man.' The Duchess seemed to think highly of him. The Duke did not answer this. But before the morning was over, Rex had gathered what the old man had wanted to know. After all, the Duke and Duchess were planning to come home. The Duchess' fear of the flying boats was the stumbling block, and the Duke was going to ask for a destroyer.

So he had come out here for nothing, Rex thought. A storm in a Royal tea-cup. He left them at the house where they were lunching, a tall dignified house that suggested old money, with a coat of arms set in stone above the door, and was told to return in three hours. Not so bad, he thought to himself, for an American woman with two unsuccessful attempts behind her. Whatever Maria said, the Duchess was doing all right.

He drove about the town a little—he had never liked a big car, but the Bentley responded well. Lucky he'd got used to driving on the wrong side of the road in France. He'd been able to let her go a bit on the coast road when the Duchess—a nervous Nelly—had been too busy talking to notice, but he'd got dirty looks from the buggers who, dressed in khaki and carrying guns, looked ready to kill.

Funny to see oranges growing on trees . . . There was a lot of building and cleaning up going on, and about time too. He watched the girls prancing over the cobblestoned pavements, up and down the hills and gliding over the fancy tiled streets—one of the streets had patterns of sailing ships. What price that down Piccadilly?

Many of the girls smiled at the English soldier. He grinned back, but remembering the horrors of the meal the night before, he asked a taxi driver for a place with English food. The driver sent him to a café on the Rua Gambetta. Rex sat down hopefully at a marble-topped table, and cautiously ordered eggs and chips. The eggs were recognisably eggs, but what they did to the potatoes he couldn't imagine. Well, even the French, who were supposed to be such wonderful cooks, never could make real chips. He remembered the quiet days in Northern France, before the balloon went up, sitting at the zinc bars, teasing the old girls about their 'pommes frites'.

A man in a dark English suit, very shabby, wearing a black eye patch over his right eye, looked up at his complaints.

"No use argy-bargying," he said. "Funny thing, really. Even a woman in England can turn out a decent plate of chips, but once you cross the Channel you can forget all about it."

The man was sitting over a glass of wine, making it last. Obviously, he wanted to get into a conversation, but Rex, after a remark or two, paid his bill and left. He had plenty of time and there was one thing he wanted to do. Manuel had told him nothing, but in Cascais he had learned that the man who had called on the Duke was a new arrival, believed to be connected with the German Legation. Fortunately Maria had remembered his name, somewhat mangled, but he understood it to be von Auerbach, and that the man was a Graf. Whatever that was. At least in England a lord was a lord and that was the end of it.

A few inquiries of hotel porters, money passing discreetly from hand to hand, brought the information that the Graf was staying, not at the German Legation, but at the Avenida Palace Hotel. Rex drove round, looking meditatively at the well-dressed men and women going in and out—some of the women were very good-looking. Dolores del Rio . . . For all he knew the Graf might be here just for a dirty weekend. Not that it mattered: the Duke and Duchess were going back to England. But he thought he'd tell the old man as much about this Auerbach as he could.

As he turned the car, he saw an old fellow, limping a little, leave a small side entrance and rush along, sweating in the sticky, intense heat. On an impulse, Rex stopped and offered him a lift. Pleased but courteous, the man explained he was going to the old quarter of the Alfama. Would the kind English soldier have the time . . . ? The English soldier did.

The man, dragging a rather stiff right leg, hoisted himself beside Rex, explaining that he had been on his way to get a bus. He spoke a broken English, carefully pronounced, that Rex could understand well enough. As he directed him through the town, he explained that he was a night porter at the hotel, that his relief had not come and he was only now permitted to leave, and he was rushing home for a few hours before his next shift began. His wife, an invalid, needed his attention. She, too, would be grateful to the English *soldado*.

A few questions brought the subject round to the newly-arrived Graf—a very demanding man, it seemed. The furniture in one of the best suites had had to be rearranged to suit him. And he had sent back his cold soup the night before, because it was not cold enough. The floor waiter had grumbled to everyone about having to go up and down those long corridors in this heat so many times.

The Graf had paid a visit to the Duke at the Boca Do Inferno, Rex remarked. The old man nodded. Yes, he had summoned the car from the German Legation. It was said that the Graf and the Duke were related. One family, for the second time, on opposite sides of a war. It was very sad. Still, it was good to be grand and rich. These things rested much harder, no doubt, on the poor.

The man had taken him into a different part of the town. The streets were narrow, almost too narrow for the Bentley, and very old. They looked like something out of the Middle Ages, Rex thought, remembering some parts of London. The houses were small, the doorways a foot low for a man of his height. The doors were open, and to his amazement he saw hens stepping in and out of the houses, as perky as the young girls. Washing was strung outside, flapping over the car as he drove.

He was going very slowly now, and stopped as he came to a flight of steps that led precipitously downward. The old man thanked him again. His house was only a few steps away. The senhor was most gracious. And as he murmured 'adeus' he was already hobbling down the steps.

Rex made his turn with some difficulty, and began the drive back for the Duke and Duchess. So the Graf was a relation. There was no mystery in his visit. Nothing to trouble old Winnie about at all.

A right boy scout you are today, Rex Barney, he told himself, amused. A good deed. He was only twenty minutes late for the Duke and Duchess and thought it no reason for the Duke to carry on as if he'd been left behind at Dunkirk. Like a lot of good men. Like Larry.

Except for the part about Larry, he expressed some of these thoughts to Maria that night when they were lying, rather squashed, in his narrow bed. Maria suddenly thought again of the strange conversation of the Duke, which she had quite forgotten in the excitement of the day, but her mind was now at peace. Rex had promised her a new gold cross so she told him what she had heard. The German had said the Duke must go home because his brother the King was very ill. And much more, she said —it was already jumbled and vague in her mind.

Very ill? The King? Rex was startled. Could he be? Christ, he'd looked rotten the day he'd pinned on the medal, but no worse than plenty of others who would still be walking about on their plates of meat for a good few years yet. Still, it might be true. He thought of old Ma Corky at the sweetshop, red and plump, always had a joke along with the change, but the doctors had said she was dying of a growth, and she'd gone in a year, just as they said.

But what was it to do with the German? Of course, Rex remembered, the German was a relation. Naturally he would think it right for the Duke to go home if his brother was very ill. So, Rex concluded, it was as he had decided earlier. There was no problem. The Duke was going to be a good boy.

He yawned and rolled over, ready for sleep, enveloping his long body around Maria's short, plump one. Maria was sleepy and comfortable but she still remembered her pressing need of a few escudos.

"And the King is kept, I think—shut up," she said, searching for words. "By Churcheel. Are they lovers, do you think?"

"What?" Rex exclaimed, sitting up suddenly, tumbling Maria, and shaking his head to clear it.

"Because he thinks his daughter is too young. He has been sent away, to another country, I think."

Rex laughed. Getting information from Maria was like receiving a message passed through too many posts all the way down a chain of command. Or like that game they used to play at birthday parties when he was a kid. One person would write a phrase on top of a sheet of paper, fold it over and pass it on. The second would add another just below and do the same. When the last giggling player had added his bit, the whole thing would be read aloud to howls of incredulous laughter.

"Mrs Brown the Vicar's wife caught a slow boat to China and met Tarzan of the Apes. They made love in a lagoon and gave birth to the blues, while Britannia ruled the waves."

"No, darling," he said. "Not lovers. And the King isn't banished, I saw him a few days ago."

"You saw the King?" Maria was intrigued. "Is he handsome? More than Churcheel? But the man of the ginger, he said he was . . .' She could not remember the word 'incommunicado' but at the time she had had some idea of what he had meant.

"Ginger?" Rex said, suddenly interested. "I thought you were talking about the Graf." He'd had a look at him. A dirty blond, but certainly not ginger.

"The Duke said . . . the man come . . . to ginger." She wondered now what it meant. It was all very difficult. But she persisted. "Rex, would the Army pay some money to know this?"

"Not if I know 'em," he said absently. "Only give me twelve bob a week, and I have to go on parade to get that."

The Ginger Man. So the Duchess had been talking about the Graf. She thought a lot of him. What in the name of creation *had* Maria heard? Now it didn't seem so funny. She could get things muddled up, but she wasn't lying. But although they talked until Maria fell into an exhausted sleep, she couldn't tell him much more.

First thing in the morning it was comparatively cool. Although the sun was blazing in the deep blue sky there was a fresh breeze off the water and Rex began by enjoying his ride on the BSA down the coast road. It ran pretty well except for a slow start-up. But then those bastard traffic police were on to him like buzzards now he wasn't in the Bentley with the Duke. He thought he'd met some miserable coppers in his life but these sods were gun-happy. They'd fired a couple of shots over his head when he hadn't stopped—and he wasn't sure they'd *meant* to fire over his head either. Made him homesick for an old blue bobby.

A good thing they hadn't searched him, he thought, when they finally let him go. He had no permit of any sort for the gun he was carrying, and he was sure the Duke would never back him up. In England he'd thought he might need his Browning for this job, and he certainly wasn't leaving it at the Boca for someone like Ferdi to pinch. Too much trouble getting it. One thing he'd found out in France, and that was that the Army-issued Smith and Wessons were bits of junk compared to the German stuff. He'd used a captured Luger until he'd run out of ammo, but then he'd had the luck to win the Browning off a Canadian at pitch and toss. A beauty of a semi-automatic with a 13-round magazine. It had saved his skin more than once.

He took it easy on the bike the rest of the way—he had to get into Lisbon that morning. The night before he'd made up his mind that the old man ought to hear about this. The King was supposed to be very ill, rumoured to be out of London, and there was funny talk about Princess Elizabeth being too young for the throne. All this from a man who, even if he was a relative, the Duke had said was coming to ginger him up. What did that mean? And why were they so coy in the car about using his real name?

110

At the house Manuel listened in on every call, and who knew how many others listened in besides. There was a telephone in the café where he had eaten the day before, and there he went, though he had to wait for it to open. Rex was relieved when he called the number given to him and gave the idiotic code words to find he was acknowledged. He had had a certain fear that someone would swear at him and hang up. Though actually, whoever it was sounded decidedly rude. But that was the old man's fun.

"Bitch," a deep male voice said laconically, and there was a lot of buzzing. It took some time to get through, and then his connection seemed as though it had been bounced half way round the world. The Prime Minister had been about to leave No. 10—he'd almost missed him. Lousy police.

He told his story succinctly and with as much discretion as possible. In broad daylight, over the crackling line, it didn't sound like much. Not surprisingly, the Prime Minister pooh-pooh'd the tale.

"Oh, that's all nothing. German rumours. They're always at it. As long as Il Duce," he chuckled, "is coming back, they're really helping us."

Rex had a feeling the old man had forgotten why he'd sent him. Well, he had a few other things to talk about. It turned out his mind was full of something quite different and he soon forgot to be discreet.

"Thompson was shot last night," he informed the startled Rex. "He claims it was the IRA. Personally," he added with a laugh, "I think he did it himself. Got it in both legs. He *will* use a shoulder holster, and he's careless, very careless. Never liked shoulder holsters, dangerous things."

Rex found later that the old man was to keep up this fiction that his bodyguard had shot himself. The public mustn't be frightened.

"I'd been kept late at the Admiralty," the Prime

Minister went on, "and I sent him back to 10 Downing Street for some cigars. Says he was shot in the black-out. Likely tale."

He'd probably got himself convinced of this codswallop by now, Rex thought grimly. Of course, they were after the old man. Shot Thompson, expecting to get Churchill right behind him. As would have happened, if he were normal and not the kind of man to send his bodyguard on errands. How many times Rex had heard his father swearing. "I don't mind getting his clobber from the cleaners, or running back for his false teeth umpteen times a month, but how can I do my real job if I'm not on the spot? Tell me that."

"So he's coming home, is he?" the Prime Minister went on. "Well, then, that's all right. I've got another idea. Why don't you come back—you're attached to me now. Don't feel right without Thompson. The Yard sent me another old codger. You come back and you can help them out. Someone young for a change. When Thompson comes back, you can join a new game I've got going. Special Unit—my Leopards. Report to me when you get back and I'll tell you all about it."

There was a click and the line was dead. Rex looked at the receiver thoughtfully. It was not the reception of his news that he had expected—but the old man never did what was expected. So he wanted him for a bodyguard. If there was one thing he had always been determined not to be . . . Well, it was only for a few weeks. And God knows, the old man needed a bodyguard, someone who would refuse to go for his false teeth. If Rex had been suspicious of possible Quislings before, since he had been in Lisbon the idea had become much stronger. Whatever Churchill might think, Rex had an uneasy feeling about the Duke. And he would bet that the Duke still had plenty of friends left in England.

The plane for Bristol left the next day. He called at the Embassy for his travel papers. They were a snooty lot but for once gave him no trouble although his orders had been changed only verbally. He didn't know it, but the Duke's complaints about him had been so bitter and protracted that they were very happy to have him go. The Second Secretary, who had to be called in, privately agreed with the Duke. Not at all the type that was wanted.

At the Boca Do Inferno, the servants were slightly happier. Although the important policemen had failed to arrest Ferdi or find the Duchess' brooch, the worried-looking plump man from the Guardia Nacional in Cascais had turned up triumphantly with several of the servants' bits and pieces which Ferdi had disposed of to the local fence for a remarkably small sum. Only Manuel's gold watch and Maria's cross had already been sold and were not likely now to be recovered, so Manuel's face was long.

Rex said nothing about his leaving as yet: he would tell Maria that night and give her the cross and chain he had bought for her that afternoon in Lisbon. There had been several likely-looking fellows hawking stuff about the wharf, and he had got it for a good price. He was not wasting the Prime Minister's escudos. Idly he wondered if it was the same one Maria had lost. He had had a strange, painful twinge of emotion when he bought it. The hawker had had a gold mezuzah for sale. Very much like Larry's. Manuel's face was long not only because of his financial loss. Maria's absence from her room at night, now occupied only by the disliked Jorge, told its own tale. Besides, the look on her face when Rex came to the table —his, Manuel's table—made her doubly damned. Never had she looked like that for him. He had been brooding all day how he could get rid of the English soldier. The Duke did not want him. He stayed only because the British Army said he must. How could they be made to change their minds?

Then it had come to him. It had not been lost on Manuel that the sergeant did not like his good cooking. In

113

his own hearing, this Sergeant Barney had asked Maria to cook him a couple of eggs: foreign food, he explained, always upset English bellies. Manuel smiled at the recollection. A soldier who is ill must be sent home. He would see to it that this soldier was ill every day. It was the simplest thing in the world.

That night he took some fine beef, bought for the upstairs table, and cooked it *em sangue* as the English liked it, but with a special sauce of his own, actually two sauces—one just for the sergeant. And the hungry sergeant ate a great portion. Manuel had been amused. Maria would be disappointed for once, he thought vengefully. But he miscalculated, his special *molho* took several hours to take effect.

The next morning when Rex boarded the KLM 'plane to Whitechurch he was still feeling extremely ill. His nausea was pronounced, far more than the comparatively calm journey could account for. So violent were his spasms that other passengers commented on the delicacy of the English soldier. He drew a contemptuous glance from a tall, blond, blue-eyed man, whose papers showed him to be Peter Hainault, an English businessman, taking the last open route back to England after escaping from France. Next to the sick and sallow Rex, he looked particularly clear-eyed, healthy and strong. One of the best types of Englishmen, the steward thought. Going back to do his bit for the war. He was in fact doing just that.

The man was Horst Holstein, Admiral Canaris' chief assassin, on his way for the new Operation Green.

It was the 13th of July.

SEVEN

Black Knight

When the 'plane landed at Whitechurch, near Bristol, the officials looked over the papers of the calm, collected, well-dressed 'Mr Hainault' very quickly, and he was then allowed to make his way to the capital. Sergeant Barney was kept much longer. His obvious illness was put down to drunkeness, his surly manner did not please, and his move order, signed by the military attaché to the Embassy at Lisbon, was unorthodox and suspect. Military police were called, and Rex was still cooling his heels in Whitechurch while 'Peter Hainault' was registering at a well-known London hotel.

He had been well-briefed by Major Leiter. There was to be nothing 'hole and corner' about 'Mr Hainault'. He was to do exactly what a returned businessman without family might be expected to do. Horst Holstein, at present an Abwehr agent, once the aspiring Untersturmführer in the SS, changed into a white shirt, a discreet tie, a dark blue suit and regarded himself in the looking-glass in his room with some satisfaction.

The suit was well cut. He looked, he thought, entirely *sälonfahig*. To the man whose father had been a caretaker, the thought was invigorating. These English clothes suited his fair hair and grey-blue eyes. The Führer was right, there was a bond between the English and the German nation. Perhaps, with his mission accomplished, he might stay on. He had a happy moment, picturing himself as a great official in a large house, perhaps even a *Gauleiter* . . .

From his window he could see a fat, silver barrage balloon floating against a paling sky. He grinned. Balloons wouldn't stop the Luftwaffe. Downstairs he ordered dinner in the grill room. Leiter had explained that the menu would be in French, and he had been instructed in what he should—and should not—order. The food was surprisingly good for war-time, and the first shadow crossed his brow. He had believed the English were suffering more than this from the blockade. But then, of course, the poor were always the first to face starvation.

He ordered an expensive French wine as he had been told, although he didn't care for it. His English mother, who had been a governess in Munich before she had married his father, had never explained the preference of the English for the wines of France. Nor had she told him that white wine of the Rhine was called hock. But then, her family had been poor. She had never entered a hotel of this sort.

Holstein had another happy moment. At times there were compensations for being an Abwehr agent. Yet he thought of his former comrades of the SS with regret. He had visited the Paris headquarters and met one old friend. The SS was the life for a true man. And the Paris mansion was the height of luxury.

Still, this job was of the greatest importance, the culmination of his life in the Abwehr, the reason for his recruitment. His last job, he had been promised. If he wished he could return to his old SS regiment with the rank of Obersturmbannführer, or something even higher. His eyes gleamed at the thought.

His dinner over, he had the porter call him a taxi, and gave the name of a theatre. Should MI5 be keeping him under observation for a day or two, they would find nothing unusual about him. He bought a good seat. The show was a revue, starring a famous English actress. Holstein's English was perfect—his mother had nagged him enough —but he missed some of the jokes. The humour was not the broad kind he enjoyed.

He thought the revue very dull but laughed when others laughed. Besides, the actress was middle-aged and Holstein did not care for middle-aged women. He found them repugnant. Old witches. No good for breeding, therefore of no use. A thought came to his mind of the *Einsatzgruppen* in Poland. While the Reich was clearing away undesirables, when the SS came to the final purges perhaps the Führer would consider old women. Useless mouths. The thought soon faded. Holstein had a child's capacity to live in the moment.

He stood correctly while the orchestra played *God Save The King*. The English, he thought, were rather sloppy in this duty. They did not stand erect, a few were already hurrying out towards the exit and one woman— a silly old woman—dropped her handbag and scrambled for its contents.

Once outside, curiosity drove him to walk about the streets. Twilight lingered, but none of the theatres was lit up. The famous statue in the centre of Piccadilly Circus was boarded up. He remembered his mother's homesick talk of mighty England—well, they were soon brought low. Already terrified of the Luftwaffe! There were few men on the streets. Nearly all were in uniform except for the elderly. Obviously, low reserves of manpower. It was a wonder they hadn't been conquered long before—they would have been in his father's time, if the Army hadn't been stabbed in the back.

He had coffee and brandy in a café, all according to orders, and then took a taxi back to his hotel. He slept easily, profoundly, without dreams and woke to a fine morning. After breakfast, he inquired at the porter's desk about estate agents. He was given the addresses of one or two, and he mentioned his requirements for a bachelor flat. There would be no problem, he was told. Many people had gone to the country and were eager to find tenants. He could have his choice. The porter knew of one close by, and arranged for him to see it after lunch. 'Mr Hainault' said he would consider it, and returned to the hotel.

He dined once more in the grill room where his blond good looks were, he saw, already causing admiring comments among the female guests. At the desk he paused to settle his bill, explaining that he was catching a night train to pay a visit, but expected to return in a few days and asked that his letters be held for him. Then he went to his room, packed, and waited for the dark.

The doorman called him a taxi to take him to Victoria Station. There, regarding the sign saying, 'Is Your Journey Really Necessary?' He bought a ticket for Brighton. It was twenty minutes to train time. He had a cup of tea, which he found loathsome, in the buffet, and after a few minutes made his way to the Gents. There were three men at the urinal, and he locked himself into a booth until they had gone. The smell of urine and disinfectant assailed his nostrils, but he was not offended. He was not a sensitive man.

He removed his coat and tie. From his suitcase he took a woollen cardigan, which he pulled over his shirt, a tweed jacket and a working man's cap. The coat and tie went back into the case. He waited in the booth until a few men had come and gone. In the fly-specked looking-glass over the basins, his reflection faced him, drastically changed. He was shocked to see the resemblance to his father . . . he looked like any member of the lower classes, the shadow of the cap giving him an almost hangdog expression.

The cap was large enough to hide most of his bright hair, and so, to anyone observing, it was an unremarkable man who left the Gents. Standing with the jostling porters at the Left Luggage office, he might have been one of them, except for his youth, and the man who took his suitcase and gave him the ticket did not look up.

Then Holstein met his first problem. He had been warned of the black-out, and told where to go to catch a certain numbered bus. It was not far from the station, but the blacked-out streets of this unfamiliar city were much more difficult to negotiate than he had imagined. He bumped into several pedestrians, and at one point almost walked in front of a car. For a moment he had forgotten that driving was on the other side of the street. It would look fine in his records, he thought angrily, if he failed at the beginning of his mission through being run over by a stupid English car. Horst Holstein, one of Himmler's Teutonic Knights! Dedicated and inspired!

He could not find the bus stop. They were not lit up in any way, but fortunately some experienced black-out wanderer was looking for the same one. He had a torch, with its face covered to leave only a half-inch slit of light, which he waved at the posts to find the sign.

They bordered the bus together. A woman, hideous in a lumpy blue uniform with straps and tickets hung about her, hair frizzed under a man's cap, came to collect their fares. Holstein gave her the exact fare, which he had ready in this trouser pocket, and asked to be set down at a public-house, the King of Prussia. "You'll have to do that," Leiter had told him. "You won't be able to see in the black-out. It's a custom, so it won't be remarked."

Holstein wondered about that because Leiter himself had told him about the advanced spy mania of the British at this point. Anyone and everyone was suspect. Of the newly introduced agents, one man had been caught because he had failed to know the correct opening time for a beerhall—a public-house, Holstein corrected himself—in a particular area. Another one because he had attempted to buy butter, not knowing it was rationed. A third because he had gone to a railway station, where no trains had run for seven years. Small fry, quickly trained, it was true. Not real professionals.

Well, the man he was going to was no new agent. He was an Englishman, a British Fascist, and, he had been told, utterly reliable. Holstein was a little curious to see this English traitor. He had already met some of the men of the Legion of St George, English prisoners who had gone over to the Nazis. But they had been, in the opinion of the former SS man, a poor lot.

The journey through the dark streets seemed very long. He had been on the bus, with people boarding and getting off for almost an hour. Holstein longed to ask the uniformed woman if she had forgotten him, but he had been told to talk as little as possible on this journey.

At last she punched the bell on her outside platform and yelled.

"King of Prussia! King of Prussia, mate!"

He smiled to himself as he got off. Appropriate, indeed. But now he must be careful. He had been over the local map of this area many times so that he could negotiate it in darkness. Before him was a wide road, a main thoroughfare. He made a careful crossing. On the other side he found, where it should be, a stone wall. He could just make out the line of a spire against the sky. The church. A few steps left, and then a right turn. Cross the street. A hundred yards down, the bars of a factory gate. So far, all was well. Another two hundred yards, and a bend in the road.

On he walked, his eyes getting accustomed to the dark. A few stars glimmered. Straight ahead was the railing, separating the winding road from a grassy plot beyond. To the left three poplars, tall against the sky. Four doors before the poplars was his destination. He went to the end and walked back, counting. He was looking for number forty-six. Before him were two doors under one portico. Safely under the portico he could light a match, guarding the flame carefully behind his cupped hand.

There were two bell pushes. One bore no name. The other had a simple label saying 'Jarndyce'.

He pressed the bell cautiously and jumped when it rang like an alarm. When the door was opened he saw why. Before him was nothing but a narrow flight of stairs leading to the upper storey. Neville Jarndyce, then, lived in merely half a house. He could see little of the man in the almost dark hallway, except that he was tall, as tall as Holstein himself.

"Come in, come in," he said irritably. "Or we'll be having trouble with the warden. These ARP people are damned officious."

He followed his host upstairs to a dark passage. There Holstein paused. His host went into a lighted room before him, but Holstein made out another doorway to the right. He opened the door slowly, silently. Nothing could be seen, but his ears were sharp. If anyone breathed in that room, he would know it. But it was empty. This was not a trap. He followed his host.

He found him in a room of modest size that seemed to serve as sitting-room and kitchen. The curtains were drawn but Jarndyce pulled them back to check anxiously on the black cardboard, neatly framed, that filled the windows.

"We don't want any interruptions now," he added.

Holstein was surprised that the man had not waited for him to give the password. Probably he had been shown a photograph. He was shocked to see a woman, obviously the man's wife, seated with her knitting beside the empty hearth. Careless, sloppy procedures. But he had been told that the English were amateurs in all things.

Strangely, the woman, even the room, had a familiar look. There was a dresser along one wall opposite the fireplace, with brightly-flowered china hanging from hooks. A wooden table and chairs. There was a black stove by the empty grate, and a gas stove in the corner. From an open door he could see the scullery beyond. A coloured portrait of the King and Queen hung over the chimney breast. It might have been his own mother's kitchen, and the woman was strangely like her. Small, with brown waving hair already heavily intertwined with grey, a nervous little bird's face, very pale.

The last observation had also been made by Jarndyce for he spoke first, not to his visitor, but to his wife.

"Have you drunk your blood?"

"Not yet, Neville," she said nervously. "You know how sick it makes me feel and . . ."

He went to the scullery, came back with a large china jug filled with dark red blood that smelled as though it had been standing for some time.

"Well, get it down and go off to bed. You look like you're half dying."

The woman ran her needles through the ball of wool, put the knitting into a flowered bag, picked up the glass jug and made as if to take it into one of the two rooms off the kitchen that apparently comprised the rest of the flat.

"Drink it here," her husband commanded. "Then I know you've taken it. We can't afford doctors' bills, you know."

Holstein, though strongly condemning in his own mind this domestic interlude in his affairs, and determined to report Jarndyce to higher authority, somehow was oddly fascinated by what followed.

The woman's eyelids turned pink. Her ashen mouth quivered. Obviously, she wanted to protest but could not with him present. Perhaps she was afraid to any way. The look she gave her husband certainly was one more of fear than affection. She put the stuff to her lips and it made her gag at once. She tried again. With a quick motion she got some down, and then choked. Her husband stood over her, silent. He stood there for what seemed an eternity, though it was actually no more than five minutes, Holstein noticed.

Jarndyce waited while the woman, desperately

fighting nausea, got down the loathsome stuff. Her hands shook, a pulse quivered in her temple, a little blood and spittle ran down the corners of her mouth. Holstein found he could not stop watching it; it was somehow very pleasurable. He noticed, with amusement, that he was sexually aroused, though certainly not for this drab creature. He had a feeling that Jarndyce was also. When he left, the wife would have company in her bed, he thought.

But once she had crept away, the amusement over, Jarndyce was all business. Holstein observed carefully this tyrant of a half-house. He was dressed in a black coat and striped trousers, as a diplomat would be. His voice showed some education. Holstein had been told the man was a dedicated Fascist, and he believed it. He knew the type, the minor official who thought he deserved better. Trying to keep up the appearance of gentility in this dreary suburb in a workingman's dwelling. Believing that the Fascist state would bring him the position he deserved. Well, perhaps it would. The Jarndyces had their uses. And a man who would put a woman through her jumps the way he had done was worth something—Holstein's old comrades of the SS would have been amused by that.

Jarndyce turned abruptly and led him into a small bedroom to the left of his wife's. It looked like a boy's room, with a plain iron bedstead and wooden chest of drawers. The linen was scrupulously clean, but the room had an unused look. There was a curtain across the corner of the room and from behind it Jarndyce took a uniform and kitbag.

"Middlesex Regiment," Jarndyce said. "A mixed lot, but a good many Londoners." He took a wallet with a sheaf of papers from a drawer. "Here's your pass and paybook. Made out, as requested, to Henry Holbrook." He spoke with satisfaction, proud of his efficiency. "And you will see your description on page three. Your place of birth is Stepney, don't forget. You have a slight London accent, that's good."

123

Holstein hadn't known that. Jarndyce was quick—he'd only spoken a few words. He had told Major Leiter that his mother had once lived in Stepney, before an aunt had taken her away to send her to a better school.

"There have been a lot of changes since the war broke out so don't pretend to know too much about conditions there. You're listed as a carpenter by trade. An odd-job carpenter, so you have no particular employer that you need remember."

The brown Army Book 64, Soldier's Service and Pay Book, had a slightly worn look, just as it should. Holstein glanced quickly at the first page.

'ALL RANKS . . . BE ON YOUR GUARD and report any suspicious individuals.'

Jarndyce saw his glance, and gave him a lecture as if he were talking to a subordinate clerk.

"During the time you are in Great Britain talk to as few people as possible and as little as possible. Remember, life here changes from day to day, and from one locality to another. It is impossible for an outsider to be aware of everything. Englishmen themselves come under suspicion constantly—but *they* can clear themselves. People are very quick now to call the police. Your papers will stand up to anything except a direct query to your regiment. The pass is perfect, it was signed in blank. We had to change the name on the pay book but it is very well done—you see the small ink smudge there—and it probably won't be asked for."

He smiled grimly, thinking of the laziness of the Captain who had signed the passes in advance to leave with his adjutant while he went off on some doubtful pleasure.

Holstein, used all his life to obeying orders, did not resent his hectoring tone too much. He seemed to know his business. Who was his superior, Holstein wondered, in the chain of command? The man's cover could not be better. Well established. A son in the Army. It was highly unlikely that MI5 was still checking on Peter Hainault, but if they were, they would never look for him here.

Jarndyce, with the air of a conjurer doing a trick, showed him the false bottom of the kitbag and displayed the contents reverently. Holstein had seen many of these before, and he had had some brisk discussions with Major Leiter about this one. First he had insisted on the knife. Major Leiter had thought he wouldn't need it. In the end Colonel Lahousen himself had been called in for consultation. This might be a 'no violence' operation, but something could go wrong on the way. He wasn't going without his knife and his Walther P38. Then Leiter fussed that it should be an English gun, if he took one at all. Lahousen had pointed out that English privates on leave did not carry pistols, so if he were caught with one on him the amount of suspicion would not be much different. He might as well have a first class weapon and not get caught.

Leiter had shuddered and argued. He had arranged matters so carefully. A group of men had to be killed by the British force, but their bodies were being burnt in a manner that would seem to be the result of an accident. "We can't have bodies with German bullets in them." That had been his final word.

Holstein had had to be contented with the standard Smith and Wesson .38 revolver. He hoped he wouldn't get into a tight place with that. There was a long length of cord, very thin, but as he knew, amazingly strong. And his special kit, well-packed. He ran a thumb lovingly over the blade of the knife—at least the British could still make steel. He had a collection of knives, some of them English, in his mother's flat in Munich. The collection covered a whole wall now.

He changed into the uniform, a battle dress in his size but an indifferent fit. Holstein was vain of his looks and sighed for the glory of his SS uniform. That reminded him: he had to telephone. He had seen no telephone in the flat, and by the time he got to the station it would be too late to make his call. He asked his host, but before he could answer the doorbell rang. Jarndyce descended the steps, muttering, and returned with a large, very young girl who was arguing excitedly.

"But you said I could go, Daddy. And the whole group went for a coffee in Lyons afterwards—I couldn't come home by myself. And the buses run only every twenty minutes, but one didn't come and we waited three quarters of an hour. Susan Ballard and Mabel Walsh are still downstairs and they'll tell you."

She saw the stranger through the open door and stopped short. She must have been about sixteen or seventeen, not pretty but with shining fair hair. As she took off her jacket, Holstein saw the swell of her firm bosom under a light summer blouse, and the creamy flesh of her throat. She eyed the handsome soldier. Holstein thought she was a hot little number if ever he'd seen one. Jarndyce must have his hands full with her—he'd better marry her off fast.

Jarndyce was furious at his daughter's late and untimely arrival. Not for reasons of security: his wife knew better than to discuss his business, and Marian would think nothing of a private from her brother's regiment coming to see her father. It was what this 'Holbrook'—an agent of the highest importance he had been told—would think of him, the father of the family, that angered him.

Marian Jarndyce looked at the handsome young soldier with great pleasure. The evening at the theatre had been a bit of a change—but not much. All girls—her old school friends. She had lied to her father; after the performance they had walked round the West End, giggling, hoping to pick up some soldiers, but it had been dark and they'd had no luck. Now her father was in a snit and it would probably be months before she got a chance to go up West again, and there wasn't a young man left in miles. She was stuck all day in the Home and Colonial, trying to tell a lot of old girls it wasn't her fault every week something else went on the ration.

126

Marian's body had been mature for over three years now; she was healthy and had a strong sex drive that she hardly knew what to do with. Her mother found the subject too painful to think about, much less to discuss. Marian had done her own experimenting, which had been consummated one night on top of the roundabout in the children's recreation ground with Willy Tompkins, a fourteen-year-old who delivered the morning papers. The violence of their scrambling had set the roundabout in motion and Willy, nervous perhaps, had felt sick. Marian had not found the business all she had hoped, but her body had been prompting her strongly to try again. She thought the visitor's light-blue eyes were beautiful, his face as handsome as Leslie Howard's but he had, she thought, much more go in him. She longed to touch the sleeve of his uniform but had to restrain herself under her father's dark gaze.

If her mother did not understand Marian, her father had his suspicions. He also had his problems. Much as he would have liked to have married the girl off, there was a question of proper suitors. Her brother could introduce her to any number of young men from his regiment, but Jarndyce didn't want his daughter to marry just any Englishman. He had his own ideas of what would happen to them after the war.

He knew some young men of the British Union of Fascists—all quiet now, but he had always despised them as a rabble, except for those at the very top. And the National Socialist League was worse than the British Union. Jarndyce's anger cooled. He'd seen his guest look at Marian. This young German, almost certainly part English, might be a possibility when the day arrived. He had no doubts about 'Holbrook's' status—he must be at the top for Jarndyce to be called upon to help him. The information that Jarndyce passed on from the Ministry was too valuable for him to be compromised for an ordinary *V-Mann* or even a *Haupt-V-Mann*.

"Don't take off your jacket," he told his daughter. "Henry here has to make a telephone call before he goes. Take your torch and show him to the top of the street and the booth outside the King of Prussia." He turned to his guest. "I'll get the car, and when you come back I'll drive you to the station. Have you got plenty of change?"

Holstein nodded, and followed the girl in some amusement. As they walked down the dark narrow street she stumbled against him. She smelt of sex. Outside, instead of walking back to the main road, the girl strolled in the opposite direction, towards the iron gates.

"Your father will be coming out," he said in warning.

"No," she whispered. "We don't have a garage. He has to go out the back and down the next street, and then he fusses over the car—we call it his girl friend. His pride and joy. Only got it just before the war."

Holstein reflected that a family living so modestly, without a telephone, nor, as his sharp eyes had seen, a radio set or any luxury, would not normally have a car. Germany, no doubt, had paid for this toy. But the Jarndyce family were apparently bent on doing their utmost for the Reich. He grinned, as he watched the girl try to open the gate to the grassy field beyond and heard rather than saw her annoyance that this gate was firmly locked.

"You a friend of Tom's?" she asked as she wrestled with the padlock.

Tom must be the brother—in the Middlesex regiment, no doubt.

"Yes," he answered. As Jarndyce had said, the less he chattered, the better.

Fortunately the girl was not interested in his life history. Giving up on the gate she turned to him, not shyly. Smiling, he loosened her jacket and embraced her. Behind those delightful breasts he could feel her heart pounding. He gave her a long kiss, and he felt her back strain against the iron railings as her body arched and she thrust her pelvis close against him. He hesitated for a moment. He had a little time to spare. The street was quite empty; they seemed safe enough in the deep darkness under the trees. Below them a small brook ran through the grassy field. It ran slowly—turgid, with a rank odour. Not a romantic spot. But it could serve. He stroked her breasts methodically, and when she moaned in pleasure slipped between her already parted thighs.

An awkward business, he reflected a few moments later, as he adjusted his clothing. Fortunately the girl was satisfied. She smothered him with embraces and hung on his arm with extravagant affection as she took him to the telephone booth. An old woman came out of one of the houses, running after her dog. She hardly glanced at a soldier with a girl—Jarndyce was not stupid, Holstein thought.

It was more trouble dealing with the telephone than he had expected. For all his careful instructions, he forgot one important thing. He could hear the voice on the other end, but he could not make himself heard. Marian had been shining her torch onto the dial for him.

"Silly," she said to him as he shouted into the receiver. "You've forgotten to press Button A."

He pressed Button A. Fortunately, Marian had been well brought up by her mother in some ways, and after giving him a final squeeze in the intimacy of the booth, she skipped outside to let him make his call in peace. He was relieved, as he asked to speak to the girl in Scotland who happened to be his fiancée.

EIGHT

Sweet Dreams

Rex Barney had believed that, as a sergeant, he would have some difficulty in dealing with a Duke. But in the event, he had been able to do his job, and had reported what he considered to be vital information. He might have known, he thought ruefully, that it was to be in England that his Army rank would be a problem.

His papers had at last been released to him at White-church by the still suspicious military police. He took a train from Bristol for London, and then made a very bad connection into Buckinghamshire—as it was Saturday, the old man would certainly be at Chequers Court. At Chequers he had trouble getting past the Lodge gates. Well, he was glad someone was looking after the PM. Usually there were just a handful of local bobbies about, but things had been tightened up a bit—his identity was challenged three times before he got to the house. He had spotted a small gun emplacement very imperfectly disguised behind a clump of bushes.

Inside the house, he was told by a Private Secretary to wait in a little ante-room. Rex chafed at this prison. It was already seven o'clock. Getting towards the old man's dinner time—and he never hurried himself at the table. While he was sitting here on his duff, God only knew what that German was cooking up in Lisbon. Soon he was roaming about the house, looking for his chief.

The Prime Minister was easy to find. A gramophone was blaring:

"Run, rabbit, run, rabbit, run, run, run."

Rex followed the sound to the Great Hall where the Prime Minister was conspicuously not entertaining his guests. Rex grinned, despite his exasperation with the old man. If England's enemies could see the scene before him, they would think the old man mad and other of the country's leaders not much better. On one side of the room, in a rather small space, two Chiefs of Staff, one Cabinet Officer and Lord Beaverbrook were huddled together, looking like sheep penned up by an autocratic sheepdog.

Beaverbrook looked intensely miserable, the others were putting a good face on it. Most of the room was taken up by the old man, who was marching up and down it, oblivious to them all. He was a strange figure among the uniforms and Beaverbrook's quiet dress, for he was in his dressing-gown, a Chinese affair, padded like a quilt, embroidered with red and green dragons. Even his slippers were elaborately embroidered and his initials WSC glared up at the observer in a shimmer of red silk—lest anyone might not realise who the wearer was.

The old man looked fat and irresistibly comic, padding up and down the room in a semblance of a march, carrying his cigar, and mumbling. Mumble, mumble, mumble. He burst into a few words of '*Run, Rabbit,*':

"Don't give the farmer his fun, fun, fun."

Then he went back to his mumbling again. His marching got out of step with the rhythm and he did a little skip and a hop to put himself right. As he passed before the suits of armour that dotted the hall, he and they both seemed to belong to another time. It was his guests, very much of the present, who looked like the ghosts.

He came to the end of the room, made a parade-ground turn and marched back. This, Rex knew, could go on for hours. Probably the old man was rehearsing a speech. He had seen him at it many times before, though not in such dramatic surroundings. The guests looked as though they were trying not to notice, as though there were a bad smell in the room. Rex had an almost irresistible desire to laugh. Only his Army training kept it back, but his mouth twitched and this caught the old man's eye.

Churchill's brow darkened. It was at these times, marching, humming, fussing with the gramophone, that his best, his clearest ideas came. No-one, NO-ONE, was to interrupt him. Then he noticed: it was his man Barney. He remembered now, he'd sent him on a job. A personal job. The Prime Minister's mind had been entirely taken up with the speech he had to make in the Commons. They must understand his every move. His support must be solid! The country could not be divided. It was still disquieting to him that his old chief, Lloyd George, had declined to join his Cabinet. But these thoughts faded and he looked with surprising mildness on the young man who had broken in on his meditation.

Rex jerked his head towards the window. The Prime Minister had had his stroll for the day, twenty minutes in the gardens was all he could allow himself. But now, with a good humour that caused a certain bitterness in the long-suffering men who had had their difficulties with him that day—and on many days—he walked placidly with the sergeant out into the last light.

Suddenly in a contemplative mood, the Prime Minister pointed out various beauties in the sunken rose garden and came to rest beside a sundial, reading the inscription:

> "*Ye Houres do fly*
> *Full Soon we die*
> *In age Secure*
> *Ye House and Ye Hills*
> *Alone Endure.*"

The sentences rolled richly off his tongue. Obviously, he liked the sound. Anyone would have thought, it seemed to Rex in his exasperation, that the old man was a retired codger, living very comfortably, perhaps in the reign of Edward VII.

"The hours are flying all right and we're in trouble," he said shortly. "I tried to tell you on the 'phone, but you didn't seem to get me. I think the Duke's up to something with Jerry. Just like you thought. And from what I heard it didn't sound so good for the King either."

Anyone else in that house would have considered the sergeant's language to be displaying a lack of respect. The Prime Minister, who could be as touchy and irritable as anyone else on occasion—and more often than most— remained benevolent. He understood that his man was merely speaking in his normal fashion. Barney was not an official member of his household or office staff. Churchill was a feudal man, and if he had defined to himself exactly how he thought of Barney, which he had not, he would have considered him a favoured man-at-arms, with something of the privilege of a court jester. Besides, the news that he had telephoned had actually been reassuring. Barney had done well, as he had been sure he would. Far better than waiting about for Menzies to try to reorganise the Service. Let him stick to the cyphers at Bletchley. The country needed a new group for special missions. He would order a Special Operations section. Prod, prod. That was his chief job in this war.

He smiled up at Barney, over six inches taller than himself, with his air that made him seem the larger man.

"As long as the Duke is returning in the flying boats, all is well," he said grandly.

He remembered now. Some German had told the Duke that the King was ill. They had talked about Elizabeth, in the event of her father's death, being too young for the throne. The poor child, she certainly was. Barney had taken this to mean that the Germans believed the

Duke had a chance to regain the throne. But certainly the Duke, sanguine as he once had been, could hardly believe that! As long as the Duke was returning, he could be handled. They must find him a job with an important-sounding title and not much responsibility. Churchill's mouth turned down a little. Facts must be faced. And something would have to be done about the Duchess. Perhaps Clemmie could think of something there. Women's business. His mind shied away from that. It was natural that the Duke would want to see his brother, knowing he was ill. And he *was* ill.

The story had not been made public. The public had enough to perturb them now. It was not necessary, and thank God the illness was not of a really dangerous kind. Weakness of the nerves, that was all. Strain and overwork. A conscientious man, the King. He said that in fairness, though he knew he had not been the King's real choice.

He patted the young man on the arm, a paternal gesture that did not soothe its recipient.

"We must not worry. We must have trust in each other. Confidence in the future!"

He was off, Rex thought resignedly. The old man was probably the only man in the world who talked all the time as if he were writing a book. Of course, almost everything he said went into his books. Waste not, want not, as Rex's mother used to say.

The old man peered at him.

"You're going to join my staff as bodyguard, aren't you?"

He'd just remembered that was why he'd brought Barney up here. Not that it would go down too well with Special Branch. Still, Barney was in a way one of their own.

Rex gazed at him. He supposed now he was in the Army, he could hardly refuse. His father would have a good laugh.

"You want me to go for your cleaning, guv?"

Churchill gave a huge chuckle.

"My staff is somewhat embellished now," he said cheerfully. "I have an idea. Would you like to go down and do some training with my Leopards? I think I'll go and see what they're doing myself. Unarmed combat, hand to hand fighting, surprise attack—"

"Sounds like the fighting in Bellingdon Road School," Barney said unimpressed. "I got first prize."

The Prime Minister laughed again. This was better than worrying about his tenuous majority in the Commons.

"I, too, had my successes at school," he replied, and told him a boastful anecdote of how he had pushed a much older, stronger boy into the swimming pool when he was a pupil at Harrow.

Rex was gloomy about his failure. He could see the old man had not understood what he was trying to tell him. Too much trust in the former King, he thought. Churchill had always liked him, after all. Harrow. The trouble with the nobs was they stuck together. But he remembered Jack Kemp saying one day in the Fox that the Duke was as much German as English. More, really. Though his brother, Rex thought, seemed all right. He looked at the rotund Prime Minister, grandly waving his cigar and thought to himself, 'My God, the old boy thinks he's Drake bowling on the grass with the Armada coming.' The fact that Drake had won did not, at that moment, cheer him.

When the Prime Minister returned to his speech and his guests, Rex took up his duty and made himself known to Special Branch. Special Branch were far from delighted. They considered that they knew their business best. Arrangements had been made for cooperation with the Army on the highest level. No-one had informed them that a sergeant from the infantry was to be entrusted with all the secrets of the protection of England's Prime Minister.

Detective-Inspector Hilliard looked down his long nose, frowned deeply, muttered something under his breath and went to call his Chief. A hasty conference at the Yard bore no fruit. At last Hilliard's call was returned. Inquiries were to be put through and he would be notified in due course. The Detective-Inspector replied testily that he could neither arrest this sergeant nor permit him to wander about the grounds of the Prime Minister's residence until he had instructions. By the time the conversation was over, he was aware that he had done himself no good with his superiors, and that he, and not Sergeant Barney, was now looked on askance at Headquarters.

Eventually someone there was persuaded to put a call through to one of the Private Secretaries. The Prime Minister had to be approached at dinner, which was truly horrifying, especially for so trifling a matter. Fortunately, the old man was gracious. He interrupted his rolling periods—his monologue, for it could hardly be called conversation—to say, "Yes, yes, it's all right. Let him look about. Give him what he needs," and went on blithely with a quotation he was trying out to judge its effect.

" 'Who knoweth not of the great preparations our potent and malicious adversary did make (nay, do make) against us, intending the bloody conquest of our country, a servile thraldom of our people, a rooting out of our name and nation . . .' "

Most of the guests managed a look of polite interest, but Lord Beaverbrook was sunk into his chair, his face sallow, his eyes glazed with boredom: he was a talker himself and used to being the centre of attention. Well, the Secretary thought, Max would have to get used to a lot more of the same.

" '. . . when all our neighbours have been infested with bloody wars and massacres, blood streaming in their streets . . .' " the Prime Minister attacked his roast beef with renewed vigour.

Detective-Inspector Hilliard bore his discomfiture

better, outwardly at least, and explained to Rex the tours of duty of the Special Branch men, and some of the measures taken for the Prime Minister's protection. One thing he did not tell him—an excellent stratagem—was that sometimes when the Prime Minister was officially staying at Chequers, he was actually at a country house elsewhere.

He turned him over to the Artillery Officer, who showed him the guns that protected the house. Larger emplacements, for anti-aircraft batteries, were to be set up in the grounds to fight off low-flying 'planes when the expected barrage came.

"I trust," Hilliard said dryly, when the inspection was over, "that you think our precautions adequate, Sergeant Barney."

"Big bloody hole, isn't it?" he replied. "Only saw over a bit of it. Spotted four places I could've got in without being nabbed. 'Course, you can't get in up the drive without papers. But I wouldn't put it past Jerry to get hold of 'em."

Hilliard, who had known and respected Alf Barney, knew too much about his son. For the child of a Special Branch man to be engaged in any form of dubious enterprise was especially bitter. "We haven't, of course, had your experience in breaking and entry."

Rex grinned. "Don't say what you can't prove. You'll get yourself in trouble, doing that."

And to the detective's disgust, he demonstrated with blithe ease the scaling of a wall assumed to be unscalable, and the dodging of a sentry apparently wide awake.

Hilliard showed him some of the precautions taken inside the house. Rex seemed more interested in the art treasures of enormous value scattered about the place. He paused with a loving regard over a glass case that sheltered a magnificent ruby ring.

"Marvellous lot of stuff here," he said reflectively. "Never mind Jerry, might be worth while for someone to nip in just to knock off a few quids worth."

Hilliard was stung. "Special Branch have guarded this house with no trouble since the first war, thank you . . ."

But he was a sensible man underneath and listened carefully to the suggestions which he resented.

"Otherwise," Rex finished up, "the place is as easy to crash as Buckingham Palace." The significance of the remark struck both men and they went about their tasks soberly.

Hilliard's rest that night was troubled by more reasons than one. It was only the thought of Barney's leaving quite soon to join the Commandos that soothed him at last. A dangerous job that, he thought, and eventually fell into a happy sleep. It was the morning of July 14.

* * *

While Special Branch, formerly Irish Special Branch, of the Metropolitan Police were guarding Cabinet Ministers and Royal Personages, an almost unknown IRA soldier, Frank Purcell, was on the first leg of his return journey to Great Britain. The U-boat had proceeded with caution and it was dusk when the craft surfaced in the harbour. Purcell stood on the deck with the Commander and watched the vessel under the German flag steer confidently through these once British waters. He watched the quiet waters of the estuary, with the pearly lights shining through the mist from the peaceful fishing boats.

"Well, we are in Cork," the Commander remarked, smiling grimly. "And we have had no problems."

"Cobh," the Irishman corrected him.

It would be good to touch on home soil. Yet it was strange to be travelling alone. He had been in training at Quenzee in Bavaria with other IRA men, in Major Erwin von Lahousen's sabotage school, when Russel himself had come to see him. Sean Russel, former Chief of Staff of the IRA, now looked old and ill. He had left New York and was returning to Ireland, he told Purcell, and he wanted to arrange this one last blow against the British. The man who did this job would do more for Ireland than all the soldiers of the IRA in their long history. He chose Purcell, for his great skill in demolition and his knowledge of British aircraft. There was another reason, but there was no need to discuss that.

Frank did have an unusual skill in demolition. All his squad were familiar now with British 'planes—enough aircraft had been shot down in France, and enough papers left behind to make that easy. He was honoured at being the one chosen, and too excited for sleep that night after landing on the Irish coast. By tomorrow, July 15, he would be in Scotland, where he, Frank Purcell, would make history.

Purcell didn't know it, but his selection had been the cause for argument between Lahousen and his Chief, Admiral Canaris. Canaris' scheme was one of perfect simplicity. As he had drafted it, nothing foreseeable could go wrong. At worst, the Royal Family could change their habit and the expected opportunity would not arise. Then Röslein would inform Black Knight, his men would go back to their normal positions, the British would not be warned, and he could put into effect his alternate plan, using a different assassin for the King and a domestic 'accident' arranged for Churchill in London. Not as polished a scheme, not as likely to leave Germany entirely free of suspicion, but deadly.

When Lahousen came to him he went over it once again. The two possible dangers had been the sending in of the new agents—too difficult now—and wireless communication—too easily traced. He had eliminated both of those. His instructions to Leiter had been to use only British agents, most of them sleepers, none of whom could be suspected. With the exception of Holstein, of course, but he had a British identity ready to step into. And the agents would communicate by messenger and telephone. Fool proof, he thought. *Unberufen*.

But Leiter had worried. One part of his detailed plan called for a work of sabotage that needed great skill. The IRA was full of crude saboteurs who could leave a bomb and run, but for the smooth handling of an important task much more than that was needed. He had consulted Lahousen, who naturally wanted to use some of the men he had been training so carefully.

And so he had gone to the Admiral. The man originally chosen to tamper with the engine of the 'plane, one Michael O'Connor, could not do what the Major needed. Sarcastically, he had told the chief of the project in Great Britain that it could not be done at all. Leiter needed to know, with as much accuracy as possible, where the Churchill 'plane would come down. It had to be a deserted place where his men could be waiting, ready to do their work, before the British blundered onto it. Besides, this Michael was the brother of Sean O'Connor, who was part of the force being gathered for Scotland, code-named 'Whale'. The brothers had a bad history when they worked together. On the other hand, Lahousen had a perfect man. He had been trained in certain work with altimeters which could be just what was needed.

"But is all this necessary?" Canaris asked. "Why not destroy the 'plane at the field—an unfortunate crash on landing. A simple job."

"Simple, Admiral—but not satisfactory, if you consider," Leiter answered. "It would bring people swarming to the airfield, with our men present—not to mention the bodies of the RAF. Our man in charge over there, the Welshman, has come up with a good scheme for an 'accident' to explain their deaths, but our men will need time to change uniforms and get away. Besides, having two 'accidents' occur together could cause suspicion, the last thing we want. The plan is to have the 'plane come down in the Cairns, a desolate rocky place with a few bad roads—not much more than tracks. That will give us time. And it is more plausible for a 'plane to crash in those hills than on a grassy field. Such accidents have happened before."

The last thing the Admiral wanted was to arouse suspicion. The coup *must* remain undetected. He wished it were possible to avoid the killing of the RAF men, but there was no way. Fortunately, the group was tiny, reportedly never more than seven men at one time.

"The big house over the airfield is empty," Leiter went on. "The owner, a widower, lives in London now. No other house has the field in view. So there will be nothing to connect the two events."

The Admiral was persuaded. He considered the inclusion of Frank Purcell. Michael O'Connor would be given a simpler job in England. And sending in another Irishman was not too difficult. Purcell was young and unknown to Special Branch. And if he should be challenged, he would stand a good chance. Born in Northern Ireland, he was a British subject.

Lahousen, who had studied Canaris' requirements carefully, was curious.

"Suppose the fish doesn't rise to your bait?" he said.

"There are contingency plans," Canaris answered. He did not say what they were. It was not his way. Even Lahousen was not to know of the agent who worked in the kitchen of a house where the Prime Minister dined regularly. The agent had been instructed, but would only move if notified. Like the man in the Iraqui Embassy who would be needed if the King failed to visit Scotland. "But the fish will rise," he added. "I know this Churchill—I have studied him for many years."

The little thin man with the wispy hair sat in his nondescript office on the Tirpitz Ufer, and thought of that other, small and plump, surrounded by the panoply of office, who spoke more as his ancestors had done than his contemporaries, who yearned for glory—something of a

Don Quixote, but his sword was tilted not at windmills, but at all the might of Germany.

"He is a romantic," he said at last. "Especially he is romantic about Royalty—he sees himself as their liege man."

Lahousen, though liking the plan, had his doubts.

"But he's no fool. He might alert the whole Army, Navy and Air Force."

Canaris shook his head. His wrinkled face peered up at Lahousen, giving him a look of a wise old gnome.

"It's the last thing he would do. The only shield the British have now is their confidence—a confidence based on very little. No-one knows that better than Churchill. No, he will be discreet. He can," he said, smiling a little. "But in any case," he added with a shrug, "it would make little difference. He will trust our Britishers, and that is his death warrant. And when he arrives, the King will already be dead."

Lahousen regarded his Chief with respect. It was Der Alte's brains that were winning Germany's wars, he thought. But he brought up one last point.

"You seem certain, Admiral, that it will be a 'plane. Might it not be a car or train? Purcell could handle a car alone but a train—"

"No," the Admiral replied. "He's a Minister of Defence, and running the whole war. He would have no time now for a train. Besides, he will be in a hurry for personal reasons. He will want to see the 'dying' King."

Lahousen looked unconvinced.

"At the meeting in the Chancellery, Göring was talking of bombing trains, with great precision . . ." he murmured.

Canaris jumped up angrily.

"For God's sake, we can have no bombing! Göring is to know nothing of this. The last thing we want is that—" he muttered something under his breath, "bumbling round in this."

The spy-master, who understood too well the effect of drugs on the personality, had no use for the Luftwaffe chief and his euphoric moods. Addicts were fools, not leaders. But, though he did not know it, Hitler was already telling Göring of the plan.

It took no time at all for Reichsmarschall Hermann Göring to see the significance of Operation Green combined with the Windsor Plot. In the original Operation Green, which should have followed immediately after Operation Yellow, the invasion of the Low Countries and the Battle of France, the Luftwaffe had had an important role. Naturally. He himself had helped in the planning. The first thing that struck him about this new plan was that the Luftwaffe had been eliminated entirely. As had been Hermann Göring. He was instantly enraged.

With the conclusion of the new Operation Green, this Windsor Plot, the war would be over. If he played no part in it, he would be remembered only for his failure at Dunkirk. He would be the last and least in the victory parade. The Führer was still his friend and referred to him proudly as the 'Iron Man', but there were many envious ones, powerful enough now to try to discredit him, and attempt to take his place as the Number Two man in the German Reich.

But that, he, Hermann Göring, would never allow. And unlike the rest, he knew how to handle the Führer with high assurance and warm good-fellowship. No other man living dared to do that.

"We must send in a small force of paratroops as well —quietly, with all due caution," he said firmly. Since the Luftwaffe had gained control of the paratroops, all the credit would come to him. "A handful of traitors and Irishmen can't do it all themselves. There could always be opposition, something unforeseen. If Canaris doesn't trust his Brandenburgers, there are other crack teams."

The Führer listened without comment.

143

"And I understand that territory," Göring added. "The Eastern Highlands and Deeside. An old friend of mine, Leopold von Auerbach, used to go there to shoot. It is very similar to Thuringia—woods, hills and mountains. They say that is why the good Prince Albert chose the place," he went on, smiling, knowing the Führer would be impressed, not only with his knowledge but the reminder of his aristocratic background. "My men have been training in the Thuringerwald and in the mountains of the Vogtland for months."

The Führer beamed. The two old friends parted after much comradely laughter and talk of the glorious future, but once out of the Führer's presence, Göring's face became grim. He sent a messenger at once to Colonel Ulrich List, of Fremde Heere West, the Wehrmacht's own Intelligence Department, and obtained a copy of the same topographic chart that Major Leiter himself was using. He would make his own plan. In his mind it mattered little how the thing was done, as long as it was done. If, in the end, the British did not like it, by then there would be little they could do. Impatient with detail, as he always was nowadays, he turned the matter over to his right-hand man, State Secretary Körner.

Then, smiling, he went off to the dinner he was giving at his favourite restaurant, Horcher's. Although his guests did not know it, this dinner had become a celebration. Nor did they understand his toast when he lifted his glass to 'Operation Iron Man,' but they drank his good wine and joined in his merriment as he laughed hugely. That night the Reichsmarschall slept well.

Blissfully unaware of these discussions, Canaris had settled with Lahousen about Frank Purcell. He watched him go, Major Erwin von Lahousen, a former officer of the Austrian Secret Service who had betrayed his country to the Abwehr at the time of the Anschluss. A competent man. He believed him completely trustworthy—or almost.

144

On July 14 he sent for Major Leiter to see how 'Whaleforce' was progressing. Their main job was the assassination of the Prime Minister, but they were to be ready to assist Black Knight if assistance were needed. And they had the job of guarding the roads for the all-important few hours.

It was Major Leiter's proud moment. The organisation of the group had been entirely his work. Fortunately, he had a useful body of agents to choose from—agents he had cultivated, but kept as 'sleepers' since the Führer had talked of the first Operation Green. They were politicals, but none of them was averse to the extremely high pay either. The Abwehr had never paid as much as it was paying the men of Whale. There were English Fascists who had not changed sides when the war began; Welsh and a few Scottish Nationalists, and IRA men who were deadly, experienced killers. The group had needed little special training, except instruction in the use of the Bofors gun.

Now he smiled with satisfaction and touched his moustache.

"Already assembled," he reported. "Waiting in Aberdeen and some small towns and villages in the vicinity. Ready to move at Black Knight's signal."

The Admiral, not an effusive man, congratulated him on a piece of work well done. When Leiter left, Canaris permitted himself a moment of content. He had already received a most satisfactory report from Fraulein Bumke, the agent who had been in charge of the Lloyd George negotiations from the beginning. Mr Hindhead—Lloyd George's codename, taken from his country home—was in his glory.

Fraulein Bumke had taken him greetings from the former King.

"Cymru am Byth."

Wales forever. It was an old greeting between them. Lloyd George had been the teacher of the Welsh language

145

to the young Prince before his investiture as Prince of Wales.

Fraulein Bumke reported that there had been tears in the old Welshman's eyes. But he had shone with happiness, looking larger than life, his mane of white hair almost standing on end, his bright blue eyes beaming brilliantly. The mantle of greatness was visibly upon him. Canaris understood.

This man had been a great Prime Minister, a great war leader. Then he had been left in the wilderness, despised by his party, almost forgotten by the public. When the new war had started, many people thought he might be called again, but it was Churchill who had been called and taken office—with Lloyd George's most generous help. It must have seemed to the old Welsh wizard that he was finished and the glory of saving the country through a second desperate war would go to the descendant of the Marlboroughs and not to the son of a poor Welsh villager who had come from obscurity and seemed destined to fall into oblivion.

Now he saw that fate would have it otherwise. He would save the country, he would go down in history as the great man of his time. Power radiated from him, Fraulein Bumke reported in awe, like the charisma of a saint. A new government, a coalition, he believed, would not be difficult to form—if Churchill stepped down from office. How to persuade him to do this had not been discussed. Indeed, Lloyd George cherished the notion that the Churchill Government would fall in the normal course of events. But Canaris felt wryly that the Führer would not be willing to wait for that.

Lloyd George—'Mr Hindhead'—had discussed very fully the composition of the new Cabinet, and some proposals for a possible peace treaty. The Channel Islands, he suggested, would be a good place for the signing of the important document. Canaris made a note to have this part of the report sent on to von Auerbach. It should, he felt, put heart into the vacillating Duke.

Only one part of Fraulein Bumke's report caused Canaris to frown. It was 'Hindhead's' appraisal of the American President, Roosevelt.

"*He* won't be pleased with all this," he was reported as saying. "He longs to have us continue the war."

German agents were doing their best to see that Roosevelt was not re-elected. The Reich had already sent five million dollars and was prepared to send much more. But even if Roosevelt should win, once Operation Green was over, there was not much he could do about it.

Yes, things were going well. Tonight Black Knight would be leaving for Scotland and Röslein. Her last letter, forwarded through the Hungarian Embassy, mentioned the likelihood of a Royal visit on the coming Thursday or Friday, the 18th or 19th of July. Or the next week at the latest. It would cause Canaris much trouble if she was wrong! His alternate plan, 'B', code-named *Araby* and *Scullion* would involve a wearisome amount of contingency planning and would not serve his purpose nearly as well. But he believed Röslein was correct. Within a week or two, Black Knight and Whaleforce would be in action. King George VI would die, to be buried at Windsor with his ancestors. Churchill, distraught, would meet with a tragic accident. The country, shocked and saddened, would be glad to turn to familiar faces, traditional design.

But his last thought before he took to his bed that night was of the Duke. Death and destruction were the very stuff of war. There was little doubt as to the fate of those who stood before its onslaught. But the struggle for the souls of men was something else. He thought of the men who had been persuaded to turn traitor—the Quislings, the Lavals. And those who had been confused enough to act in Germany's interests without intending treason. He remembered Reynaud, unable to act at the vital moment because of the importunities of his mistress, Madame de Portes. It was the woman who would make

147

the difference here, he realised. First thing tomorrow morning he would telephone von Auerbach with fresh instructions. The woman held the soul of this princeling. Feeling drowsy, he thought that he must move his 'queen' to make a king. And smiling, he fell asleep.

* * *

Churchill had gone to bed at Chequers, very late, feeling sanguine enough. But once again, he found that he was troubled. A depression that he called the black dog was suddenly upon him. Like Admiral Canaris, his mind turned to Lisbon. It was Rex Barney, he thought in some exasperation, who had pricked him with this thorn. For a time he considered the young man without affection. Like so many of the lower classes, he was inordinately suspicious of his betters. Now Churchill remembered that, except for his Army service, Barney had been a nuisance all his adult days. The great man had caught what the Special Branch men had let fall about Alf Barney's son: 'That young man will go far—in the wrong direction.'

But the Prime Minister's tenacious mind, once having found a problem, had to grapple with it. Barney had reported the German telling the Duke that the King was ill. It was true, but now he wondered, *how did they know?* It was one of the best kept secrets in England. Even Queen Mary had been kept in the dark. Why had the Germans been watching the Royal Family so closely and who was their informer?

It did not occur to him that, in fact, the Germans did not know: this had been merely a story concocted by the Admiral and given to von Auerbach to intrigue the Duke. Its veracity alarmed him. He remembered that Queen Wilhelmina had been vociferous about the lack of protection of the Royal Family—as had King Haakon of Norway. No-one had paid much attention to the refugee

Royalty with their shattered nerves, but that night it teased his mind.

He would go to the Palace on Monday and see about it himself, he thought. No use leaving it to anyone else. Prod, prod. That was his job. But his mind was still not easy. Sleep would not come. Suddenly, with no previous consideration, he made a large decision.

He would *not* bring the Duke home. No reason for this decision cluttered his mind. He would not. Already he had offered the Duke the governorship of the Bahamas. He bounded out of bed and summoned a blinking-eyed secretary. His offer was changed to an order, to be sent off at once, signed by himself—as Minister of Defence! Then, smiling, he went back to bed.

Like Admiral Canaris, he fell comfortably asleep.

* * *

In Cascais, the Duchess was also happily dreaming. She dreamed, as she sometimes did, of the man she had loved. But differently. Usually her dreams of Felipe were troubled. Felipe Espil could not marry, he had told her, a divorced woman. A diplomat from a Catholic country, with his career to make . . .

Now he would see. Twice divorced, yet she would be Queen of England after all. The barriers were down. Everything she desired could come to her. She felt the touch of the man she had longed for, as she floated, deliciously, wearing her crown. The face of the man shifted, changed; her husband, wearing his crown, became Felipe, then changed once again to the young von Auerbach, dynamic, vigorous. It was a soft and pleasant night in Cascais.

NINE

Decisions [i]

The Prime Minister's new instructions to Lisbon brought about consequences that he could hardly have foreseen, though they would not have surprised Rex Barney, who was busy that morning getting the details of the assassination attempt on the Prime Minister from the injured Detective-Sergeant Thompson.

Sir Walford Selby had made an involuntary grimace when the diplomatic bag arrived. The Duke was not going to be pleased. In fact, he would be furious. And this news could hardly be imparted by telephone. It meant a call at the Boca Do Inferno. A conscientious man, despite the heat of the day and the press of other work, the Ambassador ordered his car and soon his chauffeur was driving the dignified but powerful Rolls along the blazing coast road.

The household at Cascais was somnolent when he arrived. The Duchess was still in her room. Manuel was reprimanding little Jorge for tumbling about in the kitchen and quarrelling with the Italian cook, who was trying to listen to the wireless. Maria said nothing, but wished that Manuel would be called away, down to Lisbon to their master. A month ago she had been content enough, but since then the English soldier had come. He had been kind to Jorge. She thought about his strong limbs, his dark brown hair that turned to red in the sun, his impudent, bright brown eyes. Was it possible, she wondered, that he might return?

The Duke was splashing in the pool when the Ambassador was announced. He scrambled out, frowning.

"He has no appointment," he said.

The appearance of the Ambassador certainly meant news, important news, the news perhaps for which he had been waiting. But this sudden, unheralded irruption—the Duke did not like it. Intuitively, he felt it boded no good. Before he went to the Ambassador, whom Manuel had put in the drawing-room, the Duke made his way to his only refuge, his wife.

The Duchess was fully dressed, gleaming sleekly from her shining, close-coiffed head, her silk and linen dress, to her stockings and thin sandals. Carefully made up, even her face had a brilliance, as though her skin was mother-of-pearl. Her blinds were half drawn and she was lying on a chaise-longue. The Duke, abashed, hesitated to disturb her, and felt dishevelled beside her elegance. But his emotion was too strong to supress.

"I don't know if I should see him at all," he concluded. "Darting here without warning like—like a prison visitor," he said bitterly.

The Duchess raised her heavy lids.

"Why not see what it is?" she said, not hopefully. She stared at the ceiling. "Perhaps Selby's eagerness with good news has driven him here. Humpty Dumpty is put together again." She rose. "I think I'll go and sit on the balcony. You can come and tell me there."

The interview was short, sharp and acrimonious. The Duke affected at first to disbelieve the Ambassador, and refused even to make a reply until he had seen the order in writing. Of course, the matter had been put to him before, but he had not taken it seriously and had dismissed the idea.

"The orders have come from the Prime Minister in his capacity as Minister of Defence," the Ambassador had pointed out, his face pale but his voice quiet.

Both men understood the significance of this. The Duke was still a Major-General in the British Army, having given up his Field Marshal's baton so that he could serve in France. Another trick. Another manifestation of the Windsor Plot. If he refused the order of the Minister of Defence, he could conceivably be court-martialled.

"And we're fighting a war against dictators," the Duke burst out. "Winston made himself Minister of Defence. He has given himself as much power as any dictator —more!" His oddly crooked eyes grew wide. "I don't know that he has the constitutional authority to do it. No-one has challenged him. Perhaps I will."

Selby's face remained impassive. He had known this was going to be a bad day. The Duke's words made him nervous. He might be right, after all. Suppose he went to the courts to challenge the Prime Minister? How would the Law Lords decide? Off hand, he could think of no precedent for many things the Prime Minister had done. Not, at any rate, since Cromwell. Not for the first time he wished heartily that the Duke had stayed in Spain where he had been the problem of Sir Samuel Hoare.

"I will not say another word," the Duke said, his face like a stone, "until I receive the written orders."

The bell rang sharply, and Manuel came to show the Ambassador out. The Duke ran quickly to the Duchess who was sitting on the balcony, waiting for him.

"The Bahamas, Dolly," he said bitterly. "They've ordered me to the Bahamas! Governor of the most insignificant colony in the Empire. I don't know if it was Winston's idea or the Palace's. They'll allow you to be first lady—in Nassau! What was that you said about the Channel Islands?" He threw himself into his chair. "You put it too high, my dear."

The Duchess looked displeased but not surprised.

"I suppose we're lucky your family don't own the island of Alcatraz or I'd be made first lady of the prison!"

They sat in silence for a moment. The Duchess' air of displeasure made her look older, the Duke observed, not for the first time. Every snub, every insult, quietly borne, seemed to wither something in his beloved, little by little. Each conspicuous hesitation at the mouthing of her title, each failure, or reluctance, on the part of some nobody to give her the courtesy of a curtsey added to her humiliation, deepening the frown lines. Wallis Simpson had been so blithe, so gay. His rage poured out again.

"My God, we've come to a pretty pass when a Minister of the Crown orders a Royal Duke about like a menial. It'll be France all over again. I'll be just a fancy office boy. Except that the manners of the natives won't be as good. Those broken down English out there and their dames— they can stay up at night gossiping about whether they will or will not curtsey to you since Bertie thought fit to unmake you as a Royal Duchess. By Letter Patent that he had no right to issue—"

"Please let's not go through that again," the Duchess said wearily.

The Duke went on, too intent to hear her.

"If you are not Her Royal Highness, Duchess of Windsor, then John Smith's wife isn't Mrs Smith. Bertie couldn't refuse to give you what you already possessed."

His wife shrugged. "Yes, I know. And now von Auerbach says he's ill and has changed his mind about everything, and it's Winston making all the trouble. Your Majesties," she mimicked, catching von Auerbach's solemnity. "But you'll fuss and fume and in the end you'll do what Winston says like a good boy."

The Duke looked embarrassed. Von Auerbach's story had certainly caused a stir. But on consideration he had not been able to believe it. Certainly, he had thought of taking the flying boat home, to find out for himself. But now Selby had told him that the flying boats were already withdrawn. His brow darkened. Could it be . . . ?

The Duchess was laughing, without amusement.

"Winston! Who could have believed all this when he was a nobody. Out in the wilderness, so pleased to be your friend. A has-been like Lloyd George. Worse, really, almost a never-was. And now that he's PM—*Voila!* Worse than Baldwin ever dreamed of being."

Both the Duke and Duchess believed that the former Prime Minister, Stanley Baldwin, had been one of the main architects of their downfall.

"Baldwin only got you to descend to a Dukedom. Churchill sends you out to be a caretaker."

The Duke looked lost, his fit of temper spent, his suspicion for the moment forgotten.

"He's not the only one with a short memory," he said.

The names of former friends came to both their minds. The Duchess steeled herself against remembering how she had been betrayed.

But it wasn't the first time she had seen the pot of gold taken from her when she thought she had come to the end of the rainbow. She had lived before to see her shattered hopes mended, and her enemies brought to confusion. Now she was not overwhelmed—perhaps there was still hope.

The balcony was silent except for the sound of a child calling in the distance. A frown touched the Duchess' brow. She rang for Manuel, but before she had made her complaint, he announced that the Graf von Auerbach was calling. The Ducal pair brightened. After a quick discussion, with a show of reluctance on the part of the Duke, and a light urging from the Duchess, von Auerbach was ordered to be admitted, and refreshments brought.

Von Auerbach had been ready to take the coast road earlier. But Admiral Canaris himself had telephoned, and after consultation, back and forth, von Auerbach was finally able to make his way to the Boca Do Inferno. The Admiral was eager to get the word that this part of his business was accomplished. He did not tell von Auerbach,

154

but should the Duke, after all, fail to agree, then Black Knight and Whaleforce must be pulled back. The murders alone would be senseless. And without direct radio contact, the orders to withdraw would take time to get through. He must allow at least a day. Not that he doubted von Auerbach's ultimate success—especially with the help he had just given him. The morning had brought Canaris a new idea.

Von Auerbach had seen Sir Walford Selby's car, and had waited in the village of Cascais until he had seen the car roll back down the road to Lisbon. He had known of the Ambassador's mission, for he had seen the message before Selby himself. The King's Messenger was on the German payroll and before the pouch was delivered to the Embassy, it was taken to Herbert Dobler of the Abwehr bureau. In Dobler's Lisbon house, the bag was prised open, the envelopes steamed and the contents microphotographed.

Von Auerbach was amused. The British were cooperating with him very nicely. As he drove away from the village, he reflected on the state the Duke and Duchess must be in. And he had more for them. He was in high good humour. The Admiral's latest stroke was *fabelhaft*. How he had arranged it, so swiftly—the Abwehr must have a powerful agent in Radio Roma. He smiled as he thought of his predecessor on this job, Heydrich's man, Schellenberg. Naturally, he had failed. Good enough for Heydrich's butchery, but it took a mind like the Admiral's, a knowledge of Royalty like his own, for these epoch-making tasks.

His greeting of "Your Majesties" was once again received with smiling pleasure.

He took his seat when he was invited to do so, and though he was longing to bring out his 'news' he began with calm compliments.

It was the Duchess who drew a quick breath and brought him back to the subject of their last talk, and

155

inquired about the King's health. He replied sadly that he believed the King was sinking fast.

"What is the position of the rest of the Royal Family about the succession?"

Her voice was sharp.

"It is becoming more and more divided. A curious Constitutional problem has arisen. If the first child had been a son, of course, there is no question—if King George is considered to be the legitimate King—that the child would become King, probably under a Regency. But there is nothing in British law, it seems, stating that of two daughters, the eldest necessarily inherits. Some British jurists have given their opinion that with two *female* heirs, the throne must be divided, or that neither inherits. The question has been put most discreetly, as you can imagine."

"You know, there is something to that, Wallis," the Duke said. "After all, in such a case a peerage dies out. Of course, the monarchy can't be *allowed* to die out."

"Quite so," von Auerbach remarked.

The Duchess looked as though she would like to hear more of this.

Von Auerbach continued. "*Some* people believe that it dies out only for the line established at the Act of Succession. When was that? 1702?"

The Duke looked blank.

"But in that case, the Dukes of Bavaria, as the direct descendants of the Stuarts, have the best claim. Of course, no-one in his right mind favours *that*. Queen Mary would like the succession to go to the Duke of Gloucester," von Auerbach spoke with authority. "It's hard to determine the relative positions of Your Majesty's brothers, except for Albert, King George, but it is safe to say that, with the one exception, they are uncompromisingly opposed to your return. But the worst, I regret to say, is your Prime Minister." The German coughed and looked apologetic.

"I am sorry to bring this news. I know he was your

friend. But he is no longer, you must realise that. He is tied up in his war games, which he loves, and he will let no-one interfere with that fun."

The Duke could not argue. Of all the men he knew, Winston was the greatest war enthusiast. He loved war, fighting it, directing it, the way most men loved women. War was his element, his opportunity and his delight.

"It is ironic, Your Majesty, that of all Englishmen, only you and Churchill both understand Great Britain's position, and can do something about it. Others in England know that Britain cannot win this insane war against your friend, Germany, but they are helpless. Under the Emergency Powers Act, and other new laws, even to talk against this war is enough to put a man in a prison camp."

"By order of the dictator," the Duke agreed.

"Ah," von Auerbach said. "When one thinks what has been said against the Führer, for the necessary measures he took against Communists and traitors. But Churchill, the dictator Churchill, he puts men in prison and in concentration camps for being loyal Englishmen."

The three people on the balcony looked at each other with great meaning.

"Yes," von Auerbach went on, "Churchill is ready to fight another campaign on the lines of Antwerp or the Dardanelles. Who wins, who dies, what does it matter, he will have his game of war. He still thinks back to his escapades with the Boers and longs to live the days of his youth once more.

"Churchill is part of the Royal deception," he added abruptly. "He will never let you back into England. By the way, have you heard the Italian broadcast?"

"Broadcast?" the Duke repeated. His face was pale and puffy, like that of a man who has taken a lot of blows.

"The Italians have been broadcasting all day with the news. Churchill has put a price on your head if you are seen anywhere in Great Britain."

"I don't believe it," the Duke said instantly. "That isn't true. It can't be true."

Von Auerbach shrugged.

"You can hear it yourself if you have a radio."

The Duke turned to the Duchess.

"Wallis, didn't you remark that the pastry-cook here was an Italian? That's why we get all the sweet stuff? Let's get him up here. Call for that fellow, what's his name . . ."

The Duchess touched the bell.

Manuel reappeared swiftly.

"Your Royal Highness?"

"Manuel, I suppose you have a radio down in the kitchen?"

The man inclined his head.

"Have any of the staff heard a—a broadcast from Italy?"

Manuel looked embarrassed.

"One of the cooks . . ."

"Yes," the Duchess said impatiently. "Has there been anything broadcast about the Duke?"

"I don't understand Italian too well, Your Royal Highness, but . . ." He looked from the Duke to von Auerbach and back again. He had lost his usual dignified manner and wrung his hands.

"Go on," the Duchess ordered.

"There was something about Mr Churchill . . . a reward . . ."

"I see. Thank you. That's all."

The man withdrew hastily.

There was a silence. After a few minutes the Duke spoke.

"Even if it's broadcast, it still doesn't have to be true. The Italians have fish of their own to fry." He didn't look at von Auerbach, the professional good manners of Royalty forbade his hinting at the German's possible collusion.

"Of course, you must weigh the evidence," von Auerbach said with calm. "Though I believe Signor Mussolini was always a friend to Your Majesty."

The Duke nodded, puzzled and gloomy.

"Held up the whole railroad system of Italy for me to get through on a fast train when my father, the late King, was taken ill," he said. "But still, he has declared war . . ."

"Only on the Churchill clique," von Auerbach said instantly. "It's hardly a month since he tried to help negotiate the peace, but Churchill sent back nothing but insults. The Duke had no choice. He had to protect Italian interests. The Vatican tried to use its influence, but with Churchill there—" He shrugged. "But the pattern must be obvious to Your Majesty. Your Majesties were never offered a return with honour. The plan was to humiliate you, so that you would *not* go to Great Britain. I saw this morning that the flying boats had gone. And now, if my information is correct, the British are trying to find a place to send you, some distant island far away where you would still be under the eye of the Secret Service."

The Duke and Duchess stared at each other, wide-eyed.

"And after the succession is arranged . . . who knows? As Your Majesty has said," he nodded significantly, "there can be only one ruler on the throne of Great Britain. The message will come for you any day, any moment, you will see. Some British outpost, unimportant, far away and yet secure."

The Duke's mouth hung open in amazement, as if the accuracy of the German's information was forcing him into belief.

"A secure internment place for Royalty—they're very internment-minded now in England—a respectable prison," von Auerbach concluded. "An English Devil's Island."

The Duchess threw back her head and laughed,

laughed uncontrollably. The wild peals of laughter, harsh with a metallic sound, filled the balcony, flowed out beyond and rose to meet the brazen sky.

* * *

While von Auerbach was talking of the British penchant for security, Winston Churchill was at Buckingham Palace, bemoaning the great lack of any such thing. He had asked to see Their Majesties. The King was resting; the Queen had been with a working party in one of the State apartments, making comforts for the troops, but she left this task to greet him in her own sitting room.

Flushed from her labours, her hair very slightly tumbled, she looked pretty as she smiled at the Prime Minister. Her lilac-coloured dress was feminine and becoming —the Queen might be the titular head of the Women's Services but, very sensibly for a small woman, she refused to wear a uniform.

"I have been talking to your ladies, Ma'am, and I find there is no provision for your shelter in case of air raids," he said severely.

"Well, Mr Churchill, you know we are planning to go to Royal Lodge at night, if London is bombed," the Queen replied with her usual charm but looking at him, very slightly, as though she wondered why he was there.

"I think you should, Ma'am," he said, "and I think you should begin now. The raids will start any day."

He was hoping, in fact, that they would. Far better that the Germans waste their bombs in London. If they concentrated on the airfields, England could be without an Air Force in a few short months.

"If you think it best, I will talk to the King about it. We have been there a good deal, to see Lilibet and Margaret Rose."

The Prime Minister nodded, but still looked stern.

"I have taken the liberty of looking round in the

company of the Comptroller. It seems that the House-maids' Room in the basement could be strengthened with beams. It is hardly adequate, but it could afford *some* protection, Ma'am."

If the Queen was surprised at the thought of herself and the King sharing the Housemaid's Room, it was not apparent. Only a slight frown of worry settled on her brow.

"I hope we won't have to disturb the King too often to go down," she said. "He has so many engagements, and he gets so very tired."

"Perhaps His Majesty could limit his engagements," the Prime Minister replied, knowing, with a sense of pride, that the King would not. "But for the sake of the nation, something must be done for your protection. And, Ma'am, I must say that I think *some* of your Household very careless. As I came in I saw canvas bags, addressed to the most secret destination, marked for anyone to see 'Royal Mews'."

The Queen looked unabashed. When the invasion scare had begun, a bodyguard for the Royal Family had been hastily got together under Colonel J.S. Coats, whose job it was, in the event of an invasion taking place, to escort the Royal Family to a safe retreat. Four houses in various parts of the country had been chosen as possible retreats, to which these supplies were being sent, but the Queen had not taken the idea of flight seriously, and had not inspected any of them. One of her strongest beliefs was the importance of making decisions and keeping to them. When the war began, she had decided to keep her husband's domestic life as nearly as possible what it had been. Keeping to ordered patterns was her cherished rule. Another was the importance of discrimination. She thought she could discriminate between real danger, and war-time hysteria.

"I must tell you, Prime Minister," she said firmly, "that we are taking precautions. I spend fifteen minutes every morning practising with a rifle and a revolver in the grounds."

The Prime Minister was already aware of this, as was most of the Cabinet. Lord Halifax, who had a habit of cutting through the Palace grounds on his way to Whitehall, had complained that, unwarned, he had been within inches of being shot by Her Majesty and now intended giving the Palace a wide berth.

"I don't know about the Germans," Lord Halifax had commented. "But between the black-out and the women shooting, I don't know that we will last through this emergency."

The Prime Minister had been glad to hear that someone was afraid to go in the Palace grounds. He put it as forcefully as he could to Her Majesty that the Palace security should be tightened.

"Oh, we're well protected," she smiled on him kindly. "If anything should seem amiss, any intruder appearing or anything like that, I have only to press that bell," she indicated a bell push by the mantel-piece, "and the Guard will be here in minutes."

The Prime Minister took the cigar from his mouth and regarded the innocuous-looking bell push. He took his watch from his pocket and placed it on his palm.

"Please push it, Ma'am," he said.

"Push it? But, Mr Churchill, the Guard will come."

"Yes, Ma'am. I would like to see how long it takes."

The Queen gazed at him. To bring the Guard rushing in on a false alarm! The Prime Minister had always been an alarmist, she had been told. Now she could see that it was true. She didn't think the Captain of the Guard would like it at all. Besides, her working party was waiting. Lady Bletchley had been showing her how one makes that awkward turn of a sock when it comes to the heel. She had just got it in mind and now she was forgetting. She would seem very dull-witted. But she was too well-bred to argue and, feeling very foolish, pushed the bell.

It was hard to stop her foot from tapping, a little impatiently. She thought out what she would say to the Captain of the Guard. Beneath her sweet manner and very feminine appearance, she was a tidy-minded and well-organised woman, and had a strong dislike of appearing capricious, or even worse, thoughtless. She would tell the Captain it was a rehearsal. As it was.

Winston was glaring at his watch. Five minutes passed, then ten, then fifteen, at which point the Queen was aware of one of her ladies hovering at the door. Hovering was hardly the word, the clump of her step was unmistakable. Doubtless her working party were wondering if she had deserted them. It began to seem as though her explanation to the Guard would not be necessary.

She sent the lady-in-waiting back to the working party, saying she would rejoin them shortly. The Prime Minister waited another five minutes. But still no-one came. Nothing broke the silence but the ticking of her little clock and the wind moaning in the chimney.

Mr Churchill looked grave, and when he looked grave he did it with such—such menace, she thought. He stood, his legs slightly apart, looking—as much as a man in a dark suit *could* look—like a pink porker on his hind legs. At last the Captain of the Guard was summoned. He entered, saluting, and drew himself up to attention. The Prime Minister regarded him sourly.

"Did that contraption," and he pointed to the bell push, "go off?"

"Yes, sir," the Captain answered.

"Then WHY THE . . ." the words that might have poured from the Prime Minister's lips had to be bitten back in the presence of a lady, and the Queen at that. *"Then why the devil didn't you come?"*

The Captain looked at him patiently.

"The policeman on duty, sir, said that nothing was. wrong. It must have been pushed by mistake."

The Prime Minister took his leave of Her Majesty.

Then he went to shake up the Guard, Scotland Yard, the Comptroller of the Household, and everyone else he could think of. Prod, prod. It was a black day at the Palace, but by the time the Prime Minister had finished, he felt that the Palace security was increased five-fold and was on its way to efficiency. But he was not yet finished. He fired off written notes to Windsor headed 'ACTION THIS DAY' in his capacity as Minister of Defence, and made certain that the Lodge which housed the King and Queen would be as well guarded as the Castle itself where the Princesses, praise the Lord, were safe.

The Prime Minister also checked on the Royal train, ordering the railway men, who liked to keep it bright with spit and polish, to let the outside get as dismal as all the rest of Great Britain's war-time rolling stock. No need to make it a target plain for anyone to recognise. When at last he was finished he told himself he could now go back to the conduct of the war. If the Germans had any mad idea about the Royal Family, it would be scotched now once and for all.

He said as much to Sergeant Barney that night at No. 10. Even the Queen, he trumpetted, now understood the necessity for strict precautions. He had made her aware— she was a reasonable woman after all. The Prime Minister, who was also an historian, reflected on the great, often unreasonable passion of the Hanoverian men for their women which had troubled the country before. The King had complete loyalty to the woman who held his heart, and fortunately, Queen Elizabeth was a woman safe for a monarch to love. She would obey an order for her husband's safety. But the Cockney sergeant was unimpressed.

"Never trust a woman, guv," was all he got out of him.

TEN

Decisions [ii]

On that same afternoon the Graf von Auerbach was also thinking of the Royal Family with satisfaction, though for very different reasons. The Admiral had only told him as much of the plan as he needed to know. The Duke must be persuaded to return to England under German auspices, prepared to accept the throne. But von Auerbach was not naïve. The story he had been given to tell—such a useful tale!—of the present King's illness, could only have one ending. Such, he thought with a shrug, were the chances of war.

By lunch-time he had been ready to send his signal to Berlin on the success of his mission. The broadcast from Radio Roma had been inspired. He knew it would take only a very little more to land his fish. How the Duchess reacted to his tale of a Devil's Island! It didn't occur to her that he had seen the contents of the diplomatic pouch. The Abwehr were remarkably well organised in Lisbon—it seemed every other person there was working for the Reich.

The Duchess invited him to luncheon. At the beginning of the meal, before the servant, the Duke and Duchess kept up a painfully discreet conversation, but when they repaired to the balcony, the chilled white wine had taken its effect, and by the time the servant was dismissed the only topic in the Ducal minds was well and truly aired.

The Duchess was taken again by a fit of laughter.

"Oh, Friedrich—" sometime during luncheon he had become Friedrich—"Devil's Island. Oh, how right you were. It *is* Devil's Island. Only they call it the Bahamas."

"The Bahamas!" He had made a good show of being surprised. "Then it's come already. That's your proof." He laughed. "No wonder Selby was looking so hangdog when I saw him this morning. He knew he had to come here with this insult. *I* wouldn't want to be the one."

The Duke said nothing, but his expression clearly showed that he thought all respect, all proper feeling had long since vanished from England's official representatives.

"So there we are," von Auerbach had gone on. "A seemingly senseless insult, a meaningless exile—but not so senseless, or meaningless, when the truth is known. The Bahamas for you, until young Elizabeth is proclaimed Queen."

The Duke remained silent.

Von Auerbach leaned forward and spoke passionately.

"The German people cannot let this travesty of justice continue. For our own sake, you understand that, Your Majesty."

As always, the Duke waved a hand in deprecation of the mode of address, but the gesture was becoming weak.

"Churchill the war-monger supports the claim of the young Elizabeth, with her mother as Regent. In effect, this would mean Churchill as Regent. Then he would be, not only Prime Minister and Minister of Defence but King in all but name. His power would be absolute. It would mean war between our two countries to the finish. That is why Your Majesty must do your duty to your subjects and return."

Von Auerbach's voice rang out authoritatively. For himself, he wondered actually how much difference all of this would make. Churchill's power seemed to be absolute now. But doubtless, the Führer and the Admiral knew what they were about.

The Duke frowned.

"Whatever I have done, I have done because it was my duty," he said stiffly. "People outside of great events cannot always know where one's duty lies."

"Quite so," the German agreed. "For instance, your visit to the Führer that the scandalmongers made so much of in the press, that alone saved the British armies at Dunkirk."

That visit. The Graf smiled in reminiscence. In those days he, son of an old Junker family, had not been sure whether to throw his lot in with the Nazis. His father had despised them; the High Command was still somewhat aloof. Yet he had been almost certain that the future would be with Hitler and his supporters.

Then had come the German tour of the Duke and Duchess, the former King of England and his new wife. Edward had always been friendly enough to the Führer, that had been well known. But his father had said it was Germany the Duke respected, not that pack of louts.

The tour had been a triumph for Nazism. Ley, drunken sot though he was, as the Nazi Labour leader had had charge of the tour, for the Duke had expressed an interest in working conditions and workers' housing. Ley had paraded the couple around in a black Mercedes Benz as though he were leading them in a Roman triumph. The Duke of Coburg, cousin to this man's father, had always been certain that the Nazis would prevail. He entertained the Windsors on the tour, and was the first of European Royalty to acknowledge the Duchess as 'Her Royal Highness'. All the local authorities had been warned to use that title. The Windsors had responded to these courtesies: It was noticed that the Duke had given the Nazi salute several times. They had made the pilgrimage to Berchtesgaden and waited on the Führer. At a meeting of the

German Labour Front in Leipzig, the Duke had made the statement that was reported all over Germany:

"I have travelled the world and my upbringing has made me familiar with the great achievements of mankind, but that which I have seen in Germany, I had hitherto believed to be impossible. It cannot be grasped, and is a miracle. One can only begin to understand it when one realises that behind it all is one man and one will."

At that moment von Auerbach had decided that Coburg was right. There was no sense in failing to back the winning horse, and he had joined the Nazis.

The Duke looked immensely gratified at his remark about Dunkirk. And there had been a lot of truth in it, von Auerbach reflected. The German Army could have crushed the British while they waited on the beach, but the Führer been curiously reluctant to do it. Brauchitsch had thought the Führer a little mad, but was too nervous to oppose him. General Greiffenberg, of Hitler's own operations staff, called his orders insane. But the Führer was hoping for a negotiated peace, not the crushing of Great Britain, as this present mission proved. What von Auerbach was telling the happy-looking Duke was sincere—as sincere as diplomacy could ever be.

"Your Majesty must have wondered why the Führer did not press his advantage when he had your armies driven back to the beach; why the victorious German battalions did not pursue and destroy them as they lay helpless waiting for your ships? And why the Luftwaffe hardly touched them? But I am sure you know. A statesman can reason these things. You are one Englishman who knows that the Führer has no quarrel with England; his friendship with you and his hopes for the future that friendship brings, was the one thing that stayed his hand." That, he thought, and Göring's desire to hog all the glory. Not that there was any glory: the fat man had failed. His first failure: he hadn't liked that.

"Let me say, the Führer's decision was not popular

with the High Command." Von Auerbach looked grave. "But the Führer has always been a statesman first and a commander-in-chief second."

The Duke nodded slowly, thoughtfully.

"Nevertheless, if Churchill gets his way, and England finally rebuffs his efforts to make peace, the Führer must do what is necessary to protect Germany. You, Your Majesty, know better than anyone who our real enemies are. England's as well as Germany's."

The Duke, of course, had known he was referring to the Russians. Von Auerbach saw the Duke was struggling with the fact that Germany had made a peace treaty with the Russians, and they had been happy to divide Poland, but that he was really too polite to say so.

"Of course, Your Majesty has been aware all along that that miserable treaty was only signed to protect the Reich while the Polish question was being settled. But the Führer knows that the Russians intend to break the treaty. As soon as they believe they have an opportunity, the Bolsheviks will strike."

"Just what I've always said," the Duke remarked.

"This mad desire of Churchill's for war will give them their opportunity," von Auerbach said soberly. "If the war with Great Britain drags on, the Russians will come marching through Poland and we will have a war on two fronts. Germany cannot allow this. Even the Führer, with all his friendship for England, cannot permit it. If there is no peace treaty with Great Britain, the Army will have to invade to secure it once and for all, before we turn towards Russia. The plans are already made," he informed the sober Duke. "But you understand all this."

The Duke nodded gravely.

Von Auerbach wondered if he need bother to continue, or if he should go and get his cable off that afternoon. But the man before him swayed with the wind. And he was not going to like it, when he realised how he was to travel. But it was the only way. The British would not let him board a 'plane or ship to anywhere except the Bahamas. It might be possible to get him surreptitiously on a neutral vessel, but the news would almost certainly leak out, and the British would take action. Besides, on a neutral vessel the Duke would have a chance to change his mind. No, he would have to go as planned. A U-boat out to sea, and then a sea-'plane to the Channel Islands. It would be a seal of commitment.

"Your Majesty," he said dramatically, "it must not come to this. It will be the end of England, of all your people."

He hesitated. The late afternoon sun struck horizontal rays at the group on the balcony, flooding them with a brilliance that would have been desperately uncomfortable, if they had been aware of it.

Von Auerbach went on more slowly, and his voice dropped.

"If we have to invade, the Army will take over. The plans are drawn. After our inevitable victory Britain, no matter what its own losses, will find herself heavily taxed. This will have to be so, to replace Germany's losses of men and equipment that we will need to fight the Russians.

"Your Majesty," he spoke then almost in a whisper, and his listeners had to move towards him to catch his words. "It is not part of my duty to tell you this, the information is confined to the highest echelon, but I have seen the orders. As you know, up until his death last year, my father was on the General Staff. In memory of the old friendship and the connection between your family and mine, I feel impelled to pass this on, though I might find myself in trouble with the Gestapo."

He had pulled a face, of a sort he had often practised before a looking-glass; not the grimace of a youngster, but a movement acknowledging a wry acceptance of a situation and its responsibilities.

His eyes closed and his forehead wrinkled as if he were trying to re-envision something once seen. When he

170

spoke, it was in a monotonous tone, as though reading from a dull report.

" 'All males from 18 to 45 are to be deported for duties on the Continent. All stores, agricultural products, food, fodder, oil, crude metals (including precious metals), gems, timber, everything except existing household stocks, will be shipped to Germany. Hostages will be taken for protection against guerilla movements.' "

There was also some stuff about Jews, but the Duke wouldn't care about that.

The Duke waved his hand as if he could not bear to hear more.

"A ghastly penalty," the German agreed quietly. It was. British men to be slaves in Germany. The women to be given to the German Army. "But in the circumstances, the Führer, as Commander-in-Chief, could do no less. The precedent for strict reparations was made by Great Britain and France in 1918."

The Duke grimaced. Neither he nor his family had felt anything but horror over those drastic reparations. Now it seemed those chickens could come home to roost.

After a moment's silence, von Auerbach spoke with renewed vigour.

"On the other hand," he said, "if England agrees to a cessation of hostilities now—and it could not be regarded as a surrender, for a new government could repudiate the war-mongering of Churchill, and it would be an honourable agreement on both sides—the Führer's terms are unbelievably generous. He asks for nothing! *Nothing at all!*" He regarded his listeners, beaming. "You may have noticed how little he asked from France, after her defeat. So you know his sincerity. The Foreign Office would like to discuss the matter of some former German colonies in Africa, but between us the matter is of no importance. The Führer doesn't give a fig for Africa. It would mean only an agreement to down arms and as there is no land war between our countries now—and you may

171

have noticed how little U-boat activity there has been—it comes down to an agreement to continue as we are. Germany and England can have trade and friendship and lead the world."

Beads of perspiration shone on the Duke's forehead.

"Yes, yes, very desirable, of course. But, von Auerbach, I don't know what use there is in discussing it with me. You don't understand the Constitutional limitations. For instance, even if my brother Bertie supports my right to the throne, the Bill of Abdication is now law as the Act of Abdication. Both Houses of Parliament would have to act on it to declare it null and void. And God knows who would have to sign it," he said reflectively. "But you can't see Winston getting a Bill like that through the Commons. He wouldn't do it. But, just for the sake of discussion, supposing that he would, and I were King again, I would have no real power to make peace. It would be the same Government, no change."

Von Auerbach smiled at him confidently. The Duke mopped his brow, the Duchess was coiled with tension, but the German remained as cool and alert as he had been at the start of the discussion. He had been well coached by the Admiral himself.

"I think not. If you reach your ailing brother in time, and the news is made public about the Churchill plot, Churchill will be ruined. He is deeply committed to the cause of the young Elizabeth as Queen and her mother as Regent. His major role in the deception won't sit well with the people or Parliament, or his own Government for that matter. As it is, the Government has been causing him trouble, and his majority in the House is very shaky. Almost certainly, there will be a vote of no confidence. We know English procedure, you see," he said, smiling.

"Perhaps Your Majesty is not aware that Lloyd George has been writing letters, saying in no uncertain terms that this war must be stopped. With the Government having tendered their resignations, the King must invite someone to form a new Government, isn't that so?"

"It would mean a General Election," the Duke replied.

"Not with the country still legally at war. That could be avoided. It was a National Government, a Coalition, so it would be quite normal to ask someone—perhaps a Liberal like Lloyd George—to try to form another."

"I don't know," the Duke said slowly. "This is all very startling, very strange. You must understand that we have heard nothing of this from any other source. I have heard no hint from anyone. There have only been, from various people, suggestions that we stay here, or go back to Spain. What you are telling me is all very shocking, very disturbing and requires a good deal of thought . . . And time," he added after a moment. "Certainly, it requires time."

The Duke's gaze turned to the Lisbon road, but there was no longer expectation in his look. He stared blankly as though finally he realised the messenger he had expected would not come; that the events of which he had longed to hear would never take place, but he had looked there for help for so long that he continued still from habit.

"I'm afraid, Your Majesty," the diplomat said firmly, "that time is the one thing you don't have. Your brother could die at any moment. If he does, Churchill will win in the family quarrel and your niece will be proclaimed Queen, with no-one ever knowing the truth. And then it will be too late. There will be war to the death, and England will not recover her losses in a hundred years."

Once more there had been silence on the balcony. The house and gardens and the surrounding country, all were caught in the lazy, hot, enchanted hush. Only from the shore came a distant screaming of the gulls.

"You may believe that even with the flying boats withdrawn, Your Majesties could still return to England by 'plane to Whitechurch. But I know that British Secret

173

Service agents have been ordered to prevent this—by any means. Also no British ship will let Your Majesties board —except for the destination to which you have already been ordered. And neutral shipping will be watched— there is always the fear, Your Majesty, that if you *were* allowed to board a neutral ship, the Secret Service would be informed, and the ship would be torpedoed. Apologies would be made afterwards, error would be claimed, restoration made as far as possible, but almost certainly Your Majesties would not live to see it."

The Duchess gazed at him. "Then how . . . ?"

They'd had the sweets, now it was time for the pill.

"I have a vessel waiting in Lisbon harbour," von Auerbach said briskly. No need to mention yet that it was a U-boat. Unfortunate associations. But nothing else would do. As the plan had no set time to begin, the vessel would have to wait, hidden at Cascais. He could hardly do that with the sea-'plane, it would cause as much talk as the British flying boats had done.

"You won't have to come to the town, it can come up to Cascais. You can slip away, and I will arrange that no word will get out for a few days. No-one will know that you've gone.

"It might be a good plan if Her Majesty arranged to cancel her social engagements. I think a communicable disease would be best—influenza perhaps. Officially you will be in a hospital in Lisbon—a private hospital. Once out at sea, at least ten miles from shore, you will transfer to a sea-'plane."

A quiver passed across the Duchess' face. Her fear of flying was well-known, but she took it like a soldier. Von Auerbach found her interesting. She was worthy of the destiny that would be hers.

"You will land in Alderney in the Channel Islands, and from there proceed to England in a British vessel." Taking those islands had made life easy for the Abwehr in many ways, he reflected. "You will sail with a British

174

crew and under a British flag. Once you land, your brother will proclaim you King—before the Churchill gang realises what is happening."

He paused for a moment. He had seen the Duke's brow darken at the thought of boarding a German vessel, and lightening again at the idea of going home under a British flag. Of course, once he landed in Alderney in the German sea-'plane, he was absolutely committed, whether he liked it or not. The Abwehr would have their proof and photographs . . . but he did not have to know that.

"And the sooner you leave, once the arrangements are made, the better," he had to warn them.

It was time to return to the sweets, he decided. Turning to the Duchess he smiled apologetically.

"Unfortunately, space in a sea-'plane is rather limited, so you won't need to do much packing, Your Majesty. But once you reach London your wardrobe problems should be over." He ventured a chuckle. "And if you are not satisfied, I am sure we will be able to bring the latest models from Paris for your inspection."

The Duchess, taking this seriously, nodded. She had been very still, her eyes brilliant. The 'Your Majesties' were bouncing round the balcony with a force of their own.

"I . . . I . . . I don't know what to say," the Duke muttered. His wife's nod had seemed like acquiescence. "You know, von Auerbach, this all seems so fantastic."

Von Auerbach was silent. The Duke stared into space, his crooked eyes looking washed out and pale.

"But—I would like to see my brother if he's dying." His voice was low and his words had come slowly. "As a matter of fact—" he stood up, stretched and passed a hand over his brow, the gesture of a very tired man—"I am very homesick."

The Duchess spoke then, very quietly.

"In any event, we have to go to this dinner tonight. It would cause too much comment not to go. We could always begin displaying symptoms." She smiled. "But we'll have to talk later. In the meantime, as we're going early for cocktails, we must dress. David, you take so much longer than me since you lost your valet, would you like to go ahead? You might ask that Maria, if you can find her, to draw my bath."

The Duke grasped the opportunity to leave. The forceful von Auerbach drained his vitality.

"Certainly, my dear, certainly," he assented, "I wish I knew the Portuguese for bath water.

"Goodbye, von Auerbach, I'll have to think over what you've said. You understand . . . big decisions. We'll be in touch."

He left with an attempt at von Auerbach's own briskness and military bearing, but it contrasted strangely with his casual dress and the loose espadrilles that trailed forlornly.

The balcony seemed peaceful on his departure. Von Auerbach looked at the Duchess measuringly, and was satisfied with what he saw.

"Why England? Why not Scotland, if Bertie is up there?" she asked abruptly.

It was a shrewd question. He continued to regard the too sharp-witted Duchess. Perhaps, he reflected, she had always been a little too sharp for her own good.

Her manner was quite changed. She was brisk and businesslike, with no effort to charm or to look dignified. Her slight drawl had disappeared. She could have been speaking to a servant, a secretary or a workman about a piece of business, necessary in itself, that was being conducted clumsily.

Von Auerbach's own change of manner was more subtle. His air of exaggerated deference had left. Leaning back in his chair, he had crossed his legs and taken out his cigarette case, though he carefully asked for permission to smoke. Receiving it, he lit a cigarette and slowly blew a twisting column of smoke. His eyelids were lowered slightly as he answered her questions.

"It would be a pity to waste time. If King George should die before His Majesty arrives . . . It is important that the new King be in London."

"But the proclamation?" the Duchess asked sharply.

He had looked up. Their eyes met.

"That is the point, you see. With the Duke in London, there can be only the one proclamation. When the Duke arrives, it will be made."

"You're sure?" she said.

"It will be assured as soon as His Majesty King Edward sets his foot on our vessel," he answered smoothly.

The 'request of the dying King' was already on a wire recording at the Tirpitz Ufer. A clever actor, having familiarised himself with the public speeches of the stammering King, had injected the exact degree of hesitation to the recording. The broadcasts the King had made had been immensely helpful.

The Duchess nodded, but her fingers beat a tattoo against the side of her chair.

"His Majesty has only to decide to go," von Auerbach continued, with a hint of question in his voice. "But he must decide now. There are matters to be arranged, and he must be ready when the time comes."

"But why such a rush?" the Duchess asked. "Can't your 'matters' wait a bit?"

"Because, Your Majesty—" If the Duchess had been carefully studying his tone, she might have been offended. He had become careless, and the irony at that point had been plain in his mouthing of that form of address. But she had not noticed. "Although I thought it best not to mention it to His Majesty the King—I don't want him to feel too pressured—" and he smiled with what he hoped was delightful frankness. "But the Führer will wait no longer than this summer for the completion of this plan. In brief, he has other plans for England, not including Your Majesties, which will be put into effect if you are not on our

177

vessel by the end of this month. His Majesty must make up his mind."

The Duchess balled her fists and crashed them on the table.

"His Majesty will *never* make up his mind," she said explosively. "He cannot make a decision. You know that. Everyone knows it," she said resignedly. "And I was the last to find out." She laughed her private laugh. It did not upset von Auerbach but he was impatient.

"Then you will go to the Bahamas—and perhaps have an accident on the way," he said.

"You don't understand the British as much as you think," the Duchess said, biting her lip. "They won't have us murdered. They have better ways of killing you off and yet leaving you to walk around, just breathing."

"His Majesty *must* decide," von Auerbach said inexorably.

"He won't," she replied. "His line is to go on, doing nothing, until he's pushed. Then, if he doesn't like where he falls, he will complain. In a dignified way. But he won't *do* anything. He didn't abdicate, you know," she said, in a detached way. "Baldwin abdicated him. When I lost my head and ran."

Von Auerbach shrugged.

"Then—?"

"If he were forced into it—say kidnapped—so that no-one could accuse him of deciding—"

"Who would accuse?" von Auerbach argued. "There is no doubt his action would be for his country's good." His voice rang with sincerity. He gazed at the Duchess with impatience, as if he wished he could force on her the clarity of his vision.

"He knows that," the Duchess replied, dispirited. "But you have no idea of his fear of criticism." She sighed. "He seemed such a hell-raiser at one time," she said reflectively, "that everyone was fooled. We all thought he was a rebel. But it was just on the surface. He liked to be a rebel," she searched for words, "but a rebel from a big, stuffy, solid group that still *accepted* him. Naughty David. The wild young Prince. But he never meant to be cut off," she said. "Since he has been cut off, he has nothing to rebel against. And he wants it all back. He loathes the disapproval of his family now. Especially as he's found his friends who were so happy to rebel with him have cut him off, too." She laughed. "Prince Hal rejected by Falstaff."

Von Auerbach shrugged. "They will all come running back once he's crowned King," he said dryly.

The Duchess nodded.

"And I used to think the Washington crowd servile to the rising sun," she said. "That court clique will break their backs curtseying to you one day, and pretend to be blind so they can cut you the next."

They were silent for a moment.

"Kidnapping wouldn't do," von Auerbach said, as if he had considered it. "With the plans as made, he must be publicly willing. His support in Ireland and Great Britain will fall apart if he protests too much." He looked at the Duchess, half smiling. "No, unless you want him to stay in gloomy obscurity, you must have the King ready to get on the boat the moment the signal comes. It won't be long. If he's not ready to do that, then your boat will have sailed."

He smiled widely as he watched her reaction. Springing to his feet, he radiated energy, determination and confidence.

"Yes, Your Majesty, the King must make up his mind."

The Duchess did not rise, but stayed coiled in her seat. Only her eyes were lifted to him.

"His mind will be made up," she said softly. "You may expect us."

He had bowed and withdrawn, but could not resist glancing over his shoulder as he went.

Without him, he thought, the terrace looked desolate.

The golden sunshine was fading as twilight approached. The Duchess sat in the shadow, waiting. Her tongue flicked across her lips, her square jaw set, determined. His confidence was high. He would telegraph Canaris at Berlin, he thought, satisfied. They were well within schedule, it was only July 15.

If Maria had known von Auerbach's decision, she might have thought it premature. Despite her warm and happy memories of the English soldier—Rex, the king, she called him in her thoughts, thoughts always accompanied by a delicious excitement—she had gone on stolidly with her work, of all kinds. After she had finished the luncheon washing-up and had done the rooms, she went to her listening post behind the balcony and eavesdropped until the Duke and Duchess left for their evening engagement.

The conversation began innocuously, but it made Maria nervous. The Duke was displeased. Perhaps he would report her unfavourably to her master in Lisbon. But how could she do everything?

"Oh, there you are still, my dear!"

The Duke, clad in a chequered bath robe, came loping back onto the terrace.

"I've pushed every bell in the place and I can't get anyone to answer."

Then Maria realised that Manuel must be listening as well, probably from above.

"Really," the Duke went on with some heat, "this is impossible. I've drawn your bath water myself."

He smiled.

"How d'you like having me for a personal maid?"

"Thank you," she said gravely. "Yes, this is intolerable. We have to make a move." She regarded him with a steady gaze.

"You're not thinking . . ." his face crumpled nervously, "you're not taking that fellow seriously, are you? I think that would be a mistake. You know, there were some funny stories after that shoot where his elder brother Leo was killed. Let me think, where was that? Abergeldie? Anyway, one of the beaters insisted that it was this von Auerbach's shot that had killed his brother. Friendly Friedrich. Of course, people said it couldn't have been, Friedrich is a crack shot. Still," the Duke's eyes were round and meditative. "This young fellow was known not to have much relished being the second son. Not much left for him in that family. What there was had to go with the title and the property. And he had debts . . . Younger brothers!"

The Duke massaged the back of his head with his hand and rumpled his hair badly. It was his habit when he was puzzled and one that intensely irritated the Duchess.

"Don't," she said, twitching in her chair. "What has his character to do with what he told us?"

The Duke stopped massaging with his right hand but almost immediately resumed with his left.

"Well," he said uncomfortably, "he *is* on the enemy side."

"Whose enemy?" the Duchess said, with bitterness. "You mean you don't believe that Bertie's ill and wants you back and that it's been hushed up?"

"Bertie's never been strong," the Duke said. "His nerves are so bad they affect his health. He has fits of melancholia. I don't know if I ever told you but my youngest brother died of epilepsy. P'raps I hid that from you before we were married without even thinking of it," he smiled apologetically. "Anyway, that sort of thing makes the family worry. This is a surprise . . . But it could be true."

"And they would certainly hush it up," the Duchess said.

The Duke sighed. He seemed not to hear.

"Bertie never wanted to be King. If it wasn't for Betty, I don't think he could have been persuaded to do

181

it. Harry would have got the job then."

"I think Betty was wild to be Queen," the Duchess put in.

"No, she always said she didn't want it—very strongly," the Duke replied. "She kept Bertie waiting two years after he proposed. We weren't sure she'd ever take him."

"Phoo, phoo," the Duchess scoffed. "She was waiting for you to propose. Why d'you think she hates me so much? When you took me over that day to visit at Royal Lodge she nearly stabbed me to death with icicles."

The Duke shrugged. Wallis was quite wrong, of course, in what she was saying. But he didn't reply. He found himself painfully pleased to see Wallis jealous again. She had been so extremely jealous of him before their marriage. Even after the Abdication, when they had been separated and he stayed at the Schloss Enzesfeld, she had suddenly become jealous of his hostess, the Baroness Rothschild, though she was an old friend of Wallis herself. She had not been happy until the Baroness left her own house. But since then, jealousy had been entirely forgotten.

"And you know she rules your brother with a rod of iron," the Duchess cried.

"That isn't the situation at all," the Duke said awkwardly. "Remember, she does have quite a job. Bertie is —well, nervous, you know, and she has to give him a great deal of encouragement and support. But, Dolly, even if it's all true, if Bertie is ill and wants me back, I could hardly go off with the Germans. That British boat he talks about is probably one left behind at Dunkirk. Manned by a crew of traitors from the Channel Islands. The idea is insane."

"But look at what it means," the Duchess said impatiently. "Von Auerbach wasn't lying about the alternatives for England. You've conjectured just as much yourself. We've been through it over and over again."

"This war is a crime," the Duke said grimly. "I'd do anything to save England—Europe—the whole world for that matter, from what it will do. Everything will crack," he said gloomily. "India—in spite of what Winston says —that will be gone and the whole East will go with it. But still, Wallis," he said fretfully, "if I went back in that manner, could it be considered treason?" He gave her a long look from under his eyelashes. "We're not back in the days of the Stuarts, my dear," he said mildly. "I can't claim Divine Right."

"But surely it's treason to let your country be defeated when you can save her? And you're the only one who can? You remember you telephoned me from the Schloss Enzesfeld to say you were thinking of giving up all your titles so that you could go back to England and enter politics. Before the war! And now . . . isn't it a king's duty to try to save his country? You always told me when you were King that you couldn't be a mere figurehead, a puppet of the Government of the day. Wasn't that why Baldwin was so afraid of you?"

She jumped to her feet and faced him.

"David, you could make the Crown real again, not just a dusty, fusty relic. It's your chance, what you always wanted."

His eyes were alight with interest.

"That's true, but I always intended to be a constitutional monarch. Though with my own interpretation of the Constitution, not Baldwin's or Churchill's, as it is nowadays. But never a dictator."

"Who said anything about being a dictator?" she said, and shrugged. "You'll be saving the English people from a dictator. A mad, runaway Government under a weak, sickly King, who has taken the people into a ruinous war that no-one wants. If you save them you'll be a greater hero than the Lionheart, the Black Prince and King Alfred, all rolled up in one. And future monarchs will have a hand in shaping events, protecting the people from demagogues who can persuade them to vote with lies and tricks. You'll change the course of history," she said passionately, "and you'll be the man I married."

It was a long speech for Wallis. The Duke was deeply moved, though he winced at her last words. The corollary, "not the man you've shown yourself to be," hung too obviously in the air between them.

"It sounds . . . I can't tell you how it sounds," he said at length. "But one needs time to sort these things out; to find out what really is going on, what our position actually is. Perhaps I could try again to get in touch with Bertie—"

"There is no time," she said.

"Well, my dear," he said firmly. "I can't go off at a hop, skip and a jump at the word of these Germans. I'm not going to be trapped into being a German puppet, instead of an English one. Still, there is a way we can find out what truth there is in it, and straight away."

"How?" asked the Duchess impatiently, her voice harsh with disappointment.

"I shall send a cable to Winston immediately—and I know where he can be reached because Selby said earlier that he's waiting for my reply at Chequers. I shall tell him we've decided to go home and he should send a destroyer. After all, it's just a day or two since he was begging us to go home in his flying boats. If he refuses, then . . ." he paused significantly, "then I shall be sure it's true."

The Duchess was twisting a fine handkerchief and ripped it to shreds without noticing.

"But David," she said, "you might get outmanoeuvred again."

"No, my dear. You must allow me to decide these matters."

His demeanour was such that for once she could not argue.

"I'll send the cables and then we will know."

He left. This time his dignity was unassumed. The Duchess followed. She looked very much afraid.

Both Maria and Manuel were thoughtful when they returned below stairs.

Aware that Maria had been listening also, Manuel invited her into the privacy of the butler's pantry. Since her employment she had been not only his mistress, but also his confidante—she had consoled him for the increasing dullness and plumpness of his wife. Manuel now felt as though he held the fate of Europe, if not the world, in his hands.

Unlike Maria, he had understood almost everything that had been said. As she suspected, he drew a pleasant sum from the Germans for his reports on all the happenings at the Boca Do Inferno. On occasion, he also got a small sum—very small—from a British agent whom he met, when he could get away, at a café in Lisbon, that same café to which Rex Barney had gone hoping for real English food. But there had been no money at all from that direction recently. Now he was wondering what to do with this wealth of information. Should he tell the Germans that the Duke was wavering? Should he tell the British that the Duke might be forsaking them? Or both?

He looked with sharp eyes at Maria, wondering if she had been approached as yet by either side. It would be bad if his information arrived after hers. But that was unlikely. Maria was not allowed to use the house telephone, and he did not think she knew how to do so. She rarely left the villa and would have no way of communicating with Lisbon, except for her letters, that he read himself, to her sister in the Alfama. In reassuring himself, he had forgotten the fisherman who came to the back door, and who was very inclined to be helpful.

Maria was bewildered. She had not understood much of what she had heard. While she listened, she had been tidying the Duchess' things, and as the Duchess was a hard task-mistress, Maria's mind had been much taken up by her work. The names, places and possibilities discussed confused her, and whether the Duke and Duchess meant to go, or not go, she could not be certain. Until Manuel made it clear.

Manuel put aside the silver he had set out to be

cleaned, piled up the chamois cloth unused, and on the clear space he had made on the working table, placed a bottle of good red wine and two glasses. He and Maria should drink of the best. It was a momentous occasion.

And he was perturbed. He knew that if he, Manuel, did not take immediate action, the Duchess would prevail.

"For she," he said judiciously, "is the strong one." His hands sketched out her strong square jaw, her lean and bony frame. It was not an admiring gesture.

Maria, who was herself well-curved, nodded.

"A snake in a corset," she agreed.

"And she will do it. A disappointed woman; I think she will do anything now to be Queen."

Maria nodded and tried to look intelligent, though she knew little of such matters. She had not mixed with the great like Manuel. She was not even a lady's maid, only the second parlourmaid, but her mistress had told her to serve the Duchess, and she had tried.

"So where does that leave us? And our master?" Manuel said portentously.

He sipped on his wine. The odour from the jar of silver polish that was left open from his work spoiled the bouquet, and he waved at Maria to seal it up. He could not be distracted from his cogitations.

"The Germans want him to go to England. The English want him to go to these Bahamas. I, like our master," Manuel said, "prefer the English. As you know, the Duke of Kent who was here before these people came, is our master's good friend. So perhaps I should inform our master. Slip down to Lisbon before the birds have flown. He will know what to do," he said pensively.

Perhaps his master would reward him. There was no use bothering with the Englishman in the café, with his one good eye and his empty pockets. Manuel remembered that he had been trying to sell his camera when they last met. Something was wrong. The money was not coming from England.

Maria's cheeks were flushed from the wine.

"Then you must go."

Of course, he thought regretfully, it was the Germans who were generous. Once the Duke left this house, that would be the end of their little presents. It was a pity that he could not collect one large sum before all this was done. His savings were not large. His wife was tiresome, but his children were grown. He would like to open a café of his own, without his wife, but perhaps with Maria to help him. If she would pack off that Jorge . . .

"Wait, Maria. Not so fast." Manuel held a hand up warningly. "Our master might be embarrassed. This Duke is also his friend. They dine together tonight, at a private party in a restaurant. And our master has much business with the Germans," he added thoughtfully. "From what I have seen of his papers, the bank of our master handles great deposits from the Deutchesbank. It may be that my telling him this would be an embarrassment. It may make difficulties for him with the Germans. He may be displeased with me for the interference."

Manuel refilled the glasses, placing them together, and regarded them as though they were two weights on the scale of his problem, equal, perfectly balanced. If only he could ask the Germans to pay for his silence. But he could hardly do that.

"So you see, Maria, it is difficult. A matter for grave thought. But there is no time for thought. If I am to act, it must be soon." He was almost as fretful about passing time as the Duchess.

Maria gazed at him with respect for, he thought, his wisdom, his power. It was a look she had long since learned to wear. It meant nothing, for she thought his words made nonsense. There could be no hurry. The Duke could not leave. The Duchess had not even sorted her clothes for packing, and Maria knew with an absolute certainty that the Duchess didn't go anywhere without being properly packed.

But the wine made her eyes sparkle. It made little beads of sweat form on her neck above her white collar. There would also be a little sweat on her full breasts, now covered by her black dress, and her plump round thighs. This would be a good night to stay where he was, in the Boca Do Inferno, the thought came to him, but he reminded himself of his duty. This information must be worth many escudos, to someone. The Germans. The British—not the one-eyed man, but someone of more importance, perhaps at the Embassy? He looked again at the perfectly balanced glasses of wine.

"After all, one side is as good, or as bad, as the other."

"But if you tell the British," said Maria, not quite understanding his trend of thought, "does that mean they will stay? They will not leave at all?" Perhaps in that case, she thought suddenly, the English soldier would come back. Her Rex. The thought, the wine, stirred her. Her colour rose, and she sighed.

But Manuel jumped as if stung. This was something he had not thought of. Maria—he gave her a quick pinch of appreciation—Maria had more brains than a man could reasonably expect. She had made a point. She certainly had made a point.

The Duke had refused to go to the Bahamas. He, Manuel, had heard him screaming about it. So if the Duke did not go to the Bahamas, and did not go to England, where would he stay for the rest of the war?

"He will stay here," he said. The English would guard him so that he could not escape. The Germans would soon lose interest, and that would be the end of the pleasant payments.

"The English are hypocrites," he said in gloom. "Even if we tell all we know, they will not lock up a Duke." Nor pay much for information, he thought, his sense of injury swelling. The Englishman with the bad eyes had given him nothing for his last report. "And our master is too good. After all, they were invited here for two nights and they have been already one month. They might just stay until the war is over. Why should they not?

"They will stay. They will stay and our master will leave us here with one-third of a staff to do the work of two. For these will make enough work for two full households. You will go on doing three or four jobs, Maria, and be paid only for one and at night you will be too tired . . . too tired," he said, and coughed delicately.

"And expect no tips from these so Royal Highnesses," he said spitefully. "No presents. I have heard how it was with the Duke in Austria from one of the servants of the Baron de Rothschild when he came through Lisbon. The Baroness had lent the Duke their castle. Work but no tips," Manuel muttered darkly. "And this Duchess," his indignation grew stronger, "her mother kept a pensão. And she acts like such a one herself. I had it from the man of the Duke of Kent. While this Windsor was still King, she was hated by every servant in the Royal Palaces. She made him cut wages, check every expense, told the staff they spent too much on soap. And this was while he was giving her jewels as fine as the Crown jewels themselves," he nodded in disgust. "That boarding-house keeper."

No, with the Duke and Duchess there would never be enough money for his café. He looked at the two glasses of wine and made up his mind. For any small sum he might get at the Embassy, it was not worth it. Besides— his mind caught the same idea that had come to Maria. If the Duke stayed that English *soldado* might return. He had seen his eyes on Maria. Worse, Maria's eyes on him. Vengefully, he hoped he had been ill, very ill on the 'plane home. He drained his glass.

"We will say nothing," he said with decision. "Silence. Discretion. Let the Royals go where they will, as long as they go. And let our master return." He noticed Maria's dreamy look, her high colour, the soft rise and fall of her bosom.

"Come," he said. "It is late and we have had no rest. They go out—there are others to attend them. Let us rest before dinner."

Maria went obediently, but with reluctance. For the first time she wondered why it should be that an underparlourmaid should, by some unwritten law, become the lover of the chief manservant. For so it seemed to be. Her little Jorge was the son of the butler in the house of her last employer. She wanted no more children, especially a child of the stringy, pompous Manuel. Then she wondered, with a little suppressed giggle, how it would be if something of that sort did happen, and the child had dark red hair . . .

That night, in one of the finest restaurants in Lisbon, the Duke was very gay. It was remarked by everyone that he had quite recovered his spirits and was once more as carefree as he had been as the Prince of Wales whom so many people had known and loved. He danced all night, except when he was conducting the orchestra. He tried out all the wind instruments, and bewailed the absence of bagpipes. For a time it was thought he would join in a proposed treasure hunt to try to find bagpipes somewhere in Lisbon—a moonlight search. He almost agreed—he had been a great lover of treasure hunts—but the Duchess seemed unwell, and he was reluctant, as always, to leave her behind.

Even by candlelight she looked pale and drawn; she was both quiet and nervous and jumped at every sound. Although it was a very warm night she was shivering, and she confessed to her hostess that she had a slight fever, but didn't want to spoil the party. Her hostess sent to her house for a wrap, and her servant brought a short cape of ermine. The Duchess sat huddled into it, for once careless of her appearance. She looked as she would look as an old woman, and gazed incuriously at the Duke as he pranced and played boyishly.

Her host inquired if the Duchess would like to be taken home, but the Duke declined for her. He had drunk a good deal of champagne.

"I am expecting some news at any time," he said, rather too freely. "And it will be the cure for Wallis, I am certain. I have left word that I am here. It should arrive any moment now."

He laughed and knelt at his wife's feet, adjusting a rug that the restaurant owner, concerned, had provided. Before he rose, to the fascination of the assembled company, he pressed kisses into the arch of her foot.

"Any moment now," he said happily, and went off to demonstrate for his friends the Cockney *'Knees Up Mother Brown.'*

He had some difficulty in getting the band to follow the tune, and was assisting the ladies in their long dresses to kick up their knees in the approved style. A tall blonde slipped and fell and the Duke, caught by surprise, fell with her on top of him. Her skirt rested across his face, and her minimal underclothes exposed her fair hindquarters to view. The other guests, except for the Duchess, were screaming and laughing hysterically, when the sober figure of Sir Walford Selby appeared in the doorway. He waited a moment as the Royal Duke disengaged himself from the lady's lace garment that had become attached to him by a fallen diamond brooch. The onlookers were still shrieking, helpless with laughter, as was the Duke himself, when Sir Walford caught his attention.

The Duke waved to him amiably.

"You have my message? Good. Come over here."

The Duchess stirred. The Duke was still wreathed in smiles and gaiety.

"May I see you somewhere privately, Your Royal Highness?" the Ambassador asked.

The Duke looked round, grinning. There were couples in various corners already enjoying such privacy as could be found.

"Private? At this party? It has to be the loo. Anybody in the loo?" he called, and the party, except for the hosts, collapsed with further mirth.

"There is a small room just here," his host said rapidly, after a look from Sir Walford. "You could have a little quiet there."

He ushered the Duke through a small door into a little room that might have been the owner's office with a window to the back of the building. There was a distinct smell of rubbish that had been sitting all day out in the heat.

The host excused himself, leaving Sir Walford alone with the Duke, but just as he left, the Duchess, casting off her wraps, joined her husband. Her face was very pale and her eyes dark-ringed.

"Well, Selby, what's the good word?" the Duke said jovially. "What has Winston got for me this time?"

"I came straight away as you requested," the Ambassador said, frowning. "But I have to tell you there is no change. Your orders are to proceed immediately to the Bahamas. The Prime Minister regrets that he cannot spare a destroyer, but is sure you will be quite safe on a neutral liner."

The Duke looked as if he had been struck by lightning. His eyes bulged from his ashen face, and every hair on his head seemed to stand up separately. He said nothing but made a thick sound in his throat and stared at his wife.

"Shall I make the arrangements—I believe there is a good ship leaving on the 2nd of August?" Sir Walford murmured.

The Duchess came and took her husband's hand.

"I can assure you we will be ready to leave as soon as need be," she said.

The Ambassador was visibly relieved as he withdrew.

The party ended early, owing to the Duke's official business and the Duchess' state of health.

ELEVEN

The Fat Man Makes A Move

When Admiral Canaris received the message from von Auerbach, he was not as pleased as that satisfied young man might have expected. He had been a spymaster too long not to recognise puffery, and if a common spy was inclined to puff his reports, these diplomats were far worse.

The Duke was 'about to agree'. But the Duke was always about to agree. He was a man notorious for his vacillation. The rest of the plan was working brilliantly: Lloyd George was preparing to form a new Cabinet; Black Knight and Whaleforce were ready in Scotland, and now Purcell with them; Röslein was confident of a Royal visit very soon. But the Scottish enterprise was worse than useless if the Duke were not to be in England ready to take the throne. It would merely ensure that the young Elizabeth be Queen.

For a moment the Admiral thought of Hitler's 'one good swipe at Ekaterinburg.' He noticed, with a feeling of distaste, that at this moment the idea seemed sensible—it would lessen the problems. But in any case the Princesses were in Windsor Castle itself. Winston Churchill had seen to it that there was a regiment to protect them.

Thinking of Churchill, his brow grew dark. He had called Lahousen and given him a tongue-lashing about the

193

aborted, stupid attempt on the Prime Minister. Lahousen
had protested that the Irishmen involved had been no men
of his. True, the IRA were supposedly working with Germany, but the organisation was so split and fragmented
that none of the leaders knew all that was happening.
Canaris was no Hitler to browbeat a man for something
he was certain was not his fault. But it was maddening.

Fortunately, no great harm had been done. The Admiral put von Auerbach's telegram down and rose from
his desk a little stiffly. There had been no repercussions.
Only, he had learned, that Churchill had added a young
soldier to his team of bodyguards. Well, one soldier could
hardly stop the Abwehr. But before he could feel much
satisfaction, his orderly rushed in. Only one event ever
produced that much nervousness in his orderly. Even the
defeat of the entire German Army would not make the
slow-moving, middle-aged ex-soldier rush like that. The
Führer wanted to see the Admiral at the Chancellery. At
once!

He sighed, but of course he went. As we always do,
he thought. And if a few of us had, say, four years ago,
refused? But it was no use speculating on what might have
been.

The day in Berlin was warm and sunny; the canal
waters sparkled cheerfully. He had not noticed it earlier.
He had slept, as he so often did, on the bed in his office.
Now he could not help but notice the faces of the Berlin-
ers, soberly going about their business on this fine day.
They did not look like a happy, victorious people.

As his car drew up at the Chancellery, there were
very few people slowing down as they passed, hoping for
a glimpse of the Führer. If this had been England, if the
recent victories had been hers, what crowds there would
be before Buckingham Palace, cheering the King and
Queen! It was as if the German people, in their hearts, did
not trust their victories. Some wisdom, that warned but
could not help, had touched them.

Hitler received him in the library. His adjutant showed in the Admiral a moment too soon. Hitler was studying a map of Great Britain, peering through his spectacles. It always annoyed him to be caught wearing his spectacles, and the Admiral was nervous. The meeting was starting badly.

But the Führer smiled on him, miraculously kind, with the charm he could always summon when he wished. He asked a few questions about the progress of Operation Green, and seemed satisfied with the Admiral's careful answers. He always thought it best to let the Führer know no more than was necessary. Often the Führer's extremely sharp, probing questions made this difficult, but today all was as sunny as the weather.

The Admiral's stomach had begun to settle, and he hoped he might get back to his office before the whole morning was wasted, when the Führer asked a very close question indeed.

"You're using an airfield over there, aren't you?"

The Admiral had to pause before he could answer. His first, most uncomfortable thought was, "How did the Führer know?" There had been no mention of airfields in any of his reports. He himself had penetrated Rudolph Hess' own spy agency, the *Verbindungsstab*, and Himmler's SD. Did this mean that the Abwehr too had been penetrated—on a high level? He shivered. Perhaps Leiter had been careless in instructing the British agents. He had been told not to use wireless, but a message might have been intercepted. Though Leiter was not a careless man. He quickly formulated an answer.

"Not what one would call an airfield, *mein Führer*. There is a small grassy landing field in the target area, the property of a local landowner who formerly used it in the shooting season. Because a few RAF personnel now are stationed there, we thought it best to neutralise it."

He had other plans but there was no need to talk of them now. Remembering the conversation about Göring,

195

he added quickly, "But we are not landing anyone there. Our men are already at the location, totally unsuspected."

It was not to be that easy. While the Führer was asking a few innocuous questions, Reichsmarschall Göring was shown in. If Berlin, and the Führer himself, showed no great air of triumph, all was made up for in the person of the resplendent Reichsmarschall. He wore a white uniform, covered with medals like a harlot with fake gems. His countenance blazed triumph as if the victories had been all his own, though the Luftwaffe had failed on the beach at Dunkirk, and it had been the Army, not his airmen, who had won the great battles. Still, the Führer did not see him for what he was. Only for what he had been.

Göring greeted the Führer effusively, and turned to Canaris.

"I have a fine body of men picked out for you. Already specially trained. A small force, but highly skilled and deadly. And a Wellington bomber, brought up to perfect condition for the Fallschirm jäger, ready to fly. You have only to name the day, Admiral."

He was beaming, very pleased with his men for having salvaged the British bomber, one of several brought down over Wilhelmshaven. There the RAF had learned what it was like to meet the Luftwaffe fighters by day! He would have wished to send in a major force, using the big transport 'planes the British had left behind in the retreat, but that would cause suspicion. It had been some time since the British had transported men *to* the Continent!

"A combined operation, *mein Führer!*"

Canaris tried to mask his disgust. Certainly, Göring knew his flyers and the paratroops were not wanted, but scenting glory to come, as usual he wanted a share. The Admiral was well aware of the tug-of-war that had been going on between the OKH and the Luftwaffe, for control of the paratroops. The Luftwaffe was in the ascendant now; doubtless Göring wanted to show off his superior ability in their use.

If only the Führer had kept the business quiet! Sometimes he thought the Führer was afraid of Göring. While the Führer was doing his best to placate the French to keep them working for Germany, Göring was rounding up the finest art treasures in France. But the Führer uttered not one word of disapproval to his Reichsmarschall.

Even as the three men stood there, Göring, absentmindedly, took a handful of uncut stones from his pocket. He fingered them, let them fall to a table, admired and then scooped them up again. Hitler did not seem to notice this performance.

"Thank you, Reichsmarschall," Canaris said formally. "But our plans are complete. There would be no purpose in enlarging them. That would add much to the danger, and nothing to the success."

Göring looked annoyed, and began to bluster.

"What makes you so sure of success? You have said your force is small. In such an operation, a thousand things can go wrong and you will need my troops to fall back on."

Canaris turned to Hitler.

"*Mein Führer,* the smaller the force, the less that can go wrong. In this matter as you, in your wisdom, have ordered—" with the Führer, flattery and more flattery, laid on with a trowel, was the only thing that helped—"it is essential that the operation be completed without the British public having the least idea that Germany has—helped it along. To keep their friendship and cooperation, we must manipulate, not invade. This is no occasion for the great Panzer divisions, nor the mighty Luftwaffe. Silence and stealth, rather. All the people involved, with one exception, are British. They can hardly be challenged. None of them is known to any British security force. Even the exception is half English and has a solid identity in Great Britain. When it is all over, there can be no foreign flavour. A smooth changeover in the British Government."

The Führer said nothing. Canaris decided he had to offer him a tidbit. *"Mein Führer,* Lloyd George is already considering his new Cabinet. I have just read the report."

The Führer smiled, happy now. He had long placed great faith in Lloyd George. Many prominent Germans had wondered why he had made so little use of the British Union of Fascists, and had given so little status to its head. But he had thought poorly of the man who tried to imitate him; of his group who could not come to power on its own strength. He knew the English called the leader 'the Woolworth Duce' and in his heart he agreed. He, Adolf Hitler, had chosen the German Army over his own stormtroopers. Certainly he chose to deal not with failed revolutionaries but with statesmen of magnitude. Yes, he and Lloyd George would be meeting again soon, rejoicing that the men of both nations were not being killed in vain.

Göring attempted more argument. His pilots were so skilled, their loyalty so great—but the Führer cut him off. He had not been listening. His eyes glanced over the rows of books on his shelves, coming to rest as they so often did on the beautifully-tooled volume of *Mein Kampf.* Yes, his *Kampf,* his great plan, was going just as it should.

"Reichsmarschall, I am sure the Admiral will call upon you if he needs your men." He turned again to his map. "Show me, Admiral, where this operation is to take place."

Göring, recognising defeat for the moment, took his leave. Canaris wished to God he would stay at Karinhall, playing with his model railway. There he could do no harm. The glance that Göring gave him on parting was not friendly.

Canaris bent over the map with the Führer. He knew he had just made an enemy. If only he were as totally confident of success as he had sounded. Nothing foreseeable could go wrong, but he knew too well that the unforeseeable could happen. Certainly, he wanted no aircraft, and no paratroopers. The British RDF system, though thin in the Highlands, could spot the aircraft, unless it flew dangerously low. And even a 'plane identified as British would cause queries best never made. Paratroopers floating about would be the quickest way of calling attention to his perfectly masked operation. But he had better be successful, or his head would be on the chopping block. And not only his own.

If he were dragged down, there would be others who would go with him. His men, who had trusted him. His wife and children would not be safe.

"There is this range of mountains here, and this line of high hills, *mein Führer*. And these valleys, called glens, and these two rivers . . ."

"But it is like trying to capture the Berghof," Hitler exclaimed.

"No, not at all. It is not a war-time residence, you see. There are no fortifications. My assassin has been trained in Frankenwald and the Vogtland, very similar territory. And we have detailed charts, down to the last tree, stick, stone and stray dog."

The Führer noticed with satisfaction that the place was twice as far from London as it was from Stavanger in Norway—German held.

The Admiral's voice went on, soothingly. He hoped it was the last he would hear of Göring's involvement. Now he must certainly hurry von Auerbach. The Duke *had* to be ready, for the first possible moment when Holstein could strike. It was not only the Führer's impatience now that mattered. If the strike did not come soon, he would have Martin Bormann wishing to go on the expedition. Or his chief, Rudolph Hess. But his mind went back again to Göring. He made a silent prayer that that erratic mind would veer to some new preoccupation.

Canaris prayed in vain. Göring did go to Karinhall, but not to play with his trains. He was so furious, his nerves so jangled with rage, that his first action was to pick up a snuff box, one of his large collection, a delicate little affair in porcelain that had once been Beau Brummel's favourite summer box. The Reichsmarschall kept it filled with powder of another kind. He took a long sniff, of a quantity usually enough to soothe, but he was still shaking with rage.

He sent for Körner, and waited for him in his library, while the scene at the Chancellery played itself over and over in his mind. Hermann Göring, the second man in Germany, to be dismissed like an office boy! When he had already discussed his plans with the Führer! And by the little *'Kieker'*!

Göring had never actually disliked Canaris. He might think him a puny fellow, spending too much time, spider-like, in his wretched office, but nevertheless he was a social equal, part of the old upper class—not a slimy nobody like Himmler.

But for this—this insect to intervene between the Reichsmarschall and his Führer, to take away Hermann Göring's last chance of appearing before the people as the Iron Man . . . His indignation knew no bounds. Of course, he could not appeal along those lines to the Führer. He would merely say there would be much room for glory in Russia. But the Reichsmarschall was not at all certain that *Barbarossa* would ever take place. The Führer might be satisfied with all the rest of Europe once he had swallowed it. Privately, Göring was not sanguine about war with Russia. He had thought much of Napoleon Bonaparte. Better to leave well enough alone. Göring considered himself to be the last of the Renaissance men, with the tastes of a great prince and the mind of Machiavelli. He understood statesmanship, and he understood the use of force. Statesmanship with Russia. But with England—force! He and his Luftwaffe would not be cheated of all the glory of conquering England with their eagles' swoop. As for Canaris' protests about the safety of the mission, that was

200

mere cant, to keep all the glory for his Abwehr.

He took another sniff. He felt better. His confidence was rising. By the time Körner arrived he could talk to him calmly. He had studied again the map of the German Ocean where he had already plotted a route from Stavanger to Aberdeen for the Führer's benefit, to show him how simple it would be to avoid the RAF. Now he had Körner pull out the charts from Aberdeen along the River Dee to the west of Glen Muick.

"Admiral Canaris says he does not want our help," the Reichsmarschall trumpeted.

Körner, a quiet, cautious man, who during his years of service to the Reichsmarschall had developed a tic under his right eye, was not surprised.

"I had expected that, Her Reichsmarschall. As you requested, I have made certain inquiries."

That was one way of putting it. Lahousen owed the Reichsmarschall a debt for past assistance. The debt had been called in. Körner now knew as much about the details of Operation Green as Lahousen himself in whom Leiter had been forced to confide.

"It is really a very small affair."

He tapped his pencil at the square marking the Royal house on the bank of the Muick, the small tributary running northward to the Dee.

"The Abwehr's best assassin is already in the locality. He has easy access to the household. On the first night of the next visit of the Royal Family, he is to give the King an injection that will bring on heart attack and death. A telegram, ostensibly from the Queen, will be sent to Churchill by one of our people, requesting his presence immediately and secretly. Now it happens there is a very small airfield right in this glen, here." His finger tapped a spot in the valley, a few miles south of the Royal house. "It is the property of a man who owns all this," and he circled an area east of the Muick.

"In the circumstances," Körner continued, "Churchill will undoubtedly use this field. It is to be taken over by the Abwehr's Britishers—a mere dozen men. They will be wearing RAF uniforms. Churchill will be captured on landing and taken off to a desolate place called the Cairns, here, further east, and murdered. The 'plane he was using will be tampered with by one of Lahousen's experts so that the pilot will crash almost immediately after take-off. They have to be careful on the field itself, it can be seen from the road—a small path really—in the valley. Although it is hardly ever used."

Göring peered at the chart.

"This other house here, on the cliff over the field—"

"Virtually empty. It belongs to the landowner, but he lives in London. He is never there, except for the shooting later in the year."

"Naturally," Göring nodded. "But there must be servants."

"Just an old woman and an outdoor man when the owner is away. The old woman keeps to the back of the house, the man is about the grounds. But as you see, the spread of the estate is behind the house. It is most unlikely he would be in sight of the field at all. But in all events, the Britishers will take the field at night, and Churchill will be hustled off at once. It will appear that he dies in the wreck of the 'plane. That is the general outline of the arrangement."

Göring pushed his lip out.

"Twelve men! Suppose he comes up with a fighter escort and a bodyguard of sharpshooters in his transport? What could twelve men do then?"

"That's a very remote possibility," Körner answered, "and one dismissed by the Admiral. The Prime Minister has not been using his transport 'plane. If discretion is urged upon him, the likelihood is he will go in a small aircraft with just one or two Special Branch men. They will have to die in the accident too, of course."

202

"Remote possibility or not," Göring said decisively, "it must be taken into account. The Führer will agree with that." He smiled. The game, he thought, was his. "Certainly they need more well-trained men. We will send in one, or perhaps two Wellington bombers with crack Fallschirmjäger."

"The Admiral will argue, undoubtedly," Körner pointed out, "that even at night your men might be seen coming down over the airfield. Apart from the big house up on the cliff there are some cottages here and there."

"Then they won't come down over the airfield," Göring said shortly. His trained pilot's eye swept the chart. The Wellington bombers would follow the Dee as far as the Muick—then he saw just a little to the west, south of the Dee, there was a small clearing in a secluded wood. He measured it and checked the scale. Yes, just enough space for well-trained men, brought in by brilliant pilots, to make the landing. One of the Abwehr's Britishers could signal them down and guide them southward, up Glen Muick and across the little river to the airfield. Then *his* men would hold the field and capture Churchill. His smile broadened. Afterwards the Abwehr could say what it wished, but it would go down in the history books that Hermann Göring's Luftwaffe had captured Great Britain's Prime Minister and won the war.

"The Admiral won't agree," Körner had to say. His right cheek twitched.

Göring, euphoric now, patted him on the back. Canaris could say what he liked, but when he, Hermann Göring, had the Führer by the ear, he could persuade him; he always had. The Führer still needed him, the Nazi leader most popular with the people, their Iron Man, and the only one trusted by the old guard.

He would get Canaris out of the way somehow. But how? He sent Körner off to attend to the organization of the Fallschirmjäger, and sat back in his great chair to think. He took a little more cocaine. As always, it cleared his head and spurred his mind. Now this was not a case for force but for diplomacy, his Machiavellian side. It was like the matter of Spain that the Führer was talking about endlessly. He wanted Franco to cooperate, without the need of armed might. Only yesterday the Führer had asked Göring himself if he would go to Spain to speed up the negotiations.

Suddenly the idea came, simple, perfect. Canaris was an old friend of the Generalissimo—one of the few men that he respected. Göring would drop the idea in the Führer's mind that Canaris was the one man who could handle the project. Certainly he himself had no wish to go to Madrid in the heat of July. He laughed, thinking of the alarm on little 'Kieker's' face, when he learned that he had lost control of the great Scottish project—the most important part of Operation Green, and the whole Windsor Plot.

TWELVE

To Move A King

That same Tuesday was also a day of stress at 10 Downing Street.

The Prime Minister had finished his breakfast of bacon, eggs, and chopped beef, a mound of toast and butter which was kept warm for him under a cover, and a pot of tea, with which his household managed to provide him, despite the rationing. He had bathed and shaved, and then returned to bed as was his custom. Official bulletins were brought in, which he studied; his telephone was still cut off. Propped up in bed by a forest of pillows, with rubber pads under his elbows, he read the newspapers; and then despatches and communiqués were brought in the official yellow box that could be opened by no-one except himself. Before his appointed callers were allowed to enter, his secretaries, working in rotation, took down his correspondence and memoranda.

In the middle of a long and complicated sentence he paused, in sudden irritation. A man was outside, washing the windows. Surely that should not be done now! Worse, he was whistling. The sound of a popular song, *'When I'm Cleaning Windows,'* came piercingly through the glass.

"Get that man out of here," he roared.

The answer was startling.

"Yes, guv. I was just coming in." Rex Barney,

dressed in overalls, a brush in his hand, stepped through the open window. He had changed now to singing.

"In my profession I'll work hard, and I'll never stop."

The secretary, though she had seen Rex before, screamed.

"And stop that noise!" The Prime Minister was furious. "I've lost my whole train of thought!"

"Then shut your ears," Rex said blandly.

The Prime Minister, who had accepted this impertinence from the child, growled ominously, until the door burst open and Detective-Sergeant Hilliard, who had been stationed outside the bedroom door, came in with his pistol clutched in his hand. He, too, recognised Barney, much to his disgust.

In a quick change of mood, the Prime Minister began to laugh.

"Got you there, Hilliard, didn't he?"

Barney's duties at the moment were to find weak spots in the defence of the Prime Minister's person.

The Detective-Inspector, usually sallow, was now bright red. He glared at Barney, and forgetting for once proper procedure in the Prime Minister's own bedroom, blurted out, "How the hell did you get by—"

"I'll climb this blinkin' ladder till I get right to the top," Rex sang happily. "Window cleaner," he explained, "with my little chammy in my hand. No trouble."

"But your identification, your pass . . ."

"You can't tell 'em off out there for that," Rex said agreeably.

The affairs of the nation, the conduct of the war, were quite cheerfully put aside for the moment by the Prime Minister while he listened to the exchange.

"Showed 'em all the proper papers."

"Where did you get them?" Hilliard snapped.

"Easiest thing in the world, getting papers," Rex replied. "Nicked some old ones, and had copies made, see, with the new date."

Hilliard thought of the elaborate system of identity card, photograph, password. He would have to have a long talk with Sergeant Barney, but, of course, not here.

"I'll have a word with you outside," he said.

His thoughts showed clearly on his face. He was certain that Sergeant Barney had committed illegal acts. And the people who had helped him—naturally someone like Barney knew all the crooks in London—they might be in for prosecution under the Defence of the Realm Act.

"Well now, if the Germans were coming in," Rex said, reading his thoughts with infuriating clarity, "they wouldn't be kept back from doing something just because it was illegal, would they?"

The Prime Minister chimed in, for all the world like a headmaster in a boy's dispute.

"Yes, Hilliard. You must play fair. I have given Sergeant Barney carte blanche in this affair, and that applies to anyone who assists him."

You would never believe, Hilliard thought in despair, that we were only trying to protect him. He left the room with as much dignity as he could muster.

The secretary gathered up her papers and scurried out after him. The next secretary in the team was already at the door, but Rex waved her back. When he was alone with the Prime Minister he remarked briefly:

"Nothing in the papers yet about the Duke turning up in the Bahamas."

The Prime Minister had re-lit his cigar, he blew out a balloon of smoke, and gazed into it thoughtfully. His attention, apart from necessary political manoeuvering, had been almost entirely on the problem of aircraft production. Reconnaissance had showed that the German air force was re-grouping its formations on the French and Belgian coasts. With the harrying of British convoys in the Channel off the east coast, the RAF had already been drained. He feared it could disappear before any major assault on the islands began.

But he remembered the affair of the Duke, who seemed to have taken his orders quietly. Of course, he still asked for his valet and his wife's maid, the latter stranded somewhere in France. And he was still asking for a destroyer. It was all very annoying, but meant little. It was the Duke's way.

Barney, he thought, was a good soldier. He had been given a position to take, and he wanted to take it. He didn't like a strategic withdrawal any more than the Prime Minister. A fighter! But the Duke was no longer a problem. Selby had sent a report yesterday that he had given in. He knew he would have to go. Still the Prime Minister looked at Barney with approval. How he had dished the lot of them that morning—the police, the Army, and all the other odd bods who were supposed to be looking after him.

He didn't really need a bodyguard, but he wished he could put Barney at the disposal of Their Majesties. Of course, there was no chance. Protocol was still strong at Court. He could hardly imagine all the officers of the Guard taking orders from a sergeant. Even if he gave him a field commission, it wouldn't help. A thought, of a kind that didn't often come to him, flashed through his mind for a moment. Barney was more of a man, with more brains, than any of them. He could have made a great commander. Pity he had to be born the son of a nobody.

The thought faded, with more immediate concerns. Fortunately, the King and Queen were well-guarded now. He must get on to Public Works, though, about a properly strengthened basement at the Palace. Almost certainly, the way they moved over there, the work had not yet begun. It had to be left for him to prod, prod.

The secretary tapped on the door. The Prime Minister made a noise that she recognised as permission to enter. Rex, having given him a look that was not entirely resignation, took his leave. The secretary stared in amazement at Sergeant Barney's familiar self in the unfamiliar overalls, and he gave her a kind pat on the rump with his brush. She squealed. The Prime Minister sat bolt upright, his eyes goggling, and gazed on the nervous woman in offended majesty.

He finished the memo he had begun earlier, and then sent off a note about the air raid shelter. ACTION THIS DAY July 16. Their Majesties must be protected; their persons made absolutely secure. To the nation, they were the symbols of the power and might of Great Britain. God knows, they needed all their symbols now.

Sergeant Barney's apprehensions were justified. The Duke's decision to refuse the appointment was final. But that was not what he informed London. The Duke and Duchess played a waiting game. He continued to demand his valet, Fletcher. That request might be complied with, so he also demanded a destroyer, which he was almost certain would not be forthcoming. And to demand the Duchess' maid was an excellent strategy—nobody knew where she was except that she had never escaped from France. London could hardly produce her. He felt that he could put Winston off as long as he wished. The Duke would have been willing to go to Spain there and then, but that did not suit von Auerbach. His instructions were quite different.

After July 16, Admiral Canaris hardly left his office on the Tirpitz Ufer. Operation Green was too near the climax. He was waiting for only two things now: the decision of the Duke and the arrival of the Royal Family at Birkhall. The only thing that could upset his plan would be the Queen's confessing to the wrong person about her surreptitious weekend holidays. From what he had learned of her, he didn't think she would. Underneath her softness and sweetness was an unyielding strength and determination—which he was forced to admire. She would trust her own decision, and she would keep her silence. A wife as loyal as his own. She believed she helped her husband.

But if he was wrong—Röslein would inform Black Knight, Whaleforce would be dispersed, and Araby and Scullion put in motion. A domestic accident for the Prime Minister, unfortunately fatal. Believable, in a man of his age, known for his copious drinking. But it would involve much last minute change of detail. For Araby, his man in the Iraqui Embassy, one of his best men, would have to be sacrificed. A wild Arab, angry over British promises to the Jews, he would murder the King at a public appearance and then turn his gun on himself. The man was willing enough though Canaris would much prefer, for many reasons, not to resort to this. Nevertheless the assassination could not be laid at the door of Germany. Although he did not much care for his alternate plan, it was the best that could be done in the short time the Führer allowed. August 3! And it was feasible as long as the Röslein plan was not blown. If that happened—but it was best not to think of it.

When Black Knight got word from Röslein that the Royal couple were on their way, he was to telephone a London number. From there it would go to the Hungarian Embassy and in a few hours the message would be in his hands. The Admiral, who was always cold, found he was sweating in a sudden, irresistible excitement. He, little 'Kieker', was at a pivot point in history. And it was he who was moving the pivot. He dashed off a signal to von Auerbach in Lisbon; he must come back for a conference at once. That very day. The Duke *must* be ready to leave at a moment's notice, it was all-important. Whaleforce would probably have only one chance, and it might come in a few days. Then the Duke must go to the Channel Islands, and on to London. He would arrive to find Churchill dead, and Lloyd George taking over the reins of Government. The people would hear broadcast 'the last words of the dying George VI' and the game would be in Canaris' hands. It was time to move his 'King'.

* * *

When von Auerbach returned to Lisbon from his briefing, travelling on the night 'plane, he was entirely of the same mind. For he, himself, was determined to do just that— to move the 'King'. But his mind, a little less subtle than the Admiral's, was leaning towards a rather different method of accomplishing his goal. The Duke was not going to the Bahamas, it was true. Yet neither, von Auerbach thought with vexation, was he going anywhere else. For all his own and the Duchess' persuasions, the Duke was still spending his days peering over his balcony, waiting for the deliverance from having to decide.

Von Auerbach had come to believe that the Duke would have to have the decision made for him. He must be lured, or taken by force if necessary, aboard the U-boat. Once there, he could be soothed suitably. The decision would have been taken. A delegation in Alderney to call him 'Your Majesty', another in England and his protests would die unspoken.

Canaris had given him one more card to play. Von Auerbach thought about it and suddenly got what he thought was his most brilliant idea. He would use the Admiral's 'persuader' to get the Duke on board the U-boat, voluntarily, after all. Then he would keep him there, willy-nilly, out at sea, until the signal came to meet the sea-'plane.

He went back to the Boca Do Inferno. The Duchess greeted him with smiling pleasure and a certain expectation, the Duke with stiff reserve. Of course, the Duke was afraid he would pester him for a decision. 'His Majesty' was obviously relieved when he did not, and merely talked for a time of the local gossip.

Just before he took his leave, he gave them hesitant looks and then spoke, as if with reluctance.

"Your Majesties may have noticed that I have not

211

spoken of the matter we have discussed. There is no point in my urging it, of course, the decision must be yours. Kings and rulers must decide; people like myself can only obey. But before Your Majesty comes to his decision, there is some information, heavily documented, which I would like you to see. I have no right to show it to you since it consists of Germany's most guarded military secrets. I had grave difficulty gaining access to it myself, and in fact have put myself in a position of some danger. But it is a matter of such importance to Great Britain, that I felt that Your Majesty must be made aware . . . You are the one person in the world who *should* know."

The Duke did not look happy but he did look interested.

"Well, von Auerbach, what is it?"

"It is no use my telling you, sir. Although I am a family connection, and I hope a friend, I am a German and naturally you cannot take my word as gospel. You must see the documents yourself. But I could not bring them here, you understand. I must think of my own position. I will not say my own safety," he went on, with a noble look, "for in matters of great importance, the life of one man must often be sacrificed." He believed that to be true, providing the life was not his own. "But this is a matter of honour. For me to take these papers from German territory would be treason."

The Duke nodded. No-one at that moment was more inclined than he to weigh what was—and was not—treason.

"Yet I cannot embarrass Your Majesty by asking you to come to the German Legation. It would set all the tongues in Lisbon wagging."

"In any case," the Duke said coldly, "I wouldn't do it."

"Naturally not," von Auerbach agreed instantly.

There was a pause. The Duchess, for once, kept her silence. Her eyes were wary.

"It seems," the Duke said heavily, "that we have come to a stalemate."

Now was the time to mention the U-boat. But with the Duke before him, von Auerbach hesitated. Suddenly it seemed too large a lump for the former King to swallow —all at once. An idea came of how it could be managed in easy stages. He could have smiled; it would be simple after all.

"Perhaps, Your Majesty, I could suggest a way out. I have a vessel here at my disposal—a yacht. Perhaps Your Majesties could visit—come, say, to luncheon with me. I would be happy to return your hospitality. It would be quite proper, and I could move the yacht up from Lisbon to a quiet spot in Cascais and your visit would be quite private."

"Nothing we do is private," the Duke said in resignation. "We are spied on everywhere. Your boat will be remarked upon as it sails into Cascais."

"The *Isabella* was owned until recently by a Lisbon family," von Auerbach replied. "Everyone is used to seeing her in these waters and no-one will remark upon it."

That was true, and there was no need at all to mention that the present owner was Baron von Hoyninghen-Huene.

The Duchess' eyes met his own for a fraction of a second.

"Oh, David," she said, turning to her husband, "I am sure we can get away. We'll leave *very* early. Think how many times we've done it in the past."

She gave a delightful little laugh. Von Auerbach, even as he observed the mechanics, could not help but respond when she turned on the full battery of her fascination.

"Remember when I slipped away from Bryanston Court, and you from the Palace, and we ran quietly to Fort Belverdere."

To return to those happy memories of the time when

he had lured the wife from the husband and left his own duties was a sure charm with the Duke.

He grinned. "By God, yes. I used to climb out of my bedroom window, jump down and get away from my beastly detectives and the rest of the entourage."

King Edward, von Auerbach reflected, had perhaps been the only British King watched by Special Branch not only for his protection, but also for security reasons. Officially, of course, it had been Mrs Simpson who had been under observation.

"Oh, it would be fun to have lunch with Friedrich on his boat."

The Duchess looked so happy that the Duke remained genial. Any awkwardness about his boarding von Auerbach's vessel was passed over; the Duchess might have been speaking of visiting his yacht at Cowes.

"Tomorrow then, Friedrich? Our engagements are all cancelled, dear," she told the Duke, "because of this wretched touch of 'flu."

The Duke still looked bright.

"Perhaps we'll both crawl out through the windows, Dolly," and the three of them laughed gaily.

THIRTEEN
The Two-Level Man

Early next morning, woken by her child, Maria was standing for a moment at her window. Jorge had been fretful with a cough and Manuel had suggested, irritably, from her bed, that she send the child to her sister in the Alfama. She resented the suggestion, and her resentment kept sleep away.

The grey pre-dawn light was heavy with mist coming up from the sea. The pink-washed wall of the house looked almost grey, and her eye took it in without seeing. But below, the door to the pool opened and caught her attention—someone was creeping out early.

To her surprise she saw the Duke, fully dressed, carrying his shoes in his hands. He bent down to put them on, and then the Duchess appeared in the same state. She leaned on the Duke's arm while she slipped into her shoes. He was giggling and the Duchess tried to hush him, but she was smiling also. Maria's eyes were wide. The Duchess —the Duchess herself—had walked along the tiled corridors in her silk-stockinged feet. What kind of game was this? She watched them as they went off, hand in hand, down the driveway taking the path to the beach.

The Duchess, always so majestic. She could have slipped on the tile floor and broken her bones. It was true, then, what people said, Maria decided. The English were certainly mad. And the Americans also. But then, rich people could afford to be like children. If *they* broke their bones, other people would wait on them until their bones mended. She said nothing to Manuel. He had gone back to sleep. It was much better so.

No-one seeing the urbane, smiling von Auerbach as he greeted his guests aboard the *Isabella* could have suspected that he was in the grip of a sensation previously unknown to him—primitive, gut-clutching fear. Near as he was to victory, he could still fail. The Duke might see through the charade and refuse to board the U-boat. Or he could later cry 'Kidnap!' And in the Third Reich such failure, even for von Auerbach with his solid party record and Army support, would not be tolerated. Admiral Canaris, as an old Navy man, could be trusted, but there were others. The charge of treason was always at hand, a dossier prepared. His father and brother, those old Junkers, had too openly despised Corporal Hitler. He shivered slightly, even though at that hour it was warm in Cascais.

The mist had cleared while the Duke and Duchess were approaching. Soon sea and sky turned from silver and grey to deep blue, and the white hull and sails of the *Isabella* glistened. Von Auerbach bowed low over the Duchess' hand.

"You see, Your Majesty, how we are transformed by your presence!"

His guests were well-disposed to be amused, and he had not relied solely on gallantry. Knowing the Duke's preferences, he provided him with an English breakfast, and then showed him the yacht. It was of the 'J' class, built for luxury as well as speed, and the Duke admired both her lines and her appointments. By happy chance, the *Isabella* had been decorated throughout in Mediterranean blue, the Duchess' favourite coloure, and it seemed like a compliment to his lady.

Soon the Duke was reminiscing about the cruise

he had taken aboard the *Nahlin* with Wallis. Von Auerbach had heard all about the famous cruise when the Duchess had still been Mrs Simpson, but he encouraged the Duke to talk. He talked long, and he was still talking as the U-boat surfaced not too far off. The Duke paid no attention to it, for he was chaffing his wife, who by this time had accepted a pre-luncheon glass of champagne, contrary to their usual habit.

"Oh, David, I feel so relaxed here, for once so—so off the leash," the Duchess told him, smiling. "I am just in the mood for a party."

So of course the Duke had some too, and while the corks were popping and laughter was ringing about the deck, von Auerbach took his opportunity.

"I am afraid, Your Majesties, that we have run into a small problem—two small problems, in fact." He turned to the Duke and spoke in a low voice. "The papers we were discussing—unfortunately I have not been able to secure permission to bring them aboard the *Isabella*. She is a private vessel after all."

The Duke nodded. He understood, and did not look disappointed.

"But I have managed, just the same," von Auerbach went on cheerfully. "I had them taken under guard to the *Wilhelm II* which is a naval vessel." He waved a hand towards the U-boat. "And that has solved my other little problem. I had promised Her Majesty a delicious luncheon, but last night there was an accident in the galley. A very small fire—but a very large mess. The Captain of the *Wilhelm*, however, has invited us to luncheon on board his vessel and assures me that his cook is excellent. After luncheon we can go over the documents."

He was smiling, but he was aware that his suggestion was not well received. With a quick glance at the Duchess, he moved off casually for a word with his crew.

The Duke hardly waited for him to be out of earshot. He set his glass down, his blithe mood quite dispelled.

"Impudence, that's what it is!" The words exploded from him. "Expecting me to get on that submarine." He glared at the offending vessel.

For the first time, the Duchess thought he resembled the portraits she had seen of his great-grandmother, Queen Victoria. She moved closer to him.

"David, don't be foolish," she said in a whisper. "It's a marvellous opportunity. I don't know about his old documents, but while we're on board I'll make sure you have a chance to get a good look round that U-boat. You can make a thorough inspection and turn in a complete report to the Admiralty. It really is your duty," she added, slightly reproachfully. "I'm sure the First Sea Lord would be furious if he knew that you had refused."

The Duke's jaw dropped. He looked puzzled. Certainly, Wallis was right, as always. It *was* his duty to inspect the submarine. And yet—he did not like it.

When von Auerbach returned, the Duke's manner was cool and stiff. But the Duchess was enthusiastic, and the atmosphere soon became less strained. In the pleasant fuss of helping the elegant lady back into the launch and onto the U-boat, the Duke found himself aboard without quite noticing how he had got there.

Behind the Duchess' feminine charms was a practical, intelligent woman, von Auerbach thought in appreciation. She had already inquired of him privately about their reception on England's guarded south coast. The fishing vessel would not be remarked upon, he had told her, and a trusted deputation would be waiting to whisk them off to London. Even if they were observed, no member of a local defence force would think to detain the King's brother.

The Duchess also wanted to know about the arrangements in London, and exactly what, in Scotland, he expected to happen. Further, she asked if there were German troops present in Ireland. She made no reply when he told her there were none. A strong woman, he thought again. The idea flashed through his mind—how much such a woman might have helped the Führer, instead of that milk-and-water Eva Braun. The Führer—his mind snapped back to his mission sharply.

Now he believed he had his 'King' safe as a sardine in a tin. But—did he? Certainly once the *Wilhelm II* left the harbour, backsliding would be impossible. But the inevitable reaction when they went below and the Duke heard the engines start might be disastrous. One wrong move now . . .

Decisiveness struggled with caution. Reluctantly, for he was a man of action, he gave in to the timidity born of his knowledge of the Führer. He gave an order for the vessel to remain in the harbour until he sent the Captain word and that would be when the Duke had read the papers, he thought. For they were real enough, his trump card. They should make up that vacillating mind.

When they went below the Duke's uneasiness was plainly visible. Only the Duchess' great high spirits and newly Royal manner held him up. The U-boat Captain treated him as more than visiting Royalty, as German Royalty itself. He had served a Hohenzollern in his youth, and the great-grandson of Victoria, with his perfect German, seemed to him like a member of the German Royal House. Von Auerbach thought none the worse of the Captain for that.

It fitted in perfectly with his own wishes. He encouraged the Captain to take them on a tour of the submarine, even to see the new schnorkel equipment that was still secret and the hydrogen peroxide tanks, the fuel that was making the U-boat the fastest craft of its kind. The Duke enjoyed the inspection. His training was to inspect things, and though it had so often bored him in the past, it was agreeable to be doing it once again. As a former naval cadet, he understood for once what he was inspecting, and was genuinely interested.

He also well understood the military importance of

what he was being shown, and the fact that the Captain felt free to show it to him gave him a strong sensation, more than anything else had done, that von Auerbach was right. It was for him, the King, to say the word, and this foolish war would be over. His great-grandmother would certainly have been pleased, he thought, if she could have seen him make the peace between her two beloved countries.

All went well until luncheon was served. The Duke was shining with pride in his Duchess. For the first time, she was playing the role of Queen, and she was playing it well. Now she showed what she was capable of, how he —and Hitler!—had been right and all her enemies wrong. Von Auerbach was thinking the same thing. Her perfectly tailored coat and skirt might have been a model for what a well-dressed Queen would wear in an *Unterseeboot,* he decided with a respectful amusement, and she inspected, smiled and asked questions most royally. She certainly had the dignity of a Queen, without the paralysing tediousness of genuine Royalty. A fine example, he had considered, of the *ersatz* outdoing the real thing.

But then, between the soup and the fish, she made a major blunder. Perhaps, he thought resignedly, Royalty were dull because of their training—never ask a question unless you already know the answer. The Duchess, it was painfully obvious all at once, had never been trained at all.

While the plates were being changed she flashed her smile at the Captain and asked brightly:

"And is that a decoration? What is it for?" She nodded at his bright, shiny new badge, presented to him by the Führer just a few days before, a simple badge, a stylised form of a ship, surrounded by a wreath and mounted by the eagle and the swastika. It was indeed a decoration, conferred on the Captain for extraordinary success on his last two voyages: voyages which had, in fact, resulted in eight, probably nine, large British merchant vessels being destroyed—including the tanker that had caused Winston

Churchill so much pain at the Cabinet meeting, when he had read of the number of men killed in the flaming oil.

"To the whole crew really, Your Majesty," the Captain had passed it off, "for diligent services."

The Duchess beamed but the Duke, understanding too well, had at once lost his appetite and turned morose.

Von Auerbach was watching the Duke's pale, crooked eyes. He noticed for the first time that the right eye was actually on a higher level than the left. It was that which gave the Duke his strange gaze, the right eye looking outward, dreamy, hopeful, trusting; the left more direct, harder, more suspicious. A two-level gaze for a two-level man. And he saw the exact moment when that gaze took in the nature of his surroundings, the left eye seeing the hull as a prison wall, and the deferential companions as gaolers.

The shrewd young German could estimate almost exactly the conflict that possessed his prey, and how much soothing influence the ecstatically happy Duchess could provide. At the end of the meal, when the Duke refused coffee and brandy, von Auerbach prepared himself to remove what he was sure was the last vestige of opposition. Then a message was brought to him. Did he want the Captain to start the engines? He thought, still gripped by the strange, uncomfortable hesitation. No, he replied—not yet. He would send word.

He invited the Duke to his cabin, ordered tea for two at four o'clock and suggested if their business was not finished by dinner time, that the Duchess join them there. While the Duke was puffing moodily on his pipe, he dashed off to get his papers in order.

When the Duke came to his room, it crossed von Auerbach's mind that he looked like a man who, after indulging in a wild drinking session the night before, was trying to think how he could escape the consequences of his actions. Von Auerbach smiled on him reassuringly, seated him in the only comfortable chair, switched on the brightest light and with a flourish produced a large leather briefcase. It was heavy and black, decorated with a swastika and a German eagle, closed with a business-like brass lock, and also fastened with a steel chain and padlock.

"Your Majesty," he said, "I would not have dared to take this step, except that in my heart I believe the Führer would want me to do so. Though even for him it would be difficult to give the order directly. He is a sensitive man, and appreciates the difficulty involved in your return. I am sure that he would want me to take all steps to ease your mind, to buttress your assurance that your taking your rightful place as King is an act of duty for England's salvation—her *only* salvation. The Führer deeply understands your suffering."

He went on, in a meditative tone, "I have heard, through Vice-Chancellor Hess, of the Führer's own anguish when he realised that he must seize power. Few have understood this, but he had intended only to be Hindenberg's Chancellor. But after the Reichstag fire he had no choice, if he wanted to save Germany."

The Duke's gloom did not appreciably lighten. Von Auerbach noticed, not for the first time, that outside Germany the Reichstag fire was rarely given its proper importance. But he went on smoothly.

"To help you understand the crucial nature of the present situation, he has authorised me to give you a hint —only a hint!—as to what continuing the war would mean. No-one before has ever seen all the papers that I have here." His fingers tapped on the emblem of the eagle. "No one man alive, except the Führer, knows of the existence of all the different projects detailed in these files." That was true, excepting, of course, Admiral Canaris. "The Führer instructed me in these matters himself." It had actually been the Admiral, but von Auerbach thought that mention of the Head of State would be more impressive for the Duke.

"It took me a whole day and we ate our meals as we

222

worked. The ideas were so new to me," he added humbly, "that it was hard to take it all in. The Führer had to call in experts on the various subjects to get it through my thick Army head. Having met you, the Führer felt you would understand, not perhaps each and every technical detail, but the significance of these new weapons that our scientists, those terrifying men, have discovered, and what it would mean to your country if we were forced to use them. I knew it would mean more if you saw the actual documents themselves than if I tried to convey these horrors to you."

He bowed his head gravely. The Admiral had summoned him to Berlin expressly to get these papers and indeed had had to have technical experts to explain them. Certainly they were State secrets, and the Admiral had been taking a risk. But, as he had remarked, this would give their cautious ally the final justification for what he obviously wanted to do, enough to keep his resolution high when he had to face the outside world.

Slowly and deliberately, von Auerbach unbuttoned first his jacket, then his shirt. Round his waist, next to his skin, he wore a flat leather belt. His fingers fumbled for a moment in a hidden pocket, and at length produced a heavy, dull grey key of steel, and a smaller, but intricately notched key of brass. He opened the padlock, removed the chain from the briefcase and let it fall with a clang to the metal surface of the desk. Dexterously, he fiddled with the brass key that was connected to a combination lock. At last he opened the lid, feeling rather than seeing the Duke's fascinated gaze. The case was divided into sections, each section containing a heavy folder stuffed with documents.

"General Becker of the Heereswaffenamt had to give permission for the release of the folders," von Auerbach said with a chuckle, "even for the Führer himself!" Canaris had told him this, and von Auerbach had thought it a good point to make. It had been a long time since the man before him, he who had once had access to all the State papers of a great empire, had seen anything more important than a grocery bill. Power was the great lure, he thought. A man wants power and women. This man had given up power for the love of his woman—only to find he had lost both power and love.

"We'll start on the Wa Pruf weapons," he said. "You'll find it hard to believe, but we have—not just on the drawing board, but going into production—rocket missiles capable of destroying every city in Great Britain. Let me show you . . ."

It was an arduous but worthwhile day's work. With only a brief interval for dinner, they went through every folder in the briefcase. He had to try to summarise for the Duke rocket-powered aircraft, pilotless 'planes and flying bombs. Von Auerbach showed him the anti-aircraft shells that would make retaliation by Great Britain impossible. He showed him sketched details of the infra-red beam, which meant that German guns could shoot with almost a hundred per cent accuracy in total darkness. He showed him pictures of the remote-control boats containing thousand-pound bombs. The Duke gazed horrified at photographs of the Messerschmitt rocket fighter: he had knowledge of airplanes and a real love for the Royal Air Force, von Auerbach recalled, with their old-fashioned aircraft, their amateurish organisation.

He brought out drawings of the midget submarine, the mother-and-child torpedos with the magnetic sensors, and last of all, late at night, he showed him material on the new poison gasses, including their range and effect. The last production was Tabun, one of a group that attacked the central nervous system. Tabun had an album to itself. It contained a series of glossy photographs of the test rabbits and goats, each photograph carefully captioned as to its exact stage in the two-minute cycle, with the descriptive text typewritten below. Each subject had about twenty photographs, beginning at the first stage and showing the vision distorting and the animal blindly running into objects placed in its path.

One pretty little white rabbit especially caught the Duke's gaze, as it bumped, fell, fought pitifully to rise, then ran frantically only to fall again. Then came the drooling, the sweating, the white fur glistening under the relentless camera. He wanted to ask von Auerbach to stop, but his large square hand moved relentlessly to the next page, and the next series. The little rabbit was vomiting, its face strangely distorted with agony as its body contracted with cramp. Then the voiding of the bowels: the white fur stained and soiled, the staggering, the final, helpless collapse where the little thing could struggle no more, and then, in the last set of pictures, the final confusion and something that looked not like a rabbit at all; and at last, mercifully, death.

The Duke was a lover of small animals, and in his way, with his rigid classifications and exclusions, a humanitarian. He had loved his country and her people. They had loved him, idolised him, and he had loved them in return. After his Abdication, when that love had so quickly turned to forgetfulness, he had been hurt and sore. But that hurt and soreness were almost gone as he now convinced himself that they had not forgotten; he was still wanted, loved. It was only a few who had come between them.

He, who had not been able to face the poverty of the unemployed in South Wales during the long, economic slump, could not tolerate the thought of these horrors raining down upon his unsuspecting countrymen. In the First World War there had been horrors enough, but they had been confined to the fighting men: he himself had done his best to take his part. His grief over the sufferings of the men in the trenches, which he had seen for himself, came back to him now as if the years had never passed. He had wanted to be part of their sacrifice, but his position had forbidden it.

In his mind the tortured animals, the shattered bodies in the trenches, the faces of the miners, the working men, those who had stood outside the Palace calling for him as Prince and King, all seemed to call to him now. That position of his, so often hated, for which he had been spared the sacrifice of the first war, now surely must be assumed again for him to protect his people. He, and he alone, could do it. His duty suddenly was quite clear. Already it seemed absurd that he had ever faltered.

The Duke was a small man. 'The little man' his women and his friends had always called him. But as he rose and stood before von Auerbach, suddenly he seemed taller, regal. Fascinated, the scion of the Junkers saw before him a King.

"Of course I will go back," the Monarch spoke. "And we will sign the peace. As soon as the arrangements are complete, you will come for us at the house. My wife and I will be ready."

Just at that moment, the ensign, sent from the Captain once more to inquire about the starting up of the engines, appeared unobtrusively in the doorway. Now was the moment von Auerbach had been waiting for; obviously, it was the time to go. And yet—His Majesty had given an order. For the first time, he was not a pawn. He really was a King, von Auerbach thought with some awe. He paused, for once—as so many had been before him— under this man's spell.

There was no need to carry him off like a thief with a stolen jewel. He would come because he was wanted, needed; and with this majesty upon him, von Auerbach knew that he would sweep all before him. How right the Admiral had been, he thought, touched with a sense of destiny.

He shook his head to the ensign, and escorted the King of England and his Queen to the deck and helped them to disembark. He bowed low before them.

"As you command, Your Majesty," he said, and

watched from the bridge as the launch returned them in utmost dignity to the shore.

Next morning von Auerbach sent a triumphant message to Berlin.

"The Duke awaits the Führer's pleasure."

FOURTEEN

Röslein

While von Auerbach was triumphantly elated in Lisbon, his countryman, Horst Holstein, was in Aberdeen definitely not enjoying himself, even though he was on his pre-marital honeymoon. He disliked the city itself, that was having, as it apparently often did, a cold spell, although today was the 19th of July. The grey, granite city, between two rivers, windswept from the German Ocean, that he had to remember to call the North Sea, resembled nothing else except a damp prison. The thought was not reassuring.

His fiancée was pleased with the modest luxury of their quarters, but to Holstein, who had been instructed to stay in his room as much as possible in order to avoid dangerous encounters, it was, like the rest of Aberdeen, chill, damp and confining. Yet he should have been happy enough, for his mission was going exactly according to plan.

He had had one quick meeting in a public house with the leader of Whaleforce, the big Welshman, Dai Lewis. Lewis had given him a telephone number to memorise. As soon as Jean Sinclair was recalled to duty, the Black Knight was to ring this number from a telephone booth. The dozen men of Whaleforce were waiting in villages near the target and in the small town of Ballater.

The Welshman did not explain to Holstein but it was with the utmost discretion that he had managed to assemble the men. Some of Whaleforce were above call-up age, others were in reserved occupations: nine were on their annual holidays, come to Deeside for the fishing and fresh air like many others; two had jobs in a fish-smoking company; and one was visiting an aunt. This last, Tom Macleish, took Frank Purcell, the demolition expert, with him.

"A nice young fellow, waiting for his call-up papers," Macleish had introduced him casually. "Thought I'd let him see what real fishing is like." Macleish's cousin, Mary, in the interval of trying to get into the WAAF, thought it was a very good idea.

When Black Knight sent the word, Whaleforce were ready to move. The telephone number was to be used only for the signal, except in emergency. The code words were 'Jonah is arriving.'

The Welshman, Holstein observed, was a very different type from Jarndyce, with the manner and dress of a labourer, a miner perhaps. Lewis was actually a foreman in the coal mines, but had started as pit boy and had worked as a miner for ten years. A dour man, he spoke little. The public house, perhaps, made him wary.

"We're not being watched. I am sure of that. But it's best we all have as little connection as possible. Cut the risk."

He buried his face in a tankard of stout, and as some other patrons walked by their table, he spoke about soccer and his recent win on the pools. Before they left they went to the Gents and he gave Holstein the address of a house in Aberdeen to memorise. It was the home of a Scotswoman, a postal worker, who also worked for the Abwehr but until now only as a forwarding agent. Lewis would be there every night until eleven o'clock. Should it be necessary to meet again, Black Knight was to go there in person after dark.

Idly, Holstein wondered what had brought this

scowling man with the huge, gnarled hands into the Abwehr network. He had heard that many Welsh miners were Reds, agitating now about increased work schedules. With a war on! If that was why this Lewis was supporting the Reich, he was in for some surprises. But Holstein's mind soon went back to his own situation.

He was not an imaginative man, but when he had first received his orders—and from Major Leiter himself!—he had been awed at their magnitude. The King of England! This was not the assassination of a Polish official or a clergyman who might have roused the people against the occupation by the Reich. Nor the surreptitious murder of some recalcitrant Frenchman who did not like the idea of the peaceful settlement with the German conquerors. Even the quiet dispatch of an awkward Russian general on the wrong side of the new border seemed like child's play compared with this.

But Major Leiter had told him bluntly that this was not so. There was very little protection for the Royal Family at the best of times, except in Windsor Castle, and in his extraordinarily privileged position he might meet no opposition at all. Incredible as that had sounded, he now could see it was true.

No wonder the Führer expected to take this country easily. They were, as he had been told, decadent. Although partly a Nordic race, they had been corrupted by inferior blood. Germany would have a great cleansing to do here. If he were still in the SS, he would be working with the cleansing units now. Certainly, he thought irritably, he would far rather have been there than penned up in this hotel room with the insatiable, but so boring, Jean.

Although he knew this work was of great importance —the highest—he also knew, practically, that Abwehr agents rarely received much fruit from their labours. It was not like the SS, where honour and glory came to the brave, and the taking of booty was encouraged. Of course in the early days it had to be—the SS had got no pay. Now he was afraid that in the name of diplomacy, someone might yet decide he should actually marry this Jean.

Major Leiter had made him promises. But he didn't know that he trusted Major Leiter. For the man who brought off this coup, he had hinted, the position of Gauleiter of Scotland might not be too much. Holstein smiled for a moment—his mother would certainly stretch her eyes at that! But he soon returned to his brooding. It was true that there had been such swift promotions in the Party. But the Abwehr was tricky. He had soon learned. A mongrel gang. Nothing like the honourable band of brothers that was the SS. Not all Abwehr agents were even Nazis, and that went for men in a position of command. He had turned over a few in his time to the Gestapo. After this, there would be a few more. After this! If only it was time to move. He turned to Jean impatiently.

"Are you sure they'll call you to the telephone when the message comes?"

Jean was prancing about the room, the picture of joy.

"Man, it's another fine day," she sang out exuberantly. "Oh, they'll send someone up. Though I wish they wouldn't," she said with a grin.

Although she had not yet dressed, because of the cold she had pulled on her woollen knickers and vest. The vest was pink and the knickers were heavy and dark blue. It was not an alluring sight. Jean had had no clothing coupons to get herself a 'honeymoon' outfit and was too used to Scottish chills to consider the garments unusual. Holstein, who had spent some time in Paris before leaving for Lisbon, sighed. The young Marian Jarndyce had been better than that. He thought of those railings and grinned. Quite often, he regretted the day he had met Jean Sinclair in Munich. Certainly he regretted talking about it on that happy night in the café.

He lit a cigarette—an English cigarette which he did not like—thinking bitterly how a perfectly normal act of pleasure had distorted his whole life. A long detour, bringing him to war-time Britain. The telephone booth, where he had stood, with Marian Jarndyce outside, telling Jean the 'good news'.

The news was that he had escaped from Germany and had joined the British Army. Jean, though overjoyed, was not essentially surprised. Sanguine, she had always been sure that somehow he would manage to do so.

Her last letter, stating this conviction, had pleased Canaris, as Head of the Abwehr, immensely. As a father, another part of him was rather touched by the foolish, romantic Röslein. When it was all over, he reflected, he would do one thing for her. He would take Horst Holstein far away.

'Henry Holbrook' had told Jean he was on thirty days' embarkation leave. He had an engagement ring, and they would marry before he left. Because of his special situation, he had to get permission from his Captain; there was no doubt it would be forthcoming but as the Captain was away for a few days, he had arranged for a clerk in the orderly room to telephone him in Aberdeen as soon as the Captain returned.

And so they were on their pre-marital honeymoon, which already seemed to have gone on forever, though this was only the fifth day.

Jean had poked gentle fun at him for being a mere private. For some reason this stung.

"Are you sure they will telephone from Birkhall if you are needed?" he asked again. It was already Friday but no word had come.

"Oh, yes. I wish they wouldn't but they will," Jean said, biting the back of his neck. "And that manageress will know where to find me. She's been looking daggers at me for days." She giggled. It was an irritating sound.

Jean had told him when they went to the quiet hotel that they would have to book two rooms, as their identity cards must be shown, making it obvious they were not yet man and wife. But Jean was careless, and hated to leave his warm bed in the morning before the chambermaid came, to go and rumple her own. Holstein, too, had seen the way the manageress looked at his affianced bride. If it were not war-time, and he in the King's uniform, he had a good guess that Jean would have been asked to leave. This, too, annoyed him. He only hoped that they would never have to marry. Such a girl to be Frau Holstein! His mother, he thought, would be shocked.

"It is your duty to go," he told her.

She laughed out loud. "Oh, Henry, you do sound like a German."

He scowled.

"But Mrs Donald always calls. She won't get one meal ready without me, she'll send Arthur in the estate car. She always sends him for me at home. Henry, do you think I should give in my notice? I hate to work while you're here."

That was a bad moment. He had to show a lot of patriotic fervour to point out to Jean that she must honour her commitment to the Royal Family.

"Well, I don't suppose they could get anyone to take my place so quick," Jean said and sighed. "But after we're married, I think I'll leave. I could be more useful in the ATS. I'd really like the Wrens better, but I couldn't get in. I dearly love the wee hat," she said dreamily.

Holstein assumed she was talking about the Women's Services. Jean in 1940 was very different—except in bed —from the Jean of '36. She had become very British, forgetting the talk among her friends of England's tyranny and Scotland's shame. The Queen, her 'lady' being Scottish, and the war had driven all that out of her silly head. It made his task more awkward. In his long discussions with Major Leiter and Colonel Lahousen on the best method for this assassination—that must seem like a peaceful, natural death, unsuspected even if a post mortem were performed—they had considered Jean herself taking the active part, knowingly, or being just a little more deceived. That would have eliminated any possible risk. The decision had been left for him to make when they met again.

But now he saw *that* was impossible. Jean was very far from being a willing accessory to his plan. Despite her love for him, this Jean of 1940 might well call the police. And he did not think he could add one more enormous piece of deception. She had swallowed so many tall tales, one more might topple the whole edifice. Besides, it involved physical action on her part, and although her dreamy mind seemed to be able to contemplate anything she wished, he felt shrewdly that her common sense might assert itself if she were asked to do something within her professional competence. After all, she had been a nurse. Even a girl as love-crazed as Jean wouldn't be that stupid.

She slid her arms about his body, eagerly seeking love, and more love. He stubbed his cigarette out in annoyance. She had to be kept happy. But he had never felt less inclined for amorous exercise. From the good food at Birkhall Jean had become stouter. Her tiny nose, that had once amused him, now seemed too small for her face. Her delicate skin, with the wild rose flush, was becoming coarsened. He did his duty, making love to this patriotic Britisher, thinking grimly that it was a far cry from his days and nights of pleasure in Munich with his charming little Röslein.

FIFTEEN

The Master Moved

Foreign Minister Joachim von Ribbentrop had been delighted to receive the cable from von Auerbach. This was excellent news. The Windsor Plot he had felt from the first was peculiarly his own, although of course Admiral Canaris would want to take all the credit. It had been he, after Ambassador Hoesch, who had conveyed to the Führer the admiration, later the friendship, felt for him by King Edward. It was his conversations with the Führer on the subject that had been the springboard of this whole affair. Now, how delicious that it should be his man, von Auerbach, who was triumphant, where Heydrich's gang had so signally failed! The Foreign Minister was in such a state of excitement that he paused only to comb his thinning hair, and tease it up into a cockscomb, before rushing over to the Chancellery.

The Führer was gracious and received him in his study, with Reichsmarschall Göring present. It was the Führer's preference, as a rule, to see people one at a time. This was the bane of the Wehrmacht, who loved conferences, but the Führer was well aware of what he did, and von Ribbentrop understood. The Führer's compelling magnetism worked best in either intimate situations or before great crowds. The fact that he himself was admitted now showed how high he stood in the

Führer's good graces. And he was to go higher.

When he showed the message to the Führer, a smile broke out on his face.

"I knew it!" he cried. "He is my friend. I always knew I could rely on him." He showed it to the Reichsmarschall. "You see, we are ready."

He turned to von Ribbentrop.

"I don't know why we are waiting. Why the Admiral is holding back."

Von Ribbentrop tried to look intelligent. He had not realised there was anything being held back. Canaris had not informed him, or anyone outside the Abwehr, of the details of the plot. He had never heard of Röslein or Black Knight. But he had sense enough to know that if the Admiral was waiting for something, he probably knew what he was doing. On the other hand, he fancied that that was not what the Führer wished to hear, so he remained silent.

Göring chuckled hugely.

"You know how these old Navy men are." He used the singular form *du* which few people used to the Führer now. "Wait, wait. Caution, caution. Look how terrified they are of Sea Lion."

Von Ribbentrop wondered if the Führer really intended to go ahead with Sea Lion. To invade England . . .

"Wait for them and you will really miss the boat," Göring said with easy contempt. "The '*Kieker*' is nervous because he doesn't have enough men. I told you, he needs the Luftwaffe to take in a few paratroopers. Now you have the Duke, my men will get them in and it's all over."

Göring, resplendent in yet another new summer uniform, confident and in good humour, was hard for the Führer to resist.

"I think you're right," Hitler responded. "I have thought so all along. But the Admiral wishes to have all the glory."

236

He brooded for a moment. The Spanish situation was also dragging on far too long. Hermann's idea of sending the subtle Canaris, Franco's friend, to conclude the negotiations was a good one. Perhaps two birds could be killed with one stone . . . He slammed his fist down on the table.

"It shall be done! I leave it to you, Reichsmarschall."

Von Ribbentrop became alarmed. The Admiral had been managing very well. After all, it had been Canaris' idea to send von Auerbach to Lisbon. And the Foreign Minister knew what the Abwehr chief would think of Göring meddling in his careful plans.

He coughed.

"Perhaps you would like me to set up consultations with Admiral Canaris, *mein Führer.*"

But the Führer had already turned away to nod to his adjutant who appeared at the study door.

"I will attend to the Admiral," he said, almost absent-mindedly. "Luncheon is ready. You will stay and discuss some matters, while you are here. And you, Reichsmarschall?"

Göring, with a temerity that von Ribbentrop envied, said hastily that he was entertaining certain Wehrmacht generals at a luncheon and made his escape. And so it was von Ribbentrop who was left to lunch off the hated *Gemüsuppe.* He wondered, gloomily, how he was going to explain this to the Admiral. The very nasty vegetable soup gave him indigestion. He decided the best thing he could do would be to say nothing.

Like von Ribbentrop, the Admiral had been pleased to get von Auerbach's signal. This time he believed him; there was a note of authenticity in the message. Besides, other informants in Lisbon had reported that the Duke and Duchess were keeping close to their borrowed house, the Duchess having an unseasonal attack of the 'flu.

Now it was only a matter of waiting for the message to Röslein. According to the established pattern, it would come on a Thursday or Friday. He could not bring himself to leave his office: true, the Scottish part would go forward with no more instruction from himself—it would be over, in part, before he received word at all. But as soon as he did, von Auerbach must move the Duke—the King, as he would be. Certainly, Leiter could transmit the message to Lisbon, yet Canaris felt that he himself must be present for the climax. He, personally, wanted to take the game.

It turned out that this was not too easy to arrange. To his surprise, he was summoned again to the Chancellery. There Hitler told him, with great casualness, that he was to proceed to Madrid.

"I have decided to put 'Felix' into operation," he said.

'Felix' was the plan to take Gibralter. The Führer had been negotiating with the Generalissimo for months. The Generalissimo was the only person who seemed to be able to negotiate with the Führer, get what he wanted, and give nothing in return. The Admiral admired him. He loved Spain and often dreamed of living there when he retired. He could finally get warm. But he could hardly go now.

"But, *mein Führer,*" he expostulated, "surely von Stohrer . . ."

"Von Stohrer is a fool," Hitler said angrily. "He talks and talks and gets nowhere. It is necessary that we take Gibralter now. In a week or two, at most a month, England will be our ally. It would be embarrassing to take Gibralter then. But now, while we are still at war, it is simple. Then we will control the Mediterranean. So if any British generals in North Africa do not like the peace— well, it will be too late for them."

As usual, there was some sense in what the Führer said.

"But Operation Green is not completed," the Admi-

238

ral said in protest. "I must be here to see that all goes well."

The Führer waved his hand.

"I understand your feelings. But you have done everything. It is just a matter of time now, is it not so? I have your last report before me. And you have your staff. You must be like me, my dear Admiral. You must learn to delegate. The Abwehr has a large budget," he said, smiling. "You must have some capable men who can finish off the details."

"Colonel Piekenbrock has not yet returned from Norway," the Admiral said miserably. What the Führer said was true, of course, and yet—

"I need you as a statesman. There are few enough. I know that the Generalissimo likes you. You can pin him down, as you have done with the Duke."

What made him so sure of that? the Admiral wondered, instantly suspicious.

The Führer, turning on all his charm, put his hand on the Admiral's shoulder. "You will do this for me, my friend."

An hour later the Admiral was explaining to the stunned Major Leiter that he was going to be responsible for the day-to-day command of Operation Green, the coup d'état that was to change the history of Europe, the Windsor Plot itself.

On July 21, von Auerbach learned of the change in command. He was displeased. To receive his instructions from the Foreign Minister was normal; to be assigned to Admiral Canaris for this project was acceptable, but to take orders from a mere Major Leiter was degrading. But he consoled himself, he already had his orders. All Leiter had to do was to send the signal to move, which he probably would have done in any event.

He had no worries about his 'King and Queen' now. The Duke of Coburg, prompted by von Ribbentrop who understood the Duchess, had sent him, by messenger, some family heirlooms: a brooch with Prince Albert's hair, some letters, and a large signed portrait of his grandmother, Queen Victoria, which might amuse the Duchess. Knowing that seclusion must be tedious to such a social-minded woman, he took them up to the house just before dinner time.

The Duchess, though about to dress for dinner, had been delighted. Suddenly very gay, she had gone to stir up the kitchen, and left him on the balcony with the extremely majestic Duke. The conversation had been grave until the servant came in with a trolley of cocktail drinks and dishes, from which savoury steam was emanating.

"Aren't I clever?" the Duchess' voice came gaily. Delicious waves of scent preceded her as she came in behind the servant, dressed in a long floating garment of shocking pink chiffon and feathers, looking like a rosy cloud. She carried a matching wrap of feathers and a pink chiffon scarf. The portrait of Queen Victoria, propped against the wall, seemed to gaze upon her sternly.

The Duchess wrinkled her nose at the Royal disapproval, and covered it with her wrap.

"Pretty Vicky," she said soothingly and giggled.

Although the daylight lingered, the servant lit the lamp. It was too bright, the effect harsh. The Duchess, quick to observe a domestic disharmony, draped her scarf across the top of the shade. Suddenly, the terrace was bathed in a warm, rosy glow.

"There! Now, gentlemen, admit the feminine genius."

Von Auerbach bowed low.

"Your Majesty, were you a Roman empress, we would proclaim you a goddess on the spot."

This led to a happy discussion on the title and style of Her Majesty the Queen.

"Since your first Christian name is Bessie, you could easily be Queen Elizabeth," von Auerbach pointed out.

He, the Admiral and von Ribbentrop had thought that the best plan. The English preferred the familiar. As the new Queen Elizabeth, behaving with due decorum, she would slide unobtrusively into her role and in the minds of the average Englishman Mrs Simpson would soon be forgotten.

But the Duchess, usually so amenable to his suggestions, was unexpectedly obstinate. Bessiewallis. She had never liked her name, and had been Wallis since she was adult. Elizabeth was well enough, but if she were Queen Elizabeth, who would remember, after a time, that it was she, Wallis Warfield? Who in Baltimore would know or care? At the idea, her anger came, swift as a blow—it was as though once more her cup was to be dashed from her lips. Von Auerbach did not understand, but he saw the danger signals, the darkening of the brow, the ominous flash of her eyes. For a moment the rosy fripperies looked incongruous against her harsh countenance.

He could always return to it later. Now he had to win back her good graces, and her confidence. She was much entertained by the Coburg letters, and read aloud Queen Victoria's comments on Buckingham Palace.

" '. . . a . . . disgrace . . . not one hole to put the children into . . . the nursery is a mile from our apartments . . . Albert has to drag the younger ones in a basket along the corridors.' She complained that the drains were terrible. Few of the doors would shut. Most of the bells were broken, and all the chimneys smoked. Six hundred rooms," the Duchess added, "imagine!"

"Still the same," the Duke replied. "Hardly habitable. Buck House was built over an open sewer by a man used to designing prisons. The heating system was put in in George IV's day."

The Duchess laughed.

"You never told me that before. Were you afraid of frightening me, David? I'm not frightened a bit. I'll call in an American firm for the plumbing and heat. And an architect so that we have some rooms to live in. Structure, you have to start with that. But the White Drawing-Room sounds marvellous. I want to give a huge, super party. You'd better hurry up with the peace, or people will say, 'You can't do that in wartime.' "

Von Auerbach smiled.

"And what is that Royal Closet?" she rattled on. "It sounds delicious. Perhaps we could make a little cocktail bar."

"Why not?" the Duke said gaily. Wallis was right. And he felt even more sure she was right from seeing the very slight, quickly disguised disapproval on the face of von Auerbach. A young man, but a tiresome old Junker just the same. Queen Elizabeth indeed!

Buck House was musty and needed change. He had always called it 'the Sepulchre'. And he liked Wallis to be just as she was. He joined her in a Scotch and water, feeling that already they had begun their new life.

Then the Duchess' scarf, scorching on the lamp, smoked and made a disagreeable smell that drove them from the balcony.

"You can stay and take pot luck with us, Friedrich," the Duchess said, "but I've seen the dinner and it looks very dull. The Esperito-Santos made off with the head chef, and even the one that is left is sick most of the time from the heat."

"Why not have dinner on board the boat?" von Auerbach suggested.

It was as well, he thought, that the Duke should remain accustomed to the vessel. "I can let them know while you are dressing."

The Duke frowned at the thought of the U-boat.

"Oh, do let's," the Duchess said. "I'm so tired of the dining-room and it was fun before. Friedrich," she said laughing, "did you know we crept out in our stockinged feet? David, tell the servants I don't want any dinner. And give them the evening off. We will go very quietly while they're having their dinner—they must eat huge meals, they're at it for hours. No-one will notice we're gone."

"If you wish it, my dear," the Duke replied, as he always did, and von Auerbach rushed off to make his arrangements.

The evening went well, though not quite as well as von Auerbach supposed. The Duke had not told his wife but he had always been troubled by slight claustrophobia in a submarine. The smells of metal, oil and disinfectant rekindled it, not troubling him so much while he was aboard surrounded by the gaiety of Wallis and von Auerbach but later, back at the house, in the silence and the dark of his own room.

His mind went back to his last visit, and von Auerbach's locked briefcase full of menace. He tossed and turned, knowing he was shut into a small space from which he could not escape, shining steel, welded tight without a crack for air. It shone bright, grew wider and turned into England itself; England, a locked and airless space under a rain of fire, her people gasping and dying in the poisoned atmosphere. Total panic came and jolted him awake, sweat pouring from his body, the reality of his dark room somehow without comfort.

He lay quivering, and vowed to himself that nothing would prevent his return home. Whatever the future might bring, anything was preferable to England suffering that onslaught. He was firm in his resolution that he would save his country.

At last he fell asleep once more. But his terror resumed. This time Bertie appeared, dressed in a sailor suit as he had been long ago, a child at Balmoral. He was gasping and crying, partly from the poisoned gas, partly because they were visiting his great-grandmother, Queen Victoria, who, he believed, was a witch.

She stepped out of the picture frame, tossing aside Wallis' pink scarf, and looked on them with royal displeasure.

"Save me, David, save me," Bertie cried, holding out his hands, gasping. "Save me!" And he was in his nightshirt, dying, until he faded into Wallis who was abruptly shaking his own shoulder. Waking up was like coming through deep water.

"Bertie wants me to save him," he told the Duchess, shaking, clutching her hand.

"You will," she said, in her strong voice that always had been enough to banish nightmare. "You're going to him, any day now."

But his sleep-puzzled mind didn't know whether in order to save Bertie he should go forward or go back.

"Wallis, perhaps we shouldn't go?"

"Not go?" she said. It was hardly a question.

"Perhaps it's a mistake. Going against orders—"

"But why? We're going to do the country a service. You of all people know that."

She opened his door and called imperiously into the dark until Manuel came, his eyes still half-closed, dressed sumptuously in a dark silk dressing-gown that once had been his master's.

"Coffee. And brandy. Quick!"

Before she would let the Duke speak again, she gave him two hot, strong cups of coffee with plenty of sugar and brandy. Fully awake, but almost as depressed, he rubbed the back of his neck nervously. His mind was still confused.

"It's all so complicated," he said tiredly. "Von Auerbach is so sure—but suppose he makes a mess of everything. Think, Wallis, if we fail—"

She grinned and squeezed his wrist.

"But screw your courage to the sticking point and we'll not fail."

She had switched on all the lights. He stared at her. With her stark white nightgown and sleek dark hair she was a study in harsh contrasts. He was sure she didn't realise she was quoting from *Macbeth*—her education had

been limited. Even worse than his own. No, she would not
. . . But it was an unfortunate choice. For the first time,
in an odd, painful stirring, he felt something for this
woman that was not love.

Satisfied with her ministrations, the Duchess turned
out the lights, and stayed in the room with her husband.
She went easily to sleep but the Duke spent the remaining
night hours staring into the dark, listening to the wind off
the ocean, feeling that he was being carried somewhere
beyond his knowledge, closer, closer to—what?

But in the morning, the horrors faded. The Duchess
was once again her beloved self, chic and gay. She drank
her coffee on his bed, and in her aura of charming feminin-
ity the night was soon forgotten, as though it had never
been.

SIXTEEN

The Chocolate Soldier

After the household had been disturbed in the middle of the night, the maid Maria had felt rather sleepy the next day. But it was to be a good day. She was overjoyed to see the red-headed British soldier return suddenly, unexpectedly, to the Boca Do Inferno. Apart from her son, little Jorge, who received a present of English chocolate and a box of scarlet-painted British soldiers, she was the only one who showed any joy at all. On the other hand, Prime Minister Churchill's bodyguard had been excessively pleased to see him go.

This had been the great man's excuse for sending Rex back to Lisbon.

"I think you've harried and chivvied them long enough," he had said jovially. "I'd better pack you off before one of them breaks down and 'rubs you out' as my mother's countrymen would put it. A nice holiday in a warm climate," he added, beaming.

Rex was unimpressed.

"You want me to have another gander at what His Nibs is up to," he said bluntly.

The Prime Minister looked pained.

"You are talking about your Major-General."

He could not quite meet Rex's gaze and re-lit his cigar for the tenth time. It was hard for him to admit—

246

even to himself—the thoughts about his former King that now bedevilled him. Ambassador Selby sent comforting assurances. The Duke had booked passage on a neutral ship to Bermuda, where he would transfer to a small vessel that would take him to the Bahamas. The ship, the *Excalibur,* was leaving Lisbon on the 1st of August. Well and good. Yet rumours were coming thick and fast from neutral embassies about the Duke's new friendship with a young German diplomat, Friedrich von Auerbach. A family connection, of course, but . . .

There was nothing more he could do. Mere rumours. If there was proof of anything improper on the Duke's part, say, double dealing, a scheme to change his mind at the last minute and bolt to Spain— No, nonsense. Whenever he thought of it, he was sure it was all nonsense. But the 1st of August was almost two weeks off and he kept on thinking about it. He was tired of thinking about it. No-one was more suspicious of the Duke than Sergeant Barney. If there was any solid evidence of all this, Barney would be the one to find it. So he had decided to send him back.

"But as long as you're lolling about in the sun there," he said casually, "forgetting there's a war on, you could use what Hilliard calls your criminal talents to check on things. They're supposed to be leaving on the 1st of August," he added casually.

Criminal talents. Rex had gazed at him sardonically. He hoped nothing would happen to the old man while he was following his orders. The way Sergeant Barney was loved by the coppers, with the old man gone they'd put him away for fifty years.

He remembered his Dunkirk leave, and his father yarning one night with an old buffer he'd known from the First World War, who'd served for years in Naval Intelligence. Apart from the usual tales of the loonies in the Secret Service and the shambles it was left in, he'd talked a lot about the Germans and the way they worked. He'd only been half listening, waiting for opening time, but he remembered the geezer saying that if someone was given a dicey job, and a lot of grief might be expected from the brass, he was given something called a *Führerbefehl*. A written order saying that whatever he was doing it was all right. It took precedence over all other law. Pity for him there was no such thing as a Churchillbefehl. For a moment he had a pleasant thought or two of what a man might do with it. Walk into the Tower and out with a few of the Crown jewels . . . He supposed it was just as well there was not. Wouldn't do to have a lot of sods Befehling about.

The officials at the airport, who had shown little interest in him on his first visit, now were actively unpleasant. They held him while his papers were checked by four different people, and someone was called in from the British Embassy. Finding nothing wrong, they had to let him through, but no-one looked happy. Sergeant Barney had been making a name for himself, he thought, but how? Either Manuel had charged him with alienation of Maria's affection, or the Duke had told people he wasn't nice to know. He put his money on the Duke.

Though Manuel was sulky enough at his return, it was nothing compared to the reception he got from the people upstairs. The Duchess was the first one to see him. She was just lifting herself from the pool, the water running from her sleek head and body in a dark glistening bathing suit. To Barney there was nothing seductive in her appearance, the water might have been running from a rock, and the look she gave him was enough to change a man into stone.

The sergeant and the Duchess regarded each other for a long moment. The Duchess' antagonism was strong enough to bite. She was quick to guess that he was there to put a spoke in her wheel he thought, but it was more than that. Of course, she was used to her little man and other tame pets. Afraid of a dog off a leash—'Dirty Dog'.

Her nose quivered and her body shook.

She left silently, but she was not silent for long. For once she went straight to the Duke, and his roars were heard all over the house. He was demanding that the pool be fenced off from intruders, from peeping Toms, that the British Ambassador be summoned, and that this impudent soldier be put in the guardhouse.

Rex's own quiet presentation of his orders had no soothing effect, nor the fact that as no-one had answered the front door, his only ingress had been round by the pool. He repeated the story the Prime Minister had given him: as the Duke had again asked for his servant, and Fletcher was away on manouevres with his company, Sergeant Barney had been sent in his place.

A very nasty few hours followed. The Ambassador was jolted from his afternoon rest and had to make the journey to the Boca Do Inferno on this ridiculous matter of the soldier-servant. Rex well knew he would never be forgiven.

The Duchess had been particularly disturbed at the theft of her emerald and diamond brooch. Apart from its monetary value, it had been a gift to replace the Denmark emeralds, once hers, then so rudely taken away. When the brooch itself was taken the feeling that nothing she possessed would ever be allowed to remain her own became stronger. The Duke suffered for her and for himself. The theft reminded him, too, of the insult—of all the insults. When he learned that most of the other stolen items had been recovered along Ferdi's trail, he had suspected it was quite a different thief, under the shield of Ferdi's depredations, who had stolen the £20,000 brooch—quite out of the class of the Lisbon boy.

While Rex was in England the Duke had made some inquiries about him. He had heard a story that this Barney, before he became a war hero, had been one of a London gang of criminals. This story had been circulated, and had caused Rex's troubles at the airport. Now the

Duke, furious, bellowed to Sir Walford that this Barney was a thief. Sir Walford was embarrassed. Certainly the brooch was missing and as well as the Duchess' jewels, there were many costly things in the house, left by the Esperito-Santos. Yet the Duke had no reason to suspect this soldier, other than rumor and his own dislike. The soldier's attitude was not soothing.

"It's no good listening to him, guv," Rex said. "He's got himself into a paddy, that's all there is to it. And I happen to be here on orders."

The orders were perfectly valid. Even if the man had been a thief in peace-time, which Sir Walford thought would not be surprising, there was nothing that could be done, except to refer the matter back to the officer who had assigned the man to this duty in the first place. The Ambassador's staff knew very well how to refer any subject back to the people who must handle it. But the Duke was so vehement that Sir Walford was put to sending cables immediately. Such information as he got in return was hardly helpful. According to Scotland Yard, Sergeant Barney had no police record except for street fighting. The Ambassador asked the Military Attaché if anything could be done to get Sergeant Barney recalled from the Duke's service, and the Military Attaché, after frantic consultations, came back with a message that if the Duke would content himself with Sergeant Barney for a few days, it was hoped that Fletcher, once finished with his manoeuvres, would be restored to him in time for his voyage to the Bahamas. With that they had to be satisfied, and the Ambassador, with a sigh of relief, went home to his charming Residence, and spent the evening trying to soothe his jangled nerves.

The Duchess, who had developed a migraine, was in her room, where her suitcases, already packed, were crowding her uncomfortably. The Duke looked out over the balcony, wondering when von Auerbach would arrive. He would have to do something about that soldier before they left. If he was hazy in his mind about just what he wanted done, he was very certain that he wanted it.

Maria went to Rex in the privacy of his cubby-hole, where Manuel had once again assigned him. After a warm embrace she gave him the news of the house. The Esperito-Santo's chauffeur had returned to the Duke's service. This meant Rex wouldn't be able to drive the Duke —he wouldn't have too much chance to spot what he was up to. The cook was ill with summer fever; Manuel, who was cooking for upstairs as well as all his other duties, refused to provide the traveller with any food, and so Maria fried four eggs and brought them to him with some rolls. At least it was something a human being could eat, Rex thought resignedly.

He had observed that the Ambassador thought he might be there to nick something. After being detached from his regiment and sent all the way to Portugal on special orders. Well, there was a lot of good stuff about and no mistake. The Duchess wore enough slung around herself to look like a Christmas tree, but it was the genuine article. It would fetch a packet in London now. Thinking over the rather tempting idea, stretched out on his bed, full of food, with Maria massaging his neck and shoulders —there was nothing wrong with his neck and shoulders, but she seemed to like the work—he dreamed for a while in a land of lost content.

Then Maria was called away to the Duchess. Roaming about, Rex came across Jorge, crying. With few words understood between them, Rex nevertheless gathered that Jorge had been forbidden his surreptitious use of the pool. No-one seemed to be about in the gardens, so Rex threw a ball for Jorge to catch. Then he showed him the rudiments of kicking as used in soccer. Jorge was transformed with delight, and when Barney looked at his watch and decided it was time to go down to the village, it seemed a pity to leave the boy, so he took him along.

The young fellow who owned the motor-bike was

hunched over his dinner when they arrived. Fish and rice —it didn't look tasty. Rex had brought him a bottle of wine, which made his eyes brighten, and then quickly resumed their arrangements about the BSA. Jorge squealed in delight as Rex drove him back to the house, his small brown arms clutched firmly round Rex's waist as he did a few sharp turns to please the kid. The Esperito-Santo's chauffeur was a decent sort, and made no trouble about him putting the bike in the back of the garage. He invited the English soldier to take a glass of wine with him later. In the meantime Jorge was still full of energy, and ran out of the house through the open gates, hiding from the soldier behind the scattered pines, waiting hopefully until he was found. It was hot for such scrambling about, but Rex felt sorry for the kid who had no-one to play with. He remembered climbing the back fences with Larry, and a couple of dozen boys always ready to join in their games. He threw off his battle dress jacket and followed Jorge who was running, darting, finding cover on the territory so familiar to him, even on the sparsely covered ground. Soon they were quite a distance from the house, and he found Jorge in a sheltered cove that he had not previously noticed.

It was dusk now. Maria would be wondering about her child. He was about to pick him up and make for the house, when Jorge excitedly pointed out some object off shore. Rex peered into the gathering dusk—a fishing boat, perhaps, with a friend on board. At first he saw nothing, then a slender line, dark against the twilight.

The periscope submerged again, but soon the boat surfaced. Then the ensign was raised on the masthead, a black swastika on a white circle, set in a blazing red background. Well, there were enough of them in Lisbon harbour. Everyone knew that. But all the way up here—why? The answer came almost before the question. But surely, even *he* wouldn't do that. The old man was so certain he was going to the Bahamas. But, of course, he wasn't certain. If he had been he wouldn't have sent Rex Barney to Cascais.

His brow was creased in perplexity. The presence of a U-boat offshore, though suspicious, was not proof of anything. If he telephoned the old man, he would probably only pooh-pooh him again. He went back to the house, with a few questions in mind he wanted to ask Maria.

Maria was with the Duchess, and he had to wait. In the meantime he had his glass of wine with the chauffeur Rodrigues, a middle-aged friendly man with an olive complexion, pitted with smallpox scars, but apart from that like chauffeurs everywhere. He talked cars, his approval of his employer, his dislike of the Duke and Duchess, and how he had always had a fancy for Maria, but his wife was a jealous virago, and that Manuel was a nasty customer.

His English was good enough so that Rex could steer the conversation, after a little man-to-man sympathy, back to the Duke.

"Certainly, he is no friend of yours," Rodrigues commented. Obviously, he too had done some listening through the not-so-soundproof panel. But his next remark startled Rex.

Rodrigues bent closer. "He is afraid you are with the British Secret Police."

This took some sorting out. Eventually, Rex gathered he meant the Secret Service. He was really taken aback. Of all the people likely to be approached by the Secret Service, he was probably the last—the Duke surely knew that. Rodrigues saw his puzzlement.

"You were seen. In the café," he went on in hushed tones.

Rex could not imagine what he was talking about. Two glasses of wine later, he had learned that the café to which he had gone in all innocence, hoping for eggs and chips, was known to be a meeting place for secret agents. Another glass, and Rodrigues told him that the man to

253

whom he had been talking was without doubt a British spy.

Puzzled, Rex looked at him, wondering if this was all just rubbish, a tale passed on from one kitchen to another, growing over each coffee cup and wine glass as it went. But Rodrigues, though a gossip, didn't look like a fool. Rex thought of the small café in the Rua Gambetta, and the shabby Englishman with the eye-patch. More like a tout than a spy. He might have been a stringer, peddling odd bits of information to the Service—when there was a Service. No wonder their Royal High and Mightinesses had been so upset to see him come back. Maria was a long time with the Duchess and he encouraged Rodrigues to go on talking, but he learned little more.

The Duchess was dressing and needed Maria's services. She had recovered enough to want company. Her engagements, it seemed, had been cancelled prematurely. Von Auerbach had not arrived with the summons. But in the meantime, to amuse his lady, the Duke had invited the Graf to dinner. The Duchess was pleased with that. Underneath her testiness about her isolation, she was deeply concerned that the Duke might waver. Though this time he appeared to be strong.

Von Auerbach himself had been waiting anxiously. Perhaps he should have carried them off last night when they had come aboard the U-boat. Or even last Thursday. But Admiral Canaris had been so very strict about the timing. The last thing he had told von Auerbach was that he must wait for the word from Berlin. The Admiral had been afraid for the Duke to land too soon. They must wait for the precise moment. Canaris had been sure it would come. That it would be, if not this week, then next. But almost certainly this week.

After Maria had dressed the Duchess, she had to go straight to wait at the table. She heard little of interest, the talk was general until the servants withdrew. Then the

254

Duke went to the only subject that mattered and asked about his brother's health and why they were not leaving.

"He is lingering, but there is no chance of recovery. The end will be very soon." Von Auerbach went quickly into what he thought of as the sweetmeats. "Your Majesty's proclamation is being arranged. Lloyd George wants one to be made at Caernarvon Castle simultaneously with the one at St James's. There is great enthusiasm, I understand, among the Welsh. And the Irish—even the Free State is being cooperative. They are prepared to give, if not allegiance, immediate recognition. Of course, we've had to make *them* a few promises."

"What?" the Duke asked, his eyes a little prominent.

"Not to put too fine a point on it, their wretched six counties," von Auerbach shrugged. "Of course, we will have no authority after the peace treaty so don't let it disturb you."

The Duke cleared his throat with a cough like a controlled explosion. He sounded so much like his father that, were he not so angry, he would have been taken aback himself. His new majesty was very much upon him.

"You won't need to be bothered about the Irish," von Auerbach said, misunderstanding. "The Führer would never encourage them far. Quarrelsome and untrustworthy. If they cause any difficulties, the Führer will assist in dealing with them."

"That won't be necessary," the Duke said, very coldly.

This von Auerbach was disgusting, he thought. How Leo ever came to have a younger brother like that! A fine old family. Soldiers, statesmen. And now this. He looked at his plate grimly, not noticing that the food that Manuel had been at such pains to prepare. Sometimes, it was recognised, promises had to be given that could not, later, be fulfilled. But this man was so blithe about his treacheries. He could make a king feel like a conspirator. Certainly, he had to be put in his place. These Nazis. For the first time he thought, with a new clarity, that Germany would have to get rid of them before all was done. The Hohenzollern line should be restored. His great-grandmother would have approved of that. But he, and England, could not use power they didn't have. He would have to use these people to get the peace, but after . . .

The Duke felt better, with his discomforts now laid firmly at the door of the Nazis. Before he could think further, von Auerbach was continuing.

"We have information that the Dominions will be happy to fall into line." He saw that somehow he had made a gaffe, and he went on to more agreeable matters. Very likely much of what he said was true, he thought. The Duke might as well have the pleasure of hearing it.

"The Dominions are not at all happy about this war. They are being drained of young men, food, supplies. There are quarrels between the Churchill Government and Canada about aircraft and defence."

The Dominions. The Duke's face mirrored his mind. Once such a problem. Refusing to agree to his marriage —after Baldwin had so impudently sought their entirely unnecessary opinion. The Dominions, where he had been, perhaps as Prince of Wales, most loved. Well, he could be magnanimous and forget his wrongs.

The room was lit only by candlelight. Von Auerbach turned on the overhead lights the better for the Duke to see some notes he had jotted down earlier.

"You might be interested in this. Lloyd George has been having some talks about the composition of the new Cabinet. Tentative of course. He expects the Churchill Government to fall in a week or two, but he feels that the lack of confidence is only in Churchill himself. For the rest, he thinks it better that things remain pretty much as they are. Attlee to remain Privy Seal and leading the House. Eden to stay at the War Office. He has to really," von Auerbach said, looking up, "Lloyd George says he is the only one that Churchill allows to know what is going on. Nobody else, no combination of people, knows the whole picture. And Lloyd George is certain that they will all agree to serve under him. Glad to do it. He feels that if you call either Labour or Conservative the country will be torn apart. French disease, he calls it. He says the word going round is, 'We hang together or we hang separately.' "

The Duke nodded. French disease . . . he had often heard the old man use that expression. "But do you think Eden is the right man for the War Office?"

Anthony Eden was very much of Churchill's party.

"For a time," von Auerbach explained. "Lloyd George said there was the question of the Eden group. It has been almost a shadow cabinet. But he is sure he can manage Eden and the rest, as long as necessary."

The Duchess was smiling. In the revealing light of the chandelier that sparkled over the table, she looked triumphant. Wallis might prefer candlelight, her uxorious husband thought contentedly, but she didn't need it. Bare-shouldered, in a summer gown of ocean green, her breasts banded with white, she could have been a sea-creature rising up from a foamy wake, her hair sleekly glistening, her skin gleaming like the inside of a pearly pinkish shell: an enchantress. He knew himself to be enchanted, and he revelled in his thraldom.

Von Auerbach's eyes were on him and he brought his mind back to Lloyd George. He was sure he could manage Eden very well. The Welshman had an unsurpassed genius for political manoeuvre.

"Matters are not quite as you might have supposed," von Auerbach went on meditatively. "Eden is personally loyal to Winston of course, but it seems that professionally they've not been getting on too well. Winston will try to run everything. Hates to let the other boys play soldier. He is dissatisfied with Wavell, and Eden believes he is doing a good job. I think Eden realises that things will go more smoothly without the old fire-eater."

"Winston is Minister of Defence," the Duke observed. He had good reason to remember that. "Will Lloyd George be taking that post himself?"

"There have been discussions about it," von Auerbach answered. "He will take the post. Eden believes he won't interfere with him too much. And I don't suppose he will," von Auerbach added meditatively, "as long as there's any war to interfere with. Lloyd George also talked about the peace treaty. Thinks he should go down to the Channel Islands for the discussion. He believes they won't take long. There isn't anything to argue about."

"But Eden?" the Duke said.

"If Eden fusses, then Lloyd George says it won't matter. There'll be no Secretary of State for War. He can glide back to oblivion. And he won't get out of it again. Lloyd George is certain that the whole Churchill group is out of favour. That mad idea of Winston's for union with France, without a word to Parliament or the people—the Cabinet was horrified."

And Lloyd George, the Duke thought. The Welshman's animosity to France was lifelong.

"Lloyd George spoke bitterly about having supported him. After all, he helped make Churchill Prime Minister, but now he says he very soon regretted it."

Von Auerbach went on to the discussion of the repeal of the Abdication Act. Lloyd George felt he could get it through without too much fuss. Nobody wanted to get into the question of whether Elizabeth and her sister Margaret Rose should divide the Empire.

"But if the Abdication Act is repealed," the Duke asked, "won't it make my brother a King that never was?"

Von Auerbach shrugged.

"Lloyd George says let the protocol people worry about it. That's what they're there for, to tidy things up after the actors have acted. He says that if he'd been in England in '36, he would have told you that then. You were badly advised. They can always refer to your brother as Regent . . . *ex post facto.* You were never crowned, so your Coronation will cause no problem.'

The talk went on happily. The Duke looked like the King who had never abdicated. The Duchess was smiling and regal, considering who would make her Coronation gown.

"David," she said impulsively, "this is great. I'll ring for a bottle of champagne. Our celebration."

"Celebration?" the Duke was slightly hesitant.

"Sure!"

"Very well, my dear," her husband answered. "If you want to, certainly."

When Manuel was called back to the dining-room to open the champagne, Maria took the opportunity to slip off and find Sergeant Barney. She found him in his room, thinking gloomily of the U-boat in the cove; the German in the dining-room.

Not much more than a month since Dunkirk. He'd been given a nice little medal for shooting Germans. Yet such were the stupidities of English law that if he, Sergeant Barney, went to the dining-room and shot the German and his friend the Duke, his ungrateful country, though no doubt relieved, would most certainly stick him in quod.

He thought of consulting the British Ambassador, but quickly dismissed the idea. That sort—he knew them too well. All starch and striped trousers. Did his job, but he wouldn't bend outside all the rules and regulations. Nor would he listen to a sergeant, Rex was sure of that.

By the time Maria came in he'd smoked a whole packet of Players. Twice he'd decided to go to Lisbon and call the old man, and twice decided it was no go. He would be at dinner, and most likely the staff at Number 10 would merely refuse to interrupt him. And if he did talk to him, the old man would only say he was fussing. A duchess with the 'flu could entertain her husband's second cousin, even if he was a German. He would probably make some damn rotten joke about spreading the germs in Germany.

Maria greeted him ardently and he responded with a rather absent-minded affection: Rex, she thought, was the most wonderful of men. Jorge could not stop talking about him, this marvellous Englishman, the chocolate *soldado*. She tried to thank him in her halting English. He waved away the thanks, and told her that Jorge was a sharp kid.

"Spotted a U-boat down in the cove."

Maria did not understand his words exactly, but Jorge had already told her of the underwater fish that had come up and turned into a large boat. She nodded in comprehension. Although she had lingered at the dining-room door, she had not understood the political talk. But there were things that a maid understood very well, and the woman knew what her soldier was eager to learn.

"Come with me," she said, "but quietly."

The dinner party, with Manuel in attendance, was continuing with talk and much laughter now. Maria took Rex up the back stairs and into the Duchess' room. She lit one candle, and carefully shaded it with her hand.

Rex watched her, puzzled. He hoped no-one found them there; the Duke certainly would have him done for attempted nicking then.

"They are supposed to be going to the Bahamas. You see, the suitcases here are packed," Maria whispered.

They certainly were.

"But you see, very few. Dozens, they came with. Always the Duchess travels with many trunks, but you see here, this is all. And look."

She opened the door of the wardrobes. "All her summer things, left behind. It is hot in the Bahamas, yes?"

Rex nodded.

Maria showed him, layer by layer, rustling through the tissue paper, fur coats and capes, woollen suits, dark leather shoes. Rex was no authority on female dress but

260

even to him it looked as though the Duchess had packed for a cool climate. And for a small space.

He looked at Maria grimly. To him, this was evidence enough. But it was not at all likely to strike the old man. Rex knew the way his mind worked. Although he was fond of his wife, he spent very little thought on women and their vagaries. To the Prime Minister, in the middle of fighting a war against almost insuperable odds, the significance of the lack of a summer dress would not appear decisive. Still, he had to try. He got his motor cycle and roared off to Lisbon. But although he tried for many hours, he was not able to reach the Prime Minister that night.

Von Auerbach, returning happily to the Avenida Palace Hotel in his Mercedes, saw the obnoxious sergeant, whom the Duchess had told him was a spy. It was far too dangerous having him about now, he thought coldly. It had been a mistake on his part to let him leave the first time. He thought the matter over carefully, and the next morning he spoke to Manuel. The money that passed between them was not the only reason for great satisfaction on both sides.

The Duke spent the night in his wife's bed. She fell asleep at once, into dreams of happiness and hope, but the Duke lay awake a long time. His mind went back many years, to the first war, the senseless slaughter that he had seen close at hand, all the stupid, ghastly suffering in the trenches. He remembered how Lloyd George had tried to end it, negotiating directly with Prince Sixtus against all precedent or even legality. But if he had had his way, Austria-Hungary would have been out of the war by 1917 and then the whole holocaust might have come to an end before Europe was shattered almost beyond repair. Well, Lloyd George and Europe were having a second chance. The last chance, he thought soberly.

His father had wanted to help Lloyd George, but was

too much the constitutional monarch to act. It was Europe's fortune that his eldest son was not. He felt at once humble—a state he had hardly ever known—and proud. Proud that it had been given to him to do this work, the work, he could see now very clearly, for which his life had been a preparation. No-one could ever say the 'Golden Prince' had not fulfilled his promise. He felt power radiating from him, to encompass all of Europe and reach the island realm that was the focus of his life. His wife stirred and smiled up at him, happily.

He drew her to him, and that night they were content.

Barney returned, very late, to the Boca Do Inferno. He checked the rooms of the Duke and Duchess and saw them sleeping like two turtle-doves. At least his birds hadn't flown. Although he moved quietly, Manuel heard him prowling, and burned with hate. Maria, from somewhere, had found a key and locked her room against him, Manuel, that night. Doubtless this soldier would find the lock opened. Upstairs, the Duke was not in his room, probably the Englishman was stealing. Manuel was very tempted to call the police, but that one was too clever to keep stolen goods about him at night. Tomorrow he would catch him out . . . But the morning brought the German, and his even better idea.

Rex was up before daybreak and made his way back to the cove. The sun came up over the quiet waters, birds sang, there were rustles in the grass. But there was no sign of any U-boat. He watched and waited for several hours, but it never appeared. Perhaps it had taken itself off—but he doubted it. Probably it was waiting offshore, discreetly submerged, but he felt very sure it would be back.

He returned to the house for his motor-bike; he would try to reach the old man again. But as he approached the house, surprisingly, Manuel was looking for him. He made a special luncheon for the staff, to celebrate

262

his saint's day. The others were already at the table, which was attractively set out for once. Maria's eyes were opened wide, and little Jorge's small brown paw stole out and quickly filched a slice of melon, elaborately cut and garnished. The main dish was a chicken paella and Manuel served Rex first, smiling agreeably.

Somehow Rex did not like that smile. He remembered how ill he had been on the 'plane the last time he had eaten Manuel's food. He was tired of foreign food. He was longing for a cup of tea. And he wouldn't mind some eggs and chips. He'd even taught some French women how to make proper chips in the quiet stretch before the balloon went up. They'd giggled when they had slapped them down on the zinc. There was that café on the Rua Gambetta where the food hadn't been too bad—whatever its reputation. And he had to get off and make his call. He couldn't hang about here.

To the fury of Manuel, after making a polite toast to him and to his saint, he made his excuses and strode off. The roar of the motor-bike broke the peace, momentarily, of the house. Muttering, Manuel picked up the English sergeant's plate and scraped it very carefully into the dustbin. Maria's eyes were wide—food was not often wasted like that. There was little enough on Jorge's plate as it was. Something was very wrong, she knew.

Manuel was sick with fury at the escape of his rival. He had put enough of his special powder into the soldier's portion to have killed him within a few hours. The German had asked if he needed anything, but he had not. He had prepared the powder himself from seeds that he knew to poison the cattle, back in his own village. If the dose was sufficient, it could not fail. He had felt very safe, very sure. No-one was going to bother about the death of this inconvenient soldier, and the Duke, doubtless, would be very happy. And now the man had gone. Manuel was no fool; he thought it unlikely he would get another chance. Well, he certainly was not going to pay back the money. A man should get something for his trouble.

The Prime Minister still could not be reached. Rex lingered in the café, eating his eggs and the potatoes cooked somewhat to resemble chips, but without the right degree of crispness. There was no tomato sauce. His mutterings drew the attention of the seedy-looking fellow that he'd met there before. His eye-patch was gone but the eye was still inflamed and gummy.

He seemed very depressed. In a rather hopeless way he offered to sell Rex a watch, a camera, and offered him three bottles of Scotch whisky, very cheap. Rex thought of the Duchess' jewels with a certain regret. He could have found an easy market in Lisbon. But the Englishman didn't strike him as a pro. Rodrigues had claimed he worked for the Service. He didn't look much like that either.

Gibbons, John Gibbons he called himself. It might even have been his real name. He was crestfallen that he couldn't do any business, and confided in Rex that things were getting difficult for an Englishman in Lisbon.

"Used to get a regular bit of money from some chaps," he said, resignedly. "But it's all gone west now. Seems like Jerry is cock of the walk. And I don't want to do business with them."

The wind had risen, a strong wind blowing off the shore. It seemed to hurtle itself against the glassed-in front of the café. Rex looked at the too-talkative stranger. His shirt was clean and white, but the collar was slightly frayed. A café lounger, reluctant to leave the wine, the shelter, the company, to face the world outside. He tried to remember exactly what his father had said about the Service. A glorious muck-up. The whole Continental organisation smashed right at the beginning of the war, its chiefs captured because of their own stupidity, and not one uncompromised agent left from Turkey to Calais. Even allowing for the bias of Special Branch against the Service, it didn't sound good. If this Gibbons had been a stringer, selling his odd bits of information, then that little income had very likely 'gone west'.

Observing more closely, Rex saw that his suit was shiny in patches and his tie was limp. He was close to being down and out. Next step, no doubt, would be trouble with the Lisbon police. Barney wondered what a Portuguese prison would be like. He made a small grimace. Didn't think he could fancy it. There wasn't any beer so he ordered a bottle of wine. Gibbons drank it down fast.

"Our lot are a bunch of idiots," he said bitterly. "I got hold of something—should have been worth a fortune." He rubbed his running eye. "Talk about doing the country a favour. I still have my friend in—well, that's neither here nor there. But I got a look at something, and I thought for certain they'd have paid at least a fair price. Would've saved themselves trouble, I can tell you that. But there was nobody. So I went to the bloody Embassy." He snorted.

"Lot of shits," he continued. "D'you think his High Mucky Muck the Ambassador would see me? Not a chance. After I waited about all day, I got to see the First Secretary. And when I told him I had something worth his while all he could say was he wasn't interested. I even gave him a hint as to what it was about—pretty broad hint, too. And even then he wouldn't pay me sixpence. And the worst of it is," he said in disgust, "I paid for it. I was so sure—"

"What is it?" Rex asked. He knew Gibbons was going to tell him, but he'd just as soon save half an hour's dancing about.

Gibbons laughed.

"When I was at school we used to say that's for me to know and you to find out."

He leaned over the table, close to Rex's ear.

"Look, it's about your gov'ner. P'raps you could do yourself a bit of good. What d'you say?"

Rex looked at him speculatively. Word did get about. But he doubted this Gibbons knew any more than he did already.

"I know all about him," he said shortly. "What have you got?"

Gibbons looked disappointed enough to cry.

"Fifty quid," he said. "Come on. You can sell it back to him for a lot more than that." He winked knowingly.

"Sell what?"

Gibbons was a timid man. His were the placating manners of the commercial traveller. Only necessity had driven him to his various sidelines, one the peddling of small bits of information that fell his way. Lately he had found himself on unknown ground. Now the friendly-looking sergeant had changed quickly—he looked damned awkward. Not menacing exactly, but the change from easy tolerance to a very sharp awareness in those bright brown eyes made him look like a tough customer. Gibbons was sorry he'd approached him. A man didn't know where he stood any more.

"A document," Gibbons replied. It was worth something, and he was going to hold out for it. Frightened or not. His firm's business had gone down and his salary had been cut to the point where he could hardly pay his rent. But he had no fancy for going back to England now, with a war on. It was going to be nasty there when Jerry walked in.

A document. Rex felt the clutch of excitement, and the salesman was aware of it at once. Rex grabbed the other man's hand, which was shaking slightly as he reached for his glass.

"What document?"

"Copy of a telegram from the German Legation," Gibbons told him. He wasn't going to say any more. Not unless the soldier tried to beat it out of him.

But Rex was putting his hand in his pocket. His pay hadn't caught up with him since he'd gone on 'special

266

leave' from his regiment, but before he had left London he'd been given another small sum from the Prime Minister. After his dealings with the motor-bike, he had left the equivalent of about thirty-two pounds ten shillings and sixpence.

"Twenty quid," he said.

"That's highway robbery," Gibbons protested. "I won't take a penny less than forty."

"Twenty-five," Rex said.

Gibbons looked at him. He thought perhaps he shouldn't argue. Anyway, that was about twenty-four thousand escudos. He could make it last. He held his hand out and Rex gave him the notes, a pleasant handful. Gibbons fished in his pocket and produced a piece of paper, crumpled, grubby, with a corner ripped.

"From the Embassy here to Berlin," Gibbons said.

"How do I know it's real?" Rex grumbled.

"It's authentic all right," Gibbons said, sighing for the mere twenty-five pounds.

It was. Actually it was one of the two messages von Auerbach had sent. One had been the signal in the Abwehr code to Admiral Canaris. But he had not been able to resist also notifying his own Chief, von Ribbentrop, in a discreetly worded message: *Our client awaits the Führer's pleasure.*

"Gawd's truth," Rex muttered. There it was. Absolute certainty. While he was thinking that even the old man would have to believe this, he was shaken by a sudden fury. The skin on the back of his neck crawled. Suddenly, a mental image of Larry came, sharp, clear, as if he'd seen the incident himself. Larry screaming as the bayonet went into his gut, again and again and again.

Sweating, Rex jumped up with such force that his chair turned over. Gibbons grasped the wine bottle anxiously. Rex pushed everyone aside as he made his way to the small enclosure where the telephone stood, and already was shouting down the line to 'Bitch' while Gibbons was trying to steady himself. But all the wine was drunk before 'Bitch' got through to London. Gibbons had gone out into the dark, not uncheerfully at last, while the disgruntled sergeant was being told he certainly could not be connected with the Prime Minister. The Prime Minister was out of London on a tour of inspection. His destinations were secret and no messages could be conveyed.

"A lot of bollocks!" Rex was roaring. Wherever the Prime Minister went, his despatches would follow him. But obviously no-one in London was going to convey a message from Sergeant Barney.

He thought quickly. He had never got on with Special Branch. He didn't like them and they didn't like him. But it was no time to worry about that. They would be able to reach the old man. The old man himself had been very cagey about the secret Lisbon-London relay. Military secret. Sergeant Barney must say nothing except to give his code words. He couldn't worry about that either. Tersely, he asked 'Bitch' to get him onto Special Branch. The line went dead.

Rex swore to himself. Military secret. Probably Military Intelligence, brass-hatted, snot-nosed—it was no use. Like arguing over the Charge of the Light Brigade.

It was hot in the café, and hotter still in the small enclosure. But that was not the only reason he was sweating hard. Now he had his proof he could not reach the Prime Minister. It was as simple as that. No intermediaries, the Prime Minister had said grandly. Straight through to London or Chequers. But the old man had forgotten to leave his communication line open. A bad error. There was only one thing left to try. And he wished himself luck doing it.

At the Embassy, Sergeant Rex Barney got a reception similar to the one described by Gibbons. Only worse. The Ambassador was in a state of simmering fury about the sergeant's continued presence in Portugal, that was causing so much unnecessary bother. The Duke continued to complain that the young man had spied on the Duchess in the pool. The Ambassador, who knew the house very well, realised that all its occupants had a view of the pool which was hardly secluded. Still, it was most annoying. He *had* notified London, but London was silent on the matter, as it so often was when matters related to the Duke.

The Ambassador wished fervently that they would send the Duke's man, find his wife's maid, and detach as much of the British Navy as was needed, to get him off to the Bahamas. A good diplomat, he was engaged in negotiations of the first importance to Great Britain, that if completed would resound to the success of his Embassy. Yet here he was, with the Duke in Lisbon. The affair of the Duke was awkward, the worst kind of awkwardness, where the Embassy would get all the blame if there was trouble, and no credit if it went as well as it possibly could. The advent of this extremely dubious sergeant seemed like the last straw. And now he had the impudence to come to the Embassy itself.

The sergeant was told to report to the Military Attaché, who had left Lisbon for a few days on a visit to the Azores. When Sergeant Barney insisted that his business could not wait, his insistence was met with a polite but stony calm. But he was a wretched, persistent person, and absolutely refused to leave the Embassy.

He could have him arrested, of course, the Ambassador thought, but that might cause complications. Certainly he wanted no more complications. The Second Secretary was sent to see Sergeant Barney, and the Ambassador took his hat and left. He decided to go for a day or two to Estoril. The Second Secretary refused to discuss the Duke, and referred the sergeant to the absent Attaché.

Rex, furious, thrust the copy of the telegram into his hand.

"You stupid bloody bastard, read it!" he shouted.

The Second Secretary looked down at the dirty crumpled piece of paper that was so disagreeably thrust upon him. His expression was a politely mild blend of pain and boredom. Oddly enough, despite the guarded language, he knew what this was about. He had heard this rubbish before. As, of course, the Embassy always did. If only people realised, their 'news' was invariably an old, old story to those whose business it was to be informed.

The First Secretary had had dinner with him one night and had amused him by telling the story of a shabby little wart who was in the business of smuggling certain rubber articles—illegal in Portugal, but with a market in Lisbon—and who had come to the Embassy trying to peddle some ridiculous gossip.

"These types," he'd said, smiling, "they always spoil their own game by trying to sound over-important. They have no idea how an official communique is written. '. . . awaits the Führer's pleasure.' It's a wonder he didn't say it was signed David Windsor."

They both had a little giggle. Well, they'd deserved it. It was bad enough these days when creatures like this came to the front door and demanded to see Ambassadors.

Rex was quick-tempered, but he tried to control himself. He knew the sort of man he was dealing with. He remembered when he had taken a party of men in the lorry down to the beach at Dunkirk, a more miserable, shot-up knocked about, thirsty, hungry lot of buggers you could ever see. By luck their company was due to embark, but some sod of an Embarkation Officer wouldn't let them board because they weren't on any manifest. No manifest, no go. Manifest? They'd lost their officers, their equipment, their food and water—there wasn't a manifest form, or any other form, within miles. Not even paper or a pen. So he'd taken some lavatory paper that he kept folded up in his pocket, found a pencil stub, and, heading a sheet 'Manifest' just under the perforation, laboriously wrote out the names, ranks and serial numbers of the men. Then he'd saluted, handed it to the officer, and said "All present and correct, sir."

The Embarkation Officer had glared at him in fury, but a document was a document. He'd taken it and passed the men aboard.

But this bastard wasn't even interested in his nice little document. He wasn't going to do a thing. Sergeant Barney's only course now was to get back to England. He *must* warn the Prime Minister before the Führer decided to avail himself of the Duke's services. Rex knew he could find the old man soon enough once he was on the spot. 'The Führer's pleasure'—God knew what else was going on. The Duke might get away while he was gone, but from what he had seen at the house, they didn't seem to be in any hurry. The U-boat was out at sea. And once the old man was warned . . .

He asked the Second Secretary, very politely, if he would arrange for a ticket and a move order. Without a move order, he couldn't get on the 'plane to Whitechurch. The Second Secretary smiled happily. For that, Sergeant Barney would have to wait for the Attaché.

"Then I'll see the Ambassador!" Rex shouted.

The Second Secretary, examining his fingernails, murmured gently that the Ambassador had also left Lisbon for a day or two. Rex glared at him. He could very easily knock that bastard's teeth right down his throat. But it would do no good. No good at all.

Desperate, he considered blowing 'Bitch's' security— just to prove to this arse-hole that the Prime Minister wanted to talk to him. But then 'Bitch' would certainly disown him; the Embassy probably knew nothing of the secret transmitter, and he could just imagine the face before him if Sergeant Barney explained that he was really 'Dirty Dog'.

It came to him that he was trapped. A ticket he could get somehow, but without papers there was no way he could get out of Portugal. It was the 24th of July, and Sergeant Barney was beached.

SEVENTEEN

Black Knight Fumbles

'Private Holbrook' was surprised when he was summoned to the telephone. The chambermaid who called him looked pointedly at Jean who was lounging on his bed. But any irritation he felt was swallowed by apprehension. Some emergency had arisen.

"Come to the house," a voice said. "You know when." Before Holstein could ask a question, the line was dead.

The voice had been that of Dai Lewis. Holstein went back to his room, with a sweet smile for the chambermaid, thinking swiftly. 'When' was after dark. There must be a change in the plan, he decided. Much as he would like to get away from the hotel—and Jean—for a while, he did not like the idea of a change in plan. It had been working perfectly, if boringly, as it was. But orders were orders.

If he had known it, Major Leiter agreed with him most heartily. The Admiral had left him with the most careful instructions. Nothing was changed. When Leiter was informed that the Royal party were on their way—'Jonah approaching Whale'—von Auerbach was to be warned, the receiving groups in Alderney and on the south coast alerted. Once King George was dead—'Jonah swallowed'—von Auerbach was to be ordered to move. At once! Leiter was to report these events immediately to Madrid.

But hardly was the Admiral out of Berlin when Leiter received a memorandum from the Chancellery that filled him with anxiety. The Führer ordered Major Leiter to consult with Reichsmarschall Göring on the planning and execution of Operation Green. Unluckily for the Major, the Reichsmarschall had left for Karinhall. Leiter made the forty-five mile journey and arrived at the former hunting lodge to find Göring cooling himself in the woods. He wore boots, a silk blouse with full sleeves, and carried a large hunting knife. His cheeks were so red that the scandalised Leiter believed he was wearing rouge, and his fingernails were tinted. But the Major quickly forgot the comic appearance.

Göring airily told the stunned Major that some alterations had been made to his scheme. A small group of parachutists were to be taken in by the Luftwaffe to ensure the success of this important mission.

"This operation," Göring informed him, "is much too vital to the Reich to leave in the hands of one assassin and a few traitors. We won't upset the Admiral's plans. We will only need one of your men to meet us at the drop to guide them to the airfield. It is all-important that this airfield, so close to the target, be held by trained men. Your riff-raff can watch the roads. The radio link—"

Leiter had argued and pleaded. Whaleforce could occupy the airfield as long as necessary and guard the road north and south of Birkhall. Paratroopers would increase the danger of discovery and bring no benefits. Then there would have to be arrangements made, extremely difficult now, to get the paratroopers off. And as for the use of radio—the Admiral had particularly wanted no wireless transmission. In such a simple, well-planned matter . . .

He might as well have spoken to the wind. The Führer, Göring pointed out, had already given his sanction.

It was dinner time, and the Reichsmarschall was becoming bored with Major Leiter.

"Take up these details with Körner and the Fall-schirmjäger. All these things can be arranged."

Returning at once to the Tirpitz Ufer, Leiter was close to panic. Admiral Canaris might be able to deal with this, but the Admiral was en route to Madrid. By the time he could reach him, it might be too late. Besides, the order had come from the Führer himself. If the Führer thought that he, Major Leiter, was trying to circumvent his order . . . The Major's flesh crawled.

The best thing he could do would be to thrash it out with State Secretary Körner, and try to make this 'assistance' as small and as unobtrusive as possible. At once. Göring listened to Körner, and Körner was sensible enough. The Reichsmarschall could have his way, perhaps, and yet—the Major's mind worked feverishly. English-speaking men, from an English aircraft, wearing RAF uniforms—it would cut the risk.

He would notify the Admiral discreetly. As the Major issued new orders, he would send the Admiral copies, in the normal way. Including enough so that he would understand.

Yet the Major was haunted by the fear that something would go wrong with Operation Green. He remembered nostalgically the simple days of Operation White, the invasion of Poland; Yellow, the invasion of the Low Countries and France. In retrospect, it seemed that there the mighty Abwehr had been all-powerful and could do no wrong.

Körner was as reasonable as he could be in the circumstances. He agreed that the Major should handle the additional force in his own way. A small force, one 'plane only—the requirement of English-speaking men would help there. But he had to insist, as it was Reichmarschall Göring's orders, on one radio contact. The Major had to concede, but asked that it be through Black Knight, whose discretion he trusted. So they came to an agreement.

The Major visited Telefunken and came away reasonably satisfied. Yet he felt helpless, trapped in his office in Berlin. The Haupt-V-Mann in charge of Whaleforce was competent within his limits. He had managed well, integrating his original small Welsh group with the other diverse members, and he had supervised the training, supplies and movements. He was an honest and prudent paymaster. And he had shown he could command his killers and saboteurs with a natural authority. But the military was something else. There could be a clash of authority between him and the Captain of the Fallschirmjäger. Then the Major remembered he had yet to work out the business of taking off the Germans.

He had seen no active service in the Army, but Major Leiter was not without courage. There was only one thing he could do to ensure the success of his mission. He had to be on the spot. Should something go wrong, it was his duty to withdraw Black Knight, and proceed with *Scullion* and *Araby*. That could be done much better from London.

With the thoroughness and speed of a man well-versed in the rituals of his work, he delegated all other business to his subordinates. He said good-bye to his wife and daughter, saying he would be gone a few days, and called at the Hungarian Embassy. A Dornier took him to Lisbon, and from there the new Commercial Attaché to the Hungarian Embassy in London took the first 'plane to Whitechurch leaving on the morning of July 22.

Following him, in the diplomatic bag, was the device he had had prepared for Holstein, and the wire recording for the Abwehr agent at the BBC. If all went well, that little spool would be the final flourish of Operation Green. For a moment, as the aircraft circled the landing field, and he had his first view of war-time England, it struck him how blithe the English were in their confidence. Nearly all the people they had detained were aliens. It did not seem to occur to them to suspect their own, unless they went about waving swastikas. And yet he knew that Germany was not the only country with a spy in the BBC. The Soviets had a man there also . . .

From the time Leiter landed and was passed by the authorities, it was a little over thirty-six hours before Dai Lewis received his package and his instructions. Dai had wasted no time in telephoning Black Knight. Then he visited a trawlerman who owned a diesel in the Albert basin. It was an old diesel. The trawlerman had been a stringer for the Abwehr in the past. He had often said he would sell his soul to the devil for the price of a new boat. Now he was to have his chance.

Holstein opened the door of his room, wishing he would find it empty, but of course, Jean was there. She had managed to borrow a few clothing coupons from an old friend who was still nursing in the hospital, and bought herself a pink silk garment trimmed with lace that she called cami-knickers. Now she was parading round the room to be admired. Certainly whatever it was, it was better than the navy-blue knickers, but his mind was too troubled for enjoyment.

He thought suddenly: What would happen if Jean's message came that afternoon? The 'when' that the Welshman referred to was after dark. If Jean's summons came, he was supposed to go with her. But he could not go without seeing the Welshman. Somehow he must prevent her leaving without him—

Jean noticed his distraction, and teased him that he was tiring of her before they were even wed. Such remarks had to be dealt with, but he was tense and nervous until night fell.

He could not think at first how he could get rid of Jean long enough to make his way to Dai Lewis' house, and then he was inspired.

"I hate to go out," he told her.

She giggled and made the inevitable remark.

"Apart from that, I was hoping to hear today from my friend in camp. The CO ought to be back, and if he's signed the papers, we can get married this week, or Monday. No-one will ask to see them; there's nothing in my pay book about being foreign-born."

Jean was thrilled, and twisted her modest diamond engagement ring that had been bought with Abwehr funds and supplied through Neville Jarndyce.

"Oh, I can't wait to put on the gold band," she said. "And we could give up the other room. Such a waste of money."

"I wonder—" he said. "Look, I have to go out for an hour. I'd promised to meet one of my squad who came up today from Aldershot. Old Scotch Tom—remember my telling you about him? But I hate to miss the call. We could start arranging for the Special Licence. Jean—" he stopped as though he were struck by an unpleasant thought—"You can *get* a Special Licence in Scotland, can't you?"

Jean looked blank. She didn't know. Never had she known anyone who wanted to get married quickly.

"I'll find out," Holstein said. "But that girl downstairs is too stupid to trust with a message."

Jean would have liked to go out for a time and meet 'old Tom', or almost anyone else, but she was an obliging girl. Besides, she certainly wanted to get the message. It would be great fun if she were married before Their Majesties arrived and she could tell the Queen she was Mrs Holbrook.

"I'll stay here," she said. The cami-knickers were actually a little tight. She could let the seams out while she was waiting.

The streets were dark but he found his way to the bus stop without much trouble. Dai Lewis had given him clear instructions on their first meeting. Holstein sat shoulder to shoulder with two old men from a fish-smoking factory and wrinkled his nose in disgust. But Jarndyce had explained to him very emphatically that usually a private travelled by bus. "Remember," he said, "you earn fourteen shillings a week—about fourteen marks." Holstein, as always, meticulously followed orders.

Lewis was waiting for him in a dingy bedroom which was usually rented in the summer to a luckless visitor by the landlady who worked in the post office and also for the Abwehr. The Welshman was a careful man, and this was not his known holiday residence. He was booked for bed and breakfast in a large boarding house not too many streets away, where it was assumed he spent his days in the usual summer pleasures. A quiet, neat man who paid without being asked every Friday—the boarding house owner liked him.

But his business was conducted from this room where he sat, while waiting for Black Knight, going over his plans which had been so suddenly and drastically changed. Or perhaps—he considered carefully—not so drastically. Next to the bed on which he had to sit as there was no chair, was a rickety bamboo table. On this table was the area chart he had drawn himself, after his own inspection; not as elaborate as the chart the Germans had used, but containing all he needed. There was only the overhead light; he himself had inserted a new bright bulb so that he could see to work, but the glare was uncomfortable and from long habit he wore a green eye shade.

As he went over his original scheme, which had been agreed upon with Major Leiter, at first he saw no use for this embellishment. It had all been so thoroughly planned. He had the two sets of uniforms waiting for his men, the Air Force uniforms they would need on the field, and the RAOC which they would wear for all other duty. That had been his best idea, he thought dispassionately. People were used to seeing the Ordinance men everywhere, doing all sorts of jobs. No-one would think to challenge them. He had a lorry in readiness, a light van, an old estate car and the motor cycles. The lorry would carry all their heavy equipment. Concealed in the van would be the men's civilian clothes and papers. The motor cycles were perfect for messenger work, if necessary. For all of these he had two sets of plates. The estate car would only be used once.

The unsuspecting RAF men—a singularly slack lot —would be no trouble for his trained killers. Churchill's pilot could suspect nothing; the old man would expect transportation to be waiting for him and indeed it would be. Lewis gave a grim smile of satisfaction as he thought of Churchill being carted off by Maloney like a pig to market. Maloney would enjoy that job. Depending on the size of the escort, other men would be sent as guards—the estate car had plenty of room. He would still have enough men to watch the road to make sure all was well for Black Knight.

Nevertheless, there might be an advantage in having the Germans also. As they were English-speaking, and would be wearing RAF uniforms, he could turn over control of the airfield to them, leaving him more men to be ready for their job in the Cairns. The placing and the burning of the bodies was the most exposed part of the operation and despite the remoteness of the Cairns, the most dangerous for his men. He would be glad when that was over.

For the twentieth time he worked out how long it would take for Maloney to get the Prime Minister's body to the wreck. The 'plane would crash almost immediately after take-off. Maloney would have to take a winding path around the rocks. Difficult driving, even if it didn't rain. Time for the execution. If the old man slept while travelling as he so often did, Maloney could take him alive to the place Purcell had targeted for the crash. That would save a few minutes. But of course Churchill's escorts wouldn't sleep.

Probably twenty minutes. At the worst, half an hour.

He himself would delay the pilot almost that long. And Frank Purcell might need the time for his work. Lewis had already marked a small cross on the chart showing the crash site, which he and his men referred to as the 'Reception centre'. Now he marked a cross where the Germans were to land.

He studied it thoroughly. It was hidden well in a patch of woods, though the clearing was so small they would need to be skilled to land there. And it was rather close to the Royal House, Birkhall. He would have to escort them himself, as he knew the area best, taking a wide circle round the house—that was Black Knight's territory, and the less he had to do with it, the better he would like it. Then he would take them south, over a small footbridge at a narrow point of the Muick, close to the airfield. Even in moonlight there would be no-one about to see them cross.

Though the house was not his business, except for guarding the approaches, his eyes went back to it, fascinated. Logically, reasonably, he was certain that the plan he and the Major had evolved was foolproof. But Dai Lewis had come from a family of miners in a small village in South Wales. Some part of him found it hard to believe that England's King and Prime Minister could be killed with no suspicion aroused, no hue and cry. Though he was a stout republican, he found himself at times touched by an emotion he would not admit, a certain shadow of the Royal awe. And then the question would come to haunt him. *Could they get away with it?*

But now it would be the Germans on the field with the dead bodies of the RAF men. His own force would be free to move. He was certain that no-one could ever pick up their trail. If anything *should* go wrong, it would be the Germans who would be in trouble. He shrugged. So be it.

Bending over his chart, he sketched in the path that he would use to guide the Germans to the field. Orderly-minded, he noted the date of this change to the approved plan. It was Wednesday, July 24. Very close to the deadline. If the Royal couple did not travel up this weekend or the next, the plan would be postponed. Leiter had not informed him that it would never be reactivated. But as it was, Lewis had no wish for a postponement. He folded his chart, which was drawn on the thinnest of paper, and tucked it into his big, worn Bible. The door bell rang, and as he walked down the stairs to admit Black Knight, he devoutly hoped the Queen would soon desire mountain air.

Holstein did not take the news of the change as well as Lewis. Paratroopers. Wireless. It was rare with Holstein to criticise his superiors, even mentally, but in a job like this he preferred to work alone and in silence. Nevertheless he accepted the orders in silence. He suspected, from the Welshman's calm, that he understood little of the danger to incoming aircraft from the RDF towers. Doubtless, he had not been told of the loss of so many agents after wireless communication.

Lewis did know, of course, of the problem with detectors, but the likelihood of a detector tracing back a brief transmission from a man moving about in the mountains was too remote to consider. He couldn't know of the more dangerous problem. Admiral Canaris himself did not know precisely what the trouble was, which was simply that many of the German codes, considered invulnerable, had been cracked by the cypher unit at Bletchley. But the Admiral, aware of the number of agents lost or compromised, had become cautious. A message passed from hand to hand, memorised and then burned, or better still, from lip to ear was now, as in all the long history of espionage, the safest. But Dai Lewis was only interested in the history of Wales, that once independent country.

In any event, he was intrigued by the wireless set that had been brought in the diplomatic pouch from Lisbon and then delivered, via a cut-out to him in Aberdeen. The handy little suitcase transceiver—Agenten-Funk-Geraet,

281

or AFU—that Telefunken had developed before the war for the Abwehr, had needed to be adapted to fit into the gas-mask bag carried by British soldiers. Fortunately, it was a minor job that Telefunken had managed for Major Leiter in a few hours.

To anyone casually opening the bag, all that could be seen was the usual mica face plate. The technology involved was something that Lewis had never seen. Like so many men in the mines, he had been unemployed for years before the war. He was impressed by what such work must cost and felt a respect for the country that could afford to spend so freely. The amount he was to be paid was beyond anything he had ever dreamed. He had been informed that it was a measure of the respect in which he was held by Berlin.

He thought of his own wireless set at home, a clumsy thing that his wife dusted with love, but which mostly produced nothing but the atmospherics. And he had to take that great accumulator, full of acid, up the steep road every month to Davis the oil shop, to have it re-charged. After this war it would be different, he promised himself and his wife Bron. Some of the money would go to the movement, but not all . . .

He gave Holstein the call letters and the code with which he would communicate to Leiter in a safe house taken by the Embassy. Leiter's instructions were to transmit only in cases of extreme urgency. Air traffic was very heavy, but a radioman who was familiar with his transmissions would be standing by all through the time of the operation. Holstein did not expect he would need the transceiver. His problem was how to keep it from the eyes of Jean who already had the proprietory attitude of a wife towards his belongings. He left his real gas mask with the Welshman with a certain sinking of his spirits, and took the next bus back to the hotel.

The slight gloom on his face was the excuse for another soldier to accost him. The Tommy had got on at a stop the conductor called 'Union Street' and he quickly addressed Holstein.

"Down in the mouth up north, cock?" he said. "This place is a pain in the arse. Seven days leave and I came up to see my sister who's had a baby. Her husband's off in the Navy and nothing but women, tea and biscuits morning, noon and night. Except for the baby and its milk and that's a bloody girl."

Holstein saw that the man was wearing the insignia of the Middlesex, 'his' regiment. He answered as briefly as possible, but the Tommy rattled on. He was loud and boisterous and the Aberdeeners were watching with their eyebrows raised at the racket, but with a certain tolerance for a soldier, probably in drink. The bus proceeded very slowly in the black-out. Holstein felt he could walk faster. The soldier was being funny at his sister's expense.

"All across the parlour, knickers on the line, but no bloody good to me, mate. The women go about in squads and all you hear all day is their war work. War work! If you ask me, women's war work should be—"

The conductor, a very elderly man, was looking daggers. At any moment he was going to come over and protest. The Military Police might be called. Holstein decided to get away, and murmuring something inconsequential he jumped off at the next stop.

It was hard to make his way without a torch which all the civilians carried. He wasn't sure exactly where he was, but on the way he had made a mental note of the bus' twists and turns. If he kept walking west on this main road until it branched off to the south, he estimated it should not take him more than forty-five minutes to regain the hotel.

"Middlesex, hoy," he heard an exasperating voice behind him. The loud-mouthed Tommy had also jumped off, after the bus had begun to move. "Come on, mate, let's have a drink."

The last thing Holstein wanted was a drink with him,

but the Tommy threw an arm round his shoulders, and began to propel him masterfully to the door of a pub that unfortunately stood a few yards away. A few loungers were by the door, carelessly spilling light onto the pavement, eyeing them curiously. Holstein couldn't risk a scuffle here, and moved quickly with the other man into the crowded bar where the bright lights were softened by a cloud of smoke.

"Charley's the name," the Tommy said amiably, leaning against the bar.

"No spirits," the barmaid informed them, "only beer and ale."

"A pint of old and mild for me," Charley said, "what's yours, mate?"

"I'll have the same."

Holstein was taciturn, but that did not stop the Tommy, pleased with male company of his own regiment, from chattering on. Having learned that his new 'mate' was called Henry, he asked if he was a Londoner.

"Yes," Holstein said, remembering his papers. "Stepney."

"Go on," Charley said, interested. "I have an uncle what lives in Stepney. I'm from Brixton myself. It's all right, south of the river, but I could fancy Stepney."

Holstein was relieved when Charley got off the subject of Stepney, though he was little inclined to ask questions, and was more pleased to talk. The information imparted by Jarndyce would serve well enough with this lout.

"I been to the pictures a few times," Charley went on. "Seen everything, even *The Four Feathers*. Load of rubbish."

His noisiness didn't seem so out of place in the pub, and the two drew little attention. Holstein soon bought Charley another pint, and thought of getting away. It was dull in the hotel with Jean, but it was not worth endangering his mission for an hour in the pub. He despised the man before him, with his round shoulders and pimply skin, his badly polished boots, with lint on his battle dress; and yet his bawdy talk, his desire for male company, gave Holstein a swift, keen nostalgia for his SS days.

"Time!" the barmaid was rapping on the counter.

"Suppose I'll have to go," Charley grumbled. "Or I'll miss the last bus back. And once my sister's locked up, she carries on like Gawd Almighty if I have to knock her up. One more quick one, darling, for me and my pal, here."

The barmaid, who apparently had responded either to his affectionate remarks or to Holstein's shining good looks, bent below the bar and came up with two whiskies which she slid towards them surreptitiously.

"Bless you, me darling," Charley said in delight. "What's your name?"

"Catriona," she said, giggling.

"Little cat," Charley said. "Go on the tiles for you any day."

The barmaid was small, thin, in her forties with grey in her hair. She giggled again, but her eyes were on Holstein.

"What's the name of this place?" Charley said. "Can't see nothing in the bleedin' blackout. I'll be back tomorrow."

"The Arms," she said.

"The Arms? What Arms?"

"Not allowed to say. They've painted it out."

"Parachutist mad, everybody's parachutist mad," Charley said in disgust. "How am I supposed to find a place called The Arms? Every pub on the street is the Arms, now, I s'pose."

But Catriona's attention was not on his words. Even to the exuberant Charley it became obvious that it was his pal Henry that she was ogling. He was struck with an uncharacteristic malice.

"Wonder they don't arrest you," he said to the startled Holstein. "Fair hair, blue eyes—he's a German in disguise," he chanted to Catriona, who was still giggling.

"Time," she called again, resuming her official voice.

After Holstein's unpleasant moment, he was glad to see that Charley was ready to go.

"Gawd," he complained as they reached the door, "I've been walking round for hours in these boots. Don't feel like getting up on my plates of meat, 's truth."

In the last spill of light from the bar he could see his pal's face clearly. He was watching him intently, to see if he was making any signal to the barmaid. But what he saw was something quite different from anything he had expected—instead of a salacious wink, or a jerk of the head that might indicate Holstein was going to wait for the woman outside, he caught a look first blank with incomprehension, then of puzzlement, to be replaced with his usual blandness.

Holstein's mother had been born in Stepney, as Major Leiter knew, but she had been taken away too young to have learned any Cockney rhyming slang, and if she had she certainly would not have passed it on to her son, any more than she would have done to her German pupils. The small drink of whisky Charley had taken had not dulled his senses. The oddity of a Stepney man unfamiliar with 'plates of meat' connected in his mind with his own jocular remark about a German in disguise.

His expression showed his reaction clearly enough. Before the press of other customers leaving jostled them, the two men were locked in a meeting of their eyes, disquieting to them both. Holstein didn't know quite what had happened, but he knew he had made a blunder. A bad blunder. As they spilled out onto the pavement, Charley began to ask questions with elaborate casualness.

"Where were you in training, chum?"

Holstein, well-primed, managed to answer easily. He mentioned a Colonel Brown, now at Aldershot. Charley had served under Colonel Brown, and his suspicion seemed to subside. But Holstein could take no chances.

They walked along the dark street, until they had left behind the last of the pub patrons, and no little beam of torch light heralded any other pedestrian. Holstein paused. Charley was in the middle of a sentence, still on the subject of Colonel Brown. "Though not such a bad old fart as some . . ."

Charley hardly had time to feel the swift efficient blow that severed his cervical spine without making a sound. His body crumbled into the gutter and Holstein walked on at an even pace. Charley had been drinking before they met. He had had two pints in the pub and then whisky. When the corpse was found the assumption would be that a drunken soldier had fallen in the black-out and broken his neck. Probably not unusual. But when inquiries were made, the barmaid would remember the two of them. He didn't expect a hue and cry but he would stay close to the hotel until that message came.

Jean didn't observe the changed gas mask. Fortunately, the case they'd given him didn't look new. The masks were so much a part of every day British dress, military and civilian, that she, like most people, hardly noticed them, except when one of the chambermaids had walked into the hotel with a new, fancy case to match her handbag and was reproved by the manageress, who was also an air raid warden. Jean, like most women, did not believe in the threat of poison gas, and would squash her gas mask by putting odds and ends into the case on top of it.

She had other irritating, female ways. One was to make his room look more homelike. He hadn't minded when she bought a tin of shortbread and left it at his bedside, but his spirits had sunk when she put a large, framed photograph of the Queen on his dresser.

"Bonnie, isn't she?" Jean had said admiringly.

He remembered, gloomily, Major Leiter's hope that Jean might be willing to do his job. It seemed comic, now. Jean babbled on about 'her lady' until she went to sleep.

She was positively doting. But perhaps that had its advantages. Certainly she, and her lover, could never be suspected of divided loyalty. His heart beat a little faster as he thought exactly how he would perform his task. He only wished now that the message would come.

He did not have long to wait. The next morning, Thursday July 25, Jean was called to the telephone. She was wanted back at Birkhall. The Family were on their way.

EIGHTEEN
Move By Scottish Knight

Despite the fact that her honeymoon had been cut short, Jean, bumping over the Highland roads in the old estate car between Arthur, the gardener and odd-job man, and her lover, was as happy as a girl could be. She was proud to introduce her fiancé to her fellow workers even though, poor lamb, he looked as shy as men usually did at such times.

Just look at him, she thought, his face as innocent as that of a new born bairn. She dimpled, thinking of their days and nights in the hotel. Not so innocent! But how he had rushed to the telephone when she was recalled to Birkhall! He explained he had been trying to reach his Captain, to demand permission for their marriage. Poor thing, he had been so mortified when his leave was cut short. To think he would have to leave the very next morning! But his Captain had been kind, and promised him another three days for their wedding before the actual embarkation—goodness knows to where. For a moment Jean was sobered, but the thought of the wedding soon to come cheered her quickly.

Henry was even more eager for the wedding than she was—everything a lover should be. No laggard in love, nor a dastard in war—as a half German, she was sure he didn't need to be in the Army but she was proud as proud could be that he had joined up. And willing to be a common private to do it. She was even more proud of him for that.

Behind them were the provisions for the Family—only a very small party, Arthur had told her. Mrs. Gordon might have been able to manage without her, he said slyly, if they'd known her soldier boy was visiting. The sun was bright and only one small white cloud danced over the mountains in the light breeze. Jean breathed in the air and felt exhilaration coursing through her body, tingling to her fingers and toes. She had had to be silent for so long about her love, her Henry—she had had to remember to call him that. Now he was in England he hated to be called Horst but sometimes she forgot. Of course he wouldn't want to think of his German side now.

In reality she had not been quite silent through all the long years of her engagement. It was too much against her nature. She had not been able to resist dropping hints to her family and her co-workers that she had a mysterious lover, somewhere . . . But as she was known to be a great romancer, no-one had taken much notice.

The Dee was sparkling, almost as bright as her diamond. She would introduce Henry to Mrs Gordon and then she would go over to old Mrs Rae, the window of a former ghillie on the estate, and ask if she would give Henry a room until the Family left. Mrs Rae often put up visitors for the servants, or even an overflow from the house when it was full. As they turned south from the Dee to follow the Muick to the Royal House at Birkhall, Jean felt that life was a very fine thing. War or no war.

The Welshman received Black Knight's call at 8:30. It was Thursday morning. His first call was to Ballater; the second to Major Leiter in London. Major Leiter, much calmer now that he felt himself in a position to direct the operation closely, was seized by a sensation he had never known before. The magnitude and importance of Operation Green, the whole Windsor Plot, that had been so oppressive to him since he had been given the chief responsibility, suddenly showed its other side. It was of huge importance, and the man who brought it off would be of supreme importance also.

Before this, he had always assumed that one day it would be Colonel Pikenbrock who would step into the Admiral's shoes. Indeed, the thought of taking on the job himself would have been frightening. But now all that was changed. This plan, on which he had done so much work, was proceeding faultlessly. Just as had been expected, the King was on his way; on his way to Black Knight and the first stage of the coup. The Major's image of himself grew as he worked, and he was filled with an exhilaration very much like Jean's.

But he was his usual cool and competent self as he arranged for the signal to Stavanger, where the paratroopers would wait until nightfall to take off. They were not at one of the big airfields of Luftflotte Five, but a place carefully chosen where the British bomber, suitably camouflaged, had been kept under ultra-tight security. The flight was carefully planned, low, to avoid the RDF fortunately thin that far north, and well away from the regular flight path of Luftflotte Five. The picked squad, he knew, was eager.

The problem of getting them off had been solved without much trouble. The trawlerman, returning late— and alone—would pick them up at the bank of the Dee and take them *in* to the Albert Basin. At dawn they would go out with the rest of the fishing fleet and he would veer off to rendezvous with the U-boat. Major Leiter, considering the secrecy of the project, had decided that the trawlerman could not be allowed to survive. The fortunes of war.

He sent a signal to von Auerbach in Lisbon, the 'A" signal—stand ready. The Major didn't share the Admiral's almost suspicious distrust of wireless transmissions, but he was well aware of the detector problem. His radio operator was sent to a different safe house for each transmission; then that apparatus was set up in the attic of the house where Leiter himself was staying, for the use of Black Knight only. When it came to the question of notifying the Admiral, he found his first hesitation.

The amateurish security of the British, their obviously ill-prepared and rather hapless state—all these things, many of which he'd known on the Tirpitz Ufer, made a strong impression on him when, after his absurdly easy arrival, he saw them with his own eyes. Now they added to his euphoria. The Admiral, once he learned of Göring's interference, might try to postpone the project. But already it was his, Major Leiter's, conviction, that even with the paratroops this plan was going swimmingly. He would rather it went forward now while he himself was in charge. He was not old, but he was too old to be, still, a major. After this, most certainly, a colonelcy would be forthcoming.

He sent a carefully worded message by the diplomatic pouch to Madrid. *'Jonah approaching Whale. Stavanger alerted.'* That was enough to inform the Admiral both of the status of the operation and the changed plans. It would arrive too late for him to do anything about it. And in the next thirty hours Leiter would be sending the two triumphant messages that would complete his mission. *'Jonah swallowed'; 'Little Tubby sleeping soundly.'* The Major thought how his wife would be, at last, Frau Oberst.

Admiral Canaris had not stopped thinking for a moment about Operation Green. Deep in his discussions with the wily Generalissimo, he had nevertheless tried to reach Leiter in Berlin. His message to Leiter was in the diplomatic bag on the way to London. Leiter received it before his own was delivered; the blow was not to fall on the Admiral that day.

Sir Ewen MacBride, at his Deeside residence, was irritated because his morning paper hadn't come. His housekeeper had told him that since the call-up it was hard to get it delivered, and it often came late or not at all. He didn't care for the wireless, as he was a little deaf. Without a newspaper he felt very much out of things. Very much on the shelf.

He had been in London, offering his services to any branch of the Forces, only to be turned down. It seemed that everybody was needed except temporary officers from the First World War. To add insult to injury his London house had been commandeered for a Government department for no earthly reason that he could see. With half of them run off to Harrogate and such places, it would seem that they had more than enough space in London already.

His club was impossible. It swarmed with men in uniform, who looked kindly on those who were not. He couldn't stand any more kind looks as if he were senile, and he had brought himself up to Scotland too early for the shooting, and now without even a newspaper.

He went out moodily for a walk round the place, gazing at woods, hills and streams as Jean Sinclair had done a little earlier, but without seeing anything. Sometimes he wondered why he had kept the place on since his wife's death—it was she who had loved it. And he had no son. It was damned dull, and that was the truth of it.

He puffed up to the top of a hill just to show himself that walking was nothing to him, and those blasted fools who'd said he was too old didn't know what they were talking about. They'd suggested that if he stayed on he could join the LDV. MacBride swore under his breath. From the point where he stood he had a good view of his land, from the house, high above the river, to the stretch of plateau where he had set up his landing field.

He regarded it now without favour. *That* had been

taken over at once by the Air Force, as well as his private 'plane. He had only used it, anyway, when he came to shoot. In fact, he admitted to himself, he had set it up when labour was cheap, in a burst of vainglory, hoping that the King and Queen might use it. Although they were neighbours, he had never seen much of them. Naturally they liked to be private when they could. But unlike the ex-King, they were not fond of flying. And now a few airmen were idling about. He didn't know what they did there: the 'plane was gone and he could make a shrewd guess there wasn't a pilot in the lot. Not a pilot nearer than the fighter base at Falkirk. His hangar was full of tanks. Used for fuel storage.

Screwing up his eyes he made out some men in khaki there, also, dragging about some equipment. What the devil were they doing? Rather painfully, for his knee felt it these days if he went up and down hill too fast, he walked the long half mile to the strip, wishing irritably that he'd brought the car.

At the far end of the field, a half-dozen privates were digging a hole, watched by two lance corporals. The sergeant, a big, burly man, was directing them. RAOC, he saw by their patches. Immediately, he was furious. He had given no permission for digging on his land, even though it had been commandeered. He thought someone might have had the courtesy of informing him. But this whole war was very different from the last.

"What's going on here?" he demanded of an aircraftsman. The man looked bored. He did not know Sir Ewen, nor, if he did, would he have cared.

"RAOC," he replied laconically.

"I can see that," Sir Ewen snapped. "But what are they doing here?"

"Digging a hole," the aircraftsman replied and sauntered off.

The flight lieutenant who was in charge heard part of the exchange and came over.

"RAOC, sir," he said. "Arrived this morning. Going to build a small barracks."

"Building a barracks," Sir Ewen said. "Why on earth do you need a barracks?"

The men who, in his opinion, wasted their days on his field were billetted and well fed in cottages in Girton and Braemar. Which didn't stop the men from making tea and snacks all day in the lean-to they'd thrown up.

"Orders, sir," the flight lieutenant replied.

It was just like this war. Wasting money on a barracks for men who were perfectly happy as they were, sleeping with any village women whose husbands were away. At least the sergeant and his men were workers, MacBride observed. Some good tradesmen in the RAOC. Not like these RAF. The sergeant certainly knew how to handle a pick and shovel, and wasn't above demonstrating exactly how it should be done, when they got down through the topsoil to the outcroppings of rock. He saw MacBride's eyes upon him and made a gesture that might have been a salute, or merely the touching of his cap. Sir Ewen was mollified.

Wondering if he would be paid compensation for all this when the war was over, he made his way back to the house.

"Pompous old fart. Who does he think he is?" the aircraftsman remarked, but nobody bothered to answer.

Sir Ewen, after a glass of sherry, thought perhaps if those men made a decent job of it, he might find a use for the barracks one day. Still, he should lodge a protest. Not that he knew anyone in the RAOC, but he could call General Pettigrew at the club—he knew some of that lot. It would be an excuse to talk to Pettigrew anyway about his own appointment. He remembered hearing that the Royal Marines weren't as difficult about older officers.

He caught Pettigrew at lunch-time, not pleased at being called away from his table.

"I'll get on to someone," he promised, after hearing

MacBride's complaint. "Sorry I can't help you out just now on the other business, but it's a matter of time. We're all needed now. It would be a good thing if you organised the Home Guard in your area." Pettigrew put the phone down and went back to his lunch.

"You know Potter at Ordinance, don't you, Johnny?" he said, after he had finished his pudding. "It's that awful bore MacBride. Fussing about a barracks on his property."

"Damned lucky he doesn't have the men billeted in his house," his companion replied. "We've got some Fusiliers down at Malham and the grounds won't be the same in fifty years."

"See if you can find out something about his beastly barracks," Pettigrew said, rising. "I've got to go off for a briefing. I've promised to let him know."

The inquiry slowly wound its way about London, from office to office, and down the chain of command. It ended on the desk of Staff Sergeant Mullins RAOC at 5:45 that afternoon. Staff Sergeant Mullins was due to go off duty at six o'clock. He eyed the message with a mixture of contempt and loathing. It was a job that could take hours, days, if he wasn't lucky. God knows where that order originated. It was probably just one item on a long list and could be filed anywhere from Aldershot to Edinburgh. If it was filed. Very likely it was a note in a tray that hadn't been sorted out yet.

The clock over his head ticked on inexorably. He had booked seats for *Gone With The Wind* at the Leicester Square Ritz that night—he'd got Ethel to go out with him at last. And after all—he made a decision that would come to haunt him—there was no point starting the hunt now, with everyone going off. Tomorrow would do. Or, better still, Monday.

When Sir Ewen telephoned London again, he was unable to reach Pettigrew who had given orders to his adjutant that he was not, under any circumstances, to be found for Sir Ewen. "Tell him something—anything—if he phones again," General Pettigrew had said.

"Your enquiry is well in hand, sir," the adjutant informed Sir Ewen. "Looks like orders came down from Brigade. And the General spoke to Colonel Hawtrey in Aberdeen. The Colonel is having a conference about expanding the Home Guard in the whole sector. It's to take place at the Custom House. It would be a good thing, they both thought, if you could attend. Not supposed to say this," the adjutant's voice dropped confidingly, "but I know that a shipment of rifles and mortars is earmarked for north-east defence. Can't say where they're coming from, of course. They're going to need all the trained officers they can get."

The wind was rising, causing interference on the line. Sir Ewen could just make out what he said. After the adjutant had hung up, before Sir Ewen could telephone Aberdeen, a sudden gust blowing in from the Coyles tore down the lines, as it so often did. Soothed somewhat by this talk, Sir Ewen gazed out into the twilight. The melancholy of its beauty prompted him to go and get his car. He might as well drive to Aberdeen for dinner and the night. Perhaps, he thought, with a rising feeling of importance, he might make Aberdeen his war-time HQ.

Taking the valley road, he got another glimpse of the airfield. There was no sign of the RAOC men. Downed tools already, only a few blue-clad figures doing whatever it was they did. He would have been surprised, but perhaps not completely enlightened, if he had been told that one thing they had been doing was to tap his telephone line.

They saw him leave with a lot more interest than they showed, the sharp-eyed Frank Purcell noticing the suitcase thrown into the back seat. The wind stirred the newly thrown earth in the excavation, where seven men of the Royal Air Force lay, their dead eyes covered by a foot of Highland turf.

NINETEEN
Royal Move

Thursday was busy and exciting for Jean. She had the joy of introducing Henry to Mrs Gordon, and see her eyes grow wide at this handsome, fine young man in the flesh. Mrs Gordon had never put much stock in Jean's haverings. If the cook-housekeeper had not been so busy she would have felt surprised—what Private Holbrook could see in Jean she could not imagine. The girl was no beauty, and would never rise above being a parlourmaid. She would never learn to cook any better than a crofter's wife, and she hadn't the brains to run a household. Marriage to some long suffering soul was Jean's future, she'd had no doubt, but this young Lochinvar could do better than that. But then she thought of all the holidays that Jean had spent away from home with some 'girl friend' here and there. Doubtless, the poor lad had been drawn in. He wouldn't be the first.

But they were all too rushed off their feet to think much. And on top of everything, the wind had risen and blown down the telephone lines. Jean had to escape from Mrs Gordon to take Henry over to Mrs Rae and arrange for his room. She was painfully proud to see the same look in Mrs Rae's eyes that had appeared in Mrs Gordon's. Admiration and wonder. And she had been proud, in a calmer way, to show Henry round the house, the King's room, the Queen's room—she had, for some reason she did not know, wanted to show off the importance of her job.

Holstein's mind had been noting the layout of the house; access to the King's room would be absurdly easy. He had commented briefly on there being no guard surrounding the place.

"Oh, they'll bring their policemen," Jean said. "Though they're a bother to the poor King and Queen. Who wants some great policeman about when they fancy to be a little private?"

"Not many bedrooms," he said casually. "Where do you fit them in?"

"There won't be many," Jean said confidently. "And the policemen stay up at night. They take odd naps in the daytime."

Holstein thought back to the day when he had first got his instructions from Major Leiter. He remembered his own awe at the magnitude of this enterprise with a certain amused contempt. It was all so easy. The only moment of danger had been with that clod of an infantryman. Tonight his mission would be completed. Tomorrow he would be leaving as planned—openly by train for London, then picking up his suitcase and becoming, once again, Peter Hainault. As Peter Hainault he would wait for further instructions, but he fondly hoped that Henry Holbrook would vanish forever.

For Jean's pleasure, he dutifully admired everything as a lover should, but he was unimpressed. The simple laird's house, with its plain pine furniture, struck him as a poor place. SS officers were frequently better housed than that, in rich mansions taken from Jews. The only wireless set was in the kitchen. Even the telephone didn't work. He didn't have to cut the lines, but he was a careful workman, and he would cut the main line to make sure, though he doubted that these people would begin the repair quickly enough to make any difference.

Jean had to leave him to be given his dinner by Mrs Rae while she went back to her duties. It would be the first meal they had not shared since his arrival in Scotland. And the first night they would be apart. If only he could have stayed in the house. Perhaps, she thought to herself, smiling, he would come quietly and visit. Well, hardly that, under the very nose of the policemen and Mrs Gordon. But the teasing, happy thought sustained her through the work of the day.

* * *

Winston Churchill had not been available to receive Barney's frantic calls from Lisbon on the 23rd and 24th of July because he was on a tour of fighter bases in the south-east. He was certain that the Luftwaffe attacks on shipping and the raids along the coast were only the harbinger of worse to come. His face was dark as he saw fighter base after fighter base totally stripped of operating aircraft. This was Göring's plan, he knew, to destroy Great Britain's remaining force before the real onslaught began.

The Prime Minister was in constant touch with 'Stuffy' Dowding, Commander-in-Chief, Fighter Command, who agreed with him. The orders were given, to the frustration of local flight commands. No matter how great the odds against fighters in combat, a certain percentage of aircraft was to be held in reserve. They must be kept away from the main airfields, the prime targets, under camouflage. No-one, *no-one*, was to take up these aircraft.

In all his activity, he had quite forgotten Sergeant Barney. Shortly after he had sent Barney off to spy out the land, further reassurance had come from the Lisbon Embassy. The Duke was still asking for his man and his wife's maid, but no longer made it a condition of his travelling. He was completely involved in his preparations, and had

asked the Embassy to use its influence to secure two veran-
dah suites, on the already heavily-booked ship, for himself
and the Duchess. There was no question that he was sailing on August the 1st. Relieved and thankful, the Prime
Minister had put the Duke out of his mind.

But he still had some anxiety about the King and
Queen. The King was pale and not looking at all fit. And
—he felt a flash of irritation—despite his own personal
orders, nothing had yet been done about the reinforcing
of the Palace basement. The Palace people were so slow
—he remembered the ex-King complaining about them
bitterly. He sent off a new order, 'ACTION THIS DAY'.

The way things were, once the raids began, Their
Majesties were sitting targets. Fortunately, they had left
for a few days at Windsor. There, at least, he could be sure
they were safe. Something teased his mind for a moment
—something that brought a sense of foreboding. What
was it? Something that young Barney had said. Then he
remembered. Merely his nonsense, Cockney soldiers' talk.
'Never trust a woman'. Well, despite Sergeant Barney,
barring a successful invasion, there was no way the Germans could touch a hair of a Royal head.

* * *

The King and Queen of England were motoring the last
few miles of their journey from Windsor up to the Highlands. They travelled with a tiny party in two small, un-
distinguished cars. The King, in anticipation of this
snatched, quiet holiday, already felt more relaxed. He had
much to be thankful for, he thought soberly. Even the war,
with all its horror, had one bright side.

He had never believed in his heart he could be accepted by the British people as their King. When the blow
had fallen, and the throne became his, despite the previous
warning signs, he had been almost overwhelmed. If it had
not been for his wife . . . Even the crowds at his Coronation

had meant nothing except that they preferred him to chaos.

But since the war began, something had changed. During the dark days of the evacuation from Dunkirk, people had drifted to stand before the Palace looking for some ancient comfort. In answer to their unspoken wish, he had appeared on the balcony. The cheers that went up then, though muted by anxiety, had for him a gratifying ring. He knew that his presence gave them solace and he was humbly and deeply grateful for that. Slowly the British people began to take him and his charming young bride to their hearts.

And he was grateful, in a smaller way, that he had not let his family down. The Royal line would go on and on through his children. He thought of his own small family and smiled. Yes, the Firm—for so he always called them—were all right.

He had been happy to see Lilibet and Margaret Rose so well in the safety of the Castle. The military bustle didn't trouble their young nerves. Lilibet—he must remember not to call her that, she was too big now and he could see the look of irritation on her face when he forgot —Elizabeth had been immensely enthusiastic about getting into some active service herself. It was *one* reason he was happy to get away. Sometimes it was wonderful to know one's children were perfectly safe and happy and *somewhere else.*

The Queen saw the slight smile on his face and could have hugged herself. She knew she was doing the right thing. The past week with all the worry and strain— sometimes she wished she could do the red boxes instead of Bertie so that he wouldn't have to know everything that was going wrong—had left her frightened for her too-conscientious, never strong, husband. But Birkhall, where they had been so happy as the Duke and Duchess of York, always rested him, and even the prospect of their visit had smoothed those worrying lines from his forehead. She saw

302

the increase in his grey hairs at the temple and sighed.

It was wonderful to be alone in the car together—well, almost alone. Her maid was in front with the chauffeur. At least she had arranged it so that the two Special Branch men were both in the other car with Bertie's equerry and his valet. She felt a little guilty because they must be rather squashed, but it would not be long now. And they *would* come.

She had managed to slip away from them once, but only once. Since then they were like glue. You would think, she brooded in some exasperation, that even policemen would realise that a family wanted privacy *sometimes*. But they were so obstinate about 'doing their job'. Well, she understood that. Winston, of course, had everyone worked up. But she had come to an understanding with the Special Branch men. They could accompany her to Scotland as long as they didn't give away her little scheme. As far as everyone knew—except for her household at Windsor's Royal Lodge, who would loyally keep her secret—she and Bertie were at Windsor still. A picnic basket had been packed, and when they came to a smooth stretch of road Donaldson, her maid, opened up the basket resignedly. Donaldson had always hated travel by car. Nor for that matter was she fond of Deeside. An Edinburgh woman, she grumbled that it was cold and damp, and that the house itself was poky and inconvenient. And that Mrs Gordon, though a decent housekeeper, was a poor excuse for a cook.

"Thank you, Donaldson," the Queen said sweetly, rather amused at her maid's lowering expression, and took a mug of tea and a scone.

"I hope it agrees with you, ma'am," Donaldson said. "If we'd stayed in the train you could have had a proper meal."

The Queen had no intention of arriving in the Royal train, and blazoning her intended whereabouts to half the country. She had been *much* cleverer than that. After an early breakfast with their daughters at Royal Lodge, they had slipped away before it was light and taken their train to Scotland. It was actually the Prime Minister's train now —she and Bertie had decided to offer it to him, it was absurd to reserve it for their few journeys. And very dirty and battered it looked on the outside—no-one would recognise it now. Only her own porters knew who was aboard; even the engine driver was told merely that it was an official party.

Giles, the equerry, and the chauffeur had gone up the day before to meet them at a small, disused station not two hours from Ballater. It was dark when they got there and everything had gone off perfectly, as it had the last time. Although she didn't take much notice of Winston's fusses, she must think sensibly of her husband's safety and there was no better protection than travelling incognito to an unknown destination.

The King was smiling again at Donaldson's familiar complaints. Although the Royal husband and wife did not mind eating simply, and in war-time had a frugal table, Donaldson felt it deeply. She believed it to be a falling away from due standards. She regarded the thermos flask in her hand, and the plastic mugs, as if they were enemy weapons. The King's eyes met those of the Queen whose eyes shone in perfect wifely understanding.

And so while a regiment guarded Windsor, the King and Queen made for the small, unprotected house that had always been the Queen's favourite, their private family refuge at Birkhall. It was the one place where she was sure the King would be in perfect safety. No-one knew he was coming except the tiny Birkhall household. The odd-job man, the cook, the maid. All from old and trusted families from Balmoral. Arthur Brown, Mrs Gordon and, or course, Jean Sinclair.

TWENTY

Check To Black Knight

Shortly before midnight Horst Holstein rose from his narrow bed. He was already wearing his underclothes, and quickly he pulled on his socks. Now the time to act had come, he was calm, his mind clear and centred on his purpose. From his kitbag he took his knife, the despised Smith and Wesson and the light shoulder webbing, the length of cord, and the leather case containing the syringe and ampoules. A beam of moonlight through his small window glittered on the tiny glass containers.

So innocent-seeming—but Major Leiter had told him that just one ampoule caused death almost at once. A simple heart attack. Holstein was not given to wonder, but he had a moment's respect for the chemists of the Reich. There was no end to their ingenuity.

He strapped on the webbing, and inserted his gun and knife. The leather case went into his breast pocket. Then he finished dressing, except for his boots. Remembering Jean, he poked the cord into the gas mask case—he would have to carry it anyway. It was a nuisance, but orders were orders. An extra pair of socks fitted into his trouser pocket smoothly.

Carrying his boots, he made his way along the passage, silent in his stockinged feet. Carefully, he descended the stairs, and heard his landlady snoring in her down-

305

stairs bedroom. Outside it was dark, cool with a rushing wind. He hoped the parachutists had made their drop. Dai Lewis would be waiting for them. Though it seemed no additional men were needed. This job was so simple—it seemed too good to be true.

He had been in the kitchen with Jean and Mrs Gordon when the Royal party had arrived. The Special Branch men had soon been in the kitchen demanding tea. They knew Jean, and he was introduced.

"This is the lad our Jean's been courting so long. Come up to make her an honest woman."

Jean had shown her ring, and both she and 'Henry' came in for some chaff. The men were both in their fifties and looked old and clumsy to Holstein. Two *alte Narren*.

"Glad to see the Army's here," the one called Bailey said jovially.

"That's it," the other, Harwood, agreed. "If Jerry decides to invade Scotland tonight, we'll be all right, eh?"

It had been too early for his business, and he hadn't prepared himself. Jean was rushing about with the cook, serving a light meal to Their Majesties and the rest of the party—two men with the King, the Queen's maid and the chauffeur. What an entourage, Holstein thought with a mixture of relief and contempt! Surely the Führer and Eva Braun travelled in more state than that.

He left, murmuring that he mustn't get in the way of the kitchen, and Mrs Gordon gave him a quick, approving look. Holstein knew with cold sureness she was completely caught by his charm. Silly old woman. She wouldn't get in the way of the plans of the Reich!

This was his hour. Despite the scudding clouds, there was enough moonlight for him to be able to make his way easily enough. The birch woods were not thick on these mountain slopes and he had watched the path carefully as he had traversed it twice earlier that day. There was the winding stream below to guide him. He moved silently, for when he had pulled on his boots he had drawn the extra pair of woollen socks over them. So silent was he that Jean Sinclair, coming round a bend in the path, almost fell into his arms.

"Oh, you were coming to me!"

It was her daydream come true. It seemed to her that she must be the luckiest girl in the world. Never was there such a man, she thought with joy, Prince Charming, real, hers, here.

"You foolish one," she said fondly, tender to the recklessness that flattered. "I would lose my place if Mrs Gordon heard us."

She saw his face was pale and hugged him to show she didn't mean her cruel words.

"I couldn't sleep in my bed either," she confessed. "Not alone, on our last night, our honeymoon . . ."

Holstein was calculating. He could kill her now and get on with his work. But his orders were to kill no-one but the King unless it was absolutely necessary. Particularly anyone of importance. Jean was not important; on the other hand it was not necessary to kill her. He would have to get her to bed and to sleep, that was all. One hour, perhaps. Fortunately for her, she was too busy gazing at his face in the moonlight to notice the state of his boots. He whipped off the heavy socks when she walked ahead on the narrow path.

He got her up the stairs to his room without incident. They began to undress in the dark. Even so, it was an awkward moment when he had to remove the loaded webbing and somehow stuff it into his kitbag. But the girl was a natural fool, and giggling, she tripped over the chamber pot and laughed out loud. Not surprisingly, the voice of their landlady was heard, in Scottish wrath, from downstairs.

"And what is going on? Who is up there?"

"Oh, my God," Jean whispered. "She'll tell auld Gordon for certain."

"Be quiet," Holstein said tersely. "I'll go down and take care of her."

Placating landladies was one thing he knew well. Pulling his shirt on again, he ran downstairs and charmed the old hag. He'd just knocked into something in the dark. He was so sorry he had disturbed her; it was the last thing he wanted to do after all her kindness.

Mrs Rae was by no means deceived. She knew the voice of a giggling girl when she heard one and knew quite well what was going on. But even in her indignation, she stopped to arrange her wig before confronting the fine young man. Now she looked at him sternly, more sternly than she felt. He was a handsome fellow if she had ever seen one, fresh-skinned and clear-eyed even at midnight in the glow of her lamp. Obviously a healthy, decent-living soul, and his expression all as innocent as a new-born bairn's.

Doubtless it was that Jean, man-mad as she was, who was leading him astray. Poor young man, cannon fodder for the Germans as her own son had been in 1916. She would not, even in her own mind, have expressed the thought, 'let him have his fun' but she allowed herself to be persuaded that all was well and went to her own room, to dream that she was young again, and being courted by a lover whose face was more like Holstein's than her somewhat dour, long-dead husband's.

Upstairs, Jean was thinking very different thoughts. For the first time, her belief in her lover had suffered a staggering shock. Ashamed of her foolishness that had caused the trouble, and guilty about the mess she had made with the chamber pot, she had quickly lit the oil lamp and cleaned it up as best she could. When she had finished and washed her hands, she saw Henry's battle dress jacket flung on a chair and picked it up with the neatness of the trained servant to hang it on the hook.

Then she paused. Henry had given her the engagement ring on their first day in Aberdeen. But she was certain that he had bought the wedding ring also—had he not mentioned a Special Licence? This was the last night of his leave, the leave that was supposed to be their real honeymoon. True, his Captain had promised a few days soon for the wedding, but Jean was wise enough to know that the Army could be unreliable. The next thing she might hear was that Henry was already overseas. She had waited so long, after the joy of the past weeks she could bear not being Mrs Holbrook for a while longer. But it would be fun to wear the ring and pretend, just for the night.

She longed to put it on. Very likely he had put it in the pocket of his jacket. With it in her hand she could hardly resist taking a look. But the right pocket contained only his leave pass and service and pay book. She noticed, with regret, that his leave had indeed been intended to last another two weeks, as he had told her, always with the provision that he might have to report back in an emergency. Turning over the pages of his service book she came to 'Next of kin'. Poor Henry, the pages were blank. He had no-one but her. But, she thought happily, the next time she saw that book her name would be there. Next of kin, Jean Holbrook, wife.

A slight shadow touched her at the thought of *one* use the Army had for the names of next of kin. But nothing would happen to Henry. He wasn't the ordinary soldier. Certainly, he was unusual. She was sure he would be made an officer very soon and given a special job where he could use his good brains and be out of danger.

While she was thinking these soothing thoughts her hands were already in the left pocket. There *was* a slim case, but long, more the size to hold a small fountain pen than a wedding ring. Curious, she opened it anyway. The former nurse had no trouble in recognising a syringe and a set of ampoules when she saw them. Without any conscious thought, she was struck, instantly, by a wave of doubt, a feeling that something was terribly wrong.

It was only a syringe, she told herself. No reason suddenly to feel sick—it was absurd. But why a syringe? Her head felt curiously woolly, she couldn't seem to think clearly. Henry had no illnesses. He was the very picture of good health, so much so that she teased him about it —the bright blue of his eyes, so dear to her, his wonderful digestion that had taken Scottish oatmeal and finnan haddie as though he'd eaten them all his days, the regularity of his bowels that sent him down the hall at exactly eight o'clock each morning, the rock-like splendour of his manly parts.

Why a syringe? He wasn't a medical orderly. But there must be a reason, any one of a hundred reasons, why he should carry one. Pinched it from stores, perhaps for a friend who needed it—but what was it, who would need it? A drug? Jean had been in the hospital long enough to know about drugs. But her Henry would not involve himself in anything like that. Henry was—what was he?

She could not have said why she was struck with a strange foreboding. Half thoughts, mental pictures pressed in on her in a dense cloud like that of swarming insects, each with their own dreadful sting. She sank down on the bed, her knees trembling too much to hold her up. What was Henry? Who was he? For the first time it was borne in on her who she was. Not just Jean, but Jock Sinclair's daughter, both trusted servants of the Royal Family . . . Henry Horst. She had met him as an SS man. It was he who had told her he was working for the Secret Service—no-one else. And then he came to England and said he was a soldier. But, now that she thought about it, as a half German wouldn't it have been more likely he would have stayed in the Service—if he had been in it at all? What kind of foolish, havering creature was she?

Her frightened gaze took in his kitbag—but there was nothing to enlighten her there. She had been through it a couple of times, taking out things to be washed. Although her knees were like jelly, her hand still clutched the case with the syringe. Her mind froze, she could not think straight. But she took out the ampoules and the syringe, glittering almost golden in the yellow lamplight. She had been looking for gold. A wedding ring. And instead . . . The glittering things dazzled her eyes, and then dropped through her fingers to the floor.

Carefully, she ground the ampoules and the syringe down into the wooden planks with the wide, flat leather heel of her sensible maid's shoes.

She was still staring at the ground-up glass when Henry re-entered the room. He was struck with a horror almost as great as her own. The wretched female must have been through his kitbag. Obviously, she had discovered his purpose. That hardly troubled him. He was confident that he could manage Jean—she had not screamed or run for the police. But his syringe . . . His orders were so very definite. The King's death must appear natural. Now what was he to do?

The Black Knight did not lose his head. First, he would take care of Jean. He would contrive *something* with the King when the time came.

"Darling," he said easily, his voice light. "Everything's all right. Mrs Rae's gone back to bed." He peered down as if just noticing the mess on the floor. "Oh, you dropped my syringe."

As she looked at him, with his manner so unembarrassed, his voice so soothingly familiar, some of the strange feeling lifted. This was her Henry . . .

"What was in it?" she whispered. His mind had already checked through the possibilities. Asthma, diabetes —but she had been a nurse and knew too much. Besides, she had probably seen the other things. Better to tell something close to the truth.

"Now you're asking, aren't you?"

He gave her an affectionate, quizzical smile, and a little squeeze.

"I told my CO you'd never believe I was a private,"

he said ruefully. "My girl's too sharp for that, I said. But he ordered me not to say anything. But I know I can trust you, Jean. My God, if I can't trust you, there's no-one in the world I can. I might as well be dead."

Her soft, pink moist mouth was open and her eyes were half-pleading, half-wary. But he had seen the way she shuddered at his last, dreadful sentence, with its subtly hinted threat.

"You knew I was in the Secret Service. Well, I still am. The powers-that-be are afraid the Germans might find out that the King and Queen are coming up here. They're a bit obstinate about having proper protection, you know."

Jean did know. She had heard her lady say many times how Birkhall would be spoiled for them if they had to have the Army milling about at their very windows.

"So they sent me up here to organise a few people quietly, and to watch and see if there were any strange people congregating in the area. But everything is all right. That's why I have to go back," he said with another rueful twist to his lips. "Another little job. As soon as it's over, I think you'd better come down and meet me in London for the wedding—there's always the possibility they might decide to drop me back behind enemy lines."

That did it, he could see. The threat of danger to his person . . . For Jean, along with this new anxiety there was also a slow tide of relief. Of course. It was what she had been thinking, she told herself. Naturally Henry was still with the Secret Service. M16, the Special Branch men called it. Or was it M15? But another question came off her tongue before she had finished the thought.

"But what was that?" she pointed to the glass on the floor.

"Well, nobody really expected any trouble," he said. "But just in case, if we had to move the King quickly— you know how they are," he said, in resigned tones. "He would make a fuss, and he's not well. My CO had a talk with his doctor—this is just some stuff to soothe the nerves. Works faster than the same dose in water."

She knew that that was true.

"Doesn't matter now," he said. "It won't be needed. Everything's snug and safe."

He could go back to Aberdeen and buy a syringe. Even without the stuff they'd given him, he could make a death look natural enough. He'd done it before. The Russians had shown no sign of thinking anything was wrong, although that awkward *Polkovnik* had been a thick-necked, healthy-looking specimen.

But he had to dismiss that idea. The job was scheduled for tonight. Any delay would hold up the rest of the plan. He didn't know all that was happening, but the exact nature of the timing, once his call had been made to the Welshman, had been dinned into him as an absolute.

Jean was relieved to hear her Henry's explanation. She was now almost back to her normal feeling of security, and the thoughts that went with it.

"I'll have to get you a ride to the station in the morning," she said. "As soon as the telephone is working I'll get Arthur to bring up the van to take you."

She gazed at him with her usual trusting look. But he had to get her to sleep so that he could leave. She was still fidgety and excited. There was always the one way to deal with Jean. His mind was ticking away the seconds. By now the paratroopers should be at the airfield, part of Whaleforce was already guarding the road to Birkhall. But he would have to take the time.

Confidently, he drew her to him. He removed her print dress. Underneath she wore the silk cami-knickers, awkward things but he had learned how they fastened with the two silly little buttons underneath. Soon his hands and tongue moved about her body as expertly and mechanically as if he were starting up an engine according to instructions, and he entered her while his mind was calculating exactly how long she would take to come to a climax.

It was soon over, and Jean subsided onto the pillows. In a moment of relaxation after his own climax, as inevitable and unexciting as a sneeze, he closed his eyes. He would wait ten minutes to be sure she was asleep. Jean was a deep sleeper. Once her breathing was regular, she had to be prodded and goaded to wakefulness.

But for once, though Jean lay still, sleep would not come. The lovemaking, although it had provided physical release, had not been soothing. It had not been soothing at all. Instead, once again she was troubled. With the lamp out, in the darkness, her fears began to rise again. She was not analytical; she had never made love to another man, but something in that carefully calculated, thoroughly accomplished arousal and satisfying of her passion, left her chill.

It was not Henry who made her feel like this, she argued with herself despairingly. It was her own faithless, wicked thoughts. But faithless, wicked, as it was, the uneasiness remained. She could not think why. But her whole edifice of love and trust had been built on a romantic dream, and the dream had faded next to the reality of such a little thing, a small case containing something hard and real, the smooth glass of the tiny syringe.

Henry had explained everything . . . A shaft of moonlight came through the window and touched his noble, gleaming head. His face was white and still—he might have been a dead man, a knight entombed. Her mind was blank as she slid silently from the bed. Snatching up her dress she moved like a ghost to the door and, taking the key, stepped outside and swiftly locked it. Barefoot, she ran down the stairs, out of the house and along the path to Birkhall.

TWENTY-ONE

Black Knight Takes King

The Fallschirmjäger in the Wellington were in high spirits. The run from Stavanger had been what British airmen called 'a piece of cake'. The route had been carefully plotted well away from Luftlotte Five and kept them from any blundering encounter with their own fighters, who would have made for the 'Wimpy' like bees to honey . . . it was wretchedly vulnerable to attacks from the side.

The moon shone clear. The coast patrol was thinner than they had expected; they saw no RAF at all until they were almost over the coast. There a Spitfire was limping back, bullet-ridden, losing fuel, the pilot wondering whether or not he could make it back to his base. Suddenly clouds scudded across the sky: a strong wind had blown up from the west. He was having far too much trouble to concern himself with a lone bomber, straggling home.

Young Willi Schurmer, of Augsburg, was elated. He was not part of this crack group: it was a great honour that he had been chosen to replace Sergeant Wachter. Fortunately, his training had been completed. In peacetime he had been an ardent mountain climber . . . that, and the fact he had some English was why he had been chosen. The Captain had explained. He had been very kind, and the whole group had done a practice drop for his benefit. They had just had sandwiches and coffee, strong coffee laced with a little Schnapps.

Captain Stangel watched him carefully. Fortunately, the boy was a good type. It had been damned bad luck that Wachter, after all the jumps they had made together, had cracked his knee cap sliding down a rocky pass in the Vogtland. Out of all the possible replacements, there were few who had any English. According to plan, only the Welsh Haupt-V-Mann should have to do any talking. But Stangel knew that plans were inclined to alter slightly when they became operational. The simple record of 'objective taken' covered a lot of improvising. He smiled down encouragingly on the lad.

"These Players aren't too bad," he remarked.

Schurmer was smoking an English cigarette like the others, though he really didn't enjoy it very much. But the red glowing points were comforting in the dim light of the fuselage. Secretly he wondered how these veterans managed to be so unconcerned. Corporal Becker was arguing with Dietz about the promotions expected after the job. Schurmer coughed on the Player's. He wished he had a good German *Reval*. But they were already dressed in RAF uniforms under their flying overalls, with British papers, money, photographs and even letters in their wallets. His photograph was of a very pretty girl—he wished he had a girl like that.

The parachutes were British also. He'd tried one out on the practise drop. The cords helped in manouvering but the 'chute was very different from the one he was used to. The Captain had insisted on it. Even the pistols they carried in their supply bags, on the line clipped to their waists, were British. He had trained with the Webley six-shooter and with the .303 Lee Enfield rifle and the Bofors machine-gun of the type they expected to find at the airfield. He was competent with them now.

The Captain reflected that their all-British gear would give them a good chance even if, by very bad luck, they were intercepted before reaching the airfield. Of course, if searched, the weapons would give them away—but they would not wait to be searched. It was a pity they couldn't have landed on the field itself, but it was too conspicuous; the house above still occupied. But with any luck they should be there half an hour after landing.

The navigator was not as confident. Bad enough flying into the mountains, he thought, but they were also flying low. The low level RDF did not extend over the area, but any reasonable altitude might show them up on the plotting room screen in Aberdeen. At the moment he would rather have taken the chance—it wasn't always reliable. And the girls they had on duty might be asleep, or painting their fingernails. But the pilot, Meister, had said they had to go low anyway. Six men had to be dropped on a clearing not more than three hundred feet. He had bragged to the Fallschirmjäger, "Nothing to worry about. I can drop you on a *pfennig*." Meister was one of Göring's men all right. The navigator himself was slightly older and he had joined the Luftwaffe for the pay. He had been chosen for this job for his skill, but he had very little desire to be a hero. Mostly he was worried about the return flight. Stavanger was supposed to be warned, but he didn't trust either the brass or those fools on the guns. Lucky that this awkward, obsolete old tub could get up to 18,000 feet. They would go back flying high, under oxygen, and Meister, who was good when his mouth was shut, would land as steep and fast as made sense.

The pilot was still confident. From his side Plexiglass panel he saw the moonlight, intermittent now, turn the Dee into a glittering silver arrow leading across the valley. As the nose of the plane dipped, already he could see the little Muick flowing to the Dee. His target was very slightly south, into the wooded slopes, just west of the tributary. He was flying very low now. Captain Stangel had squeezed his way up to the front gunner's turret and was the first to see the torches in the clearing and gave the signal 'action stations'.

Moving back, he pulled away the boards that covered the dropping hole and turned on the red light. He tapped the shoulder of Dietz, the first man to drop. In a moment he was in place, and Stangel himself clipped the loose thong of his parachute to the static line, testing it with a quick pull. The man looked down where two torches were flaring, then the tree tops waved beneath him.

The pilot grunted in annoyance. He had miscalculated and overshot the clearing. He swung the aircraft into a slow turn and Stangel clutched Dietz's arm and switched off the warning light. Below the valley, a village tilted skywards and the seasonal veteran Dietz felt a familiar clutching at his gut. As they moved in again for the pass the warning light glowed red once more, and the flaps went down to cut the speed. As the light turned to green, Dietz was gone before Stangel finished the call.

Smoothly, one by one the men descended, six parachutes flapped open and hung, staggered, a perfect drop except for the pushing winds. Schurmer was the last to go before the Captain. Seeing the trees come closer he had a moment's attack of nerves and hung back.

"Jump!" the Captain shouted and he went.

He was thrown back horizontally by the slipstream. A hard jerk at his groin and below his armpits—his 'chute had opened all right. He saw the Herr Hauptmann follow him; the roar of the twin motors of the departing Wellington filled his ears, then, in a moment, silence. Tongues of flame from the exhaust pipes lashed into the night, but he at once forgot the craft. From beneath him a freakish air current, swirling from the mountains, filled his 'chute and lifted him along. He struggled with the cords—his newly acquired knowledge half-forgotten in swift panic as the current drove him inexorably into the woods, out of sight of his more skilful captain, and the rest.

Luckily, the trees on the wooded slopes were not

318

thick. Recovering, he made a swift pull on the forward set of cords, and manoeuvred himself backwards over a tiny open patch of ground, and he drifted down, knees bent, ready for the impact. His dangling supply bag caught on a projecting branch, and the line twisted about him so that he made a clumsy fall, his body crashing on the ground. Suddenly his parachute was like a live thing, pulling, billowing and evading his grasp to rip itself against the nearest tree.

Cursing softly, wishing the others would come and help him, but too well-trained to call, he struggled to get out of the harness, only to freeze as he heard a voice speak, saying something softly in English. It was not a familiar voice.

"That you, Johnny?"

He was very still. The voice spoke again, another replied, too low for him to hear. There was whispering. The steps seemed to move away—but that could be a trick. He stayed silent a few moments longer. Then, with shaking hands, feeling very sick, he hid the parachute as best he could under some windblown leaves and branches, using the spade from his supply bag. Impossible to take the time and start digging now—too noisy. Besides, the English party were to collect the 'chutes for burning later.

Nor did he dare strike through the woods to meet the others, doubtless only a hundred feet or so away. Between them were the unknown men—policemen on patrol, no doubt. Fortunately, his instructions covered the situation. If separated, he should make his way with caution, to rendezvous at the target airfield a little less than two miles south-west of the drop. As quietly as a young man of a hundred and seventy pounds could move, he struck out southward and very slightly east. Soon he should see the river.

Dai Lewis had been searching for him, while the other paratroops had quickly and quietly buried their overalls and 'chutes. Both he and the Captain had seen Schurmer drift off into the wood and expected he would be caught in a tree. Fifty feet away, he too had heard the talk of the Scotsmen in the woods. He paused.

Unlike the terrified Schurmer, he was certain that these men were not policemen—nothing was more unlikely. A couple of local men, perhaps more, doing a little poaching, still one of the great Highland occupations, he'd been told while he was in Aberdeen. Lewis was Chapel and a non-drinker. He thought poorly of most Scots, including the ones in Whaleforce. Though not as poorly as they thought of the Irish. He hadn't wanted to work with them at all, but they had needed hard, experienced killers who could help train the rest.

Listening to the Scots, it was obvious they were afraid of being caught themselves and were unsuspicious. Luckily, they'd seen nothing. Still, they were a nuisance. If they came across a group of Air Force men in a clearing in the middle of the night they would certainly go blabbing. They must have heard the 'plane. It was the very last thing he wanted. He returned to the Germans and quickly got them started on the safest path to the south, and then made his way back to where he'd heard the voices. The poachers, frightened no doubt, had taken themselves off. He searched for a time for the missing man, but the moon was almost completely hidden now; heavy rain-bearing clouds were pressing down. Probably he had freed himself and started for the rendezvous.

Lewis made a decision. The party of airmen would be much more likely to attract attention than a lone wanderer, who would be thought the usual amorous airman, returning from lovemaking in a neighbouring cottage. He made a mental note to send Evans, a good man—his own son-in-law, in fact—up at dawn to scout around. The German might have left scraps of silk in the branches. He hastened after the main group and led them along the bank away from the road, crossing by the old footbridge near Alt Chernie to the field. His own men changed back into their RAOC uniforms.

Before they went to take up their positions, he went over their instructions once again. A small party would guard the road both north and south of the house, setting barricades and 'road up' signs. Tomorrow, Maloney in the Churchill car would branch off before the south barricade. Then the road party would join the five men waiting at the 'Reception Centre'.

"Remember, no bullets," he repeated. "The old man and the pilot 'die' in the crash. Very likely there won't be a post mortem but we have to be sure."

He turned to Purcell, and asked him the question he had already asked at least twenty times.

"Are you sure it'll come down in this area?"

Purcell peered at his topographical chart in the shaded light of the hut, and for at least the twentieth time, answered patiently:

"This is roughly the perimeter he will reach." His finger marked a circle round the field. "If he is going south, he must come down about here." He tapped a small arc. "Depending on the wind there can be a slight variation, but not much."

"He'll do that," Lewis said. "Even if he gets other instructions, I'll make sure they're changed before he takes off. But you're sure that other thing will work?"

Purcell was sure. He had helped develop the K13 unit at Quenzee. It was simple enough to use, except that no-one knew what 'plane Churchill would be taking. Some small adaptation might be needed when it was inserted.

"I'm sure," he said. "But Maloney's lads had better see that the craft is well and truly burned. Later on people might start looking at that wreckage. If there's time I'll take a look at it."

The miner gazed at the technician. He had to assume he knew what he was doing.

"Don't worry, Frank lad," Maloney interjected. "My

boyos could burn up half of what the RAF has left in no time at all."

He thought of the neat job they'd done at the armaments factory in Waltham Abbey. He'd tell Frank about that some time, but not in front of the Welshman.

Lewis ignored his bragging, but remembered another job. "We'll move the tanks in the hangar up against the lean-to wall tonight. Captain Stangel, while we are finishing off the 'plane tomorrow, have your men dig up the bodies and get them in there."

Those RAF storage tanks would prove convenient. The dead men would be the victims of a nasty accident, for which, however, inquiry would hold them to be responsible—the tanks were much too close to the lean-to. The men had probably been smoking. Purcell was being very helpful about the time fuse.

He paused. Fervently he hoped the lost man would turn up soon. Before the forward parties left, he took Evans aside and gave him the job of searching the trees for the parachute scraps.

"We'll collect the rest if there's time and if not, they're well buried," he said.

Evans saw his concern and offered to go at once and hunt for the missing man. There would be two men on the barricade without him, and probably they would not be needed for hours yet. Lewis was beginning to feel about the Fallschirmjäger much as Admiral Canaris had done. He hoped they wouldn't make a mess of firing the hut. Now he had to send a man out looking for their stray sheep, putting himself in danger.

Lewis had no son of his own, but Evans took the place of the son he might have had. The two of them had been ardent Welsh Nationalists, but had broken from the Welsh Nationalist Party at the beginning of the war when the Party had decided on no action against England for the duration. He and Evans had built up a small but effective group of their own, and there was no man he valued more highly. The Germans were armed. He could imagine a young frightened foreigner in the woods at night with a gun. Hearing a man's tread he might shoot first and question later. Lewis was brave for himself, but he had no desire to make his daughter a widow.

He shook his head.

"I'll go and take a look. Purcell can stay with the Germans—though I doubt there'll be any traffic by here tonight. And I don't expect to have much to do until morning."

In the morning his sometime landlady, the post office worker in Aberdeen, would receive confirmation of Churchill's whereabouts from Leiter. She would send the telegram, and their real work would begin. He said nothing more to the Germans, but Stangel had caught his look of annoyance. He was beginning to worry about Schurmer himself, but, he reflected, a man without a guide would take longer on these wooded hills.

Schurmer had not got too far. His instructions had been explicit: directly south about two miles, and then slightly east over a footbridge. But as he tried to make his way, he decided that the instructions must have been made up by a man who had never seen this country. The lie of the land pushed him inexorably to a direct path to the east, unless he was to waste all night scrambling over hills and and inclines. It was now so overcast that no-one could see him; he could not see his way himself. Better to get down near the river and follow it south, as any man who knew the country would.

As he came to a rise of land over the river the going became easier. He was in a grove but the ground was fairly level. Congratulating himself on his decision, he went on. There was no way he could have known he was approaching Birkhall House, nor would the name have meant anything to him if he did. Quiet as he thought he was, a twig broke beneath his tread, and a dog in the dark house above broke into an excited barking.

The Special Branch men, though with no idea of trouble, were punctiliously making their patrols. The noise of the dog meant nothing, the slightest sound of a rabbit hopping to its burrow would set him off but Bailey, at the back of the house, had heard the snapping of the twig and moved in the direction of the sound.

Schurmer heard his heavy tread approaching. His orders had been to attack only if absolutely necessary. He knew he should stand his ground and present his papers if challenged. But the boy on the dark, lonely windswept ridge felt his flesh creep. If he did not pass the challenge —what then? In his British uniform he was a spy. Spies were shot. But not at once. They would want information. The English Gestapo—his knife was in his hand. Suddenly the death of this enemy seemed essential.

Some part of Schurmer's training had been thorough. The Englishman had a torch, from which a thin slice of light was approaching. Schurmer, hiding behind a bush, waited his moment. Before Bailey was aware that a man was there at all, a knife was at his throat and he fell, with only a small, inarticulate gurgling sound onto the grass. Schurmer, dizzy with relief, began to run.

"Bailey?" a voice called, and a torch flashed onto Schurmer, still holding the bloody knife in his hand.

Detective-Inspector Harwood was shocked, but not too shocked to tug the Webley from his shoulder holster. Schurmer, terrified by a second voice coming from somewhere behind the light, was slow to recover and found himself with the Webley at his head.

"Drop the knife," the voice said in a tone of command, and it slipped harmlessly from his grasp.

The man moved the thin pencil of light and saw Bailey on the ground. He gasped but it was the last breath he ever drew. Two hands closed about his neck like steel bands. Schurmer looked, unbelieving, as an English soldier choked the man with silent efficiency. Holstein picked up the light and looked at the man he had saved with grim rage. Schurmer recovered his senses enough to give the password.

"Jonah," he whispered.

"Clumsy idiot," Holstein said savagely. He kicked the dead men into a clump of bushes. The Welshman would have to dispose of them somehow. He couldn't stop now. Why had they sent this young fool to blunder about? He pointed out a path down to the river and left him to his fate. He had his own work. Silently he made his way up through the terraced garden to the sleeping house.

Earlier Holstein had heard the click of the door as Jean had left and sprung up. He could have smashed it open, but it was better not to waken Mrs Rae again. Instead he let himself down from the window, only a ten-foot drop to the ground. The moon kept disappearing now behind the cloud but he could still make out the path, though not as easily as Jean, who had lived on these hills most of her life and could have run to the house blindfold.

In the birch wood he stopped when he heard a muffled step. He approached quiet as a cat, but the other man, searching, was aware of something.

"Jonah," Dai Lewis said quietly, but to his disappointment it was Holstein who gave the answer. "Great fish."

Lewis explained quickly about the missing parachutist and went on. Then Holstein had stopped again, when he heard the running men of Special Branch, and followed them into the grove.

Jean had reached the house while the Special Branch men were hunting for Schurmer. She looked about, and went in the room where their beds were, the blankets not turned down, the pillows as yet untouched. She went straight to the Queen's room.

"Ma'am . . ." The Queen was fast asleep. Jean, her hand shaking, lit the lamp. "I'm afraid there's . . . someone

. . . coming to kill the King. And I can't find the police-men."

The Queen blinked drowsily.

"Is that you, Jean? *What* are you saying?"

"It's—" Jean felt thick, stupid and terrified all at once. "It's a German—" She could say no more, and gaped dumbly.

The Queen saw her white face, staring eyes and shaking hands. The girl was in a state of shock. Her Majesty took control instantly.

"Telephone Balmoral," she said.

"The lines are down," Jean said frantically.

The Queen had already risen. It would take time to find out what had frightened Jean. It might be a nonsense, but then she remembered the talk of parachutists that she had thought rather absurd. She also realised that if the policemen were missing, and not just wandered off, the King was unprotected. *Almost.*

From her wardrobe she selected an old tweed coat, and from the drawer of her night table she took the Webley with which she had frightened Lord Halifax in the Palace gardens. She loaded it and put it in her handbag, put on her shoes and put the coat over her nightgown. She looked at Jean, but the girl was shaking all over, as if she were in some kind of fit. So the Queen went herself to wake the house.

Burns, the King's valet, had heard Jean enter and was already up. He was startled at the Queen's appearance.

"The girl says the policemen are missing," she said quietly. "They might be patrolling the grounds. See if you can find them, will you?"

Her manner was calm but he saw her face, usually so rosy, was pale.

"I'll wake the others," she said, and he went without a word.

She woke Giles Carruthers, the King's equerry, and told him what had happened.

"The girl might be mad, or in a panic, but we daren't

take a chance. Wake Parsons, and each of you take a car and go for help. You go to Balmoral, Giles, and send Parsons to Ballater."

"Let the girl go," he protested. "I'll stay with the King."

"No, you must go." The King was in the room, quiet and calm but pale. He was completely dressed and he had a pistol in his pocket. "None of the women can drive," he said. "And the two cars are better than one."

"Then come with me," Carruthers urged. "It's safer than staying here."

The Queen spoke.

"If the girl is telling the truth, the Germans might be watching the roads for the King. It's better we go and take shelter in the woods. No outsider could find us there. But take the girl with you. Have some one calm her down and find out what it's all about. Try not to wake Donaldson. She won't let me go without being properly turned out," she added, with a smile.

The equerry went with no further argument. Parsons, the chauffeur, in pyjamas, dressing-gown and slippers, was out in the car in four minutes. Unknown to the Queen, Donaldson, woken by the movements in the house, was dressing with a speed that later made the Queen say that she must sleep in her underclothes.

Burns was stumbling about in the grounds. He was a good valet, trusted by the King, and understood what a gentleman should wear in the country. But he had been a city boy and had no idea how he was to find these policemen in the sixty acres of the Birkhall estate, even if they hadn't wandered off elsewhere. Much better to telephone for help. One of the cars should have gone to the Mac-Bride place. He began to run on the road, southward. He came to the south barricade, and was surprised but relieved to find three men of the RAOC. Carruthers was delayed in looking for Jean, but Parsons had already run into the barricade of the north party. And so of the Royal household it was two servants who were the first to die.

Jean was not to be found and Carruthers gave up—it was time he was off. If there *was* any danger—and he had always thought that girl close to a half wit—help was important, explanations could come later. The strong wind had driven off much of the cloud and the moon shone on the peaceful-looking valley. It was probably all a nonsense. But . . .

He hesitated. He could strike north-west to Balmoral over the hills. There were some rough paths he could push the car along, with luck. But then he might run out of luck. A fallen tree, or a boulder. And the car itself, he'd noticed on their way up, wasn't really up to the worst of these roads. But if he took the good road north to Ardmeanach and then the main road westward he could be in Balmoral in no time at all. And so he argued with himself, and took the same road northward as the chauffeur Parsons, to join him soon in a common grave.

Jean could not be found for she was hiding. She waited, watching from the gardens as the Royal couple departed. A little later, Donaldson came out, walking determinedly after them. This galvanised Jean into action, and she followed, hovering behind them, until they were on the other side of the river in the comparative safety of the Forest of Altcailleach. Her mind was still frozen and she moved like an automaton. But she had one driving purpose. She must go back to the house and meet Henry. It was all important that she find out—and she knew that he would come.

She was on her way back when Holstein arrived at the house. The dog barked and ran towards him, but recognised a friend. He entered under the wide-beamed porch through the door that had been left ajar. At once, with sinking heart, he guessed what had occurred, but he made a silent and thorough inspection of the house. The cook was snoring in her bed in the back of the house, but everyone else had gone. And so were the two cars.

The Black Knight of the SS felt as though he'd been punched in the gut. His mission had already failed in part. Two policemen, who should not have been killed, were lying dead in the bushes. The Royals had been warned—by that hysterical slut.

Not that they could get away. Dai Lewis' men were guarding the road. *If* they had taken the road. Jean, stupid Jean, would know where they had gone. But she had probably gone with them.

He hesitated. Below him was the Muick, behind and before a range of peaks met the sky. Jean's mountains—mere hills, he had thought that night, but now in the moonlight the landscape stretched alien and hostile. His was the instinct of the hunter, a hunter of man. And his mind was cool and clear.

From all that he had heard from Jean, he tried to follow the King's thinking. He was a sportsman, a country lover. No town-minded fool, to rush for the roads and be taken in an ambush; he had known this country all his days, and it was there he would seek refuge, quietly, on foot. But where? To the west was Balmoral, where he would find protection, but it was too far over the wide range of hills for a man of his years, in poor health. To the east was the river, but he would not attempt to cross by moonlight.

Holstein gazed about him. Southward, the sparse trees gathered themselves into a dark stretch of forest. All his hunter's knowledge told him that that was where his prey had gone. He struck south, ready to stalk the king through the wooded slopes into the Forest of Altcailleach.

The King and Queen, though alert, were in no state of panic as they walked the hills. The night was mild and they knew this country as well as the gardens of Buckingham Palace. After some quiet talk, it seemed to both of them most likely that Jean had been taken by some form of hysteria. She was a good girl and a willing worker, but

329

not, the Queen knew, very intelligent. Her new importance, as maid to the Royal Family during war-time, had perhaps gone to her head. Somebody might have been teasing her.

"They've probably been talking of nothing in the kitchen but spies and parachutists," the King remarked. "Everyone has parachute mania now."

"They do . . . indeed," the Queen answered.

She thought of the dire warnings of the Prime Minister, and felt both guilty and yet still believing there was nothing really wrong. All a lot of fuss that would turn out to be nothing, and she would feel silly for having heeded a foolish girl. On the other hand she also knew that all of England—and the Western world—looked to them as they stood alone against the enemy.

If only the telephone line had not blown down! And when it went it always put the service out for the length of the glen. Once the cars got to Ballater and Balmoral, all the police in the country and half the Army would be swarming round Birkhall. Perhaps she should only have sent to the police station in Ballater. Sometimes the police could be discreet, but once the Army was parading about they might as well go back to London. It was the end of their peaceful holiday. Still, she had had to do what she did. Never would she take a chance with Bertie's safety.

She looked at her husband anxiously, searching for signs of strain. But the walking and climbing seemed to invigorate him. He laughed. "This is better than sleeping after that long journey. I haven't been getting out enough."

Their holiday was certainly starting with an adventure, she thought, if it really was . . . all right. No use to fret, and worry Bertie. She smiled. It was a long time since they'd been walking anywhere, truly alone. He thought the same thing, perhaps, and squeezed her arm gently.

"I wonder what did set that girl off," he said.

The Queen believed, most likely, Jean had heard

some too ardent Scottish Nationalist, flown with whisky, indulge in some wild talk. There were such people around and about. A Scotswoman herself, the Queen understood these things and firmly believed they meant nothing. No harm could come from her people. Just Highland havering. Whisky talk. But she was a little reluctant to say so.

"She is very young, and her soldier was in action. She sees Germans everywhere, I expect. And imagines things when we're here. I hope Mrs Gordon won't dismiss her. She will be annoyed, that is, if everything . . ." She didn't finish the sentence.

The King pulled a little face.

"It will be you and I who will be kept under guard after this, I'm afraid."

They felt gloomily certain that this was true. By their next visit, the Royal Guard would be in barracks at Ballater. Birkhall House would be no more private than Royal Lodge.

Each was more nervous than they admitted to the other. When a firm footfall sounded close behind them, they both started violently. But the voice that came strongly was not alarming, though very unwelcome.

"Ma'am, Ma'am, wait." It was Donaldson, for once hatless, her hair in some sort of net, but otherwise fully dressed. She gazed at the Queen's costume with an air of affront. "Ah heerd the commotion," she said grimly. "And here ah am." She sounded much more Scottish in her agitation.

The Queen felt a slight pang of annoyance. Certainly, here she was, and what good she could do, no-one could tell. Donaldson complained of walking the corridors of the Palace, and with her rheumatism was very conscious of draughts. She was the last person in the world to be of use on such a night. But doubtless she meant well.

As if reading her thoughts, Donaldson continued.

"I can do ma bit," she said. She opened her bag and

showed the Queen a long knife that she had purloined from the kitchen.

The Queen felt a rush of gratitude for her and the love and loyalty that she and all her people lavished on both of them. But Donaldson complained at every step. The woman who had once been Elizabeth Bowes-Lyon of Glamis could have walked all night easily. She would have preferred to do so—although she could not believe there was real danger, yet she felt safer in motion in the woods. It would take a small army to find them there. But Bertie would get tired.

Donaldson hit her foot on a stone and groaned softly.

"We could go up to MacBride's," she said, "or is it the cottage you have a mind for?"

The Queen gave her a sharp look, but the King seemed to agree.

"I suppose we'll have to find somewhere to sit after a while. Should we go to the cottage, or make for Allt-na-guibsaich?"

The glen was dotted with houses built by Queen Victoria; there was shelter enough. But the cottage and Allt-na-guibsaich, or even Glas-allt-Shiel at the head of the Loch, were too well-known. As for MacBride's place, that was the first house that would be searched—if there was anything in Jean's wild tale.

"Let's stay in the woods—if you think that a good idea . . . ?" she said. It was her way, and part of her charm, that she presented her firm convictions in a questioning, deferential form. "By the craig at Loinmuie there's an old shooting bothy—only a hut—but there should be a chair or two to sit on. Hardly anyone knows of it, and no-one would expect to find us there."

"Ah hope that someone finds us in the morning. The police or the soldiers," Donaldson said gloomily. "I should have stopped and made up a thermos of tea. It's no so warm, now."

"Perhaps I can make a fire?" The King was smiling.

332

"After all, I ran the Duke of York's camps. *That* seems so long ago," he added, "I wonder if I can remember . . ."

Jean had got back near the house in time to see Holstein leave and look about him. She watched him strike out south, where the King and Queen had gone. Moved by an urgency she could not understand, she took a few steps towards him, hesitated, and jumped back. Holstein's sharp ears caught the slight sound, and he looked up to see her on the slope above him, a pale figure, wraith-like under the moon.

"My darling," he said, "why did you run away? What on earth has happened? Where is everybody?"

Jean looked at him. Her gaze seemed vacant. She's really turned idiot, he thought, with cold annoyance. But she saw Henry's figure, heard Henry's voice, and then Henry's firm hand took hers.

"I—I was afraid," she said. Her mind recovered from its stupor, and she felt she must have been mad indeed. What had she done? For no reason. Because Henry had had some medicine for the King. Now she remembered seeing a bottle of pills by the Queen's bed. She had seen it when she lit the lamp, but had thought nothing. Yet the Queen never took pills; she, too, must have brought something for His Majesty in case he needed it. The poor King, so tired, and she had driven him from his bed to go wandering in the woods.

"Thank God you were afraid," Henry said surprisingly. "And thank God you came back. Or I might be in my bed yet, fool that I am. Jean, there's trouble. Bad trouble. But where is everyone? Where are Their Majesties?"

"Hiding," she whispered, holding onto his hand.

"Jean," he said urgently. "On my way here I saw parachutes coming down, all over the hills."

"Dear Lord!" she moaned, struck with this new ter-

333

ror, that somehow was not as bad as the unknown fear before. She held his hand so tight her fingernails dug into him.

"They sent for help," she told him.

A lot of good that would do them.

"It'll never get here in time," he said. "The enemy are in the grove and the woods. They've been here, Jean. Look what I found."

He took her to the bushes where he'd left the bodies of the two detectives.

Jean looked down at the bodies, flung like great broken dolls across the earth. Harwood's face was in the dirt, but Bailey, who had admired her ring and teased her, was staring up, a great black hole across his throat, a broken branch dragging at his eyeball.

"Their Majesties aren't safe for a second," he said, with proper impatience. "Where have they gone, Jean?"

The wind blew her print dress and set it billowing up from her naked body. She hesitated, agonising over unnamed doubts. But the dead men were real. There was real danger. And here was Henry, her beloved Henry . . . His wide blue eyes, his familiar ingenuous face looked down at her with hope and trust. Four years of deep and fervent love stirred within her.

"Poor little Jean, so frightened," he said tenderly. "But we must find them. I must get there first."

"The Germans won't find them," Jean whispered. "I'm sure. Not at night. The Queen's a bonnie walker and she'll know where to hide."

"But they must have protection," he said urgently, "just in case. A party can come upon them by accident."

Jean stared upon poor dead Bailey. He and Harwood should be buried or the animals—her duty at last seemed plain.

"I don't know," she said slowly. "Perhaps to Glasallt-Shiel—but that's a long climb. I would fancy . . ." She paused.

334

"What do you think? Where would they have gone?" Holstein watched her intently, a snake with a rabbit.

"I wouldn't go to any house," she said. "And I don't think the Queen would either, nor the King, they've too much sense for that. If they take shelter, it'll be in a wee bothy." She looked up at him, struck by a thought. "There's one not much more than two miles up the glen, deep in the woods. On the side of a big craig, just before the stream that comes down off the Coyles. I used to play in it, years ago, and so did the Princess, so the Queen knows it well."

Holstein looked at her consideringly. The usefulness of Jean Sinclair was over. He would track the King down faster alone. She would only be a nuisance. But there were too many killings already. His orders were to refrain, if possible. And then . . . she seemed very sure but she could be wrong. The King might, after all, have gone to some other hut, on some other mountain. He might need Jean once more. But he could not take her with him, nor could he leave her to wander about, coming across God knows who, with all her silly tales.

"*Röslein,*" he said, smiling, drawing her to him with one strong arm. Even as she smiled a tremulous smile, his other arm was already raised behind her and swept down across the crown of her head with stunning force. She went down like a good-sized heifer, he thought, heavy, noisy. But there was no stir or sound about them on the quiet slopes.

He took his knife, and opening the top of his gas mask case, he cut a length of the thin, strong line. He tied her tight, although the line cut cruelly into her flesh, and stuffed his handkerchief into her mouth, binding it with a strip torn from her print dress. Carrying her well away from Birkhall House he threw her into a rocky gulley and strongly hoped he would never need to see her again.

Just before dawn it seemed that hope might be fulfilled. The way had grown harder, he was climbing now. Nothing really to trouble a man with his youth and agility, but he noticed, with annoyance, the slight slackness of his muscles after nearly two weeks with Jean in the hotel room.

The trouble was finding the bothy. Once he came across a house and had to lie low—a dog was barking. Although these mountain woods were not like dense lowland forest, they were thick enough to hide dozens of huts. He made out the craig not by sight, but by the sudden steepness of climb. Without Jean's instructions the search would have taken days. If only she was right . . .

As it was he nearly missed it, though already the darkness had turned to misty grey. It was the sound that caught him, a heavy, rhythmic snore. He turned, and behind him, in the shelter of the two leafy, bending trees, was a dark and squarish shape. He reached for his gun and approached, silent, on cat feet.

The door was slightly open. Seated on the floor was the snoring woman. He could make out a handgun at her side. It was the Queen's gun, and Donaldson's turn to stand guard. But her habit of sleep had been too much for her at last. Holstein's gaze accustomed itself to the dark of the hut. Two seated figures—and he caught the dull gleam of the barrel of a rifle. He took it from the knees of the lightly-sleeping man who was stirring uneasily, not from Holstein's feather-light touch but from the noise of his wife's maid snoring.

He opened his eyes and saw Holstein. Close enough to touch, Holstein gazed back. There was no doubt at all. That famous face, the postage-stamp profile—no doubt at all. This was the King of England, and he, Horst Holstein, had him under his gun.

TWENTY-TWO
Messages

That night Sergeant Barney had managed to get out of Lisbon. His method was crude but it had worked—up to a point. He had hung about Lisbon Airport before the evening flight and followed a passenger into the men's room. There were not too many men taking the 'plane to Whitechurch that night and this was the only one who used the place. He would have to do, Rex thought. A crown and pips, but it couldn't be helped. He was a lieutenant-colonel returning in advance of the rest of his party from a secret military mission to Salazar, but Rex couldn't know that, nor would it have troubled him if he did.

The 'plane was already on the runway waiting for take-off when the officer had darted in, and Rex had to act quickly. His victim was strongly built but he had no reason to expect the stunning blow to the jaw, and he was out cold when he hit the tiled floor. The engines were revving up, and the stewardess was standing by the open door of the craft looking about. The men were ready to take the steps away.

"Just a minute," Rex hollered.

The official at the desk glanced at his papers. The ticket was in order and there were diplomatic credentials. He waved him on and the 'plane taxied down the runway. It struck the official that the English soldier with the reddish-brown hair did not look much like a diplomat. Perhaps he should have . . . but then, if there was anything wrong it was the business of the English. By morning, the Embassy had found something very wrong, and frantic messages were on their way to England.

* * *

During the night Dai Lewis had got all the bad news of Operation Whale. He had found Schurmer, limping on a strained ankle, and on the way back to the field learned about the two dead Special Branch men. He felt a quick spurt of anger against the Germans. Part of the scheme was irrevocably spoiled, the apparently bloodless change-over. The death of the airmen could seem a convincing accident, as well as the Churchill 'plane. But now two Special Branch men also.

Worse was to come very quickly. Evans came himself to report what had happened at the barricades. Three more dead men, and that wasn't all. The victims had been glad to see the RAOC men on the road and had excitedly told of the danger to the King and Queen, and Their Majesties taking to their heels.

Lewis was aghast, but he remembered that Holstein must be close behind them. Doubtless it was Schurmer's murder of the detectives that had sent them off. The King was probably dead by now, but there could be a hue and cry, as he had always feared. In spite of the careful work of Whaleforce the bungling of the Germans had put them all at risk. Trying to make the best of it, he ordered Evans to bring the bodies in the lorry. A roadside burial would be too obvious; perhaps the Germans could manage to burn them before they left and bury their ashes away from the field. They might as well do something.

He spoke in English, but most of the Germans understood, and Captain Stangel understood very well. The Captain was white with anger. He and his men had made

338

an almost perfect landing, under very difficult circumstances. The native force had thought fit to send only one man to set the flares and act as guide and he, on some specious excuse, had abandoned the one missing man. That man had been making his own way and, meeting opposition, had handled it. The Fallschirmjäger were in possession of the airfield, ready to capture the Prime Minister and destroy his 'plane, which was their mission. This miserable peasant, who had been obstructing them and behaving boorishly all along, now was talking of crack German troops as if they were grave-diggers.

The two men wrangled about the replacement of the missing detectives. Lewis pointed out that if the sleeping cook woke up to an empty house, her first instinct would be to go gadding over the mountains spreading her tale in every little inhabited cottage. But his men were unsuited to act as policemen—only he and Maloney, both indispensable, were the required six feet.

Captain Stangel, who did not want to break up his very small unit, coldly offered two men well over the required height with excellent command of English. Dai Lewis, who was very far from having the quiet night he had expected, had to arrange for suitable clothes. Fortunately Maloney had both a suit and a tweed jacket and trousers in his lodgings and was persuaded to give them up, with reluctance, and the men's Air Force shoes were good enough. They had been despatched with instructions to leave the old woman alive if possible; to hold the King and Queen if they returned; to talk as little as they could. If questioned, they were to say that they had been sent from Newcastle as reinforcements and that the Special Branch men, who had left with the King and Queen, had told them nothing. Lewis explained that there was a certain rivalry between different branches of the police, and the old woman would believe that. And if she noticed a trace of accent, she would put it down to their dialect. The Fallschirmjäger understood inter-service rivalry. Lewis took the two men to the house, looking enough like the real thing. Their Webleys were all right, but he removed the silencers which would give them away. They didn't like that, but at least there was an apparent restoration of harmony between himself and Captain Stangel.

Dai Lewis spent the morning of the 26th of July recovering from all his unexpected activity. Horst Holstein, meanwhile, was trapped in a seemingly endless wait. Dawn had been breaking when he took his prey. With the old maid at the door sleeping, he had no trouble with the Royal party. He had rendered her unconscious with a blow, gathered up the weapons, and tied the Royal couple to their chairs with a minimum of violence.

His intention had been to take them to the nearest cliff and arrange their 'accidental' deaths. The 'heart attack' of the King would no longer serve: the Queen had seen him, and must, therefore, die too, together with the wretched hag whose appearance complicated the matter further. The Major would have to understand that that was the best he could do. But Black Knight had hesitated —for such a little thing. A little thing, but it would make the idea of the party taking a night-time walk and meeting with an unfortunate, but quite likely accident, impossible.

The Queen of England had come out in her nightdress. Such an idea had never occurred to Holstein. He eyed Donaldson, but she was thin and stringy. He could never get her clothes on the Queen. His instinct was to kill the three of them and get away. His retreat as planned, openly by train to London, was no longer feasible. The two Special Branch detectives were dead. Jean missing, perhaps dead by now. Soon the telephone line would be mended, or the alarm given some other way. Perhaps he should have killed that cook.

He would go off with the Fallschirmjäger, he decided. But while he was planning the kill, he was still hesitant. The habit of following command was very strong. Major

Leiter had told him of the existence of another plan, if his own task proved impossible. Then he had sent him the AFU set. Obviously, the command intended that in a case like this, he should question before proceeding. With the bright, furious eyes of the Queen upon him, he tapped out his message. But although someone was supposedly waiting for his signal, there was no reply. Holstein was irritated, but not especially alarmed. From his experience, transmissions were picked up more easily at night. At daybreak, the airwaves would be full of signals. He would repeat at intervals. He did so, with somewhat diminished confidence as the day wore on.

Major Leiter, in his careful way, had done everything to be sure that there could be no slip up. The 'secretary' he had brought with him was one of the best radio operators in the Abwehr, a man who for years had been familiar with Holstein's signal. The operators, Leiter knew, got to recognise a man's individual touch—a more certain identification than any call letters. His man, Eckhardt, had worked with Holstein since the Black Knight's joining the Abwehr.

Certainly he hoped that Eckhardt would not be needed. Remembering the Admiral's instructions, he had ordered Holstein to telephone on the completion of his assignment before returning to London. He was only to transmit by wireless if something went awry and he needed help and could not reach a telephone.

From six o'clock on Thursday, Leiter sat close to the 'phone. After midnight, anxiety drove him up to the attic room from time to time to check whether or not Eckhardt was receiving any signal. It was not until 3 am on Friday that Leiter, still at his desk, fell into a nervous doze.

When the Lisbon 'plane landed in Whitechurch at 8 am on Friday morning, the English officials did worry about Rex Barney. They had not yet received the message from

Lisbon, but a man in a sergeant's uniform travelling with the papers of a lieutenant-colonel worried them very much. The doctor passed Barney without remark, but word went out to customs, who held him for a careful search, turning up his own service book and a St Christopher that had been pressed upon him by Maria. The Security men were waiting for him, grim-faced. His tale of a special assignment for the Prime Minister did not impress them when they found the documents he was carrying were not only stolen but from a most secret mission. He was detained under guard pending inquiry.

Rex was in no mood to wait. God knew what was going on in Lisbon while he was penned up here. Or in England. He could not help wondering who else might be involved. He looked about him now, still angry that the Security officers had not even attempted to call Hilliard or any of the Special Branch men who knew him before locking him up. Rex had a feeling they would take their time before turning up anything in his favour.

The room he was in had no window, and the door had a stout lock. The rear and the left wall were solid, but Rex soon found that the right wall and the front were wood. And not heavy wood, either. He had been hustled into the room rather quickly for observation, but he had noticed the Security offices occupied a large concrete outbuilding that might have been converted from a warehouse. This room, like the rest of the row, had been scooped out with wooden partitions. There had been four men pushing and arguing with him as they shoved him in there, and he tried to recall what had been in the big space in the front.

A lot of dark green filing cabinets. Two desks and chairs, and a man—a policeman, not Army—had been sitting in the chair. With any luck he might still be the only one. The brass would have gone off to their private offices.

"Hey, mate, you got a cigarette?" he called.

"Don't try it on, lad," the voice of an old copper was

unmistakable, weary, know-it-all. By his voice he hadn't moved from where he was sitting.

It was quiet out there, no murmur of any other voice agreeing with the first, even by a grunt or a sigh, no fidgeting of chair on the concrete floor, no rustling of papers.

Rex stood in front of the door to his make-shift cell and, ignoring the lock, with all his force gave one swift kick at its centre. The thin wood split and parted on the left from its frame. Rex pushed his way through the mess in a bound that left splinters of wood on his shoulders and part of the door frame on his neck, and was on the startled policeman before he could rise from the desk where he had been placidly eating a cheese roll. For all that, it took a considerable pounding, even by the former local boxing champion, to knock the man unconscious. It was a bit of luck that none of the other back rooms was occupied. The brass had their offices in more comfort.

As he brushed off the splinters, it flashed through his mind that he had assaulted an officer and a policeman in one day. He shrugged. He couldn't worry about that now. But he hoped he hadn't broken the jaw of the old bluebottle. He looked out of the window. No military police. No-one seemed to be watching the warehouse building with any interest; travellers off a newly-arrived 'plane, just getting through customs, were going out of the gate. He ambled out casually, at the side of a woman with two children, who was loudly wondering if she had done the right thing in bringing the children home in war-time. Did the soldier think they would be safe at Harrogate? Rex wasn't sure that any of them were safe anywhere but was reassuring and helpful with her things, assisting her onto the train at Bristol and all the way to London.

All through that same Friday morning, Eckhardt was in the attic room, waiting for Black Knight's signal. He was not too sleepy, though he had been waiting all through

Thursday night. The Major was correct, Eckhardt did know Holstein's signal well. He picked up the first one that Black Knight transmitted. The trouble was he also knew Black Knight. Eckhardt, in his late forties, had been in the Abwehr since the First World War. Like many Abwehr men, his loyalties were divided. He trusted the Admiral, but had no great love for the Nazis. He had disliked Black Knight from the beginning, but when seasoned Abwehr agents had been denounced to the Gestapo, and all evidence pointed to Black Knight as the informer, his dislike had intensified to something much stronger. The greatest blow had been when Johann Metz, an old and trusted friend, had disappeared, never to be heard from again. Johann Metz had been the man who brought Black Knight into the Abwehr.

Eckhardt, when he had been briefed for this job, had made no conscious decision about the man he still knew only as Black Knight. His feelings about Leiter, his job, the man, were still ambivalent. In any case he had been given no choice. He was ordered and he went.

At dawn on that morning of what looked like being another fine day, Eckhardt, wearing his earphones, had been idly watching the London sparrows on the sill of his low window. He had been told nothing about the mission except of his own job, and he wondered how long it would be before he came back here in the wake of the all-conquering German Army. He was wondering too why he, Leiter and Black Knight were there now. Before he left Berlin he had found out that Admiral Canaris had been called away. It was most unlike the cautious Leiter to intervene physically in a mission. Eckhardt had known him since Leiter's Hamburg days, and disrespectfully considered him a mere bureaucrat, taking the credit for other men's work. Most likely this mission, cooked up in the Admiral's absence, was merely a ploy to glorify Leiter— the murder of some Britisher before the invasion ended the war and his chance of distinction. Leiter had been a major far too long—it was his last chance. And if they were caught . . . Leiter had diplomatic immunity. As for a mere radio operator, if he were detected, the English police might shoot first and question later. He decided that he didn't like his job.

The first transmission that came through was very weak; the air was crowding up and some atmospheric disturbance blurred the signal, but that caused no great problem to Eckhardt, who had received Black Knight for years in the communications room at Wohldorf. He took the message down:

'Discretion compromised. Subject and wife present. Advise if proceed openly or abandon. Urgent. Danger.'

Eckhardt had no idea of Black Knight's prey. It was the last two words that irresistibly caught his attention. Black Knight was in danger. He needed his instruction urgently.

Johann Metz had been in danger from the day he found Black Knight. But there had been no-one to help him.

Eckhardt could not have said afterwards when he made his decision, or if his first failure to take the message to the Major was meant to be final. The transmission was so weak that he might not have caught it. And this was not Wohldorf—there was no-one here to say what he should have been able to do. He was quite alone, except for the London birds.

The message came again and again, at half hour intervals he believed, but during the crowded hours it was, in fact, often obliterated. If Black Knight should be caught it was his bad luck. The chance of his trade. Eckhardt could not believe it would make much difference to the Wehrmacht. Yawning, he called downstairs for some food and coffee, and considered the possibility of a short nap— the Major, impatient, *might* come up again.

It was at that moment that a telegram sent from Scotland was delivered to the Prime Minister at Hawkinge.

345

TWENTY-THREE

Churchill Dead Or Alive

It was one of England's loveliest days—there had been many that summer. The Prime Minister was at an airfield by the south-east coast where the smell of fuel was dispersed by a fresh salt breeze. The sun shone from a bright blue sky. It was the kind of day when English children go by the thousand down to the seaside, escorted by harassed parents, to eat ice-cream and sticks of rock and play all day in the sand with gaily-painted buckets and spades. But not today.

Today the Prime Minister was staring up at that pretty sky, where a dogfight was going on almost directly overhead. Seven Junkers 87's, accompanied by fighters, had been dive-bombing a convoy right off the coast. Five fighters were up there now, it was hard to see which was which—just little silver flashes. He could hear the distant bursts of gunfire. A 'plane came diving down, a streak of scarlet against the blue. Of course he asked the question; of course he had to be told. It was one of ours.

It was also one of their best pilots and newest aircraft, but it was a Hawker-Hurricane, and outclassed by the ME 109's. The Prime Minister saw the burning 'plane on the field, and he watched the efforts of the ground crew to remove what was left of the pilot, while the tears ran down his old face. He told the Air Vice-Marshal at his side that he could hardly bear to watch it. The Air Vice-Marshal and other senior officers wished he wouldn't; it would be so much better if he left. It was one of the worst days Hawkinge had had; the week had been a nightmare for Eleven Group on the coast.

The Prime Minister's policy of reserving aircraft had been put into effect. Naturally, the pilots could not understand this, and were angered at being sent up in such small sections to combat such overwhelming odds. Their life expectancy was measured in days. Most of their aircraft, already obsolete, simply should not be in the battle. Though Hawkinge was not as badly off as the west coast, where they were still using Gladiator biplanes, their Boulton Paul Defiants were no match for the Messerschmitts. A group of Defiants had been shot down last week and replacements sent from Scotland. Today all of those pilots were dead.

Churchill, though he still wept, had his mind on even weightier matters. Great Britain had lost command of the Channel. A convoy of twenty-one merchant ships had been ruthlessly harried, many crippled and many sunk. Three accompanying destroyers had gone to the bottom; a flotilla of E-boats insolently put to sea in daylight to attack what was left of the merchant ships. In humiliation, the remaining destroyers had been withdrawn to the relative and temporary safety of Portsmouth. Churchill, the former First Lord of the Admiralty, was grief stricken. The Prime Minister could only hope that the Germans would not pick this time to begin the invasion.

He marched over the field to talk to a young pilot who had just landed but who would be going up again when his 'plane was refuelled. The ground crew were gawping instead of getting on quickly with their job, and the Air Vice-Marshal wondered how he could get the great man off to his next point of inspection—Manston. Let Manston try and cosset him for a bit. When the telegram came, he had it sent instantly to the Prime Minister who, obviously very emotional, was still talking to the pilot. The Air Vice-Marshal noticed that his bodyguard was starting off down the field. Bored, no doubt, he thought with an unreasonable resentment born of fatigue and a great sense of loss. Hilliard, whose own son was a pilot, was interested enough, but his professional attention had been caught by something out of the way.

When the Prime Minister first read the telegram he thought it was a hoax. A cruel, impudent, stupid hoax. The message was short.

'General Lyon mortally ill at Muick. Come at once. All discretion advised. Signed Mrs Lyon.'

One of the safety precautions he had urged upon the King and Queen, for their personal security, was that in any crisis, all telegraph communication should be conducted under a *nom-de-guerre*. The Queen herself had suggested part of her maiden name, 'Lyon', with the King to be referred to as 'General'. It was a great secret between the three of them, and the Prime Minister had entrusted the Queen with this duty. No-one but themselves could know of it. And indeed no-one had, except Donaldson, who had heard the King laughingly protest at his reduction in rank. She happened to mention it, a good Scottish joke, to Mrs Gordon, in the hearing of Jean Sinclair.

Yet the message could not be true. He was about to expostulate angrily at this nonsense when he thought better of it. All discretion advised. He glanced up, but neither Hilliard nor the pilot had noticed his reaction—they seemed more interested in some aircraftsman who was idling about than the Prime Minister of England. A rumour that the King was seriously ill could do great harm to the public spirit just now. No need to spread gloom and despondency for what must be, he hoped, a piece of nonsense.

Yet he could not go on to Manston without speaking to Her Majesty. Certainly the Queen should be warned that her code name had been discovered—irritably, he wondered again, how? The telephone lines at Hawkinge were very busy, but a line was cleared for his use while he stomped off the field, chewing his cigar irritably.

The Wing Commander gave him a telephone and some privacy in a hut marked 'Out of bounds to all ranks'. It took time to get through to Royal Lodge, and at first the connection was abominable. In the circumstances he hardly wanted to shout. Then it took an inordinate amount of time to find either the King or the Queen. He was informed by a courteous voice, after a long wait, that Their Majesties had gone out, probably to the Castle to visit the Princesses.

There was another long delay while he was put through to the Castle. Still no member of the Royal Family came to speak. The King, of course, disliked the telephone—always embarrassing for a man with a speech impediment—but the Queen would surely not refuse to take a call, an urgent call, from the Prime Minister! But another polite voice told him that the Princesses had gone for a walk. Perhaps the King and Queen were with them. Or perhaps they had returned to Royal Lodge for an early luncheon.

It was an hour after he first took the receiver down from the wall that the Prime Minister at last spoke to a member of the Royal Household that he knew, only to be told that the King and Queen had gone off for a round of croquet—the speaker believed.

The Prime Minister broke into a famous temper, the temper not only of the King's Chief Minister, Leader of the Commons and the Minister of Defence, but that of Winston Churchill, private citizen. This outpouring so alarmed the courtier that eventually, with much apology and humming and hawing, he confessed the truth. "But you will keep our little secret, Prime Minister," he ended, on a more jovial note. "It is the Queen's special wish."

The second outburst of temper that might have come from the great man, whose careful plans had been so lightly swept aside, never came. The Prime Minister wasn't angry. The potential for anger was swallowed up in sudden sorrow and anxiety. He tried to get through to Birkhall, but as so often happened up there, the telephone service was out.

The telegram could not be a hoax. The King was mortally ill and wanted to see him. The Prime Minister poked his head out of the hut and demanded a 'plane— at once. He had lent his own York transport to General de Gaulle for some business about Dakar—worth it, he had thought, to be rid of his cross. And he had been making his tour by motor—simpler, Fighter Command had told him. Safer, with the coast fields embattled, they did not add. But now there was no time for motoring.

The Wing Commander was sending up what was left of the squadron to head off the Stukas who were causing havoc among the colliers coming into port. Another Hurricane, slightly damaged, crash-landed on the runway. The wounded pilot could not free himself in the sixty seconds before it, too, went up in flames.

Detective-Sergeant Hilliard began enumerating the requirements of an aircraft that was to carry the Prime Minister.

"I'm afraid we have no transport 'planes here, Prime Minister," the harried Wing Commander replied.

"Signal Biggin Hill," the Air Vice-Marshal interjected. "No—Northolt."

The Prime Minister was already striding over to the pilot he had spoken to earlier, who was just climbing back into his Defiant. The Prime Minister plucked a cap and scarf from a startled airman and made to haul himself into the rear turret.

"This will do," he boomed.

"But, sir, you can't—" the Wing Commander was aghast.

The Prime Minister was curt. He had no intention of this business being bruited all about Fighter Command.

350

"A personal journey, this is quite good enough. It does fly, doesn't it?"

Neither the Wing Commander nor the Air Vice-Marshal could argue with the Minister of Defence. Nor could they get any sense out of him, they said later. A foolish whim. Detective-Sergeant Hilliard had no such inhibition. If the old man wanted to go somewhere in this most unsuitable aircraft, no-one in the world could stop him, though the detective was bitter at being left behind. But he could hardly cram himself into a two-seater, and it had happened many times before. Impulsive, thoughtless old devil. Refusing to tell the Air Vice-Marshal his destination. The Air Vice-Marshal and the Wing Commander had moved a few steps off in hasty consultation. Hilliard plucked the old man's sleeve and spoke in a low voice.

"I *must* know your destination, Prime Minister."

First flushing with annoyance, the Prime Minister then became somewhat reasonable. He asked Hilliard to adjust his cap. While the pilot started the engine, he told Hilliard he had to go to see the King at Birkhall, near Balmoral in Scotland.

"But this is a *private* matter. Their Majesties don't wish it to be known where they are, and it is for their own safety to leave it that way. So for heaven't sake, don't go blabbing to anyone—not even your people at the Yard. That's an order—from the Minister of Defence," he added grimly.

The Detective-Inspector thought of what that meant, as he helped hoist up that portly person. I'll be lucky, he thought, if I'm not thrown out of the Force, or shot for treason by the time this war is over. Cantankerous old devil. He had to step back when the 'plane taxied down the runway. The Prime Minister's last words were that he would be back tomorrow, and that Hilliard should meet him at Chequers.

In his gloom Hilliard forgot for a moment an oddity that had occupied his mind before all this started. He had thought he recognised an aircraftsman that he had seen the day before at Biggin Hill. Of course, they moved these fellows about, but it was the kind of thing that caught his attention. He had been asking about him when the PM got this mad idea of going up unprotected. Before he left the field, it suddenly came back to him, but by then the man was gone.

If Hilliard thought the Prime Minister cantankerous, and the senior officer considered him to be taken by a freakish whim, his pilot found him most congenial. Churchill asked searching questions about the aircraft he had been watching, displaying a pilot's knowledge. The pilot explained that the new Hurricanes were outclassed by the Messerschmitt 109's. They were slightly slower, and their firing power could not be used to best advantage without more manoeuverability. And as the Prime Minister had seen, there wasn't much time to escape after a crash landing. As for the poor old Defiants—

"We had our day at Dunkirk, sir," the pilot told him. "But these old jobs aren't good for much now. Still we manage," he said carefully.

With great insouciance, he demonstrated a few dives, rolls and turns, which the old man admired with great calm. Despite a stop to refuel, where the muffled-up, helmeted Prime Minister was sure he was not recognised, they reached their destination in something less than two and a half hours. By that time Hilliard had contravened most of the Prime Minister's orders. First he had to have a word with the worried Air Vice-Marshal and the Wing Commander, explaining that the Prime Minister had taken the aircraft for a private visit and would be returning to Chequers, or possibly London, the next day—for the old man didn't always do what he said he would.

Then, very disgruntled, he had to consider his own position. He could not ask for a 'plane to follow the Prime Minister against his express command. An order from the Minister of Defence was absolute and yet—Hilliard was a policeman and a detective. His *legal* obligation was one thing. His duty as a detective, his loyalty to the man and the country he served was another. One would have to bend a little. He was not a man who liked bending the law in any way, shape or form. But he picked up the telephone and tried to reach the police station in the little town of Ballater. There was a delay—trouble on the line—and while he waited he wondered what was the very private, very personal business the Royal Family had to see the Prime Minister about. Probably the Duke, he guessed shrewdly. That was the only thing to be hushed up. Something they wanted to keep quiet.

He got through at last, wondering how he would be received. Too often there was a layer of thin ice between the Scottish constabulary and Special Branch, if not worse, but fortunately the Ballater force seemed benign.

Hilliard salvaged his conscience by not mentioning the Royal Family. He said that the Prime Minister would be staying the night, on a private visit, at Birkhall, and he had left without his usual bodyguard. Could Ballater help? Ballater, used to the presence of the great, took it calmly, and promised to send a man. Hilliard sat back, somewhat relieved, wondering if he should go on now to Chequers. He felt rather strange at having disobeyed a direct order for the first time in his life. For some reason he thought of Rex Barney.

On the crowded train, full of servicemen as well as civilians crammed into every carriage and blocking the passage outside, no-one asked for Rex's papers, which was lucky, for his Service book and other papers, together with those of the lieutenant-colonel, were firmly locked up at Whitechurch. Before the train reached London, Security would certainly have an alarm out for him, and it was not beyond them to assume he might be taking the London express. But so near London, Rex was not too concerned. He was on his home ground now.

Still, he had no fancy for running into the M.P.'s at the barrier in Paddington Station. He wedged himself and his kitbag in front of a door in the passage, and when the express slowed down almost to a halt at a suburban station, with a cheery word to the other men about, "Well, this is where I live, mates," he was off the train and up on the platform almost before anyone could observe him. A porter at the station did notice a soldier come up from the tracks where he shouldn't be, but it wasn't so unusual. These young Service chaps didn't have the time, or the patience, to follow the rules. Didn't want to waste some of a twenty-four hour pass going into London and taking the local back. Couldn't blame 'em.

Like Hilliard, Rex wondered if he should go straight to Chequers. It was Friday, he would probably meet the old man there. But it was early yet. He'd go first to Number 10. He found a taxi, the driver at first making some witticism when Rex said '10 Downing Street'. "Sure you don't want Buckingham Palace, Sergeant?" But Rex, too swept up with his sense of urgency for much humour, gave him a baleful look with his disconcerting bright brown eyes and, subdued, the driver took off smartly.

At Number 10, Hilliard was still uneasy. True, Ballater had agreed to comply with his request, but now he had leisure to worry that a country policeman was hardly trained for this job. True, it was quiet up there . . . He wished he knew which airfield the old man would use on his return. Birkhall still could not be reached. It would be just like His Nibs—as Hilliard privately termed his charge —to go to Chartwell instead of Chequers, or even Ditchley Manor, and fail to notify his bodyguard of his arrival. He had just put in a call to Chequers to find out if they had word yet from the PM, but the lines were busy. It was ridiculous that the official residence of the Prime Minister had only two lines. Then he was disturbed further by the eruption of that pest, Sergeant Barney.

Barney had disappeared one day without a word—

the PM had said the sergeant had embarked for overseas —Hilliard had presumed with his regiment. God knows what he was doing back. He toyed with the idea that Barney had deserted but reluctantly he had to give that thought up as unlikely. Nevertheless he was furious. It was more than he could bear to let that interfering young nosey parker know that he, Detective-Inspector Hilliard, one of the most respected officers of the Yard, had been summarily abandoned by the Prime Minister. He looked at that arrogant head with the untidy mop of red-brown hair—it even had a curl in it, the policeman thought in disgust. If there was one thing, secretly, he could not abide it was a man whose hair curled. Barney was marching into the most illustrious address in England as if he belonged there.

He himself had had an awkward time at Number 10 without the Prime Minister. Officially, he should have gone back to Headquarters, but that would have caused a lot of questions that he couldn't answer. Here he had had to suffer discreet, inquiring looks from Private Secretaries, an open remark or two from the servants, jovial and not so jovial—'Let a policeman in the kitchen and you can't get him out.' But Sergeant Barney, much too familiar, might have owned the place. He would be damned, he thought, if he would tell *him* anything.

Rex Barney's argument with Hilliard was short and sharp. Rex's suspicion and anxiety met Hilliard's own. Despite his first irritation at a man he thought of as an intruder, the detective's feelings soon changed. There was almost something comforting in the presence of the young soldier, who did not feel himself confined by the Prime Minister's order. He might be a rogue but, after all, he was a VC. And Alf Barney's son could be trusted with something like this. Putting aside his respect for orders which had ruled his life for over thirty years, he told Rex where the Prime Minister had gone.

"I don't like it," Rex said at once. "It smells funny

to me. Why would the King pull him away at a time like this?"

"A family matter perhaps," Hilliard said cautiously, "but important to the country."

Rex gave him a sharp glance.

"He could have told him just as well in London. No, I don't like it."

Hilliard didn't like it either, but—"The Family were up there, you see."

"I'm going up after him," Rex said with decision. "I'm not leaving him with no-one but some Scotch country bobby. And I've got something to tell him that can't wait."

Suddenly Hilliard felt an immense tide of relief.

"But he'll be back before you get there," he pointed out. "If you take the night train—"

Rex was already striding off.

"I've a pal at Biggin Hill. I'll get him to take me up. National emergency."

Hilliard jumped up and caught his arm.

"Are you off your chump? I've told you, it's absolutely hush-hush. From the Minister of Defence. *You* probably won't go to the Tower, but you'll get me kicked off the Force. Besides, d'you think your pal is going to be sitting on his duff, waiting there for you with a nice transport? The PM himself had trouble finding one this morning—you'd have to put in an official request to Fighter Command. And I don't see them stopping the war to accommodate Sergeant Barney!" He stopped for breath. "Very likely they won't even let you on the field, unless you hop the fence, and then you might get yourself shot. Or are you planning to stick them up?"

Rex paused.

"If that's the only way," he said shortly. "Look, there's no time for 'official requests', don't you understand? You've got that car of yours hanging about outside, I saw it. Let's take it out to Biggin Hill. Police business,"

356

he said with a gleam in his eye. "You're Special Branch."

To his astonishment Hilliard found himself persuaded by this forceful young man; on the way to Biggin Hill in his own car with Sergeant Barney at the wheel he even found himself warming slightly towards him.

The Prime Minister, who enjoyed fiddling with the speaking tube, was still chatting with the pilot when they made the approach for landing. But he had been looking about him, observing the RDF towers along the coast. A wonderful advantage, the RDF, but not working too well against the low-flying 'planes. He would have to see if something could be done about that. Prod, prod. They came down low over Loch Muick and the pilot deposited him, as carefully as an egg in cotton wool, on a small landing field a few miles from the house.

"You do your stuff," Rex told Hilliard, when they arrived at the base. "Tell them what you like. But don't bugger about. I've got to get off. You can explain for hours afterwards."

Fortunately, the Wing Commander recognised Hilliard from the Prime Minister's tour. Urgent communication for the Prime Minister, to be delivered by hand only, Hilliard said. The Wing Commander had a long face. Eleven Group were not only short of 'planes, but also short of pilots.

"To the Prime Minister as Minister of Defence," Hilliard went on. Lying came easier, he noticed, once he'd got started.

The Wing Commander gave in. This had to be top priority. But there were few two-place craft about. A Squadron Leader, who had stopped in to see him before take off, solved his dilemma.

"Groupie came over from Manston this morning in a Stringbag," he said. "It's still on the field."

"You'd better take it," the harassed Wing Commander told Rex. "It's not fast, but at least you won't have to stop to re-fuel."

He summoned a pilot and they went out to the field to regard the old Swordfish bi-plane. The pilot grinned at Rex.

"She doesn't have her torpedo, but I'll show you how the Lewis operates in case we run into Jerry."

They all laughed. The sun was still bright in the sky when the pilot took off for Scotland, with Sergeant Rex Barney in the radio operator's seat.

A few men in Air Force blue looked up, curious, when the Prime Minister landed in the Defiant. Captain Stangel was taken aback; he could hardly believe his eyes. This was Winston Churchill, come up in a two-seater, with no escort in sight. In a blue suit, and an Air Force cap too big for him. No wonder the Abwehr had thought they could manage with a handful of men. For the first time he could comprehend. He looked at the Boulton Paul Defiant scornfully. If that was all the RAF could give the Prime Minister, they weren't going to last long. But the pilot was a skilled man.

Dai Lewis, in an Air Force uniform, was watching from the lean-to. He, too, was surprised at the Prime Minister's manner of travel, but he merely felt relief. It made his job that much easier. He caught Stangel's eye and gave a small shake of his head. There was no need to send the waiting Kleist as escort. Maloney could manage this.

The Prime Minister had rather enjoyed the flight. He thanked the pilot courteously, and gave him the hat and scarf to return to its owner. But then his brow darkened. A young private, RAOC, was waiting for him with a car. It was the car that provoked his wrath. It was a vehicle with its uses no doubt for transporting men and goods about the mountain paths, but hardly suited to an ageing notable whose stomach was already slightly upset from a bumpy ride in a small aircraft. He ignored the back seat that the obliging driver was holding open for him, and marched round and took the more stable seat next to the driver.

The pilot watched him go, smiling. He was really one for the book. The men were already refuelling his aircraft —a competent lot, though uncommonly quiet. Scottish, perhaps. "You'd better get back, my boy," the PM had told him. "They need you at Hawkinge more than I do. Thirteen Group can take me back tomorrow—they're not so hard pressed, up here."

The leading aircraftsman was a friendly sort, and invited him inside for a mug of tea. He had the kettle on. It had been a long time since breakfast in the mess and the pilot was glad of it. The aircraftsman, whom he soon noticed was Welsh—just like this war to send a Welshman to Scotland, Wales was probably crawling with Scots— saw him wolf down a couple of biscuits and without a word very decently got him a scratch meal together.

While the pilot was eating and talking, he was well away from the small window and couldn't possibly see Frank Purcell. Purcell was working with swift dexterity inside the motor cowl of the Defiant, punching in the K-13 unit, fitted to an adhesive suction cup. The unit had an air pressure gauge like a simple altimeter. At a thousand feet it would activate a solenoid, transmitting an electrical charge to a detonator, connected to an explosive capsule. Purcell was proud of Quenzee's K-13; it had never failed.

The pilot had another mug of tea, and then took off, with a wave of thanks to the mechanics. It must be dull up here, he thought, for they watched his take-off with great interest.

Churchill's wrath melted as they drove along. The driver made himself agreeable. He gave no news of the house and the Prime Minister did not ask. This young man was no old family servant in whom anyone would confide. And no news in this case was good news—perhaps His Majesty's illness was not so serious after all. The doctor might have given good news already; there could have been a second telegram to Hawkinge after he—somewhat precipitously he thought now—had commandeered the 'plane.

The Prime Minister had never been greatly concerned with spit and polish. And so he did not concern himself too much about the appearance of his driver: the lumpy pockets of his battle-dress, the trousers that seemed a trifle short for his long legs. Supplies were a problem everywhere.

There was the sound of an explosion coming from the hills.

"Artillery exercise?" he inquired.

"Ah, I wouldn't know," the driver said cheerfully. "They put me in the motor pool, and they'll hardly tell me the way."

The Prime Minister laughed. Leaning back, he was enjoying the soft, golden light that bathed the grass and the woods that covered the hills. Grass, not the heather of Balmoral he remembered. He had been on a shoot here once—it seemed a long time ago. They crossed a pretty little bridge. Not far now. He relaxed, half closed his eyes and listened to the soft Dublin brogue of the private. It filled him with a sense of warmth and well-being. He had been a small boy in Dublin and it had been one of the happiest times of his life. In the Viceregal Lodge, with his mother flitting about like an exotic butterfly, he had known nothing of any hostility of the surrounding Irish, only friendliness, great sport and enchantment.

He half slept as they bumped over the narrow winding road, thinking of the folly of his fellows. There were those who had wanted to bar these fine boys from Southern Ireland from joining up—too dangerous, possibly hostile. What nonsense. Like the absurd Aliens Act that he had agreed to, with reluctance. It affected mostly Jews, who, after all, hated Hitler more than anyone. And which one of the Intelligence branches had come up with the tale of Operation Green?

Operation Green. What was it supposed to be, an insurrection? Based on a few Welsh Nationalists, some Hitler lovers in England who used to call themselves, quite openly, The Link. Its members had included a former head of Naval Intelligence, he remembered. Rumours of plots in Ireland. Some claiming it was the IRA, some deValera himself. All topped off by reports of conspiracy with Lloyd George. He even had a code-name, that rather worrying man. Mr Hindhead. The PM had made a joke of it, saying that it suited a man whose head was screwed on backwards. In the event, nothing had come of it.

But he hadn't liked the tales about Lloyd George. He wished the old man would be willing to go to America as Ambassador. After all, there were plenty of people in England who thought the war a mistake. There was always a chance they might rally round the old Welsh Wizard, to topple his own fragile coalition. But he had respect for his former leader and master. He didn't think he would turn traitor.

As for Ireland, it wasn't he who had wanted to give up the Western ports. But no-one had listened. Such thoughts were disagreeable, and the Prime Minister had trained his mind not to indulge in useless and disagreeable speculation. He turned his thoughts back to the pleasant memories of the Dublin of his youth.

"And where are you from, my lad?" he asked his driver genially, wondering if he could still remember the names of the streets.

"Belfast," the driver answered promptly. "Off the Alexandra dock."

Maloney had been well-primed for his role. As his life had been spent in England and Ireland no-one had stressed to him that he should talk as little as possible, nor, being by nature a talkative man, would he have taken much notice if they had.

361

With an effort the Prime Minister kept his face and body still. He continued to breathe deeply as though almost asleep.

"Good boys, all of you," he murmured, as if from the depths of a nap. It was a trick he had found worked well for him. His reputation for cat-napping gave him a chance to observe people without their awareness. He was rewarded now, seeing quite clearly through the lashes of his drooping eyelids as the young man glanced round to observe him.

"Ah, we're all for the mother country in Belfast."

The Prime Minister considered. As a boy and a youth, he had been plagued by his inability to learn any language other than English. He had been caned and flogged, but to no avail. Only English could he speak, hear and write. But this lack had its compensations, because he wrote English well. He also heard it with discrimination. Could he be mistaken now? Decidedly, he could not. Operation Green . . . No. That was nonsense.

The boy probably lied because he was tired of being teased by his fellows. When is Ireland coming in on our side; is de Valera making a deal with Jerry—he'd heard it went on. And to the Irish a lie wasn't the same as it was to the English, any more than it was to the Welsh. Celts and Gaels had a view of such things different to the more stolid Anglo-Saxons. Suddenly, for the first time in days, he thought of Sergeant Barney. Yes, most likely it was Barney that had started him worrying about plots like an old woman.

For the moment, the great man forgot that he had snatched Barney into his service because of his own suspicions. That had nothing to do with Operation Green . . . He'd been sorry he'd ever told Barney about that. Just mentioned it one morning on the drive in from Chequers, but that was enough. He could shut off the bleatings of M15, and he didn't have to listen to all the stuff from the clever boys down at Bletchley, but he would never hear the end of it from the suspicious sergeant. All the Special Branch men were nannies by nature, including Hilliard with his long nose, hatchet jaw and huge feet; Thompson, dour and disapproving; Alfred Barney, cheery and worried at the same time. And Rex Barney, champion athlete, winner of the Victoria Cross—no different.

He had never made this journey by car, and was vague about how far the airfield was from the house, but they should be nearly there. In plenty of time for dinner and, he hoped, good news. The driver was making a good pace on the road, which was not much more than a path winding around big rocks and hills—doubtless he was looking forward to a meal himself. A very good pace—surprised by a sharp curve, he made a violent but skilful turn. His eminent passenger was thrown against his left shoulder, but sank back again, unharmed.

"Ah, I'm sorry," the young man apologised, all Hibernian charm. "Don't know this road at all, you see."

"You did well," the Prime Minister said coolly. Behind the half-closed lids his brain was working at full tilt. No wonder the young man's battle-dress was bulging. As his own right arm had bumped against him, he had felt the unmistakable bump of a pistol in a holster. Having put on this repulsive harness himself at Hilliard's request, he had no doubt at all as to what it was. Since when, he brooded, did the British Army issue shoulder holsters so that privates could conceal weapons under their coats?

He glared out of the window at the afternoon sun, and started. It had moved. Surely they should have been going due north, but with all the winding and turning they were now heading east and slightly south. He remembered the shooting of Thompson in the black-out, when he himself might have been expected to be behind him. His mind was suddenly very sharp and clear.

"Be so kind, young man, as to stop at the nearest thick clump of bushes," he asked, in his best, shy old

363

voice. "That aeroplane was ill-equipped and I don't want to appear at the house in straits."

The driver laughed and stopped obligingly. The Prime Minister watched the driver's arm keenly, but he did not reach for his gun. Apparently, he was not being 'taken for a ride', American gangster fashion. This man's orders, he guessed, were to deliver him somewhere alive. Did they think he would notice nothing, or was it planned to knock him unconscious in some suitable spot off the road? He saw the young man's eyes on him and quickly, for all his bulk, the Prime Minister hopped behind the nearest clump of bushes and did what he had to do.

"It's still warm," he remarked, "I don't need this." He had taken off his coat and held it casually on his right arm. With his left, he pulled open the door by the back seat.

"I'll just sit here and doze for a minute," he said, getting in at the back of the driver.

He thought the young man hesitated for a moment, but his own sleepy voice reassured him. The private gave him a quick, obliging smile and turned the key in the ignition. His passenger, who as well as being a statesman had been a soldier, a sportsman, and was the descendant of soldiers and sportsmen, held his pistol steadily at the back of the young man's neck and fired. When the smoke cleared he looked carefully and saw through the mess of blood the young man's brains in a sort of pink frothy sauce oozing through the front of his head. He grunted, searched his pockets, but found nothing at all except a dirty handkerchief and a crumpled packet of Woodbines.

The private was a lanky young man, and it was quite a task for the Prime Minister to pull him out of the driver's seat and dump him in the bushes. But it was done and, panting and hot, he considered his next move. He wanted to get to the house and see what was going on. Was the plot against him alone, or were Their Majesties involved? Almost certainly, it was merely himself. He could think of no IRA attempts on the Royal Family, nor did he believe they had any animus against the Throne itself. Probably they had learned by chance of his sudden journey and had taken their opportunity. Someone in Post and Telegraphs —unless they sent the message themselves? No, they couldn't know the code. His mind darted on. As he hadn't been killed at once, did that mean he was to be held for ransom? He could hardly guess that Maloney should have killed him as soon as they were off the north road, but he had been amusing himself with his blarney and kept it up a little too long—he would deliver the old man to the spot alive, he had thought, really to die on the fire. Equally sanguine, the Prime Minister considered the notion of ransom and grinned. Just as well he wouldn't have to find out how much his Cabinet considered he was worth.

Hilliard, or even Barney, would say he should go back to the airfield and get those RAF boys for an escort and make a report. But he could hardly take this car. If there were other potential kidnappers, it might be recognised and stopped.

In fact, he need not have worried about meeting any of Whaleforce on the road north. Once he had stepped in such a docile manner in the car with Maloney, Lewis had signalled both barricade parties to withdraw and take their transport to the Cairns. There the work was to be finished and then the men of Whale, excepting Lewis, were to return to their lodgings, and gradually fade into their normal daily lives.

The Prime Minister was weighing all the possibilities. He was so close to the house. He would use commando tactics, he thought. Had he not learned them from the originators? He would go to the house stealthily, observing all the way.

He crept along in the shelter of rocks and bushes, startling nothing more than a bird from a branch. Soon he could see the house, but still moved with caution. But his spirits had risen. To the old warrior, there was an *élan* about being in personal combat again. His outwitting of the young Irishman was intoxicating. He was not so old yet! And the man who had lived by his pen thought it would make a good journalistic piece one day.

By now he did not expect to find much amiss with the King. His thoughts were too much on how he would describe his exploit, to the wonder of the household. The Queen had probably been unduly nervous about her husband. The King, never strong, was undoubtedly suffering from strain which brought on despondency. He would cheer them up, stay to dinner, and tonight or tomorrow morning take a 'plane back. There would be from Saturday to Monday at Chequers to catch up on his work.

The appearance of the white-washed house, mellow in the afternoon sun, and peaceful among the trees, bolstered his expectation. There was no bustle of illness to be seen. No ambulance, no doctor's car. Still rather enjoying playing commando, he looked about and saw no cars at all. He was about to hail the plainclothes man guarding the front door, dropping some casual remark about his exploit—of course something would have to be done about the body, he hoped that wouldn't mean a tedious time with the Scottish police—when he heard the sound of music coming from the kitchen quarters, quite loud, stirring martial tunes. He liked martial tunes, but this struck him as odd. The Royal Family were informal at Birkhall, but the Queen would hardly permit the servants to make such a noise if the King was there and ill. Perhaps he had been taken to a hospital? But then, why was there no message at the airfield?

A dozen questions, and answers, sprang to his mind. Perhaps the driver of the car had been bringing a message, but had been waylaid by the Irishman. Perhaps . . . He did not hail the plainclothes man after all. Instead, surreptitiously he made his way to the side of the house and climbed in through an open window.

Mrs Gordon was setting down a tray. She stared at

the Prime Minister who had got one leg over the sill with ease, but was having some trouble hauling in the second. She looked dismayed.

"Oh, sir," she said. "No-one told me you were expected."

His means of entry apparently did not surprise her; she had more important things on her mind. She had not yet started dinner, for she did not know what was wanted.

"We're all at sixes and sevens today," she grumbled. "Nobody's telling me anything. I dare say word was left with young Jean, my housemaid—she does the early morning tea. But the silly creature has run away, sky-larking about with her soldier. The whole party went off and the policemen with them. Breakfast trays not touched. Of course, I thought they would be dining out tonight—now I might have dinner for four in the dining-room and four more in the kitchen, and no idea of what time or anything. I *asked* those two extra policemen that came to please go up to Ballater and see what they could do about the telephone but *they* won't budge. Not their job, you see. Can I bring you some tea, sir? I dare say Their Majesties *will* be back if you're expected."

The Prime Minister said very calmly he wouldn't want any tea. He rather regretted that later. Mrs Gordon went back to her kitchen and her music, while he took quick stock of the position. The Royal party had disappeared before breakfast, with their detectives, and had not been heard from since. Communications were cut. The men guarding the house were 'extra'—that meant unknown, possibly hostile.

He was chilled. This was no last minute, lightly-planned attempt on himself. From the cook's words it was obvious that the King was not ill at all—the telegram had been sent by the enemy. He wished fervently that Hilliard wasn't the sort of man who took a command at face value. If only he'd had the sense to telephone ahead and send help!

* * *

The police station at Ballater had fulfilled their promise to the maligned Hilliard, though the force was small owing to so many men leaving for the Army. A policeman had been armed with a revolver and, feeling important, had gone on his bicycle up the road. He had run into the north barricade, already edgy because of their encounters the night before.

The policeman had chatted with the RAOC men, pleased to see they were mending the road. It was a terrible road. In Ballater they hoped the Army would build a new one. He said he would ask the Prime Minister when he saw him.

Evans had had to make another quick decision. He didn't falter. The body of the policeman would have to join the others at the airfield. But afterwards it was hard to keep his men working there calmly, until the signal to leave was gladly received.

The Prime Minister remembered the explosion he had heard coming from the Cairns. Now he doubted very much that it was from an artillery exercise, though at that moment he did not think of his 'plane. For all he knew Their Majesties could be dead already. In a sudden spurt of grief, he forgot to be angry with the Queen, who, he felt, had misled him after all. He pulled himself together. Whatever the situation, he had to go at once for help. Back to the airfield. Probably he himself was not being looked for yet; he was expected to be with the young kidnapper. Leaving the house surreptitiously, he crawled back to the nearest footbridge and crossed the Muick. Then he began to run. He would have to take his chance on an ambush now; there was no time to creep the whole way. He would have taken the car, but the driver had gone too far off the northerly road. When the PM had made his way to the

368

house he had seen no-one either on the road or in the valley, but nevertheless, once within a half mile of the airfield, some new spirit of caution made him creep again.

The Fallschirmjäger, in spite of the imperturbable appearance of Captain Stangel, were beginning to wonder what was happening. They had had to open up the pit and throw in the bodies of the policemen and the three civilians, so unceremoniously dumped upon them by Dai Lewis. They felt, like Captain Stangel, that they had not come so far to act as gravediggers, but they had done the job. By now all the bodies should have been exhumed and dowsed, ready for burning. They had heard the explosion: the 'plane had been downed; the Welshman should have returned by now to take them to their hiding place near the river. At nightfall they were to board; at dawn they would go out with the trawler fleet. Their submarine would be waiting, well off-shore. Bruner, the eldest, and the father of small twins, was particularly worried. The Welshman was late.

Captain Stangel was even more unhappy. They dare not stay much longer. Even this scrap of a field would probably be under Fighter Command. And the absence of its normal occupants could not pass unnoticed for long. He was also concerned about the rendezvous with the trawler. They could make their way without the Welshman, but then they might have trouble with the master.

Nevertheless, the discipline of his men was perfect. When the Prime Minister approached stealthily from the cover of the trees, he saw nothing but a group of aircraftsmen going about their normal activities: cleaning the Bofors gun, checking the petrol tanks, some of the men drinking from big mugs. It was their tea-time. He was getting thirsty himself. He decided to join them.

He was about to hail them sharply when the lone officer gave an order. Leaning over the gun, he demanded it be cleaned again. The gunner stood and gave a smart salute as he walked off. The Prime Minister stayed in his sanctuary, thoroughly frightened. Discipline in the Air Force was notorious for its sloppiness. He hadn't seen a salute like that on an airfield in the whole of his recent tour —not even to the Commander-in-Chief. Had these men saluted when he landed? He had not noticed, he had been looking at the car. The salute was an English salute; the words were English, but the men, he knew with a dreadful certainty, were not. And neither were they IRA, he thought, from their bearing and meticulous appearance. *Germans.* He recalled suddenly the 'Special Branch' man he had seen at Birkhall. That fresh, youthful face—almost certainly another German. Was this, then, a full-scale invasion?

With his face scraping the bark of a tree, Great Britain's Prime Minister had to try to take in the extent of this coup while he cursed himself for his past senseless follies. This airfield, at least, was occupied. The telephone lines were cut. There was no way he could estimate how many parachutists may have landed, how many other airfields and vital points had been taken. The country might be saturated with enemy troops. He remembered, with a welling horror, the Irishman in the car, the Scottish cook at the house . . . How could he know how many people had turned traitor?

Almost against his will names rushed through his mind. He *had* been warned—and not only of Operation Green. Just before the fall of France he had heard a tale being told by the American Ambassador in Paris. Great Britain was full of traitors. There was a plan to divide it into eight zones, each under the control of a well-known Fascist leader. He had, with his usual lack of caution, pooh-pooh'd this tale without investigation—he thought it a typical war-time fantasy, with as much substance to it as the Angel of Mons.

Now the likelihood was no longer remote. It was as close as the men before him, real and grim. One thing, however, was certain. To show his famous face was to risk being shot on sight. Very quietly for a plump man, he

370

retreated deeper into the wood. The damndest thing of all, he thought grimly, was that he had ordered Hilliard to tell no-one of his destination. And it was Friday. His staff would imagine he had gone to Chequers, Chartwell, or even Ditchley, and a discreet muddle would ensue. It was possible that there would be no real search for him until Monday—and what might have happened by then?

Physically, the Prime Minister was already miserable. He hadn't eaten since breakfast. He had missed his afternoon nap. And although he was the same man who had made his way from the internment camp near Pretoria to Lourenço Marques with only four bars of chocolate and a price of twenty-five pounds on his head, he was now four decades older.

Scrambling about on mountain paths, sometimes on all fours, had made him realise it sharply. Middle-aged, people liked to say. A man who could call himself middle-aged in London knew exactly how old he was when he was left with no civilised comforts in the Highlands. Hungry, thirsty, rapidly growing tired, he was still willing to put up a fight. But where? Even he was not sanguine enough to take on the half dozen young Germans on the airfield.

After his first moment of shock, calmer reflection brought him hope that help would be on its way. The cars, he had remembered, were gone from Birkhall. Surely that meant the Royal party had taken them. A kidnap would have woken everyone in the house—the Germans would not have left the cook alive to tell the tale. Probably the King and Queen had received some warning and rushed away.

It was only a short distance to Ballater. Troops were probably pouring into the area now. Most likely some would be landing at this very field. That gun ought to be put out of action, but there were three men hanging about it, no doubt well armed. At least he could fire a warning shot. Certainly, as he was well concealed, this was the best place for him to stay.

The one place the now desperate Whaleforce did not look for Winston Churchill was at the airfield held by the Fallschirmjäger. It had seemed at first that their task was very easy. Purcell and the Quenzee K-13 had done their work with chilling efficiency. The Defiant had come down precisely in the area marked out by Purcell, so that the first men to arrive, those who had comprised the south ambush, saw the full descent. The north party, plus Purcell and Lewis, were not needed for the firing of the 'plane; it burned when it hit the ground. Purcell had a little trouble poking through the smouldering bits of motor to find anything left of his device.

Before he finished his search, the other men were getting nervous. Why wasn't Maloney there? He had left with the Prime Minister at the same time as the south party. He should have arrived at the same time. Allowing an interval for him to subdue the Prime Minister if it had been necessary, he still should have been there.

Sean O'Connor, another IRA gunman, but the sort that Lewis thought of as the miserable Irish, not the cocky ones like Maloney and Purcell, began whining.

"There's a curse on this job. I don't like it. First the Krauts bugger it up at the house. And now the old bastard's not here. It's not like Frank to be late, he drives like a madman."

"Probably got lost," Lewis said testily. "He's mad all right."

The two men glared at each other.

"Most likely something happened to the car," Evans said. "But what should we do?"

They stood about by the smoking wreckage, uncomfortably exposed on the bare slopes. A 'plane falling from the sky must attract attention. Even now Authority could be plodding on its way. They had uniforms and papers, but Authority was precisely what they wished to avoid. Still Maloney and his passenger did not come.

Macleish, a big raw-boned man from Glasgow, who

had been drawn in through politics and was still frightened from the violence at the barricade the night before, was already tasting panic. The real thing had been very different from his bloodless training in unarmed combat on a quiet little farm.

"We're waiting here like a lot of fules," he said shortly. "Ah think we'd better be off."

"It's the truth he's tellin'," O'Connor supported him. The tension in the group was worsening rapidly. "What are we waiting for? MI5?"

Lewis was not in a panic, but he knew he couldn't hold the men much longer. The exposed situation in the Cairns was terrifying. And people would be gathering here soon. Where the devil *was* Maloney? He'd never liked him —now he'd shown himself unreliable. The Welshman's gaze raked the bare hills—and saw a small car approaching. But it wasn't the estate car Maloney should have been driving.

This also occurred to the terrified Macleish and he was ready to bound off when Lewis' iron grasp caught his shoulder.

"Don't run, you idiot," he said.

There was no reason to run. The car pulled up by the soldiers, and the driver got out. He was a short, plump, middle-aged man, a local farmer by his looks, his face creased with concern for the tragedy.

"I saw it come down. I was over at Corrach. The poor lad!" he said, staring down at the burned body.

Dai Lewis got his idea and made the decision at almost the same instant. There was really no choice. They could wait no longer, and Major Leiter's instructions had been very plain. The body of the Prime Minister *must* be here. In a moment the metal rod that Purcell had been using to poke in the wreckage was in his hand and in the next it cracked down across the skull of the farmer.

"Get the petrol," he ordered tersely. "Burn the body."

Evans, who caught his glance, did what he was told.

"We can't get away with that," O'Connor stared at the crumpled body. "They'll know it's not him."

"Not once the body's burned to nothing. And they'll be thinking it is. That's the 'plane he went up in. And he's disappeared."

The body was already flaming. The smell of petrol mingled with that of scorched meat. The men fell back, but when the flames subsided, Evans threw on more petrol and burned the remains again.

"But what about the real one?" Macleish whispered, though there was no stranger in sight.

"We'll find him and bury him. We'll split up into two's and comb the area from here to the Muick. O'Connor, go with Evans in the van, and Macleish will come with me in that." He nodded to the farmer's car. "We'll drop it into the river. Jones and Callaghan take the big lorry. The rest search on foot. The first man to see him, kill him. It's all right to shoot now. But make sure he's buried deep. And remember—no-one, *no-one* is to know of the switch."

They nodded. They understood. Apart from any other considerations, they would not be paid the fifteen thousand pounds apiece that Leiter had promised if he learned the job was bungled.

Lewis paused for a moment. He was to have made the call to Leiter as soon as the job was done. If he didn't do it soon, Leiter would be suspicious. Better he did not become suspicious.

"We'll meet by the footbridge on the Muick. Assemble at seven o'clock sharp. By then we'll have found Maloney and the old man. And it'll be time to be off."

"Ah, Maloney's probably killed him and took to his heels," O'Connor said, brightening.

Lewis thought that nothing was more likely, but they had the little matter of the corpse to worry about. And he knew that he and his men had no time to lose. He had planned for them to be gone before this. Macleish made a tidy job of dumping the farmer's car in the river, but Lewis didn't like the look of him—he knew what fear could do to a man. When he left the glen by motor-bike to report his 'success' to Major Leiter he took Macleish with him. They had to go as far as Aboyne to find an operating telephone line. Before he reached it, while his men were searching the hills, the first policeman arrived at the wreck.

It was Evans who found, not the Prime Minister, but Maloney's body beside the road, not far from the estate car he had been driving. Evans did not tell his partner, the jumpy O'Connor, what he had seen, but made for the rendezvous early. O'Connor was willing enough to stop the search. When Lewis arrived from Aboyne, one glance at Evans told him that something was very wrong. It was the work of a moment to send off O'Connor and Macleish.

"Go and find out, you two, if there's any word at the airfield from Black Knight."

Evans gave him the bad news without comment. Dai Lewis, a practical man, knew the game was over. With the old man escaped from Maloney, he could have gone anywhere. He cursed himself for moving the barricades so soon but he would never have believed that Maloney, whom he'd seen with his own eyes overpower four men of the RAF Regiment Section, one after the other, killing them without a sound, could lose an old man. Now the whole area could be crawling with troops—it was his duty to move his men out as quickly as possible. He was filled with a sudden, racking chagrin, worse than anything he'd ever known. Leiter wouldn't pay for utter failure. As leader, Lewis was to have received more than the others—twenty-five thousand pounds. To make that at the colliery he would have had to work exactly a hundred years. And all for killing the hateful old man who'd sent Hussars to crush the strike at Tonypandy. The blood of the dead had never been avenged. He would quite gladly, if there were no risk, have killed the old swine for nothing. And now it was all over.

Obstinately, hope refused to die. Perhaps, he told himself, it was not quite over. After all, the stupid old fool had left the car. Perhaps one of the searchers had come across him wandering in the Cairns. But as his men drifted back, pair by pair, no-one brought the glad news. Only O'Connor and Macleish were still to come. Uneasy, in an ugly mood, the men of Whaleforce waited for the two remaining men—or seven o'clock.

Before Dai Lewis had felt his first bitter draught of disappointment, a lot of eminent people had been equally dismayed. The constable had reported to the local police station. The Chief Constable had happened to be there, and the Chief Constable was very spy conscious. His first call was to MI5 to come and look at the wreckage and its occupants. Some MI5 men came from Aberdeen, and identified the wreckage as a British Defiant. A simple question put to Thirteen Group brought an answer that sent spies out of everyone's head; the Defiant flying in the area was carrying the Prime Minister, travelling incognito. He had refuelled at a base in Yorkshire.

The MI5 agent who got this answer was for a moment too overwhelmed to speak. When he recovered, he thought it was as well not to blab everything to Fighter Command; first he had better report to his own Chief. But his Chief could not be reached immediately. The agent returned to the site of the accident and consulted his colleagues. They and the Chief Constable stood there, regarding the small charred figure with helpless horror.

The moment was solemn, but the solemnity did not prevent the officials from knowing this was a national disaster. Once the news got out, and it became known that the country was leaderless—to the men gathered in the Cairns, the moment seemed the most fateful in Scotland since the Battle of Bannockburn.

So heavy was the matter, it was quickly decided that the news should *not* get out. Not immediately. Nothing could be done for the dead. The investigation of the tragedy and the ceremonials could come later. The Chief Constable decided, and the Security Service was to agree, this affair must go immediately to Cabinet level. It was for the Government to decide on the necessary steps.

The Chief of MI5 brought in Air Chief Marshal Dowding himself to silence any queries from Fighter Command. And of the Cabinet Anthony Eden, as Secretary of State for War, was the first to get the news, not just because of his importance, but simply because he was the first to be found. At six o'clock on Friday evening, the exodus from London to the country had already begun.

At the airfield, an open quarrel had broken out between Captain Stangel and Sean O'Connor. Stangel had reported, as was his duty, that he had heard nothing from Black Knight. O'Connor, who was worried about his friend, Maloney, and dejected about the outcome of the venture, got off a few remarks about the general inefficiency of the German force. Instead of sitting on their arses after coming all the way to Scotland, he suggested they help in the hunt for the Prime Minister.

It was the first that Stengel had heard of Whaleforce losing the Prime Minister after he had been secured by the Fallschirmjäger. He was furious at the blunder; furious at the undoubted bad mark on his own record, and in no mood to take orders from the lowest, meanest riff-raff in the IRA. Nothing had been said about sending his men out under the Welshman's command. *He* had succeeded; the Welshman had failed. His own orders had been to hold the airfield against possible enemy action, to capture the Prime Minister, to assist the Quenzee-trained operative in sabotaging the Prime Minister's craft. If called upon, his men were to render assistance to Black Knight. Before leaving, they were to fire the Air Force bodies and the hut. Then he was to get his men on the boat to take them out to sea. He sent O'Connor back with a flea in his ear, but he felt a little uneasy afterwards about his sharp words.

To Stangel the mission already had the rank smell of failure. He and his men would need the Welshman to get off. Without him, they could find the vessel, but the skipper might not be willing to take them aboard. Yet he was reluctant to weaken further his force. No craft had yet approached, but they must hold the field until close to nightfall. He did not believe they would ever hear from Black Knight now. His job had been scheduled for Thursday night. Friday night was approaching fast and no word had come. Dead or captured, most likely. Captain Stangel wondered, if Black Knight were alive, how long it would be before he talked. He did not doubt that eventually he *would* talk—Security men were doubtless the same the world over. But Black Knight had the reputation of being a first class man. The Captain hoped he and his men would have time to get away. Of course, he could not help thinking, as soon as word of trouble got out, troops would be pouring in. Troops—and aircraft—doubtless.

He had looked forward to some action—added glory for him and his men. But there would be no glory now. Lucky if they got away with their skins. The last thing he wanted to see was any aircraft making an approach.

He looked up at the sky where rain clouds had gathered again—soon there would be more accursed rain. Then through the cloud, to his dismay, he saw the descending Swordfish. His men's orders were quite clear. They were to allow any craft to land, and deal with the airmen afterwards.

But Schurmer, taking his turn on the Bofors, panicked. Seeing the Swordfish diving down between patches of cloud, with Sergeant Barney behind the Lewis gun, caused his sudden terror. Without thinking, he opened fire.

Meanwhile, the Prime Minister, tired of inaction, had left the proximity of the field to make his way to the MacBride house and, he hoped, help, thus putting himself at considerable risk of capture by the men of Whaleforce. It was fortunate for him that there was not much eagerness in their search. By now nearly all the men were frightened and, anxious to reach the rendezvous, they arrived there before the appointed time, heavy with failure. They heard the rattle of gunshot from the airfield. Dai Lewis kept them calm.

"Your civvies and your identity cards are in the lorry. Bury your uniforms and take yourselves off. Split up, some go in the van and some in the lorry, but don't take either vehicle into the villages. The van can go in the river. Take the plates off the lorry and abandon it. Those of you with jobs, go back to work on Monday, and don't leave too soon. The rest of you finish the holidays you've paid for. You've had some money on account. I have to tell you I don't expect to see any more, but if there is, you'll get your shares."

The men, once more legal, law-abiding citizens, gloomy but glad to be getting away, dispersed under Evans' guidance.

"I've got another identity card for you, Frank. Destroy the one you used at the Macleish's."

Lewis turned to Purcell, feeling guilty. Purcell's work had been perfect but he would get no reward. Worse, he, unlike the others, had no established British identity and was very much at risk.

"It's good enough to get you by if you're challenged. Frank Porter of Kilburn. Take the motor-bike south to Dundee, much safer than Aberdeen. Then make your way cautiously to Liverpool." He wrote a name and an address on a scrap of paper. "Memorise this."

Purcell nodded, and Lewis burned the paper.

"He'll get you back to Eire. I'm sorry, Frank." He was silent for a moment. "You'd better keep your mouth shut tight about where you've been. There's going to be a lot of curiosity from all quarters about what's been going on up here."

The guns were still barking. After Frank roared off, the Welshman made a quick decision of his own. Those fools at the airfield must have panicked; their row would rouse the countryside. He'd already lost the reward that was due him; he saw no reason to be shot as a traitor as well. If any of the Germans survived, which he doubted, they could take care of themselves. The trawlerman would be disappointed, no doubt. Well, he'd had some money and no risk. Lewis got on his own motor-bike and made his way back to his lodging in Aberdeen where he was passing a blameless summer holiday.

The trawlerman was bitterly disappointed—he would never get the money for a new boat now. There was no way he could know of his good luck. The abandoning of the Germans had given him another twenty years of life.

Only one of the party ignored Lewis' instructions. O'Connor, in the safety of his lodgings in Ballater, began to brood on the money that should have been his. Only a miserable hundred and his expenses had he had so far. He lay on his bed and looked thoughtful. True, the job had not been done. But it would not be the first time the IRA had hoodwinked the Germans and got their money anyway. Long before he had reached the airfield with Macleish, he had got out of him the whole story of how Lewis had called the Major from Aboyne with the tale of their success. Doubtless Lewis would collect the pay. And he'd said if he got anything he would give them all their share . . . The lying, stingy old bastard. He jumped up, went to the nearest public telephone, and put a call through to his brother on the Edgware Road.

380

TWENTY-FOUR

Death Of A Prime Minister

While the men of Whaleforce had their weary work, Holstein was still suffering from inactivity. That Friday afternoon stretched on endlessly. The time he'd spent with Jean Sinclair in the Aberdeen hotel was nothing compared to this. It was almost certain now that his signal would not be picked up until nightfall. And even in the godforsaken hut, it was not safe to stay so long. Soon someone would start to look for the King and Queen. Probably they were searching now.

Then he had the gloomy idea that perhaps the receiver of his AFU set was defective. *Klamotten,* the Abwehr men called the AFU's Junk. But no, he thought. For Black Knight, for this job, all care would have been taken. The rain came down spattering the roof of the hut. He wondered how long it took these Scots to repair a telephone line. And then there was Jean—Jean who knew where he was. Someone might find Jean. He should have killed her, he realised.

Perhaps he should kill the King and go off. Not wait for the Fallschirmjäger. Steal some other man's clothes and papers—he'd done that in France, where he didn't even have real command of the language. Yet, interwoven with his sense of self-preservation were still the habits of a man in a chain of command. These habits had served him well in the past. His orders had been so definite. 'The King must appear to have died of natural causes.' Heart attack, Leiter had said specifically.

Looking at the man tied in the chair, face down, pale with exhaustion and worry, it seemed as though he might have a heart attack naturally. Holstein quickly turned over in his mind all the things that might induce such an attack. The King was regarding his wife anxiously, and it gave the Black Knight an idea.

Grasping a gun—not his, that wretched Smith and Wesson—he thrust it to the Queen's temple and made as if to pull the trigger. The effect was more than Holstein could have hoped. The King turned from pale to deadly white and he struggled frantically. He was not a strong man, but his struggle would have burst any ordinary bonds. However, the thin line with which he was tied could not be pulled apart by mortal man. All his struggle, fury and terror only served to overturn his chair and hurl him to the floor. His head crashed against a log lying on the dirt floor and he lost consciousness at once.

Holstein had examined him, half-hoping he was dead, wondering what the Major would say about a head wound. But the King was breathing. The Queen saw that, too. Small as she was, that woman was made of strong stuff. She had not eaten and drunk all day, but still she looked alert and angry. Holstein had refreshed himself with water from the burn that was clear and good. He had provided himself with shortbread from the tin that was Jean's gift and munched hungrily, with the Queen's bright blue eyes blazing at him.

Holstein could feel no emotion at another's suffering, but at this moment he was touched by a sensation unusual to him. For the old servant who lay groaning near the door he cared about as little as a buzzing fly. When she first regained consciousness, she had kicked at him with her bound feet and had caught him painfully on the shin bone. He had only just restrained himself from killing her, but

382

he had taught her a lesson, as he knew well how to do.

But to see that postage-stamp profile in the dirt—the King's photograph had been in the kitchen of the Jarndyce's along with that of his Queen. It was this man's father whose photograph had been in the kitchen of his own home in Munich, next to that of the Kaiser. His mother—always the teacher—had bored him for years telling him that they were cousins, grand-children of Queen Victoria.

All of Holstein's loyalty went to the SS, and the Führer. The Führer in his mind took the place of God. But he had been born in 1913. Some of his earliest memories were of his father speaking with reverence of the Kaiser. It was not the Kaiser's fault, his father had insisted, that the German army had been betrayed . . . And this man in the dirt at his feet was the son of the Kaiser's cousin. The Queen's eyes were brilliant as much from anger as fear.

Holstein was used to fear in others. It made him comfortable. But this was unfamiliar. This mountain pass was strange and lonely, and yet unnerving. The drum of the rain, the constant rustle of wind, the water of the burn slipping over the rocks, small animals scuffling about the hut set him on the *qui vive*.

It was getting close to evening. His transceiver before him was like a dead thing. He felt in his bones that he should wait no longer. Kneeling over the fallen King, he grasped his throat with his thumbs, sliding them up to the smallest, weakest point in the cervical spine.

Holstein could not have heard the burst of gunfire that greeted the Swordfish at the field, but if he had it would have startled him less than it did Sergeant Barney and his pilot. For all of Rex's suspicions and anxieties, he had never guessed that the field could possibly be in enemy hands. His concerns had been the pilot's concerns, getting through the mountains with the sudden rain squalls and heavy patches of cloud, finding the field at all.

They had been circling about helplessly, until a sudden, narrow parting of the cloud revealed the bright windsock, shaking from the pole. Then there was the matter of bringing the 'plane down on the wet grass. Rex was congratulating himself that his pilot had been a keen amateur before the war—"Could fly you up in a Sopwith Camel," he'd said—and not one of these new, quickly trained kids.

It had been interest, not a feeling of necessity, that had caused him to look over the Lewis gun on the journey. The pilot had idled his engine and they were almost gliding when they met the sudden burst of gunfire. Later Rex was to learn that the forward gun had jammed, but at that moment his reflexes were swifter than thought. Before his mind had quite taken in what had happened, he had the Lewis in position and was raking the field. Firing the rear gun, he saw two men go down.

One was Schurmer, the other was Captain Stangel. Stangel was dead. The firing could have been heard for miles. The Fallschirmjäger knew there was nothing for it but to fight and run.

Rex heard the groaning of the pilot. Two of the bullets that had ripped the fuselage had broken his thigh. He was sweating and his face had turned sickly white.

"It's all right; I'll get her down," he said tersely.

Rex was still firing. The group scattered, but Dietz had taken Schurmer's place at the gun and held his ground. The Bofors was chattering again. Bullets whistled over Rex's head as he was twisting the Lewis round.

"For God's sake, get out," the pilot said, but Rex was still shooting. Somehow the pilot taxied the 'plane into position so that Rex could get a clear shot at the gunner, a salvo that sliced Dietz in two, but not before another line of bullets had ripped the 'plane. The three remaining men drew back, afraid of an explosion.

"Leave me and run, you idiot," the pilot said. "She'll burn." But Rex was pulling him from his seat. He covered both of them with his Browning as he sheltered behind the crazily tilted wings of the 'plane. Weirdly it struck him as being like Dunkirk in reverse, the dead sprawled as the English had been on the beach, their faces still distorted with pain.

Becker, the bravest of the remnant, approached cautiously, dodging round the 'plane. He saw Rex's gun and dived; slipped on the wet grass and fell, to have his head sliced off by the propellor. Rex, dragging the pilot, began retreating to the line of trees. There was a burst from the Bofors and a bullet went into the fuel tank. In a moment the grey damp evening was lit with a flash and the 'plane flared up against the Highland mist. Behind the protection of the flames Rex shouldered his burden and ran with all the speed and strength he had in him to the sanctuary of the trees.

The roar was heard and the flash seen on top of the steep wooded hill where the Manse of Sir Ewen MacBride stood. The Prime Minister had been as restless as Holstein. No aircraft had come to the field. He heard no rumble of heavy vehicles that might have been carrying troops, coming from the road. Once he had seen a lone lance-corporal on a motor-bike, but he had been too far off to be approached, and the hidden man dared not shout.

But the advent of the soldier decided him; he could not just skulk here while the country was possibly being taken by the enemy. The Manse was on a pinnacle, a weary height above the landing field, but he determined to make his way up there. He didn't know Sir Ewen, or whether the house was occupied, or if the telephone was working, but he had to try. And although he was taking a chance to go there, he thought it a reasonable chance. The Germans could hardly have taken every private house in the country.

And during his long enforced wait, another idea had come to him. Perhaps this invasion was a small, local affair. A plan to kill the King and himself, very quietly.

Otherwise—why the telegram? In spite of his bravado to the detectives of Special Branch, the Prime Minister was well aware that if the Germans had really wanted to kill him, they could have done so. Unless he wanted to spend his life in an underground chamber, he could never be really safe. Apart from any more subtle means, a suicide squad of parachutists dropped on Chequers at night could take care of him nicely. Just as, with greater difficulty, it was possible that a group of men, willing to give their lives, could kill Hitler at Berchtesgaden.

And that was the reason for his safety. One head of government was very loath to order the killing of another —such chickens were liable to come home to roost. Nevertheless, if Hitler had decided to kill him, there was no need to go to all this trouble to bring him to Scotland—unless the plan was no open invasion, but a coup. The King to die, the Prime Minister in his anxiety rushing to his side and having an unfortunate accident on the road. Probably it was intended that he should be driven off some likely cliff. A brilliant stroke to leave the country rudderless.

Scheming, subtle—and not just Hitler's scheme. Churchill could guess what mind had concocted this. Admiral Canaris had defeated him in the race for Norway. He swore to himself that the spymaster would not do it again. Tired and sweating, the old man began the long ascent.

His shoes were not made for mountain country, and he was soaked from the intermittent rain. A small, indomitable figure, he had to stop and rest far more often than he could ever have believed possible. At last he gained the summit, carefully concealing himself—but it had not been necessary. There was simply no-one about.

Sir Ewen, on his departure, had given his small remaining household staff their annual holiday. Only the groundsman and the housekeeper were left in residence; and the groundsman, when the rain started, had taken himself off to his own cottage to smoke his pipe and put his feet up. The housekeeper had gone to visit her married daughter at Kincardine.

The Prime Minister had entered the house without being noticed, as the groundsman had already penned the dogs in the kennels. But to his extreme anger and dismay, the telephone lines still had not been repaired. He cursed the Scottish authorities with every oath he had ever heard in the course of his long life, including some that he had not realized he knew. The first line to be repaired would almost certainly be that to the airfield. But when it was operational he would have precious little chance of getting to that. The powers-that-be would merely make it easier for the enemy.

There was no sense in staying at the Manse. He tried to clear his mind to remember the details of his arrival at Birkhall from Ballater, years before. It seemed to him he remembered a village about half way, where there was still some cover from the trees, before the open stretch around the little town. He would have to make his descent again to the valley and creep along somehow. The high road would be too dangerous. He had no idea what he would find when he got to the village, but he must do something. Perhaps he might learn what had happened to the King and Queen . . .

He was two-thirds of the way down when he heard the sound of a 'plane and then the crack of gunfire. His heart leapt—help at last! But as he stared through the mist at the field, he could see the flames of the burning 'plane. Tiredness forgotten, filled with a tearing mixture of hope, anxiety and dread, he made his way to the field at an amazing pace, caution almost forgotten.

The rain was coming down again and from the trees on the other side of the road it was hard to see what was happening, but the report of gunfire still sounded. A man in Air Force blue was running towards him. Churchill recognized one of the men who had been on the field when he landed. With the experience of a lifetime, the Prime

Minister took careful aim—Kleist, with a bullet in his gut, lay groaning and dying on the road. The Prime Minister grinned, and then a singing shot from nowhere struck into him and the grey mist thickened and darkened, and blackness covered his eyes.

* * *

Anthony Eden took the news of the Prime Minister's death very hard, as the harassed Chief of MI5 had known he would. He had tried to break the news as gently as possible, considering the emergency of the situation. He gave the few details that were necessary.

"The experts will be there to paw over the wreckage, but it seems to have been an ordinary, though dreadful, accident."

"Why was the PM in Scotland?" Eden asked.

"He'd been touring the Fighter Bases," the MI5 man replied. "He might have decided to inspect the northern reaches, Thirteen Group. The 'plane might have got lost. But we won't hold an open inquiry until we get word from the Cabinet . . ."

"Yes," Eden said, "I see." He could see exactly what the men who had conferred by the burning wreck had seen. This disaster, widely published, could paralyse the nation unless someone took hold firmly. But, he had to wonder, who?

In the meantime he agreed with the very worried Chief. The matter should be kept absolutely secret until the War Cabinet decided what should be done. The new Government must be formed, continuity in the affairs of the nation and the prosecution of the war assured, before this blow could fall.

"Yes, the public can certainly wait for this bad news," he said quietly.

It was quickly agreed that they should both work to try to arrange a meeting of the remaining members of the

War Cabinet—Chamberlain was too ill—and others of vital importance. Such as could be found. It had been difficult enough to find Eden himself, for he was at his very private, almost secret residence on the Downs behind Elham in Kent. His telephone number there was private also and there had been a short, sharp struggle before his secretary in London had been willing to give it at all, and then only to the Chief of the Security Service.

They also agreed that the meeting should convene at Elham.

"It will cause . . . less attention," the Chief said, and Eden agreed.

When he put the receiver down, the Secretary of State for War looked suddenly like an old man. There was no-one to observe the effect of shock. The house was empty. Raids on the coast nearby had caused him to send his family away. The place was his private bolt-hole. After one long, shuddering sigh, he picked up the reins.

He sat down with his notebook, wishing he had brought his secretary with him, and began the job of trying to call a conference. No use trying to wait for a full meeting—*some* decision must be made at once. In an hour and a half, enough men were assembled at least to begin. Some were travelling and could not be reached. Fortunately, Sir John Dill, Chief of Imperial General Staff (CIGS), had arrived, though who had called him Eden did not know.

As calmly as he could, he explained what he had been told, but tears ran down his cheeks. Some of them had heard the news already from MI5. It was immediately obvious that the choice of a successor had already been under discussion. Although Eden had been in politics all his adult life, he burned with a fierce resentment. And someone had told Lloyd George, who had no business to be informed. Lloyd George telephoned while the group was taking their seats—the chairs that he himself had hastily collected from the kitchen and the bedrooms, to supplement the half dozen round the dining-room table.

"Dear boy," Lloyd George boomed, "everything will go on."

Eden's ulcer twinged.

" 'But the dead they cannot rise, so you'd better dry your eyes'," Arthur Greenwood was quoting, with his usual love for the obvious, Eden thought. The rest of the group looked pained although, with the exception of the host, they seemed to agree with the sentiment.

But whom, Eden wondered, remembering the end of the quotation, did they intend to take for their new love? Already Lloyd George had been too outspoken in his dislike of this war.

"Well, I think we all agree that until things are settled, you should take over the Ministry of Defence," Lord Halifax said calmly. "Nothing can really be decided until we have a full meeting, on Monday." He turned to the CIGS. "What is the situation? Anything urgent that must be decided?"

"The PM was meeting Dowding on Monday about the aircraft situation. To put it plainly," Sir John Dill said, "as I think you know, we simply don't have the aircraft to meet the Luftwaffe challenge. And in spite of all Beaverbrook's pushing, we are not going to have enough in time. The Prime Minister's plan was to hold a fighting reserve against a full-scale onslaught and, by certain technical means now at our disposal, to deflect the Luftwaffe from the airfields to the cities, which are to remain, to a great extent, undefended by fighters. It is the sensible decision," he said. "In cold facts, the aircraft and the fields are more important now than homes or civilian lives."

Some of the men at the table winced.

"If the Germans invade, we can't hold all of England. The south will have to be evacuated. I can say that the Prime Minister has consulted me as to whether the National Service men would be willing to embark for Canada, in case of need, and I have had to report to him that I think they will not. They will fight here, at home, but they will not leave their families to go and fight elsewhere. Regular troops, of course, are another matter."

Eden stirred uneasily. No-one could impugn Sir John's loyalty. He was merely stating facts. Eden, Secretary of State for War, knew perfectly well how true those facts were. There was no way this war could be won, except by a miracle. Winston believed in miracles. He was, in a way—had been—a sort of miracle himself. So often Eden had heard him say, 'As an Englishman one fights with valour. With daring. Without reckoning the odds.' He charged ahead and tempted fortune to follow.

He rubbed his head. A religious would put it that you can't always see after the act. God disposes. How Winston would stare, bulging-eyed, to hear himself explained in pieties!

Inevitably, the conversation moved to politics. It would be best, they decided, for the Coalition to continue. But who would lead them? Eden suggested that the Secretary of State for Foreign Affairs would be the natural choice. Greenwood glared at Halifax and said that Labour would not stick it. Clement Attlee, more diplomatically, murmured that there could be problems with the rank and file. Greenwood, not diplomatically, plumped for Attlee.

Halifax looked pained.

"After all, the Prime Minister was also the leader of the Conservative Party. Surely, an accidental death should not change the balance . . ."

This was debated acrimoniously. It brought Eden a mixture of relief and sorrow that few of the men round the table were overwhelmed by their loss. Amery, Secretary of State for India and Burma, looked tired and ill, and was not taking part in the political discussion. Amery, who had been such a firebrand. Eden remembered the cheering in the House when Amery had called: 'Who speaks for England?' He now murmured quietly to Eden, referring back to the CIGS' remarks. "All the Chiefs say the same." He seemed entirely dispirited.

Richard Law, whom Eden had asked for his own support, as one of the Eden group, the anti-Munich men, nodded in agreement. "The years which the locust have eaten. They went on longer than we knew. As far as I've been able to discover, we're rather worse off than we were last year. Produced little and lost a damned lot of shipping."

"Winston and the Narvik affair," someone said, not kindly.

The argument got heavier. It was very plain that neither a Conservative nor a Labour man could lead the new Coalition.

"We'll have to go to the country," Greenwood said, obstinate.

"A General Election. Now?" Halifax looked pained. With the Germans on the doorstep the idea was ludicrous.

Someone else mentioned Lloyd George. The Palace will have to be consulted, Halifax observed.

"But Lloyd George wants to make a peace," Eden cried with passion.

Greenwood looked at him speculatively. The Secretary of State for War might have been the natural choice for Prime Minister. He observed the handsome, weak face. If he'd been born poor, that one would have come to nothing. Couldn't see him shouldering his way up through the ranks of the TUC. He, Greenwood, didn't much like the way the wind was blowing but . . . Lloyd George, that Artful Dodger, would wrap Eden up and sell him for export. With an effort, he pulled his mind back to the business at hand. But there was very little business at hand.

The men of the group had looked away, a little, at Eden's outburst.

"Winston, of course, would never have listened to a peace offer," someone remarked.

"No," Halifax replied, in a rather bored tone. "Still, it must be remembered that we went to war because of the guarantees to Poland. But nobody supposes now that we could mount an invasion of the Continent and take it back from Germany and Russia. However, there is no reason for this discussion here and now." He glanced round, re-crossing his legs at the ankle. He seemed to wonder what he was doing in the provincial little room.

"This is not a meeting of the War Cabinet or the Chiefs of Staff," Halifax continued. "We are merely trying to decide procedure until Monday morning, when I assume that a meeting of the full Cabinet, together with the Chiefs, will take place. My suggestion is that the news of the Prime Minister's death be withheld until Monday, when we hope that His Majesty will be able to summon a new Prime Minister. I agree with the Secretary of State for War that the sense of continuity is all-important." He smiled a small, wintry smile. "As with the Royal succession." That was merely his joke.

He got up to take his leave. The rest began to follow and Halifax paused at the door for a word with this one and that. The atmosphere was subdued, but not grief-stricken. Well, Winston had made mistakes. Mistakes that caused anger. Narvik. His feuds with Dill. His intolerance of Wavell. Even his cutting sarcasm at times to Eden himself. "If you lose Khartoum," he had said, "your name will live in history."

A sharp pain had knifed through Eden's stomach because he feared it would be lost. He did not see how it could be defended if the Italians came through from Kassala. A huge force had to be kept in Egypt. But he had felt like a small boy who failed every subject in his class. Like that child he had feared for an anguished second the ultimate disgrace—he almost lost control and wept. The old man could be terrifying.

"Lloyd George said to me . . ." He could hear Ernest Brown in the hall as the door opened again for the departing guests.

It looked as though on Monday there would be a

decision in favour of the old Welshman. He could be a great war leader; he had proved that before. But now . . .

Dill was lingering. He had something to say that was only for the ears of the War Cabinet, just at that moment.

"There are Intelligence reports that Hitler is planning to invade Russia. That should ease our burden, whatever happens."

Halifax nodded. "The Eagle and the Bear can rend each other," he said in terms of great satisfaction. "A very desirable condition for the British Lion."

He had already collected his stick, hat and gloves and he made his departure. As his motor roared off, Dill said farewell and left also.

"Cheer up," Greenwood said heartily. "Old Winnie would have wanted that."

They are treating me like a broken-hearted infant, or an old invalid, Eden thought. But he could think of no way to hold them. Poor old Anthony—gone to pieces without his idol. He could see the thought written on each forehead.

The house was very quiet when they'd gone. He listened, as long as he could, to the sound of the cars driving away, as though the engine throbs were the heartbeats of England receding further and further into the night. He could have gone back to town with one of them; there was no reason to stay where he was. But there was no reason to go either.

Sighing, he gathered up the glasses that had been used by his guests and took them to the kitchen and washed them, for he was a neat man. His stomach was sore, as if with an old wound. Sadly, he poured himself a glass of milk and went to bed. He hadn't pulled the blackout but lay and watched the night sky, lit up by an occasional blur of the searchlights in the rain.

An hour passed. He was not quite awake yet he could not fully fall asleep. His tired, puzzled mind could not quite believe that Winston Churchill was dead and gone.

TWENTY-FIVE

The Major And The General

Earlier that day, Major Leiter had begun to feel anxious. He had woken from an uneasy rest with the expectation that he would hear from Holstein at any moment. He had stayed close to the telephone in the study of the pleasant house that the Embassy had taken on his behalf. As the hours went by expectation quickly turned to unease. When a man came to ask if he wanted lunch in the study, he snapped at him for no reason. Except that the man irritated him.

The Major, for his brief stay, had wanted no trained English servants with sharp ears and curious eyes about him. Instead he had a few ruffians recruited for him by an old member of the pro-German Link—members of Fascist street gangs who ignored the public exhortation of the former leader and still hoped for a Fascist Britain. Besides, they liked the pay.

Leiter despised these men, who had to be reminded to clean their fingernails so that a chance visitor—they had been called on once by an ARP warden—*could* believe them to be servants. But he soon forgot his annoyance in his growing worry. His early euphoria had vanished. The responsibility he owed to the Admiral and to the Reich loomed larger in his mind. There had been no message as yet from the Admiral in reply to his own.

Perhaps he should have waited for the Admiral to decide about the Fallschirmjäger. Yet nothing had gone wrong there, as far as he knew. He had been glued to the BBC broadcast since it began that morning, but there was no news flash about any descent of parachutists . . . Of course, the news could be suppressed.

His relief and joy when he heard from Lewis, speaking the code words in guarded tones, were so extreme as to bring the Major back almost to exhilaration.

"The bird died, but little Tubby was sleeping soundly."

Purcell had brought down the 'plane. And the Prime Minister was dead.

The Welshman had hung up quickly. Leiter had been tempted to ask for news of Holstein. Black Knight was not under the Welshman's command, and he was ordered to report to himself only, but Lewis might have known something.

The exhilaration soon faded, and Leiter began to worry again. It was already late afternoon. Friday. The attack had been scheduled for Thursday night. True, any number of things could have caused a delay. The Royal party might have decided to go by car instead of train and spent Thursday night on the road. It wasn't their habit, but someone might have pointed out that the Royal train could be a target for a precision bomber. The King might have taken more protection than usual, and Black Knight simply had to wait to get his chance. Black Knight in the past had been the most resourceful of killers, but this was a difficult, delicate task.

The telephone was obstinately silent. The Major made his way up to the attic—perhaps at this very moment a wireless message was coming in. But the attic was still and quiet, with only the muted sounds coming up from the street. Eckhardt was sitting before his transceiver, looking vacant. The Major flew into a rage and ordered him to be more alert. As he descended the stairs he remembered the man had not slept all the night before and sent up a pot of coffee and some stimulating pills.

Still the Major felt unhappy—more so than the situation seemed to warrant. The Prime Minister was dead, and that was virtually important. And with no outcry about possible saboteurs. In fact, no outcry at all. Surely his death should have been announced by now. The British might be amateurish, but they were not so lax as to fail to find a downed aircraft and identify its eminent passenger. Soon people would be flooding the area; pouring up from London, some of them by 'plane no doubt. By now the Fallschirmjäger should have fired the hut on the landing field and taken themselves off. But with no word from Holstein they would wait . . .

Of course, the news was being suppressed. And yet— Major Leiter was, as Eckhardt thought so contemptuously, an Abwehr bureaucrat, but in the past he had directed enough agents to sense when an operation was going wrong. Almost before there were any facts to support such a sense. It was only his sitting there so long by the telephone, listening to the inanities of the BBC, he told himself, that was giving him this feeling of unreality. Dance band music. Programmes for women.

Even the six o'clock news, which always gave the important war bulletins, had nothing to say of the Prime Minister. Leiter listened until it ended with the agricultural prices.

"Fat cows, all weights," the calm voice was reading, and Leiter switched it off in disgust. No-one would think that these people were on the verge of extinction.

By now Whaleforce was dispersed. Lewis would soon be taking off the parachutists—unneeded men, as the Admiral had said from the beginning. But what on earth had happened to Black Knight? He turned on the BBC Home Programme once again. Two comics, making jokes about the Führer. It made him sweat to listen to it.

Now he began to think about the Welshman's manner when he had given his brief message, his subdued and guarded tone. He had chosen Lewis to be the leader of the group for his competence, stability and intelligence. The Irish, though experienced and deadly killers, were unreliable and needed a tight discipline. Purcell was different, almost like a German in his ability to take orders. Michael O'Connor, who had been chosen first to undertake the sabotage of the plane, was surly as well as erratic but was even less able to hold his tongue than his brother, the melancholy Sean. The job he had been given of tracking Churchill round the fighter bases had been good enough for him. The two brothers were known for diverting German funds even more than was usual with the IRA, a thieving group. This time the men had been paid very little in advance as a safeguard.

But what was it about the Welshman's message that was now troubling him? It was natural for the man to have been subdued. The importance of his mission; the very real fear of the British on his tracks. And yet instinct was warning Leiter before his mind could deduce the facts. The Welshman was, very simply, a bad liar. In his own way a religious man, he was not accustomed to the direct lie, and his awkwardness had affected the timbre of his voice. Leiter still trusted him but—

The silence of the BBC on the Prime Minister's death could only have certain meanings, and he had to take notice of them all. The wreckage still might not have been found; but he dismissed that possibility. Communications were muddled, and the dead passenger was not as yet identified. That could be true. Even if they believed it might be the Prime Minister but were not certain, the news would be blacked out. Or, as he had thought earlier, they were sure but were delaying the blow until someone could take control. In Germany they would do the same thing, should something happen to the Führer. For once his mind didn't linger on that possibility. The other alternative, which had to be faced, was that Churchill still

398

lived. The Welshman had lied, or had been deceived. His orders had been to be present at the 'Reception Centre' himself and not trust the final work to the Irish killers, but something could have gone awry.

For all of Leiter's methodical mind, the possibility of two of his alternatives both being true did not occur to him. The news was blacked out, and the Prime Minister was still alive. But in his heart he felt that if something had gone wrong the Irish were to blame. Or those parachutists had bungled somehow. The Admiral, he thought belatedly, was almost never wrong.

There was no way he could reach any of the members of Whaleforce now. Yet he longed for more information. Lewis was not scheduled to make contact again. The money was to be paid through another agent after Whaleforce left Scotland. None of the other men could reach Leiter at the London house; it was secret from all of them. A usual security measure. He was almost sorry for it now.

The security measure was not as good as Leiter had supposed. The London-based O'Connor brothers had tracked the new 'Commercial Attaché' from the Hungarian Embassy and found the house easily enough. They had had no particular reason, but they were a curious pair. Sean kept back little from his brother, and Michael had been sulking—Purcell had been brought in and given the more skilled and highly paid job of demolition while he had been given errand boy's work. And now it seemed he might not even get paid for that. Sean's telephone call from Ballater to his lodging house in Kilburn had been short but to the point.

"Go round and try to collect our shares," he finished. "The Major might go for it—Taffy told him that we did the job." He paused to mouth a few obscenities. "Say you've come because you think you were spotted on the airfield, and we both want to get out of the country."

The Major, still waiting at the telephone, with half a

cold cup of coffee at his side and a dozen cigarette stubs in the ashtray, had an unpleasant shock when he heard that an Irishman who called himself O'Connor was at the door, demanding to see 'the guvner'. But he very much wanted some news, and ordered him to be admitted. When he saw Michael O'Connor he knew he was going to get the news he'd been waiting for, but he was not relieved. Somehow he knew it was not going to be good news.

The 'servants' who admitted O'Connor were men who had once been part of the British National Socialist League. They despised the Irish and made it clear. It was an already very surly man who was shown in to see the Major. The inside of the house displeased him. Behind its plain facade it was a magnificent private house whose owner had gone to the country for the duration of the war and had been happy to lease it to the Embassy to house some of the diplomats.

The Germans were doing well for themselves already, O'Connor thought sourly, thinking of his grubby room in the Edgware Road. They were no better than the English after all. They would have a few surprises if they thought the men of the IRA were really working for them. His brother Sean, though he looked as sour as a lemon, could be a great joker. He'd mentioned the mishap very briefly at the start of his telephone call to Michael.

"In case we don't find the old bastard, we want the money now," he'd said.

Michael had been a bit puzzled.

"If you didn't have the turkey, what did you put in the oven?" he'd asked curiously.

"Oh, some fine old pig that came our way, just like himself," Sean had answered and they'd had a laugh. Michael had thought that they must have a drink to that.

Major Leiter received him in the small library. It was not one of the main rooms of the house, and it was discreetly in the rear. The furnishings and the appointments of the house had pleased Major Leiter who enjoyed fine things and whose wife was a zealous housekeeper. Secretly, it pained him that the Abwehr offices on the Tirpitz Ufer were so commonplace. When the Irishman slouched in, with his muddy boots and his cloth cap, the workman's trousers that soiled the tapestry chair on which he sat without being asked, Leiter wished he'd had him shown to the servants' quarters.

He did not make any salutation, nor acknowledge Leiter's presence in any way, except for the raising of his eyelids. The eyes, thus exposed, were cold and grey. The gaze was not the obsequious half-glance of a subordinate; it was the chill evaluation of a killer.

The Major did not like him. He didn't like him at all. Germans served the Major, some from old Abwehr loyalty, some because they must. His British traitors served for money or for hope of power to come. But these Irish —this lout stared at him as if he were his equal, he, a Major in the German Army. The Major was not a cruel man and despised the Gestapo for their habitual torture of prisoners. But looking at O'Connor, he couldn't help thinking this man would be much improved by a good flogging.

"I want my share and my brother's now," O'Connor said without preamble. "Some old bastard from Special Branch spotted me yesterday; I saw him asking questions."

That happened to be true, though it had not troubled him much at the time. He had quickly faded away and got out of his aircraftsman's uniform when the detective's attention moved off him.

"Better that me and Sean get out of the country," he added, and then was silent.

"What if he did see you?" Major asked sharply. "I understood that you and your brother are not known to Special Branch."

O'Connor looked at him with something close to contempt.

"No, we weren't. But now I am, you see. He must have seen me at Uxbridge or Middle Wallop—they're not quite idiots, after all."

"Have you heard today from your brother?" Leiter asked.

He knew O'Connor probably would not tell the truth. Almost certainly he had heard—that was why he was here and not leaning against the bar in a drinking place in the Edgware Road. The man didn't reply immediately, but Leiter's practised eye took in the sudden, quickly veiled awareness in his glance.

"Why should I have heard?" he said, as if surprised. "What about the money? I don't want to stay here all day."

The French Empire clock on the mantelpiece was ticking away, minute by minute. Leiter felt that time was growing short. He repeated his question.

O'Connor spat on the Aubusson rug. "I don't know nothing of Sean's business," he said. "You know your people like it that way. Mum's the word. Sean's always been a close-mouthed bastard," he added, a manifest lie.

Leiter gave him a look that could cow his subordinates for a week.

"In the name of the Reich I order you to tell me what you know. You understand what a refusal would mean."

But in O'Connor's army every man believed himself to be a general and he was not impressed.

He laughed. "You know what you can do with your order." In case the Major didn't know he explained graphically.

Even if he got the money, he thought grimly, he wouldn't tell him the truth. Not that he thought there was any chance of getting it. If ever he saw a suspicious old devil, this was one.

Leiter, although he was white with anger, would have paid him the money if he'd thought he could get the truth. But he could read O'Connor's thoughts as plainly as he heard the insults. He knew what he had to do, and pressed a button that was fitted into the library table.

The Irishman stood up. His eyes had narrowed to steel-coloured slits, his big jaw set square and threatening.

"When Sean has something to tell you he'll tell you himself."

Leiter sat, outwardly calm, tapping a pencil on his blotter. His attention had already veered to the continued silence of Black Knight.

O'Connor was aware of the withdrawal of his attention, and took it as an attempt at dismissal. His rage burst out, uncontrollably.

"Do you think the men of Ireland have fought this fight against the English for you to take their place? For you to sit on your arses in luxury and give us the back of your hand? You Germans are thicker than we took you for. D'you think you're going to throw us out like sluts after the party's over?"

He leaned over the Major, his lips drawn back over his yellowed, crooked teeth. A smell came off him of beer and tobacco, and dank cloth that had never known the cleaner's.

Two men appeared behind him, guns drawn. He lashed out at them anyway—without thinking, he knew the Major didn't want him dead. They overcame him at last but not before he had smashed a Dresden vase, a fine fauteil, and stamped his cleated boots through the twisted rug.

The Major was very disturbed. He had to find out everything O'Connor knew, and there was no time for his usual methods. With this ox, any interrogation could be long drawn out. The men he had here were only good for one thing. He gave the necessary orders.

After a glance at the obstinately silent telephone, he went out to the covered terrace to smoke a cigar. He could hear the telephone there, and the garden scents were fresh and soothing, even with the rain still slanting down. When

403

O'Connor was ready, he would have to go and assist in the questioning, but he hated this part and let his men get on with it.

The wait seemed long, but not as long as it was for O'Connor. The men had got to work immediately, and his screams of agony as their razors sliced came even from the depths of the wine cellar clear out to the garden. Leiter, mindful of his neighbours, had to send orders for the stifling of the sound.

Actually it was only fifteen minutes later when the chief of his men left the basement entrance and came round to find him. His coat was splashed with blood. Leiter, in disgust at his stupidity, had to wave him back to the house.

He had not much to tell but it was enough. Black Knight was missing. The old man had got away and a fat pig had been burned in his place. The man, who had been told as little as possible, asked if that was enough.

"I'll finish it myself," the Major said.

The man looked sheepish.

"I'm sorry, sir, but I don't know if he'll come round. He wasn't as strong as he looked," he said in excuse.

Leiter had to go and see what they'd left of Michael O'Connor. The strips of flesh, the pools of blood mixed with the vintage wines that had been smashed on the cellar floor turned his stomach.

"Clumsy oaf," he muttered. "Get him out of here and clean the place up."

Once the fit of nausea had passed, his mind was clear and he was himself again, though not a happy self. Black Knight was still missing. Churchill had escaped. A 'fat pig' burned in his place? Probably some substitute to deceive him and get Whaleforce their money. The Prime Minister had probably raised the alarm already. No use to try and implement *Araby* and *Scullion* now. He thought of the Admiral's wrath and refused to consider his own disappointment. He paid off the Englishmen—their limited usefulness was over. He would go to the Embassy, get a new set of papers, and be ready to leave on the night flight to Lisbon.

But first he made his way up the stairs towards the attic. Eckhardt had to be ready to leave also. He could wait by the transceiver for another hour, but they would probably never hear from Black Knight now. If Black Knight escaped, he could always make his way back through Jarndyce in London.

They met on the second floor. Eckhardt had received one more message: Black Knight, to his annoyance, was still surviving. Eckhardt was nervous. The air waves were no longer so crowded. Someone else might have picked up one of the signals. He could not take any more chances. Acknowledging the signal, he tore off a piece of paper and, decoding swiftly, wrote out Black Knight's message. He was on his way down when he heard the step on the stairs. Without thinking, he stuffed the paper in his pocket.

Unemotionally, the Major told him they were leaving. Eckhardt must be ready to go in an hour. He could leave the key open until then, but it seemed Black Knight was dead. The operation was over. Eckhardt had no wish for the operation to continue. Leiter might abandon him to the British. He would much rather go home. The paper stayed in his pocket to be burned when he regained the attic.

While Leiter was at the Embassy he had a new thought. Because *Araby* and *Scullion* could not be used now, it didn't mean that they could *never* be used. If the Führer decided . . . He had better save what he could. He sent a coded message to von Auerbach in Lisbon. His previous instructions were cancelled. The client should remain where he was. Then the Major sent one more message by the diplomatic pouch to Admiral Canaris in Madrid.

TWENTY-SIX

A Crown For Queen Wallis

That Friday was, for von Auerbach, the most pleasant day of his life. Thursday night he had spent in charming company. When he returned to the hotel and received Leiter's first message his joy knew no bounds. All along he had been certain he could do his part—if only the men from the Tirpitz Ufer would get on with theirs. It was not easy keeping the Duke, like drawn butter, hot but not too hot over a candle flame. Now his reward had come. The signal he received was the 'A' signal. They must be ready to leave on Saturday. He started packing his bags at once, paid his bill and tipped the staff with such generosity that they decided among themselves there was a lot to be said for the Germans.

First thing Friday morning, before the Duchess was up, he had been at the Mouth of Hell. For once he had asked the maid to wake her mistress—the Duchess would not mind. He had a fancy to tell her the news, even before the Duke. The diplomat and the Duchess were soon in the highest of good humours. Even the heat seemed tolerable. The Duchess, who always took breakfast in her room, broke her rule and ordered it served on the balcony. She invited von Auerbach to stay and sent word to the Duke. Before he arrived—this morning the Duchess' toilet had been amazingly swift—she had a quiet word with the Graf.

"I do hope you will be the new Ambassador to the Court of St James, Friedrich, as soon as we have the peace treaty. I know the King will want it, too."

He had thanked her, smiling, and said that that was a matter for the Führer, of course, to decide.

"But you are the perfect choice!" she exclaimed. "You are partly English by descent, aren't you?"

He explained the connection of his family with the English branch, through Queen Victoria's husband, Prince Albert.

"Well, then," she said gaily, "if the Führer doesn't want to send you to us, perhaps the King can arrange an English Dukedom. You have been so encouraging in our dark times."

She smiled on him with regal charm. When the Duke appeared, fully dressed, she repeated her idea and he listened graciously, without flinching.

"I am afraid your brother's condition is now such that he is not expected to survive the week," von Auerbach said soberly, in a sudden switch of mood. "I hope, for the sake of the Throne, that the Coronation will be soon. As Your Majesty will not in fact be succeeding your brother, but resuming your reign, the usual period of *public* mourning could, and in fact should, be curtailed."

"Poor Bertie," the Duke said, as he always did. He drank some of his coffee and soon brightened. "And so you are to be Queen Wallis after all, Dolly."

To the Graf von Auerbach, the title really did not sound quite right.

"Your Majesty has definitely decided against the style Elizabeth?"

A tiny shadow fell on her beaming countenance. She most certainly had.

"It will be too confusing with the present Queen," she said shortly. "What will her title be now?"

"She will revert to the Duchess of York," the Duke said. "That is her title by right, as she married my brother when he was the Duke. I think we will let her and the girls have York House."

"David," the Duchess said suddenly, "can you fire an Archbishop?"

He knew very well whom she meant. The Archbishop of Canterbury, Cosmo Cantuar, who had insulted them both and forbidden their marriage.

"I'm afraid not, my dear. I don't think anyone can. I can't think of a precedent." He wrinkled his forehead. A hazy thought of Thomas à Becket came to mind. "The ecclesiastics do things their own way."

"But, surely, you're head of the Church? That's why there was all the fuss."

Suddenly he grinned, looking much younger.

"I think I'll be magnanimous. No heads will roll."

His amusement came from his knowledge of his wife. She had been snubbed so much by Society since the Abdication. No heads would roll—but he could well see the toppling of a few smart hats, and a few well-bred noses put distinctly out of joint. Wallis would not only be Queen of England, Scotland, Ireland and Wales, Empress of India and all the other bits and pieces, but she would be the undoubted Queen of Society. And how she would liven it up!

There was so much to talk about that von Auerbach had to stay to luncheon. As the Ducal pair had packed long since for the journey, they had little preparation to make. The Duchess pressed von Auerbach to stay for dinner and the night, but he had to pick up his luggage from his hotel, and he needed to stop in at the Legation in the morning. He was supposed to wait there for the 'B' —depart instantly—signal. 'B' meant that all stages of the journey were prepared; the sea-'plane ready for the rendezvous with the boat at Alderney, a group waiting on the South Coast. Von Auerbach had already decided not to wait too long. The sending of a message could be delayed —the 'A' was enough for his authority to move out to sea.

He knew in his bones that his time had come.

He arranged that he, alone, would bring the car for them at 2.30 P.M. the next day. The servants should *not* be informed of their departure. He would leave the car out of sight of the house.

"They'd see us anyway," said the Duchess realistically. "I'll give them the day off. Better, I'll send them to Lisbon for extra supplies. Manuel can drive the car. I'll pack them off early, it's the only way."

"Then leave a message for the butler," von Auerbach suggested. "You'll be away until, say, Tuesday. By then it won't matter . . ."

The Duke nodded.

"The Esperito-Santos will be happy to get the house back in this heat," the Duchess said thoughtfully.

"But, Dolly, there'll be no-one to carry the luggage." The Duke looked faintly perturbed.

Von Auerbach smiled.

"As always, I am at your service, Your Majesty. I will get it into the car. You will have the highest ranking porter on the Continent. And some of the men from the boat will be waiting near the cove to unload it."

The Duke enjoyed this kind of joke.

"Not the highest-ranking! You can carry my things, von Auerbach, but I will carry yours, Dolly. King, Emperor and Porter by Royal Warrant to Her Majesty Queen Wallis."

They laughed a lot that day.

He left them after luncheon in the drawing-room, where the Duchess was trying on a diamond tiara that the Duke had bought for her when he was King. The Duke was smiling at her reflection.

"Soon, my dear, it will be the real thing. A crown for Queen Wallis."

It was hard to realise, she thought, but it seemed like the end of the Windsor Plot at last.

Manuel, who had heard much of the important talk, soon got bored with the joys of others and withdrew to take his siesta. He had to look for Maria whom he found outside with Jorge. The child was flushed and cross and couldn't understand why he must no longer use the pool, or even trot around it. Certainly, he argued, he understood it was for the use of the great ones when they wished it, but why should the water, so cool, so blue, so inviting, be forbidden a small boy when the great ones were busy elsewhere?

For once Manuel was tolerant. He smiled.

"Our master and the family return soon. In a day or two perhaps. Our master is a kindly man and will look the other way, Jorge. You will bathe again."

"So soon?" Maria asked, her eyes wide. She had had no time for eavesdropping, and the conversation at table had been, more or less, discreet.

Manuel would say no more. But once in her room, he found he could no longer be enigmatic.

"They leave tomorrow," he confided at last, with great knowingness. "Tomorrow I must go to Lisbon myself, to collect supplies for our master's return. They have devoured like locusts," he added.

"But the ship does not sail tomorrow," Maria said wondering.

He raised his hand above the sheet and made a diving gesture.

"They will go like thieves. Probably they will leave no tips. Ricardo will probably drive me back."

"Can I come too?" Maria said, but without much hope. "I have not seen Lisbon for months. And I want to see my sister in the Alfama."

He would certainly have refused—he had no liking for the country-bred Maria to be loose in the Alfama. But as the Duchess was going to order her off, he might as well have the credit now for generosity, and so he agreed.

I will take Jorge for a treat, Maria thought. Manuel's arm encircled her. In the afternoon light it was old and stringy. She remembered the strong young arms of the English soldier and sighed. Certainly they would never meet again. She closed her eyes and pretended, as best she could, that it was not this man but the other. Later, while Manuel slept, her mind, restless, drifted to the other woman in the house. She, Maria, would not care about being Queen. But she would like a strong young man of her own. Like Rex.

TWENTY-SEVEN

Black Knight At The Kill

Rex Barney had left the injured pilot in the shelter of a bush and was flat on his belly on the wet ground, peering through the rain at the remaining Fallschirmjäger. As far as he could make out there had been only two left on their feet; then one had charged out into the open, firing up the slope. Like the bloody Light Brigade, he had thought, puzzled, not realising that Kleist, seeing the figure of a man on the slope, had believed it to be Rex himself. Rex had been even more surprised when he heard the crack of a gun behind him and Kleist fell to the ground. Then another shot rang out from the airfield, and he heard a slight thud.

Rex had been aware that his newly acquired, unknown ally was probably hurt, but he could not stir for the moment. The enemy had heard the shots. He lay like the dead and waited. Thank God for his Browning, there were plenty of shots left in the magazine. Bruner approached cautiously. He was well within range but Rex waited. Then he saw another dark shape limping behind the first. The Browning barked; Rex rolled swiftly down the slope; a bullet sped in the place where he had been; up on one knee he took aim again and Bruner fell with a bullet in his heart.

Then it was very quiet on the field. Rex searched

cautiously, but there were no reserves; no-one else was hiding. He looked at the bodies; all dead, he thought. He was wrong. Schurmer's left arm had been shattered by the Lewis gun; a bullet from the Browning had creased his head, but he would live. Now he lay still and for him the battle was over.

Rex went back to see who had come to his aid. The Prime Minister had recovered from his momentary blackout and was stirring. He had taken a flesh wound in his shoulder, but he found to his surprise that he was not mortally wounded. It was fortunate for him that the Fallschirmjäger had used the Webleys. With their own pistols, his shoulder would have been shattered beyond repair. His doctor would have his own opinion about the blackout, but that was something the Prime Minister was never told.

His first sight of that red-brown head, dark now from the rain, gave him an upsurge of joy. The two men stared at each other.

"Took you long enough to get here," the Prime Minister said.

Rex looked at the dark stain on the old man's coat.

"Silly bugger," he said. "Why didn't you stay back where you belonged?"

The Prime Minister's eyes bulged.

"The country's alive with the enemy." His voice was booming.

Rex swiftly reloaded his Browning. Then he scanned the misty, dripping landscape.

"Keep your voice down," he said. "We've done for this lot; there might be more about. But I don't know about the country. I've come today from Bristol through London and no sign of trouble. This might be a private party for you lot up here."

He looked at the Prime Minister's wound. Not serious, but he was no youngster. He should try to call for help. There was the pilot too; not complaining but he needed a doctor badly. He assisted the Prime Minister to the shelter of the lean-to, and tried the telephone but it was dead. The Prime Minister had followed him.

"They're out all down this glen."

"Since Christmas, I suppose," Rex said bitterly. "What was all that about the King? Why did you rush up here?"

"Telegram," the Prime Minister said tersely. "Now he's missing. And the Queen."

"Christ."

The wounded Prime Minister for the moment avoided the sergeant's gaze. Both remembered the warning Sergeant Barney had tried to give the first time he was in Lisbon. It was clear enough to the Prime Minister now. He and the King were to die and their places be taken by . . . people more amenable to the idea of peace. The Prime Minister's first joyous relief was dampened fast by the thought of Lisbon. He refused absolutely to believe that the Duke and Duchess had any part in the plot.

A coffee pot was burning on a paraffin stove. Rex took it off without thinking. He looked in the hangar, but apart from the petrol drums it sheltered only five bicycles and three motor-bikes, none of them with side-cars. He couldn't transport his wounded. They'd have to stay under cover while he made for the nearest town. It was eerily quiet outside. Except for the strewn corpses on the field and by the fringe of trees, there was no sign of human presence other than their own.

As he returned to the hut he noticed a recent excavation. It was lightly covered by rocks and dirt. He drew closer, frowning, and kicked some of the rocks aside.

"My God," Rex said. The Prime Minister, despite the pain of his wound, was quickly at his side. Rex pushed aside the cover of dirt, to reveal the bodies of six men. One was a uniformed policeman.

The Prime Minister stared down at the body on the right, a thin young man. Sprinkled with mud, strands of his hair still caught the light. The old man got on his knees and looked closer, though the smell of rot was already coming up from the corpses, and cleaned some of the mud from his face.

"Giles Carruthers," he said. "One of His Majesty's equerries."

Barney knelt beside him and they examined each of the bodies. Both of them expected to find the King.

"The King's valet," Churchill said, "and this man might be one of the Palace chauffeurs—I can't be sure."

He had reason not to be sure—some small animal or animals had found the bodies before them. None of the bodies looked like the King.

"The cars were gone when I got to Birkhall," the Prime Minister said heavily.

"Sent for help," Rex conjectured, "and got clobbered on the road."

His hands moved the corpses to find two rows of airmen underneath. The stench was sickening now but the pit had to be searched to the bottom.

"Looks like the King and Queen might have escaped. Where's the nearest town?"

"About five miles if I remember right," the Prime Minister said. "You don't have any brandy about you, by any chance?"

"No brandy, guv, but you have a sit-down in the hut. There's a motor-bike out there; I'll do the five miles before you get yourself comfy. I'll get a search party going, and send an ambulance back for you."

"I'm coming with you," the Prime Minister said. "And you can't use the bike. To my knowledge there are two more Germans at Birkhall, and you don't know who else might be watching the road. We'll go the way I came, dodging through the trees."

Rex didn't argue—in a way he would rather he kept the old boy with him, now he'd found him.

"Are you all right to walk?" he said.

"A mere flesh wound," the Prime Minister said coldly.

Rex looked at his sleeve, sticky with blood. He quietly removed the Prime Minister's coat and shirt, and felt a pang at seeing the exposed torso, frail-looking and old. The wound was merely a graze, the bullet had not penetrated. Rex had a moment's thankfulness that the German had been less than a crack shot. He didn't know that Kleist had in fact been an excellent shot, but had slightly misjudged the trajectory of the English six-shooter.

There was clean water in a barrel, and Rex washed and bandaged the Prime Minister's wound with strips of his own undershirt. Returning to the pilot, he saw he had regained consciousness but was lying very still. His leg was a mess. Rex did what he could and explained where they were going and that help would be sent.

The pilot nodded and managed a smile to the Prime Minister, who stood over him, his eyes watering.

"Brave young man," he said and patted his shoulder.

Outside the rain had lessened, for the moment anyway, to a few light drops. As they made their way northward Rex asked:

"How do you know the men at Birkhall were Germans, not Special Branch?" His mind was playing with the thought that old Hilliard might have got some men up here—though he couldn't think how.

"Positive. Fine, fresh-faced, healthy-looking young men. Not a line on their faces—might never have had a worry in the world. Not at all the look of Special Branch. Besides," he said, in a more subdued tone, "the cook told me the two officers that came up with Their Majesties had gone, and these two were 'replacements'."

They trudged along for a time in silence, cautiously watching their way, but seeing no-one. Whaleforce had dispersed.

"Too early for the shooting," the Prime Minister

remarked. "Don't suppose many people will come up this year anyway."

Rex had his own preoccupation.

"Why would the Germans stay to guard the empty house?"

"The cook was there. Perhaps they didn't want her to leave, and go chatting about in the cottages. Or to stop someone else coming in and finding the family gone."

"And they didn't spot you. Not really trained for guard duty," Rex said thoughtfully. "I think I'll go and have a look. P'raps they didn't do in the King and Queen. If that's what they wanted to do, they could have left the bodies and run. They might have them hidden somewhere near the house. After all, that squad at the airfield was waiting for something. Perhaps they expect a 'plane in tonight."

"Then why not hide them down here in readiness?" the Prime Minister said irritably, with unanswerable logic.

Rex attempted no answer. The King and Queen were *not* near the field. Except for the big house over the airfield, which the PM had already searched, there had been no shelter as far as the eye could see. And if they were under guard, almost surely one of the guards would have come out to observe the fireworks on the field.

There was unfinished business at the Royal house; it was worth taking a look. The Germans might know something of the whereabouts of the Royal couple. Glancing at the old man, Rex decided it would be best to leave him under cover, in some comfort. He wasn't looking too well, his face had turned a nasty colour. The old man could never walk the miles to the town. And the feeling was growing in Rex that he should make a search right now. Sense told him that if the King and Queen were still alive, time might be running out. And instinct nudged him that they were still here in these woods, on these slopes that might appear beautiful to a nature lover but were dank and dismal to the Cockney sergeant.

417

After crossing the bridge and leaving the Prime Minister below, he climbed the cliff a half mile from the house, and made his way, silently, carefully. As he crawled up the terraced garden, his Browning was ready in his hand.

The two remaining Fallschirmjäger, Sergeants Müller and Schmidt, were still complacent enough; they had not heard the gunfire. As far as they knew nothing had gone wrong since their arrival. The two bodies of the English detectives had been taken off in the night for disposal. Black Knight was tracking the King, and probably had found him long since. Schmidt had heard the Captain talking of Black Knight, and his deadly efficiency. Müller's faith was in Captain Stangel; he had brought them here, by now he would have captured the enemy's leader. Very soon, the mission completed, the Welshman would lead the party along the valley, and they would make their way to the river where their transport would be waiting. In the meantime their orders were to remain where they were.

But of the two, Sergeant Müller, the more intelligent, felt less easy. He understood better than Schmidt the importance of the order that the King was to appear to die naturally in his bed. But all this was a matter for higher authority to deal with. The Royal party had left before the Fallschirmjäger had arrived. They could not be criticised. And it was fortunate that their ruse was working perfectly. He and Schmidt would certainly be commended for taking in the old woman. Few Germans could so easily be taken for members of the Newcastle police! He had learned his English well in the *Gymnasium* while Schmidt had spent several years in England with his mother, a housekeeper and cook.

This Scottish housekeeper had been irritable in the morning, worried in the afternoon, but seemed to forget her anxieties in her annoyance at the disappearance of the maid she called Jean. She spent her time fussing about meals which no-one came to eat and trying to feed the two Germans. Unfortunately, for breakfast looked and smelled delicious, it was against orders to eat it. She might be suspicious, though both men were sure she was not, and have poisoned the food. And so it was left, and the lunch sandwiches buried in the ground, while the dutiful men consumed dry ration.

Schmidt was displeased with the Welshman. The natives were supposed to have the liaison duty. If Black Knight was successful, surely he could have sent someone to inform them of the good news! But, of course, he would be arriving soon. Müller and Schmidt had begun, very correctly, patrolling the house and gardens. But the day had been so quiet and undisturbed that they had become lax and kept close to each other.

Rex's approach had been silent until a small stone on the terrace crumbled and fell away under his boot. Both men spun round, guns drawn, but Müller put his hand on Schmidt's wrist. The Welshman, most likely, or one of his men.

"Who goes there?" Schmidt called.

The response should have been 'Jonah'. But instead the answer was a bullet that shattered his face. Before consciousness lapsed, one thought flickered across the German's mind: We were abandoned . . .

Müller had the same thought but, well-trained, he flattened himself on the ground and crawled for cover behind a stubby bush. No-one was in sight. The report of the gun had come from below. The light on the summer evening lingered long, but the drizzling rain and slight mist hampered visibility. Nevertheless if someone was creeping up from the lower level, now that Müller was warned, that someone had no chance. But perhaps there was more than one.

He could hear nothing else. Cautiously peering round, he strained his eyes but as far as he could see there was nobody. Nothing but the bushes and the trees. His eyes were fixed on the bushes; doubtless the enemy was hiding as he was himself. Not a party then, most likely a solitary man. He hoped the old woman wouldn't come blundering out after the sound of the shot but she was, as he had already noticed, rather deaf and no sound came from the house.

Rex had made his way down instead of up. From the bottom of the terraced garden, he worked his way round the wing at the back, passing the entrance beneath the rustic porch. The wing of the house was one storey and fairly low. He paused to pick up a few stones, and with a foot on the window sill, gained the sloping roof. Rex peered over the top. He could see the shape of a man stretched by the bush near the wall to the garden, out of range for a clear shot. He hurled his stones and they clattered at the side of the main building.

The man—no fool—jumped, not upright, but only from his belly to his knees. He was exposed to a line of sight from the side of the house and he carefully moved through the bushes to the front of the wing. He was within range now but concealed. Rex threw a stone on the path in front of the bushes, hoping to flush him out, but the man wasn't fooled. An old soldier, Rex thought, he had 'tumbled' him—a bullet whizzed by to shatter a chimney pot on the house at his back. A trickle of warm blood came from his ear. He took his forage cap off and poked it cautiously over the roof line. A bullet ripped through it and Rex groaned, sliding to the ground with as much noise as he could make. Swiftly he tore off his jacket and threw it over a bush, then flattened himself against the wall.

Müller came round cautiously. The rain was blowing straight in his face. He peered at the bush for a fraction of a second—it was too long. The Browning barked again, and Müller fell, not far from the place where the men of Special Branch had fallen.

Rex looked about but saw no sign of more opposition. He stared at the bodies. No doubt the first man was dead,

420

but he examined Müller's body. He'd taken the bullet in the chest; he was dead all right. His flesh was still warm; his eyes stared sightlessly. Rex had wanted to take him alive, but the man had been too good. A good soldier.

Rex went through the house quickly but methodically. No-one was there but an old woman in a kitchen chair, apparently fast asleep. He tried to rouse her, but with no success. Drugged, probably. And the telephone was still silent.

Twenty minutes later, a soaking wet Rex Barney was out in the rain that had come down heavily once more. He had got the Prime Minister up to the house, who had confessed he was too exhausted now to go further. He had agreed to stay where he was until Rex reached Ballater. But Rex was already reluctant to make his way to the town. He was sure there was very little time. Once Jerry saw the bodies at the field, the lives of the King and Queen wouldn't be worth tuppence. Even if they were supposed to be taken alive, their captors would kill them in panic and run.

Yet he must go for help. Gazing into the wind and rain that lashed the long, unfriendly glen, he knew what little chance he alone had of finding them in these Highlands. The city man sighed and moved on. At least he wouldn't take the road. He would go down to the valley again and keep his eyes open as he went. Unencumbered now, he took a steep rocky path down the crag that led him slightly to the north along the river. Strong and lithe as he was, he was not used to this scrambling and climbing. It had been a very long day. He paused in a gulley to catch his breath. For a moment he thought he heard his own heavy breathing over the sound of the rain.

But he wasn't breathing loudly. This sound was more like a moan, muffled, indistinct—was he imagining it, or was it the sound of a trapped animal? Rex was searching before he decided what he was searching for. A piece of printed cloth first made it clear that it could not be the body of the King. Nor did it turn out to be the Queen. It was a girl, gagged, trussed up, seemingly conscious.

His first thought was that she was an imbecile. Her eyes were open but with no understanding or even fear. But as he touched the back of her head to untie the knots of the gag, she moaned again. There was blood on his hand. Her skull might have been cracked. She gazed up at him with soft eyes like those of an injured dog.

The bastards, he thought, in a quick flood of anger. A maid in their way that they'd coshed and thrown out to lie there, very likely to die, a death that would take as long as it may. He released her gently. She must know something. He must find out, but she was in no state to be questioned. It would take time and there was no time.

Jean had been conscious for hours, in pain, thirsty, nauseous, the gag that bit her cheeks half choking her. But that had been the least of her torments. She was sick now, the green bile flooding up from her empty stomach, but in her misery she was hardly aware. Jean simply did not know what had happened to her. She had been kissing Henry and someone had struck her from behind. But who?

Henry was gone. Had he been struck too? Was he dead? The King and Queen . . . Her head hurt so much, she didn't want to think, but she could not stop thinking.

It was the enemy, the parachutists, of course, who had struck her down and taken Henry away. That had to be. And yet without Henry present—Horst-Henry, with his open face, his touch—doubt lapped up on her like an incoming tide.

When someone had come and released her, she had seen the khaki sleeve, and thought in fevered hope that it was Henry. Someone cleaned her face as gently as if she were a baby. She looked up. The face that peered down into her own from the rain was not fair and handsome and child-like, it was a strong face, with a broken nose, and curling dark hair; his eyes were not blue and frank, but brown, adult and kindly.

She was sick again, and the man cleaned her face patiently. He held her in two strong arms, cradling her sore head from the hard rock. Jean knew she was befouled all over, and was ashamed, but the man took no notice.

"Are you from Birkhall House, darling?" he asked.

His Cockney voice struck strangely on Jean's ear, but she understood perfectly well.

She gazed up at him, mute, afraid to speak, afraid to think even. He didn't look or sound like the enemy, but how could she know?

"Listen, love," he said gently. "I'm trying to find the King and Queen before they're hurt. If you know anything, for God's sake tell me before it's too late."

Jean was swept by an enormous wave of sorrow and guilt together with the paralysing doubt, while, at the same time, she wanted to speak.

Her mind, confused to the point of longing for insensibility again, took refuge in a blankness while tears welled from her tired eyes to run with the rain down her face.

Rex's almost overwhelming sense of the need for haste couldn't shield him from pity for this broken creature.

"Poor little ha'porth," he muttered. "Ought to get you inside."

His strong hand brushed her lashes with a tender clumsiness.

Jean lay back against his arm, her mind still frozen, an older sense taking control. Rex's caress spoke to her in a way that all of Holstein's love-making in the cottage had not. His voice, his warm, brown eyes, soft with feeling, drew their own response.

She spoke without thinking, but with some difficulty. The corners of her mouth were cut and her tongue felt swollen.

"They're in the forest. The parachutists came. I—I sent a man after them."

"A man?"

"In uniform, like yours. I thought . . . a friend. But —I don't know." Her gaze slid from his.

She knew all right, he thought grimly. The killer. What *had* this girl done?

Moving from the shelter of his arm, she was trying to stand, shaking her cramped limbs, testing her weight on her feet. Whatever she'd done, she'd paid. And this was only the first instalment.

His voice was calm and sure.

"Do you know where they went?"

She was standing now, trembling, her face white under the spattering of freckles. Moving behind a boulder, she tried to clean herself a little in the rain, the cramps lessening as she moved.

"I'm almost certain," she told him. "But you'd never find it. I'll have to take you there. It's up the glen. You'll have to climb a wee." Her body was still trembling.

He looked at her doubtfully, yet with a certain hope. He had seen men wounded in battle, calling on reserves of strength it seemed impossible that they could have, when courage or necessity drove them on.

"D'you think you can do it?"

"I must, man," she said and took his arm, leaning on him heavily.

The girl, brought up in the glens, led the Cockney soldier by the quickest path up the river, through the rocky wooded heights leading to the Craig at Loinmuie.

The old housekeeper had not been asleep when Rex entered the house earlier. Nor had she been drugged. She had heard the shots and until she knew if it were friend or foe she thought it better to play dead. She opened her eyes sufficiently to make out that it was a soldier searching the house—but not that nice boy of Jean's, more's the pity.

But Jean had said he was going back that morning. This man wore a British uniform, but that meant nothing. When help came surely it would be more than one lone man.

Most likely it was one of them. And there was no doubt in her mind by then that 'they' were about, and that 'they' were the enemy. The woman the Fallschirmjäger had thought so gullible had run a Royal household, though a small one, for many years. She was not easily alarmed, but she had good sense.

It had been a day when everything was awry. Yet nothing, at first, had seemed so strange that she was concerned, except for immediate domestic problems. It all started with her oversleeping, because Jean had not brought her morning tea. She had come down to find that Jean had washed up the tea-cups for everybody else, put them away and disappeared. And the Royal party had taken the cars and gone off before breakfast.

But that had not been too startling. The Royal party didn't often go visiting from Birkhall, especially starting so early, but with the war on everything was likely to change. The Queen had said the night before she didn't know when they would be able to come again. She had taken Donaldson, and Burns had gone with the King, so she could assume they meant to spend the night wherever they had gone, though she couldn't be certain.

Of course, the Queen must have instructed Jean when she took in her tea, and Mrs Gordon could well imagine what had happened in that silly head. Knowing she had a free day, and her soldier boy about to go off, all sense had rushed from her and she had gone helter skelter after him, no doubt going with him to the train in Aberdeen. Mrs Gordon hoped she managed to get off before it left— with Jean one couldn't be sure. But she would come back for Their Majesties tomorrow. Of course, even if Jean had remembered the Queen's instructions she couldn't telephone.

Then it had seemed quite right that the Special Branch men had gone off with Their Majesties—though the dear Lord knew the King and Queen were trying to leave them behind. And it seemed sensible that two more detectives had come to join them. They had arrived at night, and she had not thought to consider just how they had come, but as the day passed she became curious. Certainly they had not slept, the beds they usually used for their forty winks were undisturbed. Strangely, they had not been nosing around the kitchen for their breakfasts, when she had come down. And they had given her ration coupons without her having to ask for them—the first policemen she'd ever known to do that. They all liked to 'forget' and take them home to their families.

Then she had made breakfast. Well, never had she seen such a keen, hardworking pair—of course they were young and no doubt looking to make their way. They would hardly sit to eat, and they had jumped up, the food barely touched, leaving a full pot of tea on the table. And all to parade around an empty house. But breakfast was porridge and herring; some Englishmen didn't have the sense to relish it, any more than Donaldson who had taken up English ways, thinking herself very fine. Though in Mrs Gordon's experience policemen had always eaten anything put before them.

Still, in one thing they had sounded like all the others. She had asked, of course, where Their Majesties had gone. They had looked at each other resignedly and told her that they had been sent from Newcastle and were ordinary detectives and not Special Branch.

"Sent to give them a hand, Mrs Gordon, but you know how they are. 'You'll be told what you need to know, and your job now is to guard the house.' It's a wonder they didn't ask us to clean their boots."

Certainly one lot of policemen never liked another. Up here in Scotland they were never too happy about the English police butting in, even by arrangement with Edinburgh. Then it came to her—had Ballater made them walk from the station? There was no sign of car, motor-bike or any old pedal bicycle round the place. But surely they would not go *that* far. Most likely they had been short of transport and just dropped them off and taken the car back again.

And so she had not been too anxious in the morning. She had listened to the wireless and thanked heavens she was comfortable indoors with the rain coming down so miserable, sorry that Their Majesties' holiday was spoiled. The Queen dearly loved to go out for a long walk; she was a good strong walker. Though the King might tire. No doubt that was why they had decided to go visiting.

She had taken the men cheese sandwiches for lunch, and they had disappeared all right. Not a crumb left on the plates when they brought them back. At tea-time she had still not heard from Jean, and she carried the tea things into the sitting-room.

Then everything had begun to seem strange indeed. She had turned to see the Prime Minister himself behind her. The Queen had said nothing about his coming and she was startled indeed. She had no doubt who it was, though he was hatless and his coat was wet and he didn't look much like his pictures in the paper. He must have come in over the windowsill. Ever since the wing had been built on the house, with the entrance in the back, some people would pop over the low sill rather than go round. Feeling foolish, she had to explain that Their Majesties had gone out; she didn't know where. It was incredible to her that the Queen would have forgotten an invitation to the Prime Minister. She must have sent some message that Jean had failed to deliver. But already Mrs Gordon was very disturbed, and not merely because of the cooking.

The Prime Minister had refused her offer of tea. He had said nothing after her explanation, and she had withdrawn. But when she had gone upstairs to get a room ready she had looked out of the window, to see him leav-

427

ing the way he had come—and not going to a car with a chauffeur and a bodyguard but creeping through the bushes.

She had sat down on the bed and suddenly felt sick. Things were not just wrong—they were terribly, horribly wrong. As bad as they could be. England's Prime Minister, in the King's house, creeping about like a thief . . . Everything she had ever heard of the invasion, parachutists, spies, came flooding into her mind at once. And all the comforting reasons she had thought of for the strangeness of the day now lost their comfort.

What did she actually know? The Royal party had disappeared before she woke, and Jean as well. For a moment her mind played with the idea that the man she had seen was not the Prime Minister, that he was a double, one of the enemy himself. Certainly she had heard much of 'doubles'—people said Hitler had several. But she dismissed the idea. Mrs Gordon was not fanciful, and she had seen the Prime Minister in person before, on an earlier visit to Deeside. She couldn't be mistaken.

If something was wrong, why hadn't he told the policemen? The policemen. She stared at the clean, white linen in her hand without seeing that she was crushing it badly. Her first thought in trouble would be to call the police but . . . She looked again the way the Prime Minister had gone. Those men were watching the approach from the roads and had missed him. As she stared down she noticed some birds under a bush quarrelling round what looked like bits of bread. Neither she nor Jean threw crumbs near the house to litter the approaches, nor did they put them out at all in the summer months. She went downstairs with surprising swiftness, and with a quick look to be sure that the two strangers were not nearby, she peered down and poked the wet ground, as the bird flew off with an indignant cry. Two cheese sandwiches had been buried under the bush.

The sickness had gone. Now that she was certain, she

knew what was to be done. She returned to the house and tried the telephone again, but it was as dead as last week's mutton. She was not too dismayed by that. The telephone was new enough in the glen and people had spread the news long before it was invented. Some time soon Arthur Brown would be coming over from the Crofts in the estate car to bring her the ducks for tomorrow's dinner, and to see what else she would be wanting. Or he would if those men didn't stop him.

She made a pot of tea, took them each a cup on a tray with some biscuits.

"I don't think you know our Mr Brown," she said casually. "He'll be stopping by with some things and taking the order. So you'll let him come round to the kitchen. A thin, stringy old bean with a sour face."

When Arthur Brown arrived one of them followed him into the kitchen and stayed until he left, but she had been prepared. Arthur took no notice of the policemen at all. He came in a nasty temper—all the Browns were a bad-tempered lot. For once it was a blessing. He wore his large floppy hat and a sou-wester, but he'd got soaked anyway and his rheumatics were giving him the devil.

"It's no good your complaining I'm late, Mrs G.," he said. "Tyre went up on the Knock and a fine job it was getting the spare on. And there's a leak in the radiator. Time we got a new car, but with this war I'll be dead and in my grave first."

Mrs Gordon poured him a cup of tea, and he threw one glance at the 'policeman'.

"You'll be shrunk out of those town clothes when they dry," he said with satisfaction at seeing someone more uncomfortable than he was. "I wouldna ha come at all if you didn't have company," he told Mrs Gordon. "Fine summer weather we're having."

"Just as well you came," she replied, shoving a wicker basket at him. "I used the last of the herring this morning, so take this and bring some by early. You know how auld Donaldson is if she can't have a herring after her porridge."

Arthur Brown was not the most quick-witted of men. When Mrs Gordon gave him her favourite bread basket to bring fish—which he always brought wrapped in some handy newspaper—he thought she must be unhinged. When she chattered on about auld Donaldson wanting herring, which she couldn't stand any more than she could porridge, his first thought was that Mrs Gordon had gone daft. But the look she gave him was not daft, and she had never been a silly, Jessie-like creature such as young Jean. A Highlander born, he kept his mouth shut, took the basket, went his way and considered later.

The note in the basket sent him much faster than it was safe to travel up towards Ballater and the police station, and faster than the old estate car could be pushed. The slow leak already in the radiator and the excessive speed soon made the engine overheat and the steam poured from the bonnet. Cursing, he pulled over to the side of the road. Taking the old can from the back, he rushed out to get water, for once in his life actually running. He filled the can at the stream and rushed back, almost tumbling over his own feet. The engine had cooled enough, but when he got back in the car the ignition was dead. The damned, cursed, German-loving rain had got in the wires while he had the bonnet up. He got out again, occasionally damning the Almighty, and walked by the quickest path to Ballater.

When Mrs Gordon got word off to Ballater, the King was still alive. Holstein had been ready, with his fingers on the King's spine. Yet he had hesitated once more; perhaps he was premature. He might still receive a signal at nightfall, or the Welshman might come. Leiter might now want the Royals held prisoner.

What had lessened Holstein's tension and restored his usual confidence was the occurrence of something familiar to him. As his hands had closed on the King's neck, he had caught the Queen's glance, a look of fear and terror. At last. This was what he was accustomed to. This was what he enjoyed.

But he was on duty and must keep his mind on business, though the British had shown themselves so helpless and no-one ever seemed to come through this dull and dreary place. He would wait for complete dark, and try one last signal. If there was still no reply he would kill the three of them, and take himself off. It was not his fault if London was too lazy to receive his signal, if the weather was too bad, or if the *Klamotten* was defective. He would have done his part.

No-one would believe now in their accidental deaths. He might as well shoot them with these British bullets; it might cause some confusion. Anyway, whichever way he chose, someone else would have to explain it. It was hard now to tell if it was nightfall or not, it had become so dark due to the heavy mass of cloud throwing water almost in buckets over the glen. But there was still a greyness outside. In the windowless hut it was difficult to see.

There was an oil lamp on the shelf. The wick was damp but he managed to light it. He shielded it as much as possible with a table and an upturned bench. By the amount of water that was coming in the planks must be ill-fitting; no sense in giving his position away. If the Welshman was searching for him—that was his problem. The Black Knight cared nothing for the men of Whaleforce or the Fallschirmjäger either. They were to have assisted him if necessary—they had merely been a nuisance. If they survived he would recommend their execution.

He tapped out his last message. To his surprise, it was acknowledged. Very relieved, he sat back waiting. The message would be decoded; the operator get his new instructions. But though he waited a full half hour, there was no reply. The idea came to Holstein that he had been abandoned—by London, probably also by Whaleforce and the Fallschirmjäger. In the dim light his baby-soft face hardened suddenly into the taut look of a killer pushed by fear. He looked at his prisoners, whom it seemed someone had judged to be of no more importance. His survival instinct made his decision for him. No sense lingering to drag them to the top of the crag. He *would* shoot them with the British gun and disappear. Now. Royal or not, he thought, it was no different from shooting rabbits. No difference at all.

In the twilight and the rain, Rex, unaccustomed to the woods and the hills, would have taken a long time to follow the track without Jean's guidance. For most of the way there was no path of any kind leading to the hut near Loinmuie. Christ, he couldn't pronounce it, much less find it, he thought. But after a time he began to doubt if he would find the place before full darkness, if at all, with her.

Jean had got so far on courage and a will that she had never known she possessed, but it was obvious that she had suffered concussion. Trying to scramble along with all the desperation of guilt, she could hardly keep upright and was overtaken frequently by dizziness and bouts of nausea. Rex held and carried her where he could, pushing, pulling, knowing that the girl might well be causing herself more injury, yet knowing also that they had to continue.

At last Jean sank to the wet ground, overcome by a more violent nauseous fit, and could go no further. When she tried at first to move, her dizziness was so acute she no longer knew where to go. She lay helplessly and told Rex to go on.

"You'll find it now," she said, from her misery. "From here it's just up all the way until you reach the Craig." She pointed due west. "The bothy is on this side. You'll get there sooner without me."

Rex's battle-dress jacket was soaked through, but he

put it under her head anyway. It seemed wicked to leave the injured girl on the bare ground. He patted her on the shoulder, trying to give her as much comfort as he could.

"Back soon, darling," he said, and walked and climbed the slopes, wondering if anything could be found in the increasing gloom and the downpour.

"Hardly notice a bloody lighthouse," he muttered to himself, wiping the rain from his eyes with the back of his hand. He went on, swifter without his burden. Here the way was not so hard to follow, though the inclination was steeper. There had been an attempt at a path here, once. The hut was not yet in sight, but he was certain now it was not far away.

As he moved, he considered his best approach. One blunder and Jean's 'man' would kill the King—if he was still alive and in the hut. Jean had told him a lot on the way—when she hadn't been sick she couldn't stop talking. From her rambling he had made out that this was no parachutist, quickly trained in field combat, but Untersturmführer Holstein, a spy the Germans had been grooming for four years for this chance. A seasoned killer, not to be taken in with any old soldier's tricks, a few stones for distraction, or a cry from the trees. Except that this Holstein, though a spy now, must have come from the SS. Untersturmführer was an SS title; he remembered Larry talking about it. Lieutenant, that's what it was. An SS lieutenant. A man used to taking orders, and sharp about it.

Despite the rain, he made out a dark square shape— the hut. And it seemed as though they might be there— a few faint chinks of light glowed between the planks. Rex felt a sudden drive of strength and hope. Then suddenly there was a crash, a thump and a muffled report—a gun with a silencer.

Too late, Rex thought, sick, but he was running.

"Holstein, *halten Sie,*" he yelled. "*Achtung!*" and crashed with all his strength into the wall. Then swiftly he

433

drew back and silently moved round the side to burst in through the door while the German, startled by the sound of his name, was looking up at the shaking wall of the hut.

By the shaded lamplight he seemed to be on his knees, scrambling between two overturned chairs with bodies bound to them, a pistol in his hand. A third shape lay in a corner. Rex dared not shoot into the melée in that half light. In one bound he threw himself forward and his outstretched hands just barely clasped the man's throat.

The man flicked round, escaping Rex's clasp, lithe as a snake and with the power of a steel spring, but his gun fell from his hand and went off, sending a bullet into the wall of the hut. Rex fell to the floor between the chairs and Holstein was over him, his hand raised for the chop. Rex rolled, catching the hand and throwing Holstein to the ground, but he was up in a flash on one knee, reaching for Rex's throat. Rex butted his head with all his force into the other man's diaphragm, but although Holstein fell back he recovered with sickening speed and gave Rex a blow to the throat that sent him, winded, crashing to the ground. The chairs were in the way; Holstein kicked them aside and straddled the winded Rex, reaching again for the throat. Rex, with all the strength he had left, kicked into the groin. Holstein, grunting, landed on top of him. Over and over they rolled, twisting and grappling towards the door.

They were evenly matched in speed and power—odds on, Rex thought, grim. A groan from one of the chairs distracted him for a fraction of a second—it was too long. Holstein's hands were on his throat, the thumbs digging into the artery, and Rex felt himself blacking out. Rex's throat was thick and strong. Holstein sweated; this Englishman's neck felt like a tree trunk. His groin was afire with pain and he had no more power in him. He couldn't reach his gun—but the lamplight flickered on something by the head under his hands . . . It was a blade, kicked

434

aside in the struggle. Keeping his left hand pressing on the throat, his right hand reached down for the old woman's knife.

Rex had almost lost consciousness. His head was twisted to the left. The glimmer of light that had played on the knife showed his misty, bursting eyes the anguished face of the King. His hair was tumbled, the gag still cut his mouth, his eyes dark with pain. Perhaps he was dying —it seemed to Rex it was Larry's face beside him. Larry. This German. The pressure on his throat eased slightly as Holstein raised his right hand. Rage swept through Rex with a last explosion of strength. His body arched up, his hand caught the outstretched wrist and he came crashing down on Holstein with all his weight, twisting the body half prone beneath him, half supine across the fallen chair, while his powerful left fist pummelled the head down to the floor. Holstein's spine snapped at the waist. Suddenly it was over.

Barney scrambled up painfully, feeling bruised all over, his throat too sore for speech. His fingers felt like sausages as he untied the King. He found the old woman in the corner and released her, intending to leave her the task of untying the nightgowned Queen, but she had been badly beaten and took time to recover her wits.

The King began the task of loosening his wife. It was the Queen who, when Holstein's finger had closed on the trigger of his gun, had hurled herself, chair and all, on top of her husband, surprising Holstein so much that his first shot had gone astray. It was then that Rex's shouting of his name had shocked the usually inperturbable killer.

The surprises were not over. While the Queen was putting herself to rights and helping the dazed Donaldson, Holstein groaned. Rex and the King looked at the man, sprawled at such an impossible angle. It was a death sound, yet Holstein still moved. The King turned away. Rex lifted the gun and drilled a hole through Holstein's forehead.

TWENTY-EIGHT

The Hunter And The Hunted

When Arthur Brown had reached Ballater, as he said later, "The cat was really among the pigeons." Such a fuss was never seen before or since. Glen Muick still could not be reached by telephone but their other lines were working. While officialdom in Aberdeen was trying to decide if this was merely—surely!—a hoax, Ballater was in action.

The local force was small, but the Highlands had their own resources. Every man from Ballochbuie to Tanar was out combing the mountains, while the women tied scarves round their heads and ran to spread the word from house to house. And at last they had reached Glen Muick.

The way back down the glen was very different from Rex's manner of arriving. Despite the dark and the rain, before they had got half way help was at hand. Figures appeared quietly through the trees, shaded lanterns showed the way, strong arms were there to assist the Queen and her maid. A car was on the nearest pathway for the Royal party, but Rex and two Highland men went off to search for poor helpless Jean.

Rex had a sick, bad moment when he found his jacket but no girl. Had she been taken? he wondered. Were there more killers still at large? But she was soon found; she had crawled a few yards off in her delirium. One of the men covered her with a mackintosh and they carried her to the house.

When at last they arrived, the place was buzzing. The grounds were crawling with policemen, and one of them stopped Rex and asked for his papers—which were still in Whitechurch. The rain, now that it no longer mattered, had almost stopped. He was soaked, exhausted, pained with the bruises, and in the long wet walk with the groaning girl he had felt little sense of triumph.

The excitement and exhilaration in the house did not touch him. Mrs Gordon was the centre of a group of admirers—she was the Highland heroine. Other women were dashing about with jugs of hot water, tea and other liquids and something was cooking on the stove. He could not even get near the old man, who was an 'old man' no longer—well-fortified, he was restored to Prime-Ministership. A batch of signallers was dashing about—a transmitter had been set up for the Prime Minister to reach all major defence points in the country. And Hilliard was guarding him—Hilliard, who had followed him with proper permission, in a Lysander transport which had had to land at a distant airfield.

The King and Queen, learning that Rex had arrived, did not summon him, but came to the kitchen where he was trying to dry himself and his sopping uniform. They thanked him, with the same kind of simple gratitude that his own parents would have shown: the King for his wife and the Queen for her husband. The King, although pale and with some nasty bruises on the forehead, didn't stammer, Rex noticed. Although suffering from shock, he managed to make a joke. With the trained memory of Royalty, he remembered Sergeant Barney to whom he had presented the Victoria Cross. "We do bump into each other," he said, grinning.

Considering what they'd been through, they looked pretty well. The Queen was concerned for his comfort, and prevailed upon someone to get him some clothes while his uniform was dried, and insisted he join them at a simple dinner—just himself and the Prime Minister—"if we can get him away from his new toy," she said.

The Queen was a *lot* like his mother, Rex thought. The King had a quiet word with him. "It's all right," he said. "Winston has been in touch with the various Commands all over the country. There's no sign of trouble elsewhere. Of course, every one's on the watch. It looks like this affair was meant to be private, just for us." He paused. "I understand from Winston that you found . . ."

He couldn't go on. Rex remembered the rows of bodies in the pit at the airfield. Some of those men had been close to the King.

He nodded. The King was silent.

"Could have been a lot worse, guv—Your Majesty," he said belatedly, remembering protocol for once.

"It could have been."

The King went on to say again that he, the whole country, could not thank Rex enough, and then he was called to confer with the Prime Minister.

Rex had a feeling of unreality. Of all the people there, he was the only one that felt no lessening of tension, tired as he was. They were here, dry and safe, but he felt himself to be somehow still outside in the dark and wet, the hunter and the hunted. As did Jean, no doubt, and he went to her room where she still lay in her small white bed.

The doctor had decided she must go to a hospital, and a decision had been made to send her, under guard. Now they were waiting for the ambulance. He looked down at her, washed clean, her eyes half open but with no look of consciousness. Perhaps she was drugged. From time to time she groaned. What would happen to her? he wondered. Poor broken creature.

The Prime Minister came and found him there.

"I couldn't have done it if it wasn't for her," Rex said.

The Prime Minister nodded.

"It was her fiancé, the Queen told me. How they used the child!"

"No prosecution then?" Rex asked.

"From what the doctor says, the girl will be punished without our intervention. The brain, he fears, is injured. She will live, he thinks, but she won't be the same girl again. In any case," he said, shrugging, "we want no trial. I haven't found any other trouble from the Hebrides to Dover, except what we always have. Prahms on the Channel. U-boats in the Western Approaches. The Italians are about to attack Egypt, and we'll have to send the South Africans to secure the Canal Zone . . . I have to get back tonight. Prod, prod." They left Jean's room and the Prime Minister got them each a stiff brandy.

"I've been in consultation with the Intelligence Chiefs and Special Branch—and a few other people. And Their Majesties agree. The traitors will be pursued—but quietly. Best all this be kept from the public. To know that Their Majesties were set upon—never mind my own humble person—would cause grave disquiet. And the killer is dead. M15 were disappointed—but perhaps it is as well." One of the airmen is still alive, they can have him—*in camera.* And one good thing will come of it—Her Majesty agrees in future to be more careful.

Rex looked at him.

"We've got an awful lot of corpses for something that never happened."

"Ballater has been informed, officially, that the report was a false alarm, and they have passed that on to Aberdeen. The King and Queen are still, as far as anyone knows, at Windsor. The rest will be arranged."

He avoided Rex's gaze. "Sometimes these things have to be. A policeman meets an accident while riding a bicycle; a tragic fire at the airfield; members of the Royal Household meet with a driving accident in Windsor Great Park.

Rex remembered the quiet, torch-lit procession.

"The people here?"

"They'll hold their tongues. We'll hardly need to ask, it's their habit. It won't be the first Royal secret kept along Deeside. By the way," he added, "I believe certain Cabinet members were informed I had met with a fatal accident." He grinned with a certain pleasure. "I'll be working at Chequers till Monday morning. It will be a joy to see their looks when I walk into that Cabinet meeting Monday morning. See the happy faces—and the not so happy."

They were called to dinner, and Rex couldn't say what he had to say in the presence of the King. He realised why he couldn't feel like the others, why he still felt the pressure of pursuit. It was very simply that he knew the game was not over. He knew why it had begun, and there was no change. One attempt had been stopped, but there could be another. And another. But no-one would want to hear it.

After dinner the King and Queen retired, and the Prime Minister made arrangements for transport. The doctor was trying to prevail upon him to stay overnight. Rex, remembering his exertions, added his voice to the doctor's.

"Knew you'd turn into a nanny, they all do," the Prime Minister said. "What about you? I suppose you'd like a few days' leave after all this. Go and see your best girl."

Rex wouldn't have minded seeing Ida, but love was not on his mind. He gave a little sigh and shook himself, like a dog with fleas. The old man had forgotten, and had to be reminded.

He could talk to the Prime Minister as no-one else could, but he knew, with a certainty, just how far he could go. How far before the Great Man remembered that he was a Great Man and that some lowly Cockney was treating him in a manner not to be borne. There was one thing the Prime Minister had to hear—and heed. And the Prime

Minister would not accept it from anyone but himself; but having heard it, their strange comradeship, which had sprung from the kindness of a Great Man to a child on his doorstep, and nourished in a shared adventure, would wither, never to exist again.

The Rex Barney of a month ago would have laughed at the notion of his giving a sod, one way or the other. Now he had to admit to himself that he would care. Wryly, he thought he must be the only grafter from the East End concerned about the affections of the cousin to the Duke of Marlborough. But sentiment had nothing to do with the job.

"What about 'im in Lisbon?" he said.

The Prime Minister actually growled.

"That has nothing to do with this business," he said. His voice did not carry conviction, though it was angry enough.

"Look, guv, there's no time to waste," Rex said, his voice carrying his own sense of urgency. "The Germans have a U-boat waiting. And he's already agreed to go. Maybe he's gone already."

The Prime Minister looked down.

"He's still there." He lit a cigar and puffed on, savouring the pleasure. It was the first he'd had since—it seemed to be forever. It so happened that he'd thought to send an inquiry to Selby, and he'd received an answer. No problem, of course. The Duke and Duchess were at Cascais, preparing to leave on their chosen vessel on the 1st of August. He wished Sergeant Barney would stop fussing. Suddenly the import of what Barney had said struck him. A horrible slur on the Duke. The worst he had thought, even in his innermost mind, was that the Duke, because of his—temperament—might give the Germans ideas, a kidnap attempt or—something. But this . . .

"I tried to get you on the 'phone but you'd gone off," Rex went on. "And I came back to show you this."

He dug around in his pocket. With everything that

had happened, he had completely forgotten that bit of paper. It must have got soaked, and one of the women had just ironed his jacket. He drew it out, dirty, still damp in spots that clung together and lost part of their surface as he unfolded it. As a document it wasn't impressive but the message was more or less legible. *"Our client awaits . . ."* Rex explained shortly how he had acquired it.

"You bought the thing, whatever it is," the Prime Minister pointed out. He peered at the hateful scrap of paper. "It's only a copy—supposed to be a copy. A man in a café asks for money for a piece of paper that he probably wrote out himself. How much did he ask for this State secret?"

His tone was sarcastic and he was angry, really angry. He had been enjoying himself as he had not enjoyed himself since—he could hardly remember such a heady exhilaration. When he had become Prime Minister in May, despite the terrible ordeal facing the country, he had known a sense of joy. At last he had taken the place which he had always felt should be his—as it should have been his father's. He, Winston Churchill, had overtaken and surpassed his glorious ancestor. But that had been a satisfaction of ambition.

What he felt that night had been something deeper. It was the joy of a man of sixty-six who had fought a battle and won, not as a general, but hand to hand, with young men in the prime of their youth; his wits, his strength, his keen eye and unfaltering hand against theirs. He had outwitted them in their plots; he had slaughtered them on the field of battle just as he had as a young officer in a cavalry charge at Omdurman. He had *won*—a good omen for England, a foreshadowing of victory!

And now his cigar—the celebration of his feat of arms, a tossing aside for the moment of the burden of his years—was bitter in his mouth. He threw it down. A moment ago he had wondered if Caesar at his triumphs had felt such elation. But Barney had soured it all. For a moment he forgot Rex's part in the victory—at best he was inclined to forget his understrappers.

Barney was still talking.

"That house should be surrounded. Send a regiment if necessary—but by air! And someone to put the fear of God in him and make sure he gets on the right ship. Even if it is a fake," he said tactfully for him, "you're Minister of Defence. You've got to make sure."

Churchill's eyes were bulging. Prime Minister, Minister of Defence, and he was being given orders by a Cockney private! Such a thing had never happened in the history of the country. He swelled up visibly and looked as though he might burst in anger.

Rex saw it all. He had slept little on the 'plane the night before. The day seemed as though it had been a hundred years long. His labours had been exhausting, his combat with the killer German had left pain in almost every inch of his body. Good food and strong drink had restored him, but the sense of unreality had persisted. But now, for no good reason, seeing the old man in one of his typical rages brought a sense of the familiar—the ordinary, predictable, controllable life.

He began to laugh.

The Prime Minister's eyes nearly came from his head. His colour turned scarlet. No-one, NO-ONE laughed at the Prime Minister. No-one laughed at Winston Churchill. He couldn't remember the last time it had happened to him at all.

Rex laughed harder.

Looking at his furious elder, he threw back his head, and made the high-pitched cry that in their old game had been the sound of a gorilla. He waved his arms in the traditional battle dance. Almost light-headed with a new relief, a certainty of action, he skipped about the table.

An aide-de-camp in the next room, who was guarding the Prime Minister while Hilliard had something to eat in the kitchen, heard the cry. His nerves on edge from the strangeness of the day, he dashed into the dining-room, gun drawn. Before him were the figures of the Prime Minister and the sergeant, hooting with uncontrollable laughter, dancing round, waving their arms at each other like monkeys. Nervous breakdown he thought, and rushed for the doctor. But before the doctor came from the ambulance where he had been superintending the removal of Jean, the Prime Minister was already on the newly repaired telephone.

Once he went into action the country moved fast. Not a regiment but a large body of Secret Service men were to leave from Whitechurch on the 'plane at 0700 the next morning. They were part of the 'official entourage' on a diplomatic mission—to be led by Walter Monckton, who was roused from his bed to be given this news. The Prime Minister in motion had a sublime disregard for other people's convenience.

He burned the piece of paper with the match that lit his next cigar. There were still his old loyalties, but he was the leader of the country. Operation Green was blown, but the presence of the Duke in Europe must not tempt the Germans to try again. He had a thought of the spy-master who had outwitted him once, and so nearly had again. No, he could not take the risk.

He had work to do that night and he was already dictating a note to Wavell about the problem of troops for Egypt, when Rex interrupted to ask if he could go with the party to Lisbon.

The Prime Minister looked up.

"You couldn't go with them—you can't get to Bristol in time."

"I can if you let me go in the Lysander tonight," Rex answered. "They've cleared the airfield, we could bring her up there. I'll be in time, might even get a couple of hours sleep."

The Prime Minister signified assent with a wave of his

hand, the Lisbon matter already forgotten as his mind turned to other matters.

While he waited for the aircraft, however, Rex made sure he had a few documents signed. Remembering the way he had left Whitechurch, he had no desire to be held there again for questioning.

TWENTY-NINE

Return Of The Chocolate Soldier

Saturday dawned bright and hot at Cascais. Manuel was happy driving the big Bentley, even though he had to take Maria and that annoying child of hers, Jorge. At least they were awed enough at the experience to be silent for a time. When they entered Lisbon, Manuel drove them round a few streets and squares, before taking them to the Alfama, pointing out this place and that, letting Maria see his knowledge and experience.

She looked at the British Embassy thoughtfully.

"They will not like it that the Duke and Duchess go," she said.

Manuel was irritated. Always this talk about the British. Ever since that soldier came. And even Maria should know better than to discuss important matters before a child, even a child as stupid and backward as Jorge.

"Concern yourself with your own affairs," he said. "What are the British to you?"

Maria thought about it. What, indeed? The British were no longer her business. The soldier would never return. She would not see him again, and nor would Jorge. She looked down at Jorge sadly and his expression mirrored her own.

Major Leiter, congratulating himself on his escape, had left Lisbon with Eckhardt before the English party arrived. He sent Eckhardt on, and took another 'plane to Madrid. Although he was a cautious man, he was not a coward and he wanted to explain personally to the Admiral everything that had happened. Eckhardt had the disagreeable job of informing the Reichsmarschall of the failure of the mission. Göring was to receive the news sullenly. He blamed the Abwehr, hinting that they had deliberately sabotaged the project once they realised they were no longer to have the glory, and that they had abandoned the brave Luftwaffe men. But he soon retreated into his drug-induced dreams.

However, Leiter was spared a difficult interview. The Admiral, to Leiter's undoubted relief, was not in Madrid. He was with the Generalissimo at El Ferrol, where the Caudillo had gone on a family visit and to get the sea breezes. Still engaged in their interminable discussions, he had invited Canaris, whom he liked, to go with him. Leiter, needed desperately in Berlin, left a coded message with von Stohrer at the Embassy Residence in Madrid.

The Ambassador did as Leiter had asked him, and gave the message to the First Secretary to get through, as soon as possible, to El Ferrol. The Secretary promised to send it at once, though he could not promise El Ferrol would deliver it before Monday. It was a sleepy little place. When he sent it he included another message that had been waiting for the Admiral. It should have gone off before, he thought, looking at the date. The staff here were getting very slack. Like the Spaniards, in fact.

The Admiral, who normally loved Spain, had been at El Ferrol in a fever of impatience. He could not leave the Generalissimo, who agreed with him every day in their discussions—only to discover, the next day, that there was one more point . . . His message to Leiter had not been answered. Or more likely it had been answered, and the answer was lying about in the Embassy in Madrid. Or even in the post office of El Ferrol. He was certain that Operation Green was at its culmination, and he could bear the silence no longer. With the Generalissimo's sanction, he was at the Post Office himself that morning, dragging the postmaster to his work, and was there when the messages came in.

The first was what he had expected—almost. He had decoded it in a moment. '*Jonah approaching* . . .' But what was Stavanger to do with anything? A mistake by the telegraphist? But he was already tearing the second message from the postmaster's hand. His hand shook and his mind froze as he transcribed from the code of his own devising. But the message was there, and he couldn't pretend to himself that it was anything less than plain.

'*Röslein, Green, blown. Lisbon client excepted. Reserved for Araby.*'

Both messages bore Leiter's code name.

The Admiral was totally stunned. There had not been a whisper from Berlin that anything was wrong. He had been normally anxious but—his eyes were staring at the first message. It had been sent to Madrid on Thursday. Stavanger . . . Göring, of course. His paratroopers.

Canaris was sitting at the little desk in the postmaster's office, a small, dark room and very close. Outside there was sunshine cooled by sea breezes, but he had no awareness of comfort or discomfort.

"*Röslein, Green, blown.*" Then the English had been warned. *Araby* could never succeed now. No point in wasting his best agent in England, the brave Iraqui. The British Government would make sure the Duke sailed wherever they planned for him to go. And once he was gone the Führer would most certainly let loose *Adlerangriff*—the terror bombing that was to precede invasion.

He looked down at his hands, which lay as though

448

they were detached from him on a heap of official, buff-coloured forms. The little finger of his right hand was quivering. The war was lost. The English would not surrender. The Führer would invade Russia, and the Americans most certainly would come in on England's side. And he . . .

The Admiral knew now that he would fail in Spain. The Generalissimo was more than a match for all of them and he would remain neutral. Operation Green had failed. God knows how—but it had failed. His whole carefully constructed plan, foundered on the rock of Göring's boastfulness, and his own inability to oppose the Führer. The Führer had removed him from the Operation, but that would be forgotten. Not the failure, that was his. He was a man who had failed twice. His long record of success that had been his shield, his armour against the suspicions of Himmler and Hitler himself, was destroyed. If they had cause to suspect him again . . . In the hot little room the Admiral shivered, as though an icy finger probed him in some vital spot.

For a moment he thought of the man in England, plump and hearty, who had once been the *dumkopf* of his school, as subtle as a railway train at full speed, yet who had beaten him at last. How curious, how strange. To sit still was suddenly impossible and he sprang up and walked to the door. Canaris, devious, brilliant, Admiral and Chief of the mighty Abwehr, gazed over the sunlit landscape and saw nothing but a thick grey fog of fear, as though he could look into the future and his end in the death camp at Flossenberg. Little sailor, little *'Kieker'*, the guards would mock him, and slap his face as he was driven forward, naked and trembling to the rope.

* * *

The English party arrived in Portugal to all the tedium of an official reception. Sir Walter Monckton, as a member

449

of the British Government, was met with much pomp. Not only was the English Ambassador present, but officials of the Lisbon Government and certain leading citizens, some of whom knew him, including the Windsors' host, Ricardo Esperito-Santo. Esperito-Santo had arrived in suitable dignity in his car, which was driven not by Manuel, but by Rodrigues in his best summer uniform.

It was hot on the tarmac but most of the British bore it with resolution. The large group of Secret Service agents with Sir Walter, ostensibly part of a diplomatic mission, remained patiently through the speeches and exchange of courtesies. Sergeant Rex Barney did not.

He had woken from his snatched sleep as the 'plane came in for the landing, possessed by the same sense of driving urgency that he had felt before. The members of the mission all about him, despite the late night call, the rush to Bristol, were calm and confident. He was neither.

Drifting away from the gathering, unobtrusively he hoped, he headed for the airport building. As part of the official party, he could probably slip through ahead. Then he remembered the way he had left this airport—quite forgotten since. A man stood by the barrier, and it seemed to Rex he gave him an inquiring and unpleasant look. Rex hesitated for a moment before going in, looking about him, when a solemn, dark gaze caught his eye.

Huddled by the side of the building, watching the 'plane and looking very out of place so near the uniforms and the elegance, all the pomp and ceremony, was a ragged, dirty little boy with a familiar face. The face broke into a smile of recognition and greeting.

"Chocolate?"

Rex had come prepared for a meeting with Maria and Jorge, and handed him a large bar of milk chocolate with nuts and raisins, not yet melted by the scorching heat, which had cost not only Rex's ration coupons, but also those of some of the 'diplomats' as well. They had reminded Rex crossly that Portugal was not rationed, but

Jorge liked his English chocolate, and English chocolate he got.

"What are you doing here? How did you get in?" Rex asked, as the small white teeth dug into the sweet stuff. His eyes raked the perimeter of the airport.

Jorge understood very little English, but all his life people had been asking him what he was doing wherever he was—there was really no place except his mother's bed where he was actually supposed to be, and he was often driven from that comfortable haven—and how he had got there. He had got to the airport by hiding in the car when Manuel delivered it to Rodrigues. Rodrigues had seen him, but had let him ride, crouched down in the front. Now he saw the soldier's gaze as he stared around the field and understood.

To the side of the airport building, along the field's edge, was a stout, high, chain-link fence. Taking Rex's hand, Jorge trotted along and showed him the place where he had found a small hole, but looking up at the soldier's big body, shook his head regretfully. The fence was eleven feet high. Rex looked at it with dislike. Glancing back at the official party, it seemed that the speaker—someone in a most impressive uniform—was running down. Rex hoped he wouldn't be much longer. He looked down at Jorge.

"Mamma, bono?" he said agreeably, with the Englishman's confidence that somehow the foreigner would understand.

Jorge thought. His mother had pulled a face. And she had told her cousin that the English soldier would be unhappy that the great Senhor, the Duke, was leaving.

"*O Duque* . . ." he said importantly, and hesitated, trying to think of the English words. He waved his hand in the unmistakable gesture of farewell.

Rex nodded and looked at the boy, his eyes suddenly sharp.

"On the big ship?" he squatted down and took his

451

papers from his pocket and drew on them the picture of a ship on the waves. "Or the boat we saw?"

He drew another picture, of the U-boat in the cove.

Jorge looked carefully, and then dipped his hand as if diving. He remembered some English words. "Big fish," he said.

Rex grabbed him by the arms. "Jorge, have they gone?"

But Jorge could not be sure what he meant.

"*Brevemente*," he said.

"*Brevemente*"— Maria had asked him to come to her '*brevemente*'— soon. They had still been there, then, when Jorge left. Jerry was going to take the Duke off while the whole British contingent was listening to the speeches. Sir Walter was now making a reply.

Rex acted as he thought. He took off his boots and socks and threw them over the fence. Then he went up painfully with fingers and toes, monkey fashion. Shoving his feet back into his shoes he ran towards the line of waiting cars. The first car he came to was the Esperito-Santo's Bentley. Rodrigues was standing with all the other chauffeurs, in the only bit of shade outside the main building, gossiping and having a smoke.

He had left the keys in the ignition. Rex was in the car and was pulling away well before the chauffeurs saw this incredible happening. Rodrigues shouted in rage, and a car drew out of the line to follow. Rex plunged towards the city streets to shake off his pursuer. The sports saloon had plenty of speed and soon he was free of him. Traffic was light and he left the city with little loss of time, taking the familiar coast road to Cascais.

The sun was blazing down, dazzling the eye. The trees dividing the road provided little shade. Rex saw a car ahead of him, and blinked and screwed up his eyes—it was what he thought all right. A black Mercedes, with a pennant flying from the offside front mudguard. It seemed like a familiar figure at the wheel.

He wanted to draw closer to make certain, but it was by no means easy. The Mercedes touring car was going almost flat out, and its speed seemed equal to that of the Bentley. If it was von Auerbach, he was in the devil of a hurry. He was going to take the Duke off in the U-boat, that was certain. Catching his last chance, he would thumb his nose at Sir Walter and the whole British Empire. Damn the arrogant bastard. Rex's foot went down to the floor. He'd see what this souped-up waggon could do.

Von Auerbach had readied himself for his journey that morning in leisurely delight. He rang for a man to gather up the few belongings left unpacked, deciding luxuriously that he would never again travel without his own valet. He had slept well, and now lay in bed a pleasant half hour, considering the Duchess' various offers.

The London Embassy would be pleasant and in the circumstances it could hardly be refused him. Her other suggestion intrigued him even more. An English Dukedom would be a pleasant addition to his German title and estates—he was sure the Duchess did not mean it to be an empty honour. There was no problem in holding titles and territories in two countries—it had been done by the Hanoverian line long enough. The Duke of Coburg, the relative common to the Duke and himself, had been Duke of Albany, though foolishly he had given up his British title. Perhaps that might be the title to take—Graf von Auerbach, Duke of Albany—it had a good ring to it.

These happy ideas had been in the background of his mind as he bathed, shaved and breakfasted. With his luggage already in his car, he made his last call at the German Legation, ostensibly to say farewell to Hoyninghen-Huene, actually to send another triumphant message to von Ribbentrop. Should he mention the British Embassy? he wondered, knowing how quick others would be to put forward their own claims.

When he received Leiter's message, it was the most

unpleasant shock of his life. At once he was overtaken by a storm of anger that he could hardly control. Those fools! After all his work—probably the most clever piece of psychological manoeuvring in the history of the world —a handful of unknown bunglers had ruined everything. He wanted to storm, rage, shout—but he could hardly do that in the code room of the Embassy. A mistake— perhaps a mistake in the decoding? But of course there was no mistake. This was the message. *'Previous instruction cancelled . . .'*

But a moment's delay had cooled him. Sense began to flow back. Major Leiter had sent this message. But who was Major Leiter? He had received a communication from him before. Obviously he was someone at Abwehr headquarters. Von Auerbach had assumed he was some functionary of the Admiral. The communication had been properly sent and coded; there had been no reason not to accept it as genuine. And he had seemed to remember the name—it had been mentioned at the Tirpitz Ufer. He thought perhaps he had seen the man, possibly it was that fussing, clerkly fellow with the mousy face. But this . . . It came to von Auerbach, very sharply, that the Major, whoever he was, had no authority over him.

He, von Auerbach, was a diplomat, not a spy. He had been asked by his chief, von Ribbentrop, to assist Admiral Canaris. Admiral Canaris had given him his orders and only Admiral Canaris could countermand them. This Major, this underling, who obviously had made a botch of his own assignment, now wished him, von Auerbach, to fail in his. Doubtless to make his own failure less conspicuous.

Von Auerbach's eyes narrowed. Certainly he knew of such tricks. Many a blunder was covered up that way and sometimes turned to an inter-organisational victory. Persuade a colleague that a matter is hopeless and entice him to withdraw. Then the original blunder is presented to the authorities as an inevitable consequence to the colleague's failure. Von Auerbach was not to be taken in by such an old gambit! For there was no reason to believe that the Admiral wished him to give up on the great plan—and certainly the Führer did not. If one group had failed in Scotland, then another could be found to finish the job. His was the delicate, vital role.

This was to have been the peak of his career. All that he had hoped for was still ahead of him, brightly glittering. Should he abandon that straight path, he would march into the byways of failure with all that that implied. Failure was not well seen in the Third Reich, especially important failure. Von Auerbach had no romantic notions about the Führer. Baulked of this much desired prey, who knew what form his displeasure might take on the failed hunter? At the very least, the career of the Graf von Auerbach would be over. The fatal mark would always be against him.

The Duke and Duchess were waiting. He would go at once. There was no time to consult the Admiral. The Legation was already buzzing about the arrival of a new British diplomatic mission. The Azores, the First Secretary had given his opinion. Von Auerbach thought otherwise. They must not get to the Boca Do Inferno and the Duke. Forgetting his polite messages of farewell, he had rushed to his car and made for the coast road.

Could von Auerbach have seen the Duke, he might have been somewhat calmer. Nothing now could change the mind of the Duke. He was firm and determined at last.

All was ready. He and the Duchess had eaten the light luncheon left for them by Manuel, buffet style, and were ready to go. More than ready! For the last time, they were sitting on the balcony; the Duchess was dressed in a deep blue silk dress for the present heat, a matching woollen jacket at her side in preparation for England. Her shoes had heels low enough to manage on the submarine. Always perfect, he thought with a fond smile.

But his eyes soon turned to the road along which von Auerbach would come. Again, and for the last time. He had stood here before, for so long, waiting, hoping. Now he hoped no more. Certainty was his, happy certainty—happy except for the thought of poor dying Bertie. His mother would feel that badly. Yet in a way she must have been prepared for it. His health had always been an anxiety.

His mind quickly reverted to his own change of fortune. Certainty, and responsibility. He would make a good job of it, this time. King Edward. He liked the sound. How he had loathed the name of Windsor! Now at last the Windsor Plot was over. Soon it would seem as if it had never been. 1936–1940, to be mentioned in the history books as an interregnum in a long, successful reign.

King Edward VIII. He would be loved, more than his father had been. Rising with dignity, he stood before the parapet, as he had stood on the balcony of Buck House so many times, the crowd below cheering their favourite Prince. So they would cheer him when he made the peace and saved Great Britain and all her people. Tears pricked his eyes and his throat constricted as he heard the roaring of the crowd and saw the sea of faces in the Palace forecourt.

"We want the King! We want the King!"

He smiled and bowed, and bowed again—to the incurious gaze of a white gull off the cliffs of Cascais.

Rex Barney was gaining on von Auerbach. The overdrive in the new Bentley gave it an edge on the powerful but far too large Mercedes. Von Auerbach had glanced back and seen the Esperito-Santo's car and had assumed it was merely returning, in normal course, to the house. A nuisance having the chauffeur witness the departure of the Duke and Duchess—but it did not really matter. The Duchess could always send him back to Lisbon on some errand.

But its speed surprised him—the chauffeur was enjoying himself, going flat out. His own furious drive had slackened slightly. He had just passed the last fort in the chain along the coast before the Boca Do Inferno. He was almost there. In a half hour he would have his Duke safe as a sardine in a tin. He would take him off, and if the sea-'plane was not at the rendezvous, they would take the U-boat all the way to Alderney and wait there while the Admiral completed his new plan.

The Bentley was gaining on him. In the rearview mirror he could see the driver—not Ricardo nor Manuel, but a British soldier. It was that arrogant, red-headed lout the Duke had thought was a spy. Von Auerbach's foot jammed down on the accelerator, but the Bentley moving at full speed came up almost to his back wheels, and still came on with only inches between them.

The redhead was on his right, pulling ahead. With appalling effrontery, or clumsiness, his front wheel nudged the Mercedes. Von Auerbach moved slightly farther to the left. The maniac had plenty of room to pass. But he did not pass. He was cutting the Mercedes off. Looking up, von Auerbach saw the redhead grinning as he nudged him further and further towards the divider.

Rex enjoyed seeing the German sweat. As they approached a curve to the right, supremely confident, he nudged again. In the unfamiliar car, he misjudged by a hair's breadth. There was a scream of steel and for an instant the bumpers intertwined. Suddenly the steering wheel of the Bentley was wet with his own sweat. He was hit with a rush of panic and moved his foot to decelerate at once. Glancing back at the German, Rex saw the Mercedes spinning out of control over the grassy divider, then only the rear wheels as the car tumbled over the road's edge down to the beach.

EPILOGUE
King Of A Coral Reef

The weather, at least, was kind to the stunned Duke and Duchess. The sun shone; the sea was calm. The sea air helped restore the vigour of their bodies after the exhaustion of shock, disappointment, and the sudden physical work of transporting as much as possible of their worldly goods to a place that would be their exile for many years.

The Duchess was in a somewhat better state than the Duke, for she had had to exercise her mind with decisions, and she got on board at last with three lorryloads of baggage and odds and ends, including two golf bags and clubs, and several cases of wines and spirits. There were fifty-seven pieces of baggage in all, and space had to be found for their servants. The British Government, in a burst of gratitude for their departure, had sent at the last moment the invaluable Fletcher, and the Duchess' maid had arrived from France.

But the man who had expected to resume his role as King of a quarter of the globe and its peoples could not take it in that his destiny was now to rule over a few coral reefs and sandpits. His mind was still dazed. Sir Walter Monckton had seemed to know nothing of the illness of his brother—but then, he might well be part of the Plot. The miserable, horrible, Windsor Plot again.

Certainly, Sir Walter had tried to hide from him the fact that von Auerbach had been murdered by that red-headed criminal, the thief. The man undoubtedly was a thief, though the police had recovered the Duchess' brooch at last. The Duke would never be able to look at it again with the smallest degree of pleasure. He hoped the murderer would be hanged or executed in whatever manner they used in Portugal. But he would probably get away scot free.

But day by day, under the golden sun and sparkling seas, hope sprang again. Nothing was really changed, they told each other. The fact that von Auerbach had been murdered, that they had been intercepted before their planned departure, meant nothing. There would be other emissaries, other boats. Since it seemed they were not to be murdered at sea, the Duchess quipped, they might even survive on 'Elba' long enough to make plans.

The Duke remembered that when he had spoken to Hoyninghen-Huene—as he had felt he must after the murder of von Auerbach by a man, supposedly in his employ —he had been most gracious. More important, after that a long message had come by way of Esperito-Santo from von Ribbentrop. It stated simply that Germany still wanted peace. The Duke was to keep himself prepared for further developments, and stay in touch with his former host. Of course, the Duke told the Duchess excitedly, he would be called again. The game was not yet over. There was still time for hope.

They landed with some ceremony. But it was as always in a British possession: one of the first things they heard was that the Bishop had publicly insulted them, tearing down a poster with their image. Officials and other people, whom the Duke believed to be mostly secret agents, swarmed about them, and they had privacy only in their beds. A concerted effort was immediately under way to get them off to the Bahamas. A British cruiser had been sent for 'escort' duty. A young naval officer, their official attaché for their stay in Bermuda, stuck with the Duke like a limpet.

They consulted at night in the Duchess' bedroom, after the Duchess, only half mocking, had looked under her bed.

"You must be in touch at once," the Duchess advised.

The Duke agreed.

"If I could get five minutes alone I would telegraph. Of course, there is the code, but I don't want these people to see where it's going. The message would probably be intercepted—I would put nothing past them, Dolly."

"I told you we should have insisted on stopping first in the States. How you let them bully you!" the Duchess said, displeased.

He pushed up the hair on the back of his head.

"Well, now I have to get rid of that—that naval warder we've acquired. And I just don't see how we can do it."

"Don't worry about it. I'll manage him," she said with confidence. An impressionable young lieutenant would be child's play for her.

Next morning, dressed in cream-coloured shantung silk, looking at once frail and gay, she descended on the naval officer.

"I would so love to do some shopping," she said. "And I am terrified to go alone after—after everything. And the Duke is confined to bed with a dreadful migraine."

He smiled at her. "But, Duchess, you are surrounded by people all the time."

She sighed and gazed at him trustfully. "But I don't know them—some of these people seem complete ruffians. I don't think they're from the island at all. You can't imagine how we've been badgered and followed, spied upon—and we were nearly kidnapped."

The Navy could not refuse. The young lieutenant had

461

not thought the Duchess especially attractive, but as she gave him the full force of her attention, and the richest display of her charm, he changed his mind. No-one had ever shown such an interest in him before. He spoke of his parents, his brothers and sisters, his schooling at Osborne, his early adventures at sea, and she hung on his words. At his last birthday he had been twenty-seven, but he might have been seventeen.

He followed her from shop to shop like a little dog while the Duchess bought bathing suits and sweaters, losing his head entirely, bragging, blushing, overwhelmed by her confidence in him when she asked him to decide for her whether she should buy an expensive set of china for Government House, cleverly painted by hand with colourful Bermuda fish. She did not take it after all, but later was to joke that she had landed at least one fish in Bermuda.

The Duke, left alone at last, sent a telegram to his former host in Lisbon. A code had been agreed upon before he left—indeed, he had been told that upon the receipt of a certain word he should be prepared to return at once. But the Duchess was right, he thought—as always. Berlin should be reassured, kept up to the mark. It would be easier to return from Bermuda than the Bahamas, before they had uncrated all their things, and where, probably, his 'guard' would be even more intense than it was here. He felt very strongly that he would rather not go to the Bahamas at all.

His message said simply that he wished to be informed the moment action was advisable. Then, despite all efforts to get him away, he settled down to await his reply. While the Duchess was shopping in Hamilton, he would slip away from the entourage and take a boat to St David's Lighthouse on the far side of the islands.

Every day the small man, dressed in the uniform of a British Major-General, could be seen standing on the promontory on the eastern tip of the Western World. He gazed, with his sad yet hopeful, crooked eyes, following the sea lanes of the great ships out to the horizon, where on the other side of the wide Atlantic lay Lisbon. The sun was dazzling; his ears filled with the screams of gulls. But although he lingered a full week, no vessel, no message ever came.

The Windsor Plot was over.

Bibliography

For the actual historical background over which this story is embroidered, the following works are among those consulted:

The Rise and Fall of the Third Reich by William L. Shirer; *The Second World War* by Winston S. Churchill; *A Long Row of Candles* by C. L. Sulzberger; *English History 1914–1945* and *The Second World War* by A.J.P. Taylor; *The Game of the Foxes* by L. Fargo; *Adolph Hitler* by John Toland; *The Ciano Diaries 39–43* by Count Ciano; *Inside the Third Reich* by Albert Speer; *The Arms of Krupp* by William Manchester; *SS and Gestapo* by Roger Manvell; *Hitler's Decision to Invade Russia* by Robert Cecil; *Operation Sea Lion* by Peter Fleming; *The Ultra Secret* by F. W. Winterbotham; *Ordeal in England* by Philip Gibbs; *Queen Mary* by James Pope-Hennessey; *The Queen Mother* by Helen Cathcart; *David Lloyd George* by Peter Roland; *Cosmo Gordon Lang* by J.G. Lockhart; *Windsor Revisited* and *A King's Story* by H.R.H. The Duke of Windsor; *The Heart Has Its Reasons* by The Duchess of Windsor; *The Woman He Loved* by Ralph G. Martin; *The Windsor Story* by J. Bryan III and Charles J. V. Murphy; *Edward VIII* by Frances Donaldson; *The Collapse of the Third Republic*

by William L. Shirer; and a London *Evening News* report
of November 1978 of an interview with Lady Diana
Cooper.